Where We Went Wrong

a novel by

Kelsey Kingsley

COPYRIGHT

kelsey@kelseykingsley.com

Cover: Danny Manzella

Editor: Jessica Blaikie

To all of those battling the little devil on their shoulder—

You are never, ever alone.

A NOTE FROM THE AUTHOR

Dear Reader,

Once upon a time, I read a book by Jack Ketchum called *Off Season.* This book was so memorable to me, because it—a shock horror novel—made me so uncomfortable in the most delicious and realistic of ways. And while I don't write horror, I had always wanted to incite that type of emotion in myself through my own writing.

Because, the thing is, as unpleasant as it is to feel uncomfortable, it's also realistic, and that's exactly what I set out to do in writing this book. To depict a realistic relationship between two lost, sad people and the demons they fight together.

It's also that discomfort that makes their happy ending so much more special and sweet.

I achieved that with this book. With how raw, gritty, and real these characters are, as well as the situations they find themselves in. And for that, I am proud. In fact,

I am more proud of this book than maybe any others, and considering how proud I am of the work I've done, this is saying a lot.

I can't lie to you, Dear Reader; it's a bumpy ride. But, for me, it was so worth taking, and I hope you'll feel the same.

Kelsey

PROLOGUE

He's late again.

He's always late.

He wouldn't be late if he'd hire someone to help him out, but oh, wait. Hiring someone requires money, and that's exactly what we don't have.

He said we'd have money by now. He said we'd be well off. That was years ago.

Our youngest was pulled violently from sleep, to vomit all over the couch and pillow he laid upon. With an aggravated groan, I stood from the chair and grabbed another blanket for him, along with a rag and the nearly empty bottle of cleaner. I situated my son at the other end of the couch, patted his head and instructed him to go back to sleep, and set to scrubbing the sofa.

Dammit, I wish he was here to wipe the puke stains off of this fucking couch. I wish he was here to take care of his kids. I wish he was here, period.

"Mommy," Vinnie cried from the other end of the sofa. "My belly hurts."

"I know! I know it does!"

I shouldn't snap at him. It's not his fault he picked up a stomach bug at school. It's not his fault that he's been puking and shitting all over himself all damn night. It's not his fault his father isn't here.

"Here, honey, sip on this," I said, handing him a cup of flat ginger ale, making sure my tone had softened to something a little more motherly.

That's better. He's my son. I love him. I shouldn't be mad at him for being sick.

Vinnie's sip of ginger ale sputtered up from his lips, and it was followed quickly by another round of projectile vomit, covering his fresh pair of pajamas and the last clean blanket in the apartment. Tears spilled from his eyes as his little body heaved, contorting violently with every lurch and bout of puke. And I just stood there, watching as my youngest baby cried and gagged and threw up, begging me in broken sentences to make it better.

But I couldn't make anything better.

I need to get out of here.

"M-Mommy!" he cried, looking at me through pleading, brown eyes. His father's eyes. Not mine.

Help him. Do something. He's your son.

He's his son, too.

"You're okay. You're going to be okay." My hand touched the back of his clammy, little neck. He was so hot. His fever hadn't broken yet. "Just lay down."

"It's too hot. I can't sleep. I … I don't …" His face told me all I needed to know just moments before he vomited again, all over the couch cushions.

"Dammit," I groaned through gritted teeth, clenching my fists.

I'm done. I'm packing my things. I don't need a lot. Just a few pairs of pants, a couple shirts ... Just enough to get the hell out of here and ...

Where the hell would I even go? What else is out there?

Isn't that what I've always wanted to know? Isn't that what we were going to do? See the world and find an adventure that didn't include kids and a shitty failure of a pizzeria?

I'll just grab the jar of coins and envelope of money we've been saving for a rainy day. That'll get me away from here, away from them, away from all of this shit. I'll start over. I'll pretend they don't exist. I'll live my life and I'll be better, and they'll be better off without me.

Come on. Just walk through the living room. You just have to get through the living room and out the door.

Then run.

"Mommy?"

Goddamn him.

"Go back to sleep, Vinnie."

"What are you doing?"

"Nothing. Go back to sleep."

"You goin' on a trip?"

Ignore him. Get to the door and leave.

"Mommy, where are we gonna go?"

"You ain't goin' nowhere! Now, go back to fuckin' sleep!"

He was used to me yelling. He was used to me cursing. But I guess he wasn't used to me carrying suitcases through the living room and to the door, because he ran for me, grabbed one of the bags, and pulled as hard as his little arms would allow.

"Don't leave!"

He was crying and I panicked, not wanting him to wake his older brother and sister in the next room.

"Vinnie," I hissed. "Knock it off *now*."

"M-M-Mommy, don't go! I w-wanna come!"

"You're gonna wake them up. I swear to God, if you wake them up …"

Go. Just go.

"Mommy! P-Please! I'm-I'm sorry."

Don't listen. Just go.

"I-I won't be sick no more. I won't puke. I promise. I-I-I …"

The little shit lied and vomited all over himself and the floor at his feet. I was tempted to clean it up, but I resisted. It wasn't my problem. Not anymore.

"Go back to sleep, Vinnie," I demanded, before opening the door and leaving, all while ignoring his little boy cries.

I'm a horrible person. I'm a horrible mother.

Yes. Yes, I am. And he's a horrible husband.

But he's a wonderful father, when he's around, and they're so much better off without me.

I'm doing the right thing, for all of us.

At least I hope so.

CHAPTER ONE

VINNIE

"Someone in this area, has lost someone. A prominent, female figure." The bottle-blonde swept her hand in a circle, gesturing toward a cluster of tables that included ours. "A mother, a grandmother, a friend, or maybe even a boss."

I watched in silent scrutiny as residents of neighboring tables eyed each other with questions and accusations. Nobody wanted to own it or speak up. Even though they were all there for the same reason—they all wanted closure and affirmation. Whispered voices hit me from all directions and from the corner of my eye, I saw my brother nudge his husband in the ribs, then heard him whisper, "Your mom, man. Or what about Natalynn?"

"Nobody here has lost a grandmother? Or a close friend, or a, uh, a neighbor, maybe?"

Reluctantly, Greyson, my brother-in-law, raised his hand. "Um … my mom?" he answered timidly, his voice lilting as though he were asking a question.

Regina Miller tapped the tips of her fingers together with satisfaction as she nodded and stepped toward our table. "Is she no longer with us?"

He shook his head. "She died when I was fifteen."

"Yes." Regina closed her eyes and outstretched her long, manicured fingers, not quite reaching Greyson's forehead. "Yes, she's showing me a young boy. You were … so sad and … hurt. You were so hurt, weren't you?"

I turned to watch Greyson's throat shift with a deep, hard swallow as he nodded. "Y-Yeah. I was."

"Of course, you were. No child should lose a parent. She's showing me letters," Regina went on, touching her fingers to her temple. "She's showing me a B, or … or maybe it's an E, or, um, it could be an S—"

"My dad's name is Sebastian," Grey chimed in, more eager than before. He shifted forward, to now sit at the edge of his seat.

"Yes! Yes, she's gesturing toward a male, a father figure. He means a lot to you. You relied on him so much after her passing. And he relied on you; they loved each other so—"

"My parents weren't together," Greyson cut in, the hope in his eyes dying just a little.

Regina's eyes widened with panic. "Oh! No, I must be confusing her love for you. Of course. And how much *you* relied on *him*. You did, didn't you?"

I stifled a snort at her quick attempt at a clean-up, as Greyson slowly nodded and replied, "Yeah, I did."

A look of surprise shrouded her over-done features. “Was she sick?”

Immediately disappointed, he shook his head. “No, she wasn't.”

Pressing her palm to her forehead, Regina said, “Oh! Oh, of course. An accident. There was an accident.”

The charade continued longer than it should've, yet I successfully kept my snickering concealed behind the fist I pressed to my lips. This wasn't my scene, and it wasn't my brother's, either. We weren't strangers to loss. But that loss came with a bitterness we didn't care to face. Greyson, however, was another story entirely, and when tickets to see the infamous psychic medium, Regina Miller, went on sale, he had jumped at the chance to grab them. Unfortunately, he was also too nervous to go alone and had no problems talking my brother and me into tagging along for support.

And it wasn't that I was a skeptic. I was cool with the idea of an afterlife, and I was also willing to believe with reasonable proof. But this woman? Her façade was so transparent I could easily see right through to the fraud that lurked beneath all that caked on makeup.

“Your mother, grandmother, and friend want me to assure you that they are in a good place,” Regina concluded, repeating the information Greyson so easily supplied earlier. “They are so proud of the man you've become, and they wish you the best of luck with your band.”

Greyson nodded, his face paled with shock and disbelief. “Th-thank you so much,” he stammered, and my brother wrapped an arm around his shoulders.

With that, Regina moved on to the next sucker and left us to mull over the experience. I listened to Greyson speculate on whether she was the real deal or not. He injected doubt into his words and tone, but his dominant smile gave away his faith.

“What do you think, Vin?” Zach asked, turning to me with widened, bewildered eyes.

I silently cursed him out for putting me on the spot as I smiled and said, “Sure, yeah. She was pretty good.”

“You don’t sound convinced,” Z scoffed, rolling his eyes.

I could’ve punched him as my eyes darted to Greyson, then back to my brother. “I am, asshole. I’m just tired. It’s been a long day.”

He opened his mouth to reply, but before he could push the debate further, I announced that I needed a smoke and excused myself from the dark theater.

Outside, standing on a sidewalk in the middle of the greatest city on Earth, I took a deep breath before digging out my pack of Marlboros. The air was balmy and stifling, thick with summer and sweat, but it was still easier to breathe out here than inside, where I was forced to put on a happy face and lie to my brother-in-law.

I wasn't good at a lot of things and lying was pretty high on the list.

“Jesus fuckin' Christ,” I muttered, loud enough for others to hear, but nobody paid any attention. Because this is New York City we're talking about here. Not a whole lot fazes us, and especially not some idiot talking to himself on the sidewalk. It's one of the things I loved about this place. Nobody looks and nobody judges.

But it could also be that nobody cares, and when I thought of it that way, I wondered if that was really something to love after all.

Pulling a cigarette from the pack and holding it between my teeth, I patted myself down in search of my lighter. "Where the hell did I put it?" I grumbled, becoming more frustrated with every passing second. "I just had the damn thing. What did I do, leave it at the freakin' restaurant?"

"Well, it doesn't look like you have it on you, so I guess so."

Startled—because why would I expect anybody to actually answer—I looked up from my swatting hands to a pair of laughing, blue eyes, behind a pair of thick-framed glasses and a glossy smirk. She stood against the side of the building, her back to the bricks and her hands dipped casually into her pockets. The smile she wore shrunk when she realized she had my dumbfounded attention, and she shook her head, breaking out in a nervous laugh.

"Sorry," she said. "You asked a question, so I thought I'd answer."

Chuckling brusquely, I nodded. "Yeah, thanks," I replied, suddenly remembering the cigarette between my teeth as it tumbled to the dirty sidewalk. I stared at it, lying sadly in a puddle of rainwater and filth, and muttered, "Well, fuck."

"Eh, you shouldn't smoke anyway," she answered, and I looked up to watch her shrug. Her bare shoulders glistening with a golden tan beneath the venue's lights.

"Yeah," I answered in a hoarse voice, clamping my lips shut before I went into a spiel about how it wasn't any of her damn business what I chose to do. Instead, I headed back toward the door and said, "Well, have a good night."

"Oh!" she exclaimed, just as my hand started to grip the metal door handle, surprisingly cool in the middle a heatwave. "You can't get back in."

"What?" I tugged at the door to find it locked. I tugged again. "Why the hell not?"

"You can't leave the venue during a show," she explained, wincing with apology.

"But, I have a ticket." Then, I produced said ticket from my pocket and showed it to her, as if she needed proof. As if she could actually do something about it.

She stepped forward and took it from me, then pointed somewhere in the fine print. "Once ticket is scanned, you must remain inside the venue until the show is over. Re-entry will be denied," she read.

"Get the hell outta here." I took the ticket from her and squinted my eyes to read the tiny font, determined to catch her in a lie, but sure as shit, there it was. "Well, son of a bitch."

"I thought you already knew that, since you were out here."

Peering through the glass door and into the nearly empty lobby, I mumbled, "I just needed a smoke."

"I guess this isn't your night."

"Yeah, guess not."

With a heavy sigh, I pulled my phone out and called Zach. What was to stop him from just opening the door and letting me back in? The one fat, old security guard? We'd just give him the truth and tell him I'm an idiot and didn't realize that I couldn't step outside for a minute. No big deal.

Except that Zach wasn't answering his phone. "Are you fuckin' kiddin' me?" I growled, staring at the call screen as it went to voice mail. "Thanks for putting your phone on silent, asshole," I said, before hanging up and jamming the thing back into my pocket.

"There's no point to going back in there, anyway."

I had almost forgotten about the woman, dressed in a pair of denim shorts and a white tank top. I looked back to her and asked, "Why not?" The question came out as an accusation, not letting on that I didn't even want to be there in the first place.

She shrugged and shook her head. "Because she's a fake. I mean, I honestly can't believe I even spent money on her in the first place, but, whatever."

My eyes narrowed as I cocked my head. "How do you know?"

The woman scoffed and crossed her arms over her chest. I trained my eyes only on her face, desperate to ignore the way her cleavage deepened. "You didn't hear her talking to that guy in there? She was spewing the most generic garbage, that could apply to *anybody*. And I mean, of course, he ate it all up, because that's exactly how she makes her money."

It didn't matter to me that I knew she was right, or that I'd been thinking the exact same thing. From the moment I knew she was talking about Greyson, my chest puffed with the immediate need to defend, and I said, "Yeah, well, if she's helping people to make peace with whatever, then what the hell does it matter to you?"

"Because *that*," she pointed at the door, "isn't helping people to make peace," she mocked, deepening her voice, before continuing, "She's a predator. That's what she is. And she preys upon pathetic guys like that, who are so desperate to know that their loved ones are safe, or still with them, or whatever."

Lowering my brows, I growled, "You're talking about my brother-in-law here."

For a second, she looked like she might apologize, but her resolve to argue her point was greater than her need to be sorry. "Yeah, well. Whatever. It was *so* nice chatting with you. Hope you find your lighter."

With that, she abruptly turned her back to me, lifted a hand in a flighty little wave, and walked away.

"Yeah," I snorted, rolling my eyes as I began the walk home. "Have a nice night."

***

"What the hell happened to you?" Zach asked, entering the apartment with Greyson on his tail.

Closing the door behind them, I said, "Oh, I always love spending eighty bucks on a ticket and then leaving in the middle of the show. Didn't you know that?"

"Ha-ha, you're a funny guy," Z jabbed before turning the corner into the kitchen.

"For real though," Grey chimed in. "Where'd you go?"

I led the way into the living room and dropped down into my recliner. "I got locked out of the place."

Greyson sat down on the couch and pulled his sneakers off, before propping his feet up onto the coffee table. "You could've called," he pointed out, grabbing a pillow and tucking it behind his head.

"Shit," I slapped my forehead, "why the hell didn't I think of that?"

Zach snorted as he emerged from the kitchen, with a glass of soda in hand. "Oh, is that why I had a friendly voicemail from you?"

"Uh-huh." I eyed him as he sat down beside Greyson.

"My bad, man. And I'm sorry you missed the rest of the show. It was pretty fuckin' crazy."

Grey nodded. "Seriously. You should've seen this one—"

"Junior! You out there?"

"Yeah, Pops!" I called before muttering, "He knows I'm here. He was sitting right there when I came in."

"You wanna come in here a second? The clicker's not workin'!"

Laying a hand over my eyes, I shouted, "Are you using the Fire remote for the cable box again?"

"What?!"

I pulled in an agitated, deep breath and raised my voice. "Are you use—"

"For the love of God, Vincent! Can you just get your ass in here?!"

With a groan, I stood up from my chair and hurried down the hall to Pops's room, finding him in front of his TV and cable box. In his hands, he held every remote he owned, and his fingers continuously jabbed at random buttons while cursing under his breath.

"This fuckin' thing ..."

"Pops," I sighed, entering the room, "give 'em to me."

"If you'll just show me—"

"I have," I interrupted, shooting him a knowing glare as I took the remotes from his wrinkled hands. "That old noggin of yours just can't retain the info."

"Ah," he spat, slashing a hand through the air. "Just put on my show, will ya?"

"You got it, old man." I smiled, pressing buttons and passing through menus until I got to the Netflix listing for *Breaking Bad.* "Damn, Pops. You're already on the third season?"

"What can I tell ya? It's a damn good show," he said with a chuckle, climbing into bed. "Maybe I shoulda gotten into makin' meth instead of pizza. We woulda been a lot better off."

"Yeah," I snorted. "And you woulda been in prison."

"You don't know that."

Heading over to the bed and handing him the correct remote, I said, "Nah, I guess not. Here, press *this* button to play, *this* one to stop, and when you're done, just leave it and I'll turn it off before I go to bed. Okay?"

Pops took the remote and laid it on the bed. Then, before I could leave, he took my hand in his and said, "You're a good boy, Vinnie. You know that, right?"

"Yeah, Pops. Sure."

He squeezed my hand and released it, before taking the remote and pressing Play, and I took that as my cue to leave. But before I could close the door, he caught my attention with an, "Oh, Junior! Wait a sec."

Glancing toward the bed, I asked, "What's up?"

"I found this earlier."

"What's that?"

I went to stand beside him as his hand dipped into his shirt pocket, and came black out with something in a fist. "Here," he said, opening his hand to reveal my black Zippo.

"Oh, shit, where was it?" I asked, taking it from him to tuck into my pocket.

"Found it at the pizzeria. Almost threw it out."

"Well, thank Christ you didn't," I laughed.

"You woulda lived." His eyes bore into mine, raising his brows.

"Maybe." I winked, before clapping a hand against his shoulder. "Thanks, old man. Enjoy your show, all right?"

"What are you gonna do?"

I chuckled as I walked to the door. “Well, I was gonna hang with Z and Grey for a while, but first, I think I'm gonna have a smoke.”

CHAPTER TWO

VINNIE

"I don't know what the hell is gonna happen. But what I *do* know is, that man has never held a hammer before in his life. I'm willing to bet good money that he's gonna lose a thumb before the bathroom is done."

My sister, Jenna, blew out a breath and sent the thick, curly hairs laying across her forehead flying. An expression of annoyance held firm to her face, but the look in her eyes betrayed her. She was worried, and I couldn't blame her. Her husband, Nicky, wasn't the most handy guy on the planet, and he'd been doing a great job proving that point ever since they bought their house on Long Island.

"Get Grey to help him out," I suggested, slathering a ladle of sauce onto a perfect circle of dough.

"Yeah, okay," she fired back sarcastically. "In what spare time? They're talkin' about adoption, Vin. They don't got time to help my idiot husband."

"Kittens, Jen. They're adopting kittens."

She leveled me with a stern glare. “Yeah, and once they see how cute fur babies are, you know a real baby is comin' A-S-A-P.”

“Okay, and adopting a kid takes time. They can help Nicky put in a damn tub.”

“Who said anything about adopting?”

I shot my sister a questioning look as I slid a peel underneath the pizza. “How else are they gonna have a kid?”

“There are other options, Vinnie.”

Carrying the pie to the oven, I said, “Sis, I dunno what you know about the birds and the bees, I know it's been a while for you, but uh, two dudes can't exactly have a—”

“They’re thinkin’ about a surrogate, you moron.”

With the pizza now in the oven, I turned back to her and cocked my head, intrigued by this new bit of information. “You're shittin' me?”

She shook her head. “Nope. I mean, they haven't made a firm decision yet or anything. They’ve mentioned checkin’ out a couple adoption agencies, but ...” She shrugged, casting her gaze downward. “They asked me if I'd be willing, just in case, and I said yes.”

“Holy shit,” I breathed, shocked and wondering why my brother hadn't said anything to me. “You're actually willing to have another baby?”

“Well, I mean—”

“Are you pregnant again?” Pops asked, hurrying out from the kitchen.

Jenna shot me a look, one that said she needed a change in subject, and *fast*. So, I said, "Nicky needs help redoing the bathroom."

"Oh." Pops's speculative glare volleyed between us before saying, "Why isn't he asking Greyson for help?"

I barked an obnoxious "ha!" into Jen's face, before heading into the kitchen, where Moe, our employee and friend, sat with a bottle of soda and a slice of pepperoni pizza. He scarfed it down with an air of gratitude, the way he always did, and nodded happily toward me by way of greeting.

"Hey, man. You know you don't have to eat pizza every day, right? We won't be insulted if you wanna grab a sandwich or something," I said as I opened the fridge to grab some more dough.

Moe shook his head. "I'll never get tired of eating this."

"Whatever you say, man."

"When you remember going days without eating anything at all, you learn to not take what you get for granted," he pointed out, before licking the remaining sauce and grease from his fingers.

Shame wrapped its icy hands around my throat. It was easy to forget that, before we'd hired him years ago, Moe had once been homeless. I could still remember his dirty, tattered clothes, but now, after seeing him every day, clean and put together, the memories from before had faded like an old, vaguely familiar photograph.

"Sorry, I—"

"Vin," he said, smiling as he stood. "Relax. It's all good. Now, what was I hearin' about babies?"

I chuckled, shrugging. "Zach and Greyson are apparently thinking about having a kid."

"Oh, nice. I can see Zach as a dad."

"Yeah," I practically grunted, nodding. "Same here."

Moe narrowed one eye as he took the bowl of dough from my hands. "What, you're not happy for them?"

Scoffing, I replied, "I didn't say that."

"Brother, you didn't have to," he laughed, an easy sound that was usually contagious. "You wear the truth in your eyes, my friend. So, what's up?"

"Eh, I dunno. It's stupid. I just ..." I shrugged, feeling like an idiot for even letting it bother me at all. "I guess it gets to me a little that he didn't tell me. He told Jenna but he hasn't said shit to me about this."

Moe hummed thoughtfully. "Yeah, I can see where that might sting a little. But you know, there's not a mean bone in that guy's body. I'm sure it just slipped his mind. He's got a lot goin' on."

I knew there was truth in that. Zach had just opened up his own pizzeria in Hog Hill, Famiglia Bella II, and his old farmhouse seemed to be in a constant state of construction. He was a busy guy, with a full life, and forgetting to tell me something wasn't out of the realm of possibility. But, I reminded myself, he had told Jenna. And sure, she could be the one acting as a surrogate for the guys, but I couldn't help feeling that he had purposely kept me out of the loop.

"There you go again," Moe jabbed, wagging a long finger. "I might be going out on a limb here, but maybe he didn't wanna say anything because he thought you might get jealous."

"*Jealous*?" I spat the word from my mouth and forced a laugh that instantly felt bitter. "Why would I be jealous? I'm happy for him. I'm not jealous."

His deep brown eyes narrowed with taunting acknowledgement. "You can be happy for him while still being jealous. Do you know how many times I was happy for my friends on the streets, who had lucked themselves into better situations, while still being jealous as fuck that it wasn't me? And brother, I know that there are people out there who are thrilled that I got myself outta that hole, but if their envy could kill, I'd be lyin' in a gutter right now."

"Well, I mean, that's different," I reasoned weakly.

"Okay, then you tell me what you got goin' on in your life."

"What?" I couldn't help but laugh.

Moe hoisted himself up to sit on the clean, metal countertop. His legs swung casually, new white Nike's on his feet. I distinctly remembered a time when he always had holes in his shoes and I wondered how many of his old friends resented him for such a simple luxury.

"You got a woman?"

"The fuck?" I laughed, shaking my head. "You know I'm not seeing anybody, man."

"Okay, well, love isn't everything. You got your own place?" I didn't bother replying. I simply stared at him exhaustedly, waiting for him to get to his point. "Any prospects for kids, marriage, financial progress … Stop me when I hit on something—"

"Okay, I get it. My life is shit." I took the bowl of dough and headed for the door.

"Yo, I never said that," Moe objected, hopping off the counter and stopping me from leaving. "And if you're happy, man, then that's great for you. But, your brother might be thinking you *aren't* happy, you know what I'm sayin'? And with everything going on in his life, he might not wanna rub it in that you're just …"

"Just, *what*?" I spat angrily.

"Coasting," he finished, regret blazing in his kind, sympathetic eyes.

That stung. It stung a lot. But, determined to not let it show, I concluded, "Yeah, well, maybe I'm *happy* just coasting," before I left the kitchen in a huff.

***

I once read about a woman who, even though she was on a diet, enjoyed watching other people eat dessert. She said it was enough to live vicariously through other people, indulging in the things she couldn't let herself have.

That was me with booze. After years of substance abuse and rehab, I had sworn off drugs and alcohol. But, while I couldn't drink, I enjoyed the atmosphere of a bar. I liked the grit. I liked that everyone came together with one goal in mind: to get drunk. And while I couldn't partake, I wanted to, and that was enough to feel connected with these people.

I was sat on a stool, bellied up against the bar with a glass of Coke in hand. I knew it wasn't booze, but to anyone else, it looked like it could've been. The bartender, a buddy of mine called Goose, for one reason or another, wiped down a martini glass as the beginning notes to Lynyrd Skynyrd's "Sweet Home Alabama" blared through the speakers.

"Son of a fucking bitch!" he shouted, throwing the rag down on the bar. "Can someone in this place change the goddamn song?"

"Ah, come on, Goosey. You love this song," I teased, bringing my glass to my lips.

"Oh, yeah. And you know what my favorite thing about it is?"

I placed my drink back onto the bar and gestured for him to go on. "Please, tell me."

"I love that these people insist on playing it over and over and over again. That's my fucking favorite."

I snorted, shaking my head and knowing he was partly right. The jukebox was a hot spot at Goose's bar, and he had made sure to keep a wide selection of music in its library. But for some unknown reason, the song that got the most attention was always good ol' "Sweet Home Alabama" and over the years, I had watched my friend slowly lose his sanity over it.

"You know, you *could* get rid of it," I pointed out. "I mean, I dunno if anybody has told you this before, but you *own* that jukebox."

"Yeah, except that," he leaned his elbows against the bar and came in close, lowering his voice, "what if this fuckin' song is the only reason people come to my shitty little bar?"

Chuckling, I shook my head, as I glanced in the direction of the surrounded jukebox. Drunk girls danced with equally drunk guys, singing at the top of their lungs and laughing as if it wasn't the fifth time they'd heard it tonight.

"Huh," I muttered, before turning back to him. "Maybe you're right. Maybe your success all comes down to this one freakin' song."

Goose nodded, eyes widening, as he said, "That's what I'm sayin', man."

"Maybe," I lifted a finger, "you should be more grateful, then."

"Oh, hell no." He backed away from the bar and grabbed another rag, slinging it over his shoulder. "Never gonna happen. I mean, I won't get rid of it, but I'm not gonna stop bitchin' about it, either."

"Fair enough."

The conversation drifted off, replaced by the lyrics about Birmingham and Watergate, while I stared blankly at the bubbles collecting inside my glass, remembering the conversation I'd had with Moe.

Was I jealous of Zach? I hadn't really thought about it before, but now, I wondered. Our lives had always run pretty parallel to each other, for as long as I could remember. Even when he was the first to venture out on his own, I hadn't been jealous or resentful. His place had given me somewhere to run to, when the apartment in Brooklyn I'd shared with the rest of my family became too stifling. But things were different now, and he wasn't just a quick subway ride away. He had his own house, in his own town, with his own job, and soon, he'd have his own family, too. While I was still single, and still living with Pops.

Suddenly, it felt like life had been kicked into high gear and was rushed away with everyone else, leaving me behind to collect the dust.

"You okay, man?" I looked up to find Goose, eyeing me with concern.

"Yeah, I'm good," I lied, while a sudden surge of despair settled deep in my gut.

The narrow-eyed look he gave said he didn't believe me, but he didn't press any further. Instead, he nodded his chin to the back of the bar.

"Good," he said. "'Cause there's a really hot lookin' girl over there and she's been staring at you for a solid five minutes."

That was enough to distract my worried mind, and I took a quick glance over my shoulder. Sure enough, there she was, a pretty brunette in the tightest white skirt I'd ever seen. Just as I caught her eye, she lifted her hand and wiggled her fingers in a little wave that could only be interpreted as flirty. She had cast the bait into the water, and I was biting.

Grabbing my glass, I excused myself from the bar and left Goose chuckling as I made my approach.

"Hey," I shouted over yet another round of "Sweet Home Alabama."

"Hey!" she parroted, wearing a bright grin framed by watermelon pink lips.

"I'm Vinnie," I introduced myself, offering my hand.

"Anna!"

As her hand slid into mine, her fingers brushed gracefully against my palm, and at that touch, I had a feeling Anna and I would be getting to know each other very well.

***

"Oh, my God," she moaned, gasping as my lips found their way down her neck. I licked the soapy bitterness of perfume from her skin and resisted the urge to cough. "God, that's so good. Don't stop."

Quickies in bar restrooms weren't my favorite, despite how often I found myself in that very situation. These moments always felt cheap and made me feel even cheaper, but I had no intentions of stopping. My hands skimmed the curve of her waist and moved lower to find the hem of her skirt. She used her nails against my scalp, clawing and hissing like a cat, and arched her back in anticipation. The moment was good, my fingers inched their way to the apex of her thighs, and then, my elbow hit the wall of the bathroom stall.

"Fuck," I muttered at the pain of smacking my not-so funny bone.

"Maybe we should go back to your place?" she coyly suggested, and my hands stopped moving altogether.

"I have a roommate," I replied, my mouth against her neck.

"Hmmm," she purred, pressing her hips against mine. "I'm down for a threesome, if you are."

An instantaneous torrent of visions crowded my mind. Thoughts of Pops, of him doing things I wished I'd never thought of before. My mouth pinched at the sudden taste of sour and I backed away from Anna, as far as the stall would allow.

"What's wrong?" she asked, pouting and reaching for my belt loops with waggling fingers.

I gently brushed her hands away. "Nothing. I just remembered I, uh, have an appointment tomorrow morning."

Her once friendly, sultry eyes clouded with an angry hurt. "Asshole," she growled, pushing past me and out the door.

My pride should've been hurt. I should've at least been embarrassed. But instead, I was relieved, and after waiting a couple of minutes, to allow her the time to leave the bar, I exited the bathroom and ordered another Coke.

Goose narrowed his studious eyes and asked, "Uh, do I wanna know what happened in there?" And shrugging, I casually replied, "She could tell I was lyin'."

CHAPTER THREE

ANDREA

The old man had been following me around the hospital all day. Silently watching from the end of a hallway or the corner of a room. He was angry, that was made very obvious by the scowl permanently affixed to his wrinkled face, but he was also stubborn and unrelenting.

"I don't know what you want me to tell you," I muttered impatiently through gritted teeth. He just shook his head. "I'm sorry, okay? I'm just—"

"Hey, girl," Elle, my friend and colleague, said, as she leaned against the counter of the nurse's station. "I'm starving. You wanna take your break and grab some lunch?"

With a quick glance toward the old man, I answered, "Yeah, sure, I just gotta wrap this up and take meds into three-fifteen. Then, I'm good to go."

"Cool. I'll wait in the lobby."

Elle walked away with her bag in hand, leaving just the old man and me once again. I sighed, seeing no other option.

"Why don't you see me later on, after my shift? Then, we'll talk. Okay?"

He seemed to consider the offer for a moment, narrowing his eyes and continuing to scowl through his skepticism. But after a few moments of eerie stillness, sliced with the beeps and whooshes of hospital equipment, and the static I'd been plagued with my entire life, he nodded.

"Okay, good. Find something to do in the meantime. I have a patient to tend to."

From the drawer marked Schreiber, I gathered my patient's meds. Two extra strength Tylenol, a handful of vitamins, and a couple of blood pressure pills filled the little white cup, and with my trusty computer and cart, I rolled down the hall to Room 315.

"Hey, Mrs. Schreiber," I said, turning into the room.

The old woman rolled her head against the pillow to face me. "Hi, honey," she greeted with familiarity, but I saw the confusion glistening in her eyes.

"I'm Andrea," I said cheerfully, never minding that I had given her my name five times already today. "Ready for your medicine?"

"Oh, I suppose," she replied, feigning happiness while exhaustion dimmed the brightness of her smile.

The 87-year-old mother of five and grandmother of twelve had been in and out of the hospital six times in the past year. A stroke in September, a mild cardiac event in January, and a serious case of pneumonia in March, had all left her kids wondering if this was it for their mom. But the old woman's body and spirit were tough. She had survived surgeries and broken bones. She had birthed children. She had been through more than her fair share of trauma in her time on this Earth. She had weathered the storm, but the soul can only take so much before it begins to let go, and I knew Mrs. Schreiber was losing her grip.

I placed the paper cup full of pills in her hand and grabbed the water bottle from her bedside table. "Have you seen the grandkids yet?" I asked as I uncapped the bottle and inserted a straw.

After swallowing the pills and a swig of water, she shook her head. "I don't like them to see me like this," she explained, a hint of sadness in her voice. "If I die here, I don't want their last memory of me to be of this room."

I nodded. "I totally understand."

"At least someone does," she grumbled under her breath. Then, her eyes met mine as she offered an apologetic smile. "My kids don't see any reason why they can't come down."

I sat at the edge of her bed and laid a comforting hand on her knee. "It's hard for them to understand," I replied softly. "But ultimately, you're the patient, and this is your life. You call the shots."

Smiling gratefully, she placed her hand over mine. "Thank you, honey." Then, with a quick glance around the room, she said, "I never thought it'd be like this, you know?"

"What?"

“Dying,” she whispered, as if it was a secret. “I never thought I'd want to be alone.”

“It's a very private thing for a lot of people,” I agreed, choosing not to divulge that she wasn't at all alone.

***

“I heard about this place online,” Elle said excitedly, as she opened the door. “It was ranked as like, the best pizza in the city or something like that.”

“Every pizza place says they have the best pizza,” I disputed.

“Yeah, but *Devin O'Leary* has been here,” she countered, knowing that the mention of my favorite singer would spark excitement.

We stepped inside and were shrouded with a blend of garlic and spice. It was pleasant enough, but it was also crowded. The dining area was completely packed with people, and above their racket was the familiar white noise that threatened to drive me crazy on a daily basis.

“But still, it's just pizza,” I said, resisting the urge to stuff my fingers in my ears. “We can get pizza anywhere. We could just order a pie and eat it in the breakroom.”

Elle knew I hated crowds, and with a glance around the room, her smile wilted. “I'm sorry,” she sighed. “I'm just dying to try this place, and after the night I had, I could really use it.”

Sighing and sucking down my groan, I nodded begrudgingly. “Fine. But I'm eating outside.”

The line was long, and the cacophony of voices and fuzzy static made the wait feel like torture. I tried to admire the bricked walls and old photographs of who I assumed was the owner, but I knew better than to try and distract myself. It was always impossible and every passing second felt like an hour.

Eventually, we ordered our food from a tall man with chocolate skin and warm eyes. Then, we waited some more, as he called to a Jenna to grab our slices and sodas, and we watched as the curly-haired woman bustled around to collect our lunch.

“I had such a freakin’ night,” Elle complained, crowding one of my ears, amidst the static, while the other was occupied with the now annoyed curly-haired woman.

“Dammit, we're outta paper plates,” she muttered, before calling out, “Vinnie! Grab some plates back there, will ya?”

I believe we are all born with gifts, and one of mine is intuition. I could be having the most ordinary day, until I hear a name, see a sign, or turn a corner, and intuition will strike. Sometimes it comes as a ping in the gut, or as a gentle brush against my heart. And right now, it was a flick against my brain, a sudden rekindling of a memory.

I turned my head toward what I assumed to be the kitchen door, as Elle continued, “Mike is driving me completely insane. And it's not like I ask for much. Just give me some attention, you know what I mean?"

"Uh-huh," I muttered, watching the door.

"So, last night, we're getting hot and heavy, and he tells me he really wants me to, you know, use my mouth. And I did, thinking, like, I'm gonna get the same treatment, right? But the bastard just fell asleep—girl, are you even listening to me?"

"What?" I faced her abruptly, my eyes wide and startled. "Yeah, sorry. I'm just, I dunno, distracted or something. What were you saying?"

Elle went on about her night, telling me about her night of laying awake, with her sleeping husband and her vibrator. I offered my sympathies, just as the door swung open and I heard a voice so distinctly familiar from a moment that shouldn't have been so profound.

"Here ya go."

I turned to see a tall man with dark eyes and dark hair peeking out from beneath his white cap. I would have to be blind to not recognize he was attractive, but it wasn't his looks that awakened my intuition. It was that I knew him once, albeit briefly. We had met just days ago, outside the Regina Miller show. And in a city of millions of people, what were the chances that I'd find myself face to face with him again?

"Damn, girl, you're seriously on your own planet today, huh?"

"Yeah," I answered absentmindedly. "I guess so."

Jenna plated our slices, before handing them to us over a glass partition. "Here you go, ladies. Enjoy."

We took our food, but while Elle went to find a seat on the sidewalk, I stood near the counter, watching awkwardly as Vinnie went about his business. I wanted him to notice me, to recognize me, and to make me feel a little less like a freak and more like the feeling was mutual. But he never looked in my direction before disappearing back into the kitchen, leaving me wilted with disappointment.

"Andrea, what the hell are you doing?" Elle laughed, as I headed outside and approached the table.

"Sorry," I repeated, and readied myself to eating my lunch, while trying to escape the static.

***

Finally, it was the end of my workday. I had already given my patients' report to the night shift and my purse was already slung over my shoulder. But before I could leave and find sanctuary at home, I turned to the old man.

Still following. Still watching.

"Okay, sir," I said quietly with a weighted sigh. "Let's do this."

He offered a short nod before leading the way to Room 315. Mrs. Schreiber was asleep, cuddled in her bed, with her arms around an old stuffed bear, and I imagined her in the beginning of her life. A young girl, full of possibility and hope, dreaming of what her life would be like. Wondering who she would marry, who her children would be. And now, her story had been written. Her children were grown with families of their own and her husband was already gone from this Earth. It was time to close the book on her life here and now, so that the next could begin.

It was time for her to let go.

"I'll call her children before I go home," I whispered into the room, almost dark from the setting sun.

The old man nodded gratefully in reply.

"Are you sure I shouldn't send her home first and let her die in her own bed?"

His chest puffed with a silent sigh, before he shook his head.

"I guess, in the end, it doesn't really matter, huh?"

He shook his head again and placed a hand on my shoulder. I couldn't feel the pressure of his hand against my skin, but somewhere in my soul, I sensed it there. The warmth and care in his touch. I smiled, despite hating this particular gift of mine, if you could even call it a gift at all, and he smiled back, his eyes twinkling with excitement. Then, the old man sat at the edge of her bed and silently watched as she slept. He leaned in, put his mouth close to her ear, and although I couldn't hear what he said, I saw her smile and that was enough.

Sitting up straight, he turned to me and nudged his chin toward the door.

"Okay, Mr. Schreiber," I whispered. "Take care of her, okay?"

He cocked his head and eyed me sardonically, as if to say, *duh*.

Then, looking at the old woman laying in the bed, so fragile and weak, I said, "Goodbye, Mrs. Schreiber, and good luck."

CHAPTER FOUR

VINNIE

Aaron Paul's character, Jesse Pinkman, was high again and up to no good. I shifted uncomfortably on the couch and unsuccessfully ignored the itch beneath my skin. It whispered sweet nothings in my ears and into my brain, and I shook my head to try and chase that little devil away.

Pops grunted a noise of disgust beside me. "I'll never understand what makes someone do this shit to themselves."

The devil on my shoulder begged me to reply, to defend my past decisions, to justify the cravings that still pricked against my skin. Instead, I continued watching the show and maintained my silence.

"I get that it's an addiction," he went on, thrusting his hand toward the screen. "But that addiction begins with a choice, doesn't it?"

"I guess," I said, bringing the nail of my thumb up to my teeth.

"Well, what about you?"

I glanced at him. "Me?"

Pops nodded, a little too eager. "Yeah! I know it's probably not somethin' you wanna talk about, but I've always wondered. What made you decide to … you know …" He circled his hand in the air, searching for the appropriate words.

"Snort some shit up my nose?" I offered brusquely, cocking a brow.

"Well ..." His lips pinched with consideration, before saying, "Yeah. I guess that's what I'm tryin' to say."

It had been years since my brother and I had first gotten ourselves wrapped up in our addiction to drugs, and although I had spent a lot of that time too high to remember much of anything, I could still recall that first hit. How good it felt to descend into darkness. How good it felt to escape. How, for the first time in a while, it had felt good to be *me*.

"I dunno," I lied, thinking about that party from what now felt like another life. "I guess I wanted to feel cool or some stupid shit like that."

"Did you?"

Glancing at him, I saw the disappointment in his expression, and said, "I don't remember."

"Hm," he grunted, nodding. "I don't know why I brought it up, sorry."

"Don't worry about it."

"I just realized I had never asked," he went on, shrugging.

We resumed watching the show as if nothing had happened, but my mind wouldn't allow me to pay attention. I felt too vulnerable now, watching this show that reminded me of things I had left behind and still struggled not to think about every single day. Things that only one other person in my life understood.

"I need a cigarette," I announced abruptly, standing and heading toward the fire escape.

"Okay," Pops said quietly, nodding.

While the apartment was a good size for the two of us, that didn't make it large by any stretch of the imagination. It took me no time at all to reach the window from the couch, but before I could climb outside, Pops stopped me.

"Junior, did I say somethin'?"

"Nah." I shook my head, pulling out my pack of smokes and sliding one out.

"You don't like talkin' about it?"

I laughed. "I really gotta work on my lying skills."

Pops shrugged like his shoulders were too heavy, weighed down by something I couldn't see. "Or you could just be honest."

"No," I answered his question bluntly. "I don't like talkin' about it. Not with you."

He nodded slowly, unsuccessfully hiding the insult in his eyes, and said, "Okay."

Clearing my throat, I returned the nod, feeling that we'd come to an understanding, and climbed through the window to stand on the fire escape and smoke.

With a cigarette lit, I held it firmly between my lips and called Zach. He answered on the second ring. "Hey, what's up?" he asked, breathless and clearly irritated, and I groaned.

"Were you just fucking?"

His laughter blended easily with the street symphony down below and I missed him. "No, I wish. I'm over at Greyson's dad's place, playing hide and seek with Izzy before she goes to bed. But Grey hid her somewhere and I can't freakin' find her. Like, how hard is it to find a five-year-old?"

I am not jealous of my brother, I had to remind myself, as I chuckled and said, "They're stealthy as fuck, man. And small. Small fits in small places."

"And it doesn't help that this house is so damn big," he grumbled. "If we were at the old place in Brooklyn, this wouldn't be a fuckin' problem, you know what I'm sayin'?"

I smiled at the mention of our childhood home and how funny it is that the places we grow to despise, become the places we miss the most. "Yeah, well, you can find anything in a shoebox," I said, before taking a long drag from the cigarette and pinching it between my fingers.

Smoke filled my lungs and I imagined I could feel them twist and char from the poison before I exhaled into the dark night. It painted the sooty, black sky with a swirl of grey, before fading into nothing, like it had never been there at all.

"You got a point there," he grumbled, then asked, "So, what's up?"

"Can't I call my favorite big brother?"

"I mean, you *can*," he said, "but you don't. You're too cool to call. You *text*."

Sniffing a laugh, I nodded to the sky. "It's true."

"So, tell me what's up while I look for this kid."

Suddenly, I couldn't remember why I thought calling would be a good idea. Z and I had gone through the war together but, from what I could tell, he wasn't fighting those demons anymore. I knew there was some residual temptation—that's what kept him from drinking or partying, too—but I doubted it was still a *battle*. Not like it was for me, regardless of how infrequently I was drafted into combat.

"Pops just asked me why I used," I admitted quietly, feeling uncomfortable but seeing no point in lying to him.

There was a pause on the other line, then Zach said to someone else, "Hey, tell Izzy I had to use the potty." Then, I waited what felt like an eternity for him to close a door and say, "He actually asked you that?"

"Yeah."

"Holy shit," he muttered. "Why did he say anything?"

"I dunno. We were watchin' *Breaking Bad*, and out of nowhere, he just brought it up."

"That's really fuckin' weird."

Years ago, Pops had walked into the old apartment, just as Zach and I were in the middle of our former favorite pastime, snorting coke. He threatened to kick us out if we didn't get ourselves into rehab, and afterward, there had been some understandable trust issues. He had eluded to things and had silently speculated, but he had never talked about it or asked questions. I'd always just assumed it was simply that he wasn't much for expressing himself verbally, which was just fine because I wasn't either. So, why he had brought it up after so long like that was really fucking weird, to say the least.

"Yeah, man, I dunno. I mean, he's been on a *Breaking Bad* kick, so maybe that's all it is," I offered weakly, studying the swirls of smoke coiling from the tip of my cigarette. "I just needed to tell you about it. It was so fuckin' … I dunno ..."

"Weird," Zach repeated, and I nodded a silent reply.

***

"Junior."

The voice came to me in sleep and I stirred, shaking my head against the pillow. I couldn't tell if I was awake or dreaming, and before I could open my eyes, I muttered a grunted, "Huh?"

"Vinnie."

It was Pops. His voice was gentle and quiet, but I couldn't ignore the hint of alarm.

Opening my eyes and turning my head toward his voice, I saw him there, standing in the glow from the hallway that streamed seamlessly into my room. One of his hands was pressed to his chest, while the other gripped the door frame. Startled by his stance, I was instantly alert and sat up.

"What's goin' on?" I asked, rubbing the sleep from my eyes.

"Something's wrong," he said, shaking his head. "I don't feel right."

"What doesn't feel right?" I threw back the sheet and climbed out of bed. "Your chest? Your heart?"

"I—" He shook his head and furrowed his brow. "I, I don't know."

The old man would never admit that he needed to go to the hospital. Years ago, when he had his heart attack, it was Jenna who'd had to talk him into going. But, I reminded myself, this time he had woken me up. He was alarmed enough to inadvertently ask for help, and so, I grabbed a shirt and a pair of sweatpants and told him we were going.

"I don't think I need to—" His words were stopped with a wince and his fingers dug into his chest. I quickly made the decision to get him on the bed while I grabbed the phone and called 911.

The paramedics came. Pops protested weakly as they got him onto a gurney and rushed him down to the ambulance. I took the ride with them to the hospital, speeding through New York City traffic, and once we were there and he was admitted, I called Zach and Jenna to tell them where we were.

Of course, they wanted to know what was wrong, but I didn't know. They wanted to know if it was his heart, but I didn't know. They wanted to know if he was stable, if he was okay, but I didn't fucking know. It angered me that they would ask, and it infuriated me even more that I was too useless to have any answers for them.

The beeping monitors put my worried mind on a fast train back to his heart attack. When he had been in Intensive Care and everything was so touch and go. Jenna had sat Zach and me down and told us we needed to make some decisions that none of us were prepared to make, in the event he took a turn for the worse. But Pops had been given his second chance at life, and now, I worried he wouldn't be granted a third.

"Junior."

With my thumb nail between my teeth, I took a glance at him, laying in his bed, so alert and aware. "Yeah?"

"You're scarin' the shit out of me, boy."

Lowering my hand, I forced a pained smile. "Sorry."

He lifted a hand slightly, as to not disturb his IV, and waved toward the door. "Get outta here."

"What?" I asked, taken aback.

"You heard me. Get outta here. Go smoke or somethin'."

With jaw slack and eyes wide, I shook my head. "What are you, crazy? I'm not leaving you here."

"I'm not sayin' to *leave*," he groaned, rolling his eyes. "I'm just sayin', get some air. You're makin' me nervous."

I pulled in a deep breath and released it as I stood up, eyeing him warily. Pops rolled his eyes again and said, "I'm not gonna die if you leave, Vinnie."

Alarmed by the D word, but not wanting to show it, I chuckled and turned toward the door before I could get choked up. "You better not," I managed to say, then left the room.

As much as I didn't want to leave, the moment I was outside in the hallway, I exhaled, unaware that I'd been holding my breath. My shoulders felt just a little lighter and my chest felt just a little less constricted. There was still a fear in walking away, as though his life was dependent on my being there at his side, but I resigned myself to moving down the hallway and to the elevator in the waiting room.

I stepped into the small room, and just as I pushed the button to call the elevator, the sliding doors opened and out stepped a woman in scrubs, looking down at her phone as she bumped into me.

"Oh!" she exclaimed and took a step back, looking up past her thick-framed glasses and into my eyes. "I'm so—" Her words were abruptly cut short as she cocked her head, her gaze flooding with recognition. "It's *you*."

As I shot an arm out to stop the elevator doors from closing, I raised an eyebrow. "Me?"

She looked at me as if I should know her, as if I should've immediately recognized her, the way you would with an old friend. But I didn't, and when she realized that wasn't going to happen, her face fell, disheartened and disappointed.

"I met you at the Regina Miller show," she said. "Outside, remember? You didn't have your lighter."

I tipped my head as recollection settled in, remembering a tight tank top and little denim shorts.

"That's right. You're the wiseass who thinks she's a fake."

She sighed. "I don't *think* she's a fake, I *know* she is. But whatever, yeah, that's me. I'm glad you remember."

Snorting, I nodded. "Sure, whatever you say. Anyway, it was nice seein' you again. Have a good night." Then, I stepped into the elevator and let the doors close, all while noticing she hadn't walked away.

***

After smoking and getting a breath of air, I headed back upstairs to find Pops asleep. At his side was a nurse, dressed in scrubs and a sloppy, blonde bun. When she heard me enter the room, she turned to stare at me with now familiar, blue eyes.

"We just keep bumping into each other," she laughed.

"You're his nurse?"

She rolled her eyes and turned back to her computer screen. "No, I just thought I'd creep on him for no reason."

Stifling a groan, I dropped back in my chair. "Do they know what's goin' on with him yet?"

"Um …" She glanced over her shoulder, biting her lip. "Well, nothing's been written in his file yet, they're still running some tests, but I could give you a guess, if you'd like."

"Yeah, sure," I nodded, "tell me what you think."

Clearing her throat, she stepped away from the computer and toward me. "He didn't have another heart attack. What's going on … or, what I *think* is going on is, your father is battling heart disease."

"Oh," I said, nodding. "So, he's gonna take some pills and be okay."

The nurse chewed at her lip for a moment before shaking her head. "Well, it's not always that simple, and with Ischemic heart disease, the prognosis isn't great. You should be prepared for that. But we can be positive and hope for the—"

"Well, you just said that they're still running tests, right?" I interrupted, instantly annoyed and defensive.

She swallowed, clutching at her hands. "Right, but—"

"Then, I guess we'll wait for the results to come back before we start assumin' anything."

Nodding, she offered an obviously fake smile. "Absolutely. And I'm Andrea, by the way. I have your dad tonight."

I nodded once, not bothering to ask how she knew he was my father. "Vinnie."

For a moment, Andrea stood, frozen in front of me, before walking back to her computer. *She's weird*, I thought. Weird and awkward, but that sarcastic wit of hers told me she was okay. *With a nice ass*, I also noted, glancing at her back, and smirked.

***

Pops hadn't slept much, and I slept even less, little thanks to Andrea and her seemingly constant vital checks. So, come morning, he and I were both running on fumes and desperate to be back home and in our beds.

Without warning, the door of the room flew open and in came my brother and sister, worried and frantic.

"I told you guys, you didn't have to come," I mumbled, seeing as Pops had only just drifted off into something kind of like sleep. "I know shit looked kinda bad last night, but we're good. At least for now."

Jenna scowled angrily. "You're kidding, right? I couldn't even get back to sleep after you called."

"I tried but there wasn't any point," Zach muttered in reply, glancing over to the bed. Then, he asked, "How's he doin'?"

I shrugged. "I dunno. I mean, he had that little episode late last night but that was it. After a while, he was feeling better."

Jen swiped a rogue tear from her cheek. "I can't believe we're back here again."

"Me neither."

Zach tightened his arms around his middle and shook his head. "He should've taken better care of himself. We knew he'd be back here again if he didn't get his—"

"Will you stop?" Jenna snapped quietly, smacking the back of her hand against his chest. "We could all talk about what he should've been doing or what he should've not been doing, but the fact of the matter is that he's—"

She was interrupted by the door opening. I thought it would be Andrea again, she was just about due to check Pops's vitals again, but it wasn't her. A doctor, short with dark hair and dark skin, entered the room wielding a clipboard. She saw the three of us, huddled together at the foot of our father's bed, and when she noticed he was finally asleep, she beckoned for us to join her in the hallway.

"My name is Doctor Singh," she introduced herself, offering a kind smile to each of us. "You are all Mr. Marino's children, yes?"

We nodded in unison as Jenna asked, "How is he?"

Dr. Singh's smile shifted to a straight, thin line as she addressed her notes. "Well, at the moment, he appears to be stable. He didn't experience a heart attack last night but—"

"Oh, thank God," Jenna breathed, gripping onto Zach's arm.

Clearly not a fan of being interrupted, the doctor hardened her glare as she continued, "*But*, after running a number of tests, we have been able to confirm that your father has coronary artery disease, or CAD."

Every vertebrae in my spine locked stiffly into place as my brother asked, "So … what exactly does that mean?"

Her expression became solemn and a deep line formed between her brows. "What happens with CAD is, plaque lines the walls of the blood vessels, making the pathways to the heart more and more narrow, until eventually the blood flow is stopped altogether."

Jenna gasped and took a hold of my arm, and I asked, "So, why can't you just clean them out? I mean, they already put in those … what were they? Stents?" The doctor nodded slowly, already exhausted with my attempt at playing doctor. "Right, okay. So, just do that again."

"That's not how it works, Vin," Jenna whispered from beside me, her voice quivering, and I looked at the doctor for confirmation.

Dr. Singh sighed. "I'm afraid she's right. If caught earlier, the progression of CAD can be slowed with treatment, but as it stands, years of damage have already been done. We can try to do what we can, but …"

Then, Zach asked the question the rest of us were afraid to ask. "So, what are you sayin' here? He's gonna die?"

She released a deep breath, and in her eyes, I saw how much she dreaded what came next. I thought about how hard her job must be, to deliver this type of news to family members. To *children*. Because, at the end of the day, that's what we were. Adults, sure, but we were still his children and he was still our father, and no amount of adulthood can prepare a child for that look.

My heart had already started to break before she even spoke.

"I'm afraid so," she said quietly, barely nodding.

Jenna's sob crashed through me and her hand released my arm to cover her mouth. "I'm sorry," she said needlessly, her voice muffled behind her palm. "I just … I need to …" Before she could finish, she was hurrying down the hall to the waiting room, and it was just my brother and me, alone with the angel of death.

Zach cleared his throat. "So, um …" He cleared his throat again and sniffled. I couldn't look at him, knowing he was crying. If I saw my big brother cry, I would fucking lose it. "How long do you think?"

"It's hard to say," Dr. Singh admitted, looking between Zach and me and maintaining eye contact. "I hesitate to guess—"

"Humor us," Zach interjected. "Please."

The doctor sighed and let her shoulders lift in a limp shrug. "If I *had* to guess, I'd say about six months."

The breath was forced from my lungs with an invisible punch to my aching gut. I reached out a hand to grapple for my brother's shoulder, as he clapped a hand over his mouth, just like Jenna had moments before. I worried he'd leave me, too, with the need to cry or scream or search for air that no longer seemed to exist. But he stayed by my side and muttered, "Jesus fuckin' Christ."

"Please remember, that's just a guess," Dr. Singh pressed, but from the look in her eyes, I could see it was more than *just a guess*. It was her professional hypothesis, and maybe it was her way of just being kind, by giving the old man a little more time.

She excused herself to speak to Pops behind the closed door of his room, leaving Zach and me in a monotonous hallway of doors, handrails, and bustling nurses with carted computers. We didn't say anything for several seconds that felt more like hours, as we fought to wrap our minds around the sudden news and the sudden reality that soon, sooner than we had ever thought, we'd be facing the world alone.

Then, Zach wiped his hand away from his mouth, letting it drop at his side. "She said years of damage," he said, his voice hoarse and strained.

"Yeah," I said, nodding.

"How the fuck is that even possible? He sees a cardiologist pretty regularly. I mean, he's not the greatest at keepin' up with his health, but he at least does *that*. How the hell can there be *years* of damage?"

Narrowing my eyes, I took in what he was saying, realizing that it didn't add up, and when the doctor emerged from the room moments later, I stopped her from walking away.

"Wait, we have a question."

"Of course." She nodded, keeping her back perfectly straight, when I knew she wanted to slump away and hide. Nobody wants to give news like that to anybody, not even someone who does it regularly.

"He had a heart attack several years ago. How can he have *years* of damage without his cardiologist noticing it?"

Dr. Singh pulled her lips between her teeth for a fraction of a second, showcasing a hesitation that did not sit well at all, before saying, "I think you all need to speak with your father." And then, she walked away.

CHAPTER FIVE

VINNIE

"What do you mean, you *knew* about it?!" Zach shouted in the middle of the hospital room.

Pops wouldn't look at him. Hell, he wouldn't look at any of us. He just shrugged and said, "I told you. I've known about it for a while."

"And at what point were you gonna tell *us*?!" In reply, Pops simply shrugged again without saying another word and I watched as my brother came dangerously close to detonation. "You gotta be fuckin' kidding me! You seriously weren't planning on saying a goddamn thing to us?! Go ahead and tell me you weren't gonna say anything to us, and I swear to God, I will fuckin'—"

"Zach," Jenna croaked, clutching a wad of tissues in her hand. "Please."

He stopped his pacing to glare in her direction. "Are you *seriously* okay with this, Jen? Because I'm sure as fuck not." Then, he glanced at me and asked, "What about you, Vin? Huh? You've been awfully fuckin' quiet."

It was true. After we had returned to my father's room and confronted him, I struggled to find the ability to speak, as I listened to Pops confess to knowing about the heart disease for several years. What could I say? There was nothing any of us could do to change what had already happened, and so, I had just sat there in an uncomfortable chair. Feeling the sadness and anger both of my siblings were exhibiting, while not knowing how to express it myself.

I dropped my gaze to the white, linoleum floor. "I dunno what you want me to say, Zach."

He scoffed, thick with bitterness. "I want you's both to have my fuckin' back right now, that's what I want. But I guess I'm not gonna get it." Then, he abruptly turned and headed to the door.

"Where are you g-going?" Jenna asked, choking on a sob.

"Home," he spat angrily, opening the door and closing it heavily behind him.

I began to stand and said, "I guess I'll go get him."

"No," Pops said, lifting a hand. "Let him go."

"O-kay," I murmured, slowly sitting back down.

The room fell into a deep, heavy silence and the space between the walls filled with everything we didn't know how to say. Pops laid motionless in his bed, staring blankly toward the window that overlooked the cityscape where the world continued, even while ours fell apart. Jenna stood awkwardly by the bathroom, holding the doorknob precariously and pushing the door an inch open and then shut, open and shut, open and shut. My sight was trained only on the floor. The seams between each tile and the grainy, beige pattern in the linoleum. I imagined every pair of feet that had scuffled across that floor. All those shoes, the different people who had lived in them. And then, there were the questions. How many of those people had walked across that floor and laid in that bed, never to get up again? Would my father be one of them? And as soon as those questions came, so did the reality of his mortality. If his heart attack hadn't driven that home, this diagnosis definitely did, and my throat thickened with the urgent need to cry.

"I gotta get out of here," I muttered, hastily standing and heading toward the door.

"Where you goin', junior?"

Junior.

Junior.

Nobody else ever called me junior, and the moment he was dead, nobody would ever call me junior again.

"I'll be back," I blurted out before the tears could come and I left the room.

***

I found Zach sitting outside on a stone bench overlooking a small garden, a gentle and natural reprieve from the morbidity inside. I dropped down beside him, heavy with grief, and frantically dug into my pocket for my lighter and smokes.

"Fuck," I said to the white and red packet. My hands shook as I pulled a cigarette out and stuffed it between my lips. Four times, I tried to light the damn thing, and four times, I failed. With an aggravated huff, Zach snatched the Zippo from my hand, lit the cigarette, and then, threw the lighter into my lap.

"Hey!" I grabbed it before it could slip through my thighs and onto the sidewalk. "What the hell are you pissed at me for?"

He shook his head. "I'm not pissed at you."

"Oh, great. Glad we cleared that up."

I took a long drag and held the smoke in my lungs until I thought I might choke, feeling warm and heady with its venom. I exhaled slowly, closed my eyes, and imagined my world the way it was a day ago. Normal. Decent. It hadn't been great, it hadn't even been good, but it was mine and it had been okay. I wanted to go back there. I wished I could.

"I just can't believe this shit!" Zach exclaimed, and startled, my eyes snapped open. "I can't believe *him*! For fuckin' years, he didn't trust us, he didn't believe us, and now, we find out that he's been lying to *us*? That's the pot calling the fuckin' kettle black right there, that's what that is." A paper napkin skittered across the sidewalk, carried by a gentle breeze. It landed on the toe of his sneaker and as though that napkin was the materialization of heart disease itself, he kicked it away angrily and shouted, "Son of a bitch!"

"I know," I said, nodding and puffing away at the cigarette. "I can't even look at him right now."

"He's a fuckin' hypocrite."

I turned to look at him and take in the anger etched in the lines on his face. My brother had been through his share of shit but never before had I seen him so mad, so hurt and betrayed.

"I know," I agreed.

"How's Jen?"

"Not great," I said, before exhaling.

"Yeah," Zach nodded. "I figured."

Our sister had always been in the unique position of never doing wrong. She was rarely scolded and almost never in trouble. Once upon a time, I had envied her for that, until I realized she'd never had much of a choice. She needed to be perfect, to counteract every fucked-up thing my brother and I had done. Once I'd acknowledged that, I just felt bad that she'd never really been allowed to live.

But Jenna had also gotten something that Zach and I never did. And that was an undying, close knit bond with our father. One she'd never had to work at.

It only seemed natural that she'd be more upset now and less angry.

"I gotta go home," he muttered. "I need … I dunno, time to think or something. You know what I'm sayin'? And I can't think with," he gestured behind us, toward the hospital looming over our shoulders, "all this shit."

"I feel you," I replied honestly, while also despising him for having somewhere else to go.

"I'll call you, okay? And if there's any update, let me know."

"Yeah," I said, nodding. "Sure."

We stood and Zach pulled me into his arms. We hugged tightly, and for a brief fraction of time, I felt about thirty years younger, wrapped in the protection of my big, strong brother. The one I looked up to, the one with all the answers. But then, he let go and walked away, and that's when he became the one who abandoned me when I needed him most.

***

After Pops fell asleep, I sent Jenna home. She'd been sitting on the windowsill, leaning in an uncomfortable position against the glass and dozing off. I told her she needed to go home and rest, and that I would call her if anything changed. She had hesitated, but eventually, she did leave.

And then, I was alone.

Alone with my dying father.

I hated being alone.

I pulled out my phone to occupy my time and soon found myself reading about coronary artery disease. I didn't get far into my research via Doctor Google before I spotted a word I'd heard before: Ischemic. It stuck out to me like a big, red, throbbing sore thumb, and that's when Nurse Andrea walked in, pushing her computer.

"Hi," she greeted, too cheerfully for my taste.

"Hey."

She cocked her head as she typed. "Everything okay?"

"Well, I found out my dad's dying, but other than that, I'm just swell."

Exhaling, then nodding, she said, "I saw in the doctor's report. I'm sorry."

"You already knew," I accused pointedly.

"Huh?" She continued typing, never looking at me.

"You said ischemic."

"Right," she replied, nodding. "Coronary artery disease. That's what the doctor—"

"You *specifically* said ischemic, that's the word you used, and that was before the doctor had even diagnosed him," I said, putting my phone down beside me and studying the firm set of her jaw as she worked. "How the hell did you know that just by looking at him?"

She shook her head. "I've been doing this for a—"

"Do you work for his cardiologist?"

Her typing stopped abruptly; her fingers laying still against the keys. "W-What?"

Bingo.

"Is that how you knew he had ischemic heart disease?"

Andrea turned toward me and shook her head. "N-No, I've only ever worked here."

"Then, explain to me how you knew what was wrong with him. Because the only thing that makes sense to me is that you work for his doctor, 'cause," I pointed to the point, "*he* already knew and apparently, so did you, so—"

One hand pressed to her chest as she gasped. "He knew?"

"Yeah," I shot at her, unconvinced of her shock. "He's known about it for years, apparently, and decided his kids didn't need to be filled in. How nice, right?"

"I'm so sorry, Vinnie."

She used my name like she knew me, like we were friends. But we weren't. She was a liar and a fraud, and the longer she stared at me, with her big, blue, sympathetic eyes, the more I wanted to scream into her face. Anything to stop her from looking at me like that, and maybe to pull the truth from her lying lips.

"Knock it off," I barked.

Only mildly taken aback by my tone, she asked, "Excuse me?"

"You're lying."

"I haven't lied to you about anything."

Her eyebrow twitched. It was nearly undetectable and if I hadn't been watching her so intently, I would've missed it. But I hadn't and now I knew for sure that something was up. I stared her down, as a thick tension manifested between us, foolishly believing that a staring contest would uncover the things she wasn't telling me. But she was headstrong, despite her subtle tell, and there was no beating down her walls without more coaxing.

I broke the hold on her gaze and turned my attention to the floor. "They gave him six months to live." I don't know why I said it, let alone to her, the lying nurse. I guess maybe I just needed to feel the words in my mouth, try them on for size and make them real. They singed my tongue with the bitter truth and flicked my brain with medical facts I couldn't pretend to understand. All while my heart begged to insist it was the biggest lie I'd ever told.

Andrea was quiet, save the gentleness of her breath. She swallowed, and then sighed, before saying, "It's just an estimate, though."

"Yeah, well." I lifted a hand and scrubbed the back of my head with my palm. "They're the doctors. So …"

"So, what?"

I looked back at her, furrowing my brow. "*So*, they know a whole lot more about this shit than I do."

Nodding slowly, she crossed her arms over her chest and took a step toward me, keeping her eyes on the floor. "That might be true, yes. But what you have to keep in mind is," she crouched down to the floor at my feet and purposefully sought my gaze, "the doctors are only going off of textbook information. They know the *science* behind your father's disease, but they don't know *him*."

"Yeah, well, science is pretty important in this case," I replied, chuckling bitterly.

"It is," she agreed softly.

"So, then, what are you talkin' about?"

One of her hands, one of her small, delicate hands, lifted to cover my knee. "What I'm saying is," she began in a near whisper, "they might know that your dad is going to die, but they can't tell you exactly when. So many people defy the odds and live years after their expected expiration date, while others are allowed a much smaller timeframe. Science tells us a lot, but when it really comes down to it, Vinnie, it's up to your dad to decide exactly when he's done fighting this."

She spoke carefully, as though every word was chosen with a firm, gentle purpose. I was sure she gave speeches like this on the regular, that it was all par for the course in her world. It wouldn't have surprised me to learn that she didn't actually care as much as she seemed to in that moment. Yet, it worked, and I allowed myself to feel comforted by the things she said.

"Thanks," I replied, nodding.

"Yeah, of course." She offered a cautious smile, then asked, "Do you live far from here?"

"Nah."

"So, why don't you go home and get some sleep?" At the question, my eyes darted toward the bed and the form of my sleeping father. Andrea's hand squeezed my knee. I had forgotten it was even there. "I'm going to be here until seven this evening. I promise to take care of him until you get back."

My gaze returned to hers and suddenly, I wasn't a thirty-four-year-old man but a little boy. I wanted to crawl into that bed and curl up beside my father, the way I used to when I thought thunder was the only thing to be scared of.

"You *promise*?"

She must've seen that little boy, the one who was struggling not to cry, because she smiled gently and nodded. "I promise."

CHAPTER SIX

ANDREA

"Good morning, Mr. Marino!" I entered the room with a cheerful smile. "What can I get for you?"

The balding man on the bed was only seventy-five, but he looked about ninety. His failing health was not treating him kindly. From what I could tell, in my experience, it usually never does.

He flapped a hand, smacking the pillow behind his head. "You call these pillows? It's like sleepin' on a plastic bag."

I fought back a laugh as I moved toward the head of the bed. "You know why that is?"

"I can't imagine," he muttered dryly.

"Because," I smiled, gently fluffing the flimsy thing behind his head, "it *is* a plastic bag."

"Humph." His scowl deepened. "Some accommodations you's got over here."

The old are generally bitter. They hate that their time is so limited. They hate that they wasted so much of it, they hate that they took so much of it for granted, and they hate how there was never going to be enough, even if they'd lived to see their one-hundredth birthday. Vincent Marino was no exception. I could see the brewing despair in his eyes, the frantic need to hold on while also knowing his grip was slipping.

"Not exactly the Ritz," I agreed. "But the food isn't terrible." I eyed the tray hovering over his bed.

"Pfft," Vincent spat, waving a hand toward the scrambled eggs and toast. "This crap is barely passable as food. You want food? You go to my pizzeria. *That's* food."

The old woman standing in the corner of the room rolled her eyes in a silent display of intolerance. She shook her head, crossed her arms, and moved to stare out the window.

"Well, I have a couple minutes," I said, pulling up a chair to the side of the bed. "Tell me about it."

"Not much to tell."

"Oh, come on!" I exclaimed, throwing my hands in the air. "You can't tell me you have this amazing pizza and then say there isn't much to tell."

Vincent sighed and rubbed his fingertips against the lines between his brows. "Ah, well …" He hesitated, dropping his hand down to the mattress, before continuing, "I opened her up years ago with my wife. We poured everything into the joint, all our money and time, and it wasn't until just a few years ago that the place really took off."

The old woman scoffed without a sound, shaking her head and rolling her eyes again, and I smiled gently.

“Better late than never though, right?”

“Yeah, well, if it hadn’t been for my son’s husband, it never would’ve happened at all.”

Son’s husband? The thought of Vinnie being taken sparked an aggravating hint of jealousy, while the idea of him not even batting for the same team left me with a shameful despair. But I knew Mr. Marino had two sons. Maybe the husband was that of Vinnie’s brother.

“Sounds like he came into your lives for a reason, then,” I said, keeping the conversation going without asking any questions, despite my itching curiosity.

“He’s a good kid,” Vincent answered astutely.

It seemed like a door had creaked open, beckoning me to just take a peek inside. I grasped at the opportunity and said, “I guess he’d have to be. All of your children seem really nice.”

Vincent’s chest puffed with just a tinge of pride. “We’ve had our ups and downs, but all things considered, they turned out all right.”

“You and your wife must be proud.” I shot a quick glance toward the old woman, just in time for her to cast her gaze downward and turn her back to the room.

“Well, I can’t speak much for my wife, but I know I am.”

***

When I was six, my parents moved my sisters and me to Long Island. They had bought an old house down by the bay, in a town called Islip, and that was where I met my imaginary friend, Jamie.

Jamie never spoke, and that had struck me as strange initially, but after a while, I welcomed her silence and learned to communicate in spite of it. At the time, my sisters were mean teenagers, and the kids at school had been even meaner, so to face Jamie with nothing but a smile on her sweet face was a nice change from my norm. She'd offered a kind, listening ear, and kept me company on lonely Saturdays spent in my room. And although I think I had always expected her to disappear when I no longer needed her around, I enjoyed our time together and never took a second of it for granted.

But Jamie never disappeared.

As I grew in years and height, Jamie stayed young and small, and it wasn't until I knew of the passing of a little girl in my parents' house that I understood why. And with Jamie, came others, old and young. In the grocery store. At the mall. At school. I couldn't go anywhere without seeing the dead, and I learned very quickly how distracting they can be, once they knew of my ability to see them. Dates were ruined, relationships failed, and I entered adulthood under the resignation that, if I couldn't turn my sixth sense off, I'd have to accommodate it, with zero room for anything else.

And when you live your life a certain way, it becomes routine. You might look at someone else's life and think to yourself, *wow, that must be nice.* But then, you just carry on living without a second thought because that's all you know to do. There is nothing else, and it's fine.

But there was nothing fine about facing Vinnie Marino.

This wasn't a fleeting thing. This wasn't a quick glance at a hot guy and a just-as-quick glance away. And I hated to admit I had a crush on him, but dammit, wasn't that exactly what this was?

The sloshing somersault my stomach performed at the sight of him coming out of the elevator told me the answer to that question.

He entered the ward, pushed along by a cool and casual air that I was both attracted to and envious of. I knew he wouldn't notice me at the desk. I knew, that to guys like him, I blended in with the plain and sterile environment, but Lord, what I wouldn't give for him to glance my way and acknowledge me. Just for the thrill and excitement of being noticed by a guy any girl would brag to her friends about.

"Hey."

The rapid process of my thoughts came to a screeching halt, realizing he had stopped at the counter and was now staring me down with warm eyes and a reluctant half-smile.

I shook my head and quickly gathered my bearings, before replying, "Hi, Vinnie. What can I do for you?"

"I just wanted to apologize for being such a dick earlier. I jumped to conclusions and—"

"Everybody reacts differently to traumatic news like this. There's absolutely nothing to apologize for."

He was quiet for a moment, as he stared at his fingers, erratically tapping against the counter. He was nervous and I was sure he had questions he didn't know how to ask. Nobody ever does.

As he struggled with words, I quickly shot a sideways glance and saw the older woman from his father's room. I had seen her periodically throughout my shift but there was a reluctance in her presence. She was cautious, moving into the room and hallway with uncertainty. I thought for a moment that she was new to this, being here but not. But, I was quick to realize that, no, that wasn't it. There was a distance between her and this family, yet she was still tethered tightly to them.

She looked at Vinnie, while clutching a hand tightly to her chest. The fingers of her other hand reached out and brushed against his shoulder. I wondered if he felt it. People usually do, but they brush it off, excusing it for something else. Wind. A sudden chill. He turned his head over his shoulder, and I smiled, wondering what he thought it had been.

"Have you lost anyone?"

The question blurted from my lips and I immediately wished I could take it back. I wasn't typically that kind of medium and didn't sensationalize my ability. I also never went out of my way to reconnect people with the spirits of their loved ones, unless the spirits were particularly adamant. But the need to connect with *him* was too great and conversation wasn't my strong point.

He looked back to me, eyes narrowed and curious. "What do you mean?"

"Have you, um ..." Jesus, what was I doing? "Um, I'm just wondering if you have experience with losing someone."

He still stared with unconvinced curiosity as he said, "My grandparents died when I was younger."

The woman wasn't a grandmother, or at least not his. She shook her head, her eyes mournful and clouded with regret.

I nodded, deciding to dig just a bit more. "Were any of them more, um, unexpected?"

"Are you asking if I've ever had it sprung on me before that I have a few months to say goodbye to someone?" He asked the question in a way that made me wince, but still, I nodded. He shook his head. "No. This would be the first. My grandparents were all old as hell. I mean, it sucked, but it wasn't like I hadn't seen it comin'."

That didn't tell me who this woman was and now, I needed to know. "Um, *both* your mom and dad's parents?" I asked, grasping at straws.

"Yeah," he drawled slowly, eyeing me with suspicion.

I nodded. "So, will I be seeing your mom? I haven't seen her come by."

Vinnie's expression hardened to stone and I knew I had hit on something. "No. My mom is dead."

The old woman's lips fell open in a silent forlorn sigh I couldn't hear and my eyes met hers with one thought.

Hello, Mrs. Marino.

“I'm sorry to hear that,” I said.

He shrugged without a single display of emotion. “Eh, it’s fine. I didn’t really know her.”

Before I could say anything else, he pushed from the counter and said, “Anyway, I just wanted to say I was sorry. I shouldn’t have taken shit out on you.”

“It’s okay,” I replied, so pathetically meek and small.

“I’ll see you around, Andy,” he said, offering a grin so genuine and beautiful I thought I would float right through the ceiling from my elation.

Andy, I thought as he headed toward his father’s room. He’d called me Andy. Nobody had ever called me Andy before. I liked it, it was casual and cute, and it felt so personal. Maybe even *too* personal for what our relationship was, but … I liked it.

I liked *him*.

And I really wanted to know more about the old woman following him down the hall.

CHAPTER SEVEN

VINNIE

"Pops, can I help you with that?"

I hurried to my father's side as he struggled to put his shirt on without snagging the tubing that hung around his neck and connected to the oxygen tank at his side. I reached out to help him with the buttons, but he quickly swatted me away. I pulled back with the shame of a puppy who'd just been scolded.

"I think I can manage to button my own goddamn shirt," he snapped, just before twisting the tube around a button and snagging it inside the shirt. He huffed with agitation, tugging at the cannula, and pulling it from around his ears. He threw it to the side and finished with the buttons. After tucking the shirt into his pants, he shot a triumphant look in my direction. "See?"

I could've fired back obnoxiously and reminded him of how I had needed to help him use the bathroom just a day ago. But I was too focused on the weighted sound of his breath, the wheezing and struggling with every rise and fall of his chest. Had it always sounded that way? And if so, how had I not noticed it?

"You need to wear this," I said, snatching up the cannula and fitting it back into his nostrils, up around his ears, and under his chin, all while ignoring his scowl.

"You need to stop treatin' me like a little kid."

"*You* need—"

"Hey!"

I turned at the sound of Andy's voice and lifted my mouth in a feeble smile. Pops had only been in the hospital for a few days, but I had found myself looking forward to every fleeting moment with his nurse. She was infuriating in her own right, like the way she mysteriously knew of his condition without apparently knowing him, but she was also endearing and sweet. It was her job to be, I understood that, but it was still a comfort I found myself needing.

"Hey," I grunted, wishing I was capable of sounding a little happier to see her.

"You guys excited to be out of here today?"

Under her arm, she carried a folder that contained, I'm assuming, Pops's discharge papers. The doctor had given him the okay to get back home, with strict instructions to come right back if he had any chest pain or difficulty breathing. Pops had nodded eagerly, ready to get the hell out of the hospital, while I wished my older sister and brother were there to handle this shit instead of me.

I shrugged. "Sure, yeah."

Pops scoffed. "What kinda question is that? Of course, I'm excited to get the hell out of here."

Andy laughed, meeting my eye. "You'll be happy to get some sleep without being woken up every couple of hours."

"You're damn right," Pops grumbled, slipping his feet into his loafers.

I sniffed a quiet laugh, not so sure I agreed. Sure, I was looking forward to my bed and trading the beeping of machines with the symphony of the streets, but I wasn't prepared to become his caregiver. I wasn't prepared to wait quietly for him to die. Nothing could prepare me for that.

"Now, you're not going to be alone, right?" Andy asked, laying the folder on his bed and flipping it open.

Pops shook his head as I said, "No, he lives with me."

Admitting that to women was always difficult, but now, it rolled off my tongue without any shame. She wasn't asking to speculate or criticize; she was just doing her job. Still, I waited for a sign of judgment. A barely-there smirk, or a nearly-silent chuckle—anything to make me dislike her. But it didn't come.

She smiled. "Is that a new arrangement?"

"Nah," I said, surprised by how easily I could tell her the truth. "I've lived with the old man my whole life."

"And you guys haven't killed each other yet?" she teased, her eyes volleying between my father and me.

“We’ve come close.” I swatted the back of my hand lightly against my father’s shoulder. “Right, Pops?”

He snorted with a nod. “That’s for damn sure.” His eye met mine, revealing a glimmer of morose. “I guess my heart beat you to it, huh?”

My gaze dropped to the floor as I forced a grunted laugh. “Guess so.”

Pops excused himself and shuffled off to the bathroom, dragging the oxygen tank behind him and refusing help from both Andy and me. With the bathroom door shut, I felt like I could breathe again, as I ground the palms of my hands into my eyes and took noisy, deep breaths, in and out. In that moment, I’d forgotten she was standing there at the foot of the bed, thumbing through the folder’s contents. I forgot she could see me, as I struggled to maintain my strength and composure, but even if I hadn’t forgotten, I’m not sure I would’ve cared.

“How you holding up?” she asked, and I dropped my hands to my sides.

It took a couple of seconds for my vision to clear and for my eyes to focus on her, but when they did, I fell momentarily silent, finding a semblance of calm in just looking at her and the messy pile of her blonde hair.

“Um, okay,” I lied, bringing my thumbnail to my teeth. “Hangin’ in there.”

Andy narrowed her eyes. “You know you can tell me the truth, right?”

“Who says I’m not?”

"Gnawing your fingernails off kinda gave you away."

With a groan, I pried my hand from my mouth. "I'm *fine*," I insisted, turning away from her and walking toward the window. "I'm just not sure I can keep handlin' this shit by myself."

"What shit?"

I thrust my hand toward the bathroom door and said, keeping my voice low, "*This*. Taking care of him."

"What do you think you can't handle?"

I growled through my frustration, gripping my hair with my fingers and gritting my teeth. "He's got a million fuckin' medications to take. He's got tanks of oxygen. He's got … I dunno! All kinds of crap to keep track of. What if I can't keep it all straight? What if, I dunno, what if I screw up and … you know …"

"Vinnie." She had this way of saying my name that felt like a gentle pat on my back, instantly capable of bringing me down off the proverbial cliff. "You're not going to kill your dad."

Immediately, my throat clotted with sadness and the reality of our situation. "You don't know that."

"Yes, I do. I'm going to run you through everything you need to do, you'll have it all written down, and before you know it, it'll become second nature. Plus, he'll have a nurse checking on him regularly at home—"

"You?" I glanced over my shoulder, holding onto that tiny spark of hope.

Andy pressed her lips together for a moment before shaking her head. "No. I don't work outside of the hospital."

"Oh." I nodded, turning back to the window to hide my disappointment.

"*But*," she swallowed audibly, "I can, um, give you my number. And that way, if you ever have a question or problem, or you know, if you ever wanna just talk about stuff, I'll just be a call or text away."

"Really?"

"Of course."

A jolt of excitement punched me in the gut, as I struggled to remind myself that it was nothing more than a professional offer of support. She didn't *like* me and she wasn't doing anything any other good nurse wouldn't do. But still, having her there in my corner, when my brother and sister felt so far away, made me feel a little less scared and a little less alone. And I needed that more than anything.

***

Years ago, when Pops and I had sold the old place in Brooklyn and moved into our apartment, I'd been pissed that it wasn't bigger. As much as I didn't mind living with the old man, I had still wanted more space to call my own. A bigger bedroom, maybe my own bathroom. Hell, just a little more than one thin wall between our rooms would've been nice. But now, with him sick at home and sleeping alone, that wall felt too thick and cumbersome. I laid in bed, desperately wanting to knock it down and straining to hear him snore, just to make sure he hadn't died on me.

Zach called first, making sure Pops was okay, and then Jenna. I felt bad for them, that they were so far away and helpless. They had their own lives now, with families to worry about and things to take care of, but they were still his kids and what kid wants to be away from their dying parent?

But I also felt bad for myself, being the one to watch over him, and wishing I'd had the foresight to see this coming when I'd decided to continue living with him.

Hours ticked by in what seemed like years, as I stared at the ceiling and listened for his signs of life in the next room. Occasionally, I got up to use the bathroom or grab something from the kitchen and I'd stand in his doorway, squinting my eyes into the darkness, to watch his chest rise and fall.

"I'm driving myself fuckin' crazy," I mumbled, quietly moving down the hall and to the living room window.

The doctor had strongly advised me not to smoke around him, and if I absolutely needed to, to keep it outside. Really, I probably should've decided then and there to quit cold turkey. But I'm not a saint, never pretended to be, and as much as I loved my dad, I knew I was going to lose him, whether I smoked or not. And there's only so much a guy can lose before he also loses his mind.

I climbed out onto the fire escape and shivered in the cool night air. Fifteen floors down, I knew the air was heavy and sticky, but the humidity never seemed to touch us up here.

I pulled the pack of Marlboros from my pocket, along with my Zippo and phone. I plucked a cigarette out and held it between my lips, as I checked my phone screen for messages, making sure my brother or sister weren't trying to get in touch with me. It irked me to find that they hadn't. It shouldn't have, it was late and they would be sleeping, but while I was here, stressing myself out and unable to sleep, they were enjoying the comfort of their beds. I wondered if I'd be like that, if I wasn't here. I wondered if I could just fall asleep, knowing my father was at home, living with a time bomb in his chest.

"Knock it off," I muttered under my breath. I wasn't going to villainize my siblings simply for having different lives than me, knowing that underneath the worry, I was only jealous it wasn't me.

I lit the cigarette and inhaled, slow and deep, only to exhale in hopes that I'd also release my stress and worry. My fingers scrolled through my phone, seemingly with a mind of their own, when I came across Andy's number.

I hadn't thought about her since leaving the hospital, not with the ordeal of bringing my father home. But now, staring at her name and number, I couldn't get her out of my head, and because I was never one to deny an impulse, I called her.

I just don't think I expected her to answer.

"Hey!" I could hear the smile in her tone, bright and bubbly, like it wasn't a quarter past midnight.

"Hey." I blew a stream of smoke into the night. "I can't believe you're awake."

"Oh," she laughed, "don't let my work hours fool you. I'm really a night owl, and I don't go to bed before three AM on nights when I don't have work the next day."

"Ah." I nodded to the night sky. "A day off, nice."

"*Two* days off," she corrected triumphantly.

"Good for you," I laughed, then sucked at the end of the cigarette.

"So, how are you? Is everything okay?"

I pinched the smoke between my fingers, pulling it from my lips. "Yeah, everything's fine."

"Well, I mean, you called, so I figured—"

"Yeah, I dunno, I guess I just wanted to talk to someone." I licked my lips, realizing how vague and weak that sounded. Like she could've been anybody, like it didn't matter that it was her. So, I added, "I mean, I wanted to talk to *you*."

"Oh," she answered, nearly in a whisper.

That one-worded response led to an awkward silence that I would've filled with a kiss, if we were together in person and if she was any other girl. And it was in that moment, I realized and acknowledged that she wasn't just any other girl. She was different, and in what way, I didn't know. But I know I liked it.

I liked *her*.

"So, um, what are you up to?" I asked, forcing myself to use my tongue for other things, like conversation.

"Oh, uh … just watching some YouTube videos."

"What kinda videos?"

"Promise to not make fun of me?"

"Nope."

"What?" She laughed incredulously. "Seriously?"

"Yo, I can't promise nothin'. If you tell me you're watching behind the scenes footage of the *Teletubbies* or some shit, you can bet your ass I'm gonna make fun of you."

"Wow," she grumbled. "And here I thought you were a nice guy."

I grinned around the cigarette, then sucked in a puff of smoke to hold in my lungs, before asking, "And that's my problem, how?"

Andy laughed, filling the space between the phone and my ear with a happiness I hadn't felt in days. "Touché. Anyway, I'm really into watching videos of John Edward."

My eyes narrowed at the street below me. "The guy who sees dead people?"

"He doesn't *see* dead people," she muttered defensively. "He's a psychic medium, and a really good one, actually."

"Okay," I conceded, nodding. "So, you're actually into that stuff?" I asked, remembering the night I had met her outside that show Greyson had dragged us to.

"I am."

"That's cool," I shrugged, stamping my cigarette out in the ashtray I kept outside. "Why would I laugh at you for that?"

"Well, considering how we met …"

"Hey, I don't care if people are into that shit. What I cared about, was you making fun of my brother-in-law for believing in it."

"I think it's nice you care about your family so much."

The compliment came from nowhere, it seemed, and I stopped the grinding of my fingers. "Yeah, well, uh … they're kinda all I have, so …"

"Oh, come on. That can't be true."

"Well, it ain't a lie."

"You don't have any friends? Or a, um, a girlfriend or boyfriend, or … I dunno …"

"No girlfriend, and I'm not into guys," I said with a smile, easily offering the information she was obviously fishing for. "I have a couple friends, but I'm not like, super popular or anything."

"Yeah, same here."

"Which?"

"What do you mean?"

My back relaxed against the side of the brick building as I pulled out another cigarette. "Friends or a boyfriend, or you know, girlfriend, if you swing that way." Grinning, I lit the cigarette and inhaled, patiently awaiting her response, and allowing her some seconds to adjust to my direct approach.

"Both," she finally replied, suddenly bashful.

"I have a hard time believing that."

"What? That I don't have friends or a boyfriend?"

"Yeah."

"I'm not really someone guys wanna date," she said quietly. "And, I mean, it's not like I don't have *any* friends. I just don't get out much, so my friends are mostly from work."

I pinched my lips around the end of the cigarette, considering how bold I was willing to be, and quickly decided that, fuck it, I had nothing to lose.

"Well, *I* wanna date you," I declared.

"Jesus," she said, barking with an abrupt laugh. "You don't sugarcoat anything, huh?"

"Eh," I shrugged, holding the smoke between two fingers, "I have too much to deal with to dance around this shit."

"Yeah, I can understand that."

"So, what do you say?"

"About what?"

For someone so initially outspoken, judging from our first encounter outside of the show, she was certainly acting clueless now, and that made me smile.

"Going out with me."

"Oh." She sighed, blowing a breath into the phone. "Y-Yeah. I'd like that."

"Cool," I replied smoothly, as if my stomach wasn't flopping around with nauseating excitement. "One of my only friends has this bar I like to chill at sometimes, if you're into that. He gives me a discount on wings and charges me nothing for a glass of Coke."

Andy laughed, easy and light. “So, you’re a cheap date, huh?”

I shrugged. “Well, I don’t drink and I’m pretty easy when it comes to food. But if you had somewhere else in mind, that’s—”

“No. Wings and Coke sound good,” she interjected gently.

“Cool,” I repeated, relaxing against the building and realizing I hadn’t worried about Pops since dialing her number.

CHAPTER EIGHT

ANDREA

When had I last been on a date? I actually couldn't remember, and as I stared at my open closet, I thought about how pathetic that was. Nothing hanging or folded on the shelves was what I'd consider date appropriate, and I wanted to kick myself for not having the foresight to be at least a little prepared for the situation.

But then again, why would I have ever thought to prepare for this?

I plucked out a drab-looking floral dress that I'd worn to my grandmother's funeral some years ago. There was still a stain over the right breast from where I'd dripped a blob of barbeque sauce, and it was the nicest thing I owned.

I narrowed my eyes at the little heart-shaped mark and remembered the meal that had put it there. "Those were really good ribs," I muttered, glancing in Jamie's direction. She rolled her eyes and cocked her head, eyeing me exhaustedly with her hands on her hips. "What? They were."

Over the years, I'd learned to listen through the silence, and right now, Jamie was tired of my procrastination.

"What am I supposed to wear?" I asked, throwing the dress into the closet and not caring as it dropped unceremoniously to the floor. "I mean, we're just going to a freakin' bar, so how fancy do I really have to get?"

Jamie held up a hand, waggling it a bit in the air.

"I'm not saying I'm gonna wear my scrubs," I replied dryly. "I'm just saying, it's a *bar*. I don't need a freakin' ball gown."

She dropped her gaze to my old, nearly-see through pajamas, and smirked.

"Knock it off," I laughed boisterously. "I'm not wearing these either! But seriously, I have nothing to wear and I don't have time to go buy anything. I'm meeting him at this place in just a few hours."

Ever since I was a little girl and started to interact with the dearly departed, I had quickly learned that there was something keeping them tethered to the land of the living and prevented them from passing through the veil. Sometimes, it was a message they needed to give a loved one, other times, they were here to help someone pass into the next life. Often, it was easy enough to figure it out, like in the case of Mrs. Schrieber's husband, who had been lingering by her bedside until the very moment she allowed her soul to let go. And although I despised not having a choice in possessing this gift, if I could even call it that, it was simple enough to help them leave.

But Jamie was another story. She never left, and while I sometimes wondered about that, I was also grateful to have a constant friend. One I didn't have to hide from. And right now, I was grateful for her assistance, as she walked across the room to my dresser and pointed to a picture of my sisters and me. Smiling, I shot her a steady thumbs-up and grabbed my phone.

***

Willa and Meredith had no problem ditching their husbands and kids to rush over with outfit options. It was an unusual occurrence for me to request date advice, so they had jumped eagerly at the opportunity.

"She's going to a bar, Mer, not a rave." Willa explained as she held up a skirt, embellished with reflective piping along the seams.

"Yeah, okay, and she's not going to a goddamn tea party, either." Meredith picked up Willa's floral chiffon top with ruffled sleeves and tossed it on the floor.

"Oh, my God," I muttered, dragging my hands down the sides of my face. "Remind me to never call you guys for help again."

"Okay, okay," Meredith said, holding up her hands in surrender. "We'll take it seriously. So, what do you know about this bar?"

I frowned. "Well … I mean, I know they, uh, they serve alcohol, and …"

"You know nothing about it," Willa stated astutely and pulled her phone out of her jeans. "What was the name of it?"

"The Thirsty Goose."

Meredith wrinkled her nose. "The Thirsty Goose? Never heard of it."

"Oh, I forgot you were the authority on bars," Willa drawled, her voice dripping with sarcasm. "Anyway, it looks like a nice place. Not one of those sleezy hole-in-the-wall type places."

"The jury's still out on this Vinnie guy, though," Mer jabbed with a teasing smirk.

I looked up abruptly from my perusal of the pile of clothes on my bed. "What?"

"I'm just kidding," she said, but her voice was so dry, I knew she was lying.

"No, seriously, do you think I should be worried?"

Meredith glanced at Willa, who smiled sweetly. "No," she assured me gently. "But just keep in mind you know nothing about him. Like, have you even looked him up on social media?"

"Well, I mean …" I shrugged, allowing my words to trail off, because I hadn't. And now I felt stupid.

Mer flopped on my bed beside the mountain of clothing options, with her phone in hand. "No time like the present!" she declared, already beginning to type. "You said his name is Vinnie?"

"Yeah," I said hesitantly. "Vinnie Marino."

It only took her a few seconds of typing and tapping before she read, "Vinnie Marino. Thirty-four—"

"Ooh, an older man!" Willa exclaimed, holding a short, black dress up to my body.

"By like, four years," I muttered, rolling my eyes.

"—from Brooklyn, now living in Manhattan. Single, good. Employed at a pizza place called Famiglia Bella, not too bad, I guess," Mer assessed, sliding her fingers across the screen. Her eyes met mine with a coy grin. "Damn, girl. He's pretty hot."

My cheeks heated wildly with my flush. "You don't have to tell me that. It's been torture having to look at him the past few days."

Willa glanced at Mer's phone screen and let out a long whistle. "I bet. Holy hell."

I continued to dig through the clothes while my sisters occupied their time by stalking Vinnie's social media. They gawked at pictures of him, with and without his family, and they looked into his interests. They scowled at his smoking habit, instructing me to get him to quit, and they cooed approvingly over pictures of him with his sister's kids. The two of them didn't seem to have much to say and I was grateful, until they began to browse through pictures he'd been tagged in by others.

"Wait, wait, wait. Look at this," Mer said hurriedly, her voice full of alarm. "He looks stoned out of his mind."

"Holy shit, yeah, he does," Willa agreed, taking the phone and shoving it in my face.

The picture in question was indeed incriminating. A younger-looking Vinnie and his brother, Zach, stared out at me from behind the glass. Sitting on a beat-up couch, with their arms around each other's shoulders, red-eyed and sleepy-smiled. What was worse than the eyes, was the joint pinched between Vinnie's fingers and the small bag of white powder in Zach's.

"Is that *cocaine*?" I asked needlessly. I knew what it was—I was a nurse, for crying out loud.

Willa turned the phone back to her curious eyes and raised her brows. "Uh … yeah. Sure looks like it."

My stomach knotted as the room fell silent. Wordlessly, I selected a tight pair of black jeans and a purple, sequined tank top, and as I got dressed, I ignored the way my sisters stared at me from the bed. I knew what they weren't saying. They didn't want me going out with him and they didn't trust him. And if I'm being honest, I wasn't sure I should either, but the picture was obviously older and who knows where life had taken him since. So, I continued getting ready for my date, trying hard to not think about the redness of his eyes or the contents of that bag.

But as I did my makeup, Mer finally said, "I don't think you should go out with him."

"Oh, come on," I groaned, shoving my eyeshadow palette back in my vanity drawer.

"He probably took one look at you and thought, oh, this is a girl I can steal money from to buy my drugs."

"You don't know that," I fired back, glaring angrily in her direction. "It's an old picture."

"Yeah, drugs do that to people. They make you look older," Willa muttered.

"Will you guys *stop*? You have no idea. Maybe it was a one-time thing. Maybe *he* wasn't even doing it, maybe it was his brother's."

"You're making excuses for a guy you don't even know," Mer pointed out, crossing her arms. "I mean, Andrea, he *looks* like a junkie, now that I think of it."

I gawked at my sisters, allowing my anger to disguise the concern I also felt. "Wow. Real nice," I snapped, shoving my feet into the black stilettos Willa had brought. "I have to go. Thanks for the clothes."

I left in a huff, with my anger toward my mean sisters fueling my drive to the train station. But once aboard and seated, I couldn't help wondering if they were right. I didn't know him or what he did in his spare time. I realized I didn't know what type of person he was, and yet I was on a train to go see him.

"What an idiot I am," I muttered to the spirit of an old man sitting beside me. "And this is exactly why I stick with ghosts and not live men."

***

"Damn."

It was the first word Vinnie uttered as I approached him at the bar. He removed himself from the stool he sat on, extending a hand toward me and helping me onto the seat beside his. He was so smooth, so chivalrous, I almost forgot about the picture my sisters had found.

"Purple is my favorite color," he said.

I glanced down at the shimmering top. "Really?"

"It is now."

I groaned, rolling my eyes back up to his. "Wow. Smooth operator."

He grinned, sliding back onto his stool and grabbing one of two glasses of soda. "Sorry, I took the liberty of ordering you a Coke. But if you wanna drink something else, that's cool."

"Nah, Coke is fine," I said, taking the glass from him. "Thanks."

"Yeah, sure." He nodded and grabbed a basket of sauce-covered wings. "Here, eat."

The bartender, a burly, huge lumberjack of a man, let out a gruff laugh. "Dude, it's like you don't even *wanna* try." He extended a hand toward me. "Hey, I'm Goose."

"Andrea," I replied with a smile.

"He's a little rough around the edges but I swear he's a good guy," Goose replied. "Don't let him—"

The bar filled with a distinct guitar intro and he groaned. "Fuck, hold on a second." Goose turned his head and shouted into the bar, "For the love of all that is holy, play another goddamn song!"

Vinnie snorted, lifting his glass to his lips. "Dude. Give it up and embrace the 'Sweet Home Alabama.'"

"Never," the bartender muttered begrudgingly before eyeing me again. "Anyway, don't let this guy fool you with his bullshit. He's a teddy bear."

"Okay, I won't," I replied, smiling warmly and deciding to push the picture to the back of my memory.

***

Vinnie, I learned, had the appetite of a garbage disposal, but after four rounds of wings, he finally leaned back in his stool, with his hands over his stomach, and blew out a heavy breath.

"Holy shit," he groaned, closing his eyes. "Why did you let me eat so much?"

I couldn't help but laugh at the pained expression on his face. "I wasn't aware I was calling the shots here."

Opening his eyes, he glared at me. "Andy, listen to me right now and listen to me good. When it comes to food, I will keep going unless someone steps in and cuts me off. So, if you're ever like, whoa, this dude's gonna explode if he keeps eating, I want you to say, Vinnie, I'm pulling the plug on this binge-fest. You got me?"

My heart hammered wildly in my chest because, oh, I liked him.

I liked him a lot.

"I got you."

"Good." He nodded his approval, then called Goose over for a fifth refill, and I gawked. Vinnie laughed. "What?"

"You were just complaining that you ate too much!"

"Yeah, but I never said I was full," he pointed out with a grin. "Plus, you didn't pull the plug."

"I didn't know I needed to control you."

"Well, I kinda need someone to control me," he retorted, and I waited for a grin or a chuckle, but they never came. When he realized I was taken aback by the statement, he said, "Okay, Andy. Let's play a game."

"What kind of game?"

"I want you to ask me a question, and then, I'll ask you one."

I studied him, with that picture now front and center in my mind. "*Any* question?" I asked, testing the waters.

He nodded once. "Any question, and the rules are, we have to answer honestly. No holding back."

"Okay," I said on an exhale, my voice heavy and breathless. "I gotta make this good."

He smiled with his lips against the rim of his glass. "You better."

CHAPTER NINE

VINNIE

"What's the one thing you would hate for me to know about you?"

When I had instructed Andy to ask me anything, I hadn't anticipated that. Now, I sat at the bar, frantically wondering how I could get out of answering.

Andy laughed. "You look like you've seen a ghost."

My own laugh came out quaking and forced. "I just wasn't expecting that."

"You have to answer," she reminded me. "Those are the rules."

"I made the game up," I said pointedly, grasping at whatever lifeline I could find. "I can change the rules."

"Oh, come on," she groaned, rolling her eyes. "You hardly even know me. What do you care if I know your deepest, darkest secret?"

And she had a point there. I didn't know her well, and she barely knew me. If she judged me, if she decided to never see me again, it wasn't as though I'd already invested a ton of time and energy on this thing … except …

I didn't *want* her to judge me. I didn't *want* her to decide to never see me again. I didn't want to ruin this thing before it even had a chance to really become something.

But.

Whether she found out now or sometime later on, she *would* inevitably find out about my past. Wouldn't it be better to get it out in the open now, before either of us wasted our time on something destined to die?

"Jesus Christ," I mumbled, wiping a palm over my mouth before dropping it against the bar. "Shit, all right. Don't say I didn't warn you, okay?"

"Wow," she uttered quietly. "You're actually freaking me out right now."

"No, no, no," I chanted, shaking my head. "Don't be freaked out. It's just, uh …" I gripped the back of my neck and held on tight. "So … I was pretty fucked up a while back. Like, I did drugs and drank a lot."

I glanced at her, expecting an expression of disgust, but I was only met with a sort of curious compassion that dared me to like her just a little more.

"Oh," she said, nodding slowly. "So, I guess that explains the picture on your Facebook."

Raising a brow, I asked, "Uh, what?"

Andy shrugged. "My sisters kinda looked into you earlier and they found a picture on your Facebook, of you and your brother and a bag of cocaine."

"Oh, Jesus Christ," I groaned, scrubbing a hand against my chin. "See, that's why I don't like that shit. The past follows you around, whether you want it to or not, and it'll always come back to bite you in the ass when you're trying to impress a pretty girl."

Then, she laughed, and I breathed a sigh of relief. "Yeah, the internet is kinda fucked up like that."

"Seriously," I muttered, grabbing for my glass of Coke. "But yeah, that's why I don't drink. I can't even have a sip of beer without wanting to drink the whole six-pack."

"And yet, you're hanging out in a bar …"

Shrugging as I took a drink, I lowered my glass and said, "I dunno how to explain it, really, but I guess being around it and choosing to not drink makes me feel better. It's sort of, I dunno, comforting or some shit."

She hummed as she nodded. "I think I get it. It's kinda like window shopping when you don't have the money to buy anything. Like, just browsing is enough sometimes."

"Yeah, sure," I said, furrowing my brow. "I mean, I'm not big into shopping but it sounds about right."

"Anyway," she sighed, propping her elbow on the bar, "now, I gotta ask—"

"Hey," I interjected. "I said one question."

"Well, you inspired another," she said, smiling into my eyes, and I conceded with a nod of my head. "It's really in the past, though, right?"

I nodded firmly. "Yes."

"Okay, then. I'll tell my nosy-as-fuck sisters to back the hell off." She blushed and said, "I'm sorry for asking, honestly."

"Don't be," I replied, my voice soft and gentle. "And your sisters were right to question that shit. Family is supposed to do that, so consider yourself lucky."

Her smile lit the dark atmosphere of the bar. "Okay. Your turn."

Without a moment's hesitation, I leaned forward, coming close enough to smell her hair. She smelled like the beach, salty and fresh.

"How do you feel about pizza?"

***

Standing beside me as I unlocked the door to Famiglia Bella, Andy giggled wildly as if I didn't have the keys and we were doing something genuinely scandalous. I had to remind myself that this was different, and that I was trying to do things right. But with every glint beneath the city lights, that damn purple top kept tempting me to throw all conviction of being good out the window. The only thing keeping me from doing just that, was the feeling she wouldn't be into going all the way on the first date.

"Can I tell you a secret?" she asked as I pushed the door open and stepped inside.

"Yeah." I nodded. "I mean, I told you mine, so I guess it's only fair you tell me yours."

She hesitated, standing in the doorway and staring at me unblinking. I couldn't imagine that I had gone too far, just by teasing her with my own confession, but hell, maybe I had.

"Andy, I'm kidding. You don't have to—"

"I saw you here. Last week," she blurted. "My friend, Elle, and I came here for lunch and you were working. I waited for you to recognize me but you never did, so I didn't say anything."

Narrowing my eyes, I tried to rack my brain and remember her being in the restaurant. But my memory came up blank and I shook my head. "Sorry," I said sheepishly. "I really don't remember. It gets so busy in here and—"

"It's fine," she said, tittering with a nervous giggle. "I just felt like I needed to tell you."

I laughed. "Whatever gives you peace of mind, sweetheart."

The term of endearment easily rolled off my tongue and tasted sweet as it passed through my lips. I hadn't intended on saying it, but there it was, now out in the open, and Andy just stood there, frozen and wide-eyed, chewing on her bottom lip the way I chew on my nails. She was what I'd call a good girl, probably far too good for me, and good girls don't like guys who call them things like sweetheart on the first date. And after my confession at Goose's, I bet she thought I was a creep.

I mean, fuck ... I felt like one.

"Sorry," I quickly said, hoping to remedy the situation.

Andy's eyes widened even more as she shook her head. “Oh! No, it's okay. I'm just ...” Her cheeks turned strawberry pink as she rolled her eyes. “Guys don't usually like me, so all of this is kinda new for me.”

“Well, I don't usually go on dates, so I guess we're even. Now,” I said, reaching out to take her by the hand and pull her into the restaurant, “I'm gonna make you a pizza.”

Her laugh bounced off the brick walls of the empty restaurant, and although we served a crowded house on a daily basis these days, no sound had ever made me feel so full.

“We just ate!”

Leading her toward the kitchen door, I glanced over my shoulder, cocking a brow incredulously. “So?”

“So, how the hell am I gonna eat a whole pizza?”

“Andy,” I laughed, shaking my head and pushing through the swinging doors, “there's *always* room for pizza.”

***

I had just scratched the surface of my troubled past, with the expectation that she’d run for the hills. Yet, there we were, leaning over either side of the counter, facing each other, with a fresh pie between us. Her smile never faltered, and she laughed at all my jokes. Every now and then, I caught myself tangled in the hope that this moment could last forever.

"How's your dad doing?" she asked, pinching an olive between her fingers and popping it into her mouth.

I groaned dramatically. "Do we *have* to talk about him right now?"

Andy cocked her head and smirked. "Why not?"

"Because …" There were about a thousand obnoxious and chauvinistic things I could've said, a thousand things to hide the truth. But with Andy, I found I didn't want to lie. "Because, for the first time in days, I haven't thought about him. And that might make me an asshole, but it feels really good to be thinking about something else."

Her eyes softened and her smile wilted as she shook her head. "It doesn't make you an asshole. You might be caring for your dad, but you have to think about yourself, too."

"Yeah, but I mean, my dad's fuckin' dying, so …" I wet my lips and steered my gaze away from her, to stare at the old picture of Pops in front of the shop when he'd first bought it. He was so young then, so full of hope. Ma hadn't left him yet, Zach and I hadn't gotten wrapped up in drugs, and he hadn't spent decades of his life trying to make ends meet. He also hadn't known then that, at the age of seventy-five, he'd be given an expiration date. I mean, we all have one, but most of us have no idea when our time's gonna run out. Pops, though …

My eyes welled up and I cleared my throat, shaking my head and turning my eyes back on the pizza. "Anyway, uh, what's your family like?"

"You can be sad, you know," she said quietly, ignoring my half-hearted question. "I deal with sad people on a pretty regular basis. You don't have to—"

"Please, don't."

She hesitated, blinking and stunned, before asking, "Don't, what?"

"Don't treat me like one of your patients."

Andy blew out a deep breath. "I'm sorry."

I immediately felt like an asshole and pushed a hand through my hair, shaking my head. "Nah, don't apologize. I'm just not good with talking about hard shit."

"Well, if you ever do want to talk, I'm pretty good at listening."

My mouth lifted in a half-smile. "I'll keep that in mind."

***

Famiglia Bella wasn't located in Times Square, the heart of the city where the lights are bright around the clock. The little pizzeria was shoved deep in a residential area, currently surrounded by dark apartment buildings and their sleeping inhabitants. So, when I pulled the metal security shutter down over the door, I winced as the metallic rattling sliced through the quiet, disturbing the peace.

"Shhhh," I hissed, as I locked it into place. But, despite my stern warning, the second hadn't made any attempt to be quieter. "Fucking hell."

Andy giggled, hiding her mouth behind her hand. “What's so funny?” I asked, and she replied, “I don't think it listened.”

“What can ya do?” I shrugged, and then, I stared at the dirty sidewalk as my mouth was sucked dry.

Now what? The distraction of the restaurant was behind us and I hadn’t thought this far ahead. I couldn’t walk her home—she lived out on Long Island—and I wasn’t going to invite her back to my place. Not with Pops there, not this time. I was clueless and I stood still, taking my time as I struggled to come up with something to occupy our time.

And just like that, as if by magic, a tune started to gently float through the sticky summer air. It came from above, from an apartment a few floors up, and it echoed softly through the narrow canyon of concrete and stone. I didn’t recognize the song, and judging from the indie sound of it, it wasn’t my thing. But it was upbeat, it felt romantic, and it was there. So, without another thought, I let the melody move my body, and I grabbed Andy, with one hand on her waist and the other fumbling to find hers.

“What are you doing?” she asked, excitement in her voice and laughter in her eyes.

“Dancing,” I replied, grasping her hand and releasing her waist, twirling her around, then pulling her back. The fingers of her other hand landed against my chest, and fuck, I liked the feel of them there. No, scratch that—I *loved* it. I loved *this*; this night, this song, this feeling I had when I was with her.

She giggled. “I wouldn’t have pegged you for a dancer.”

I pulled her body closer to mine and felt her rigid nerves dissipate and relax. “Well, believe it or not, I kinda am. I took lessons when I was a kid.”

“Ballroom dancing?”

I laughed. “Nah, hip hop.”

Her smiling eyes reflected the street lights like stars and I had to talk myself out of making a wish upon them.

“O-kay,” she drawled playfully. “Then, how did you learn to dance like this?”

My shoulders shrugged before dipping her low and whispering into her ear, “You already know my worst secret. Let me hold onto a little mystery for a while.”

Andy threw her arms around my neck and squealed loudly, drowning out the music from above and the distant sound of a street sweeper. I pulled her upright and held her close, closer than before, and pressed my nose to the top of her head. I closed my eyes and pulled in her scent, a beachy, floral blend that reminded me of the flowers in Zach’s garden upstate, and I felt so overcome by good, happy emotions, that I fucking sighed and kissed her hair. No second thought, no questions of if I should go for it or not. I just pursed my lips and went for it. After, I waited for her reaction and wondered if it was weird. Do women like that kind of thing, or is it creepy? And how was I supposed to know, when the brunt of my physical interaction with women was restricted to one-night stands in bar bathrooms?

She was quiet, and just when I thought we would both silently agree to let it pass without mention, she asked, “Did you just kiss my head?”

I swallowed, embarrassed, and said, “Yeah. I kinda did.”

“Oh.”

Oh.

What the hell did that even mean?

Oh.

Christ, she was so different from other women I’d been interested in. Sometimes, when she was cool and laid back, eating wings and sipping Coke, that was a great thing. Other times, like now, when she was so shy and awkward, it was more frustrating than dealing with my father.

As the singer went on about being saved and just wanting to repay the woman he sang about, I looked to the streetlamps for some kind of answer. What was I doing here? Why had I even asked her out? I liked her, yeah, but that one, stupid little word now made me wonder if I was fooling myself into thinking I could have anything more than dirty sex in dirty bathrooms.

Oh.

“God, you think too loud,” she groaned, her cheek pressed to my shoulder.

“Huh?”

“I said,” she pulled her head back and looked up into my eyes, “you think too loud.”

"Well, then why don't you shut me up?" I fired back coolly, lifting a brow and smirking, assuming she'd be way too chicken-shit to actually do anything.

I was wrong.

Her hands moved so quickly from my neck to the sides of my face, I didn't have time to think or react, as she pulled me down to her level and pressed her soft lips against mine, surprised and partially open. I didn't even have the time to close my eyes, even though she had, and two seconds later, when she pulled away, I continued to stare at her, eyes wide and jaw open in a silent gasp.

I always kissed women first, they never kissed me.

"How was that?" she asked, her bold act contrasted by the bashfulness of her voice.

"Lame," I countered, with my heart jittering in my chest and my hands trembling at her waist.

"And you could do better?"

"I could," I retorted confidently.

She licked her lips and swallowed hard, while her eyes watched mine with a brazen dare. "Okay," she whispered, her voice trembling.

"Okay, what?"

"Okay," she began slowly, standing higher on her toes, "prove it."

She was such a contradiction of herself. Timid and bold. Brave and terrified. Everything was so black and white for me, while she walked in a grey area I'd never delved into before. Somewhere else, somewhere … not here, and I wanted to go there, too. That place where women were simultaneously strong and needy, shy and confident. But I found I was scared of that, as I mustered my courage and bowed my neck. I was scared of *her*, as if I knew that kissing her would open the door to a world best left uncharted and untouched.

And then, when my lips touched hers with a little more passion than she had exhibited, I wondered if that fear was just a sign that I was about to embark on a journey worth taking. If maybe that queasy, terrifying feeling in my gut was my soul saying, *yo, Vin, this chick right here? She's better than dirty sex in dirty bathrooms, and you know what? Maybe you are, too.*

CHAPTER TEN

VINNIE

"Pops, let me get that," I demanded, hurrying from the kitchen to help my old man carry his loaded plate to the table.

"Jesus Christ, Junior," he grumbled, jerking the plate away from my grabbing hands. "I'm capable of carryin' my own fuckin' dinner."

I easily relented, because as much as I hated to admit it, he was right. He was more than capable. I guess I'd always figured that, when he was old and dying, he'd also be frail and unable to help himself. But this man didn't look like he was dying, even in spite of the oxygen tank trailing behind him. He looked very much alive, and that only made accepting his fate that much more difficult.

I turned back to the counter and caught Moe's sympathetic expression. And that was another thing—the sympathy. Ever since we announced Pops's disease and diagnosis to anybody who needed to know, we—the whole family—had been treated like the old man was already gone. But he wasn't. He was still alive, he was still here, and sometimes, when I was lying in bed and the grief really got to me, I caught myself wishing he wasn't. Just to make those sympathetic looks worth it. Just to get it over with.

"Am I meetin' this girl of yours today or what?" Moe jabbed, steering clear of the topics ever persistent in my stupid head.

I laughed, pushing through the swinging door to stand behind the counter. "Man, I told you, she's droppin' by on her lunch break."

"Hey," he smacked the back of his hand against my shoulder, "I'm just makin' sure she exists."

"Oh, she exists," Pops chimed in, his mouth full of pasta and meatballs. "And why she's interested in *this* guy," he jabbed his fork in my direction, "is completely beyond me."

"Gee, thanks, Pops. I love you, too," I grumbled, shaking my head.

"He just hasn't corrupted her yet," Moe said to him. "That's gotta be what it is. Once he sleeps with her, that's gonna be the end of it. Bye-bye, Andy."

"And that's the last time I confide in you, dick," I muttered, shooting my friend a mean side-eye, just as the front door chimed and Andy Bennett walked in with her friend, Elle.

"Hey," I said, nodding my chin toward them and hoping to keep my cool in front of Moe.

"Hey, yourself," Andy replied, her cheeks the color of ripe strawberries. Her gaze shifted to the dreadlocked man beside me and her smile went from sweet to shy in the matter of seconds. “You must be Moe.”

“And you must be the lady who’s got my boy all googly-eyed,” Moe said, outstretching a big hand over the counter. “It’s a pleasure to meet you.”

I watched as Andy slid her little palm against his, and I watched as she faltered, just a little, before they shook. Her throat had bobbed and her breath had tripped.

“You, too,” she said, her voice quiet as she looked up at him, her eyes wider than before. Then, she shook her head, broadened her smile, and added, “Sorry. I’m such a weirdo. You just kinda remind me of someone.”

Moe laughed good naturedly. “It’s all good.”

“What can I get you ladies?” I asked, tightening the strings of my apron. “We have a killer baked ziti pie that Jen made this morning.”

“Sounds good to me,” Andy replied, slowly diverting her gaze from Moe.

Elle, a stick-thin blonde, wrinkled her nose and shook her head. “No, thanks. That many carbs will keep me on my Peloton for hours tonight. Do you have salad pizza?”

I nodded, as my eyes met Andy's. “Yeah, you got it,” I said, as I thought about all the girls I'd been with who'd turn their noses up at a good slice of greasy, carb-loaded pizza. But not Andy. Andy knew how to live, and with a quick glance toward my father, I wondered if that was because she had seen so much death.

***

Since we'd started seeing each other, I had been making it a point to walk Andy to the train whenever I could. So, after her shift at the hospital, Andy came back to the pizzeria and sat with Pops while Jenna, Moe, and I hustled during the dinner rush and then cleaned up the restaurant after closing. I loved watching her with him, the way she held such an interest in his story and life. And although I knew it was her job to take care of the elderly, it was her heart that made her so compassionate, and I loved that, too.

"So, your parents came here from Italy?" Andy asked, her chin in her palm.

Pops nodded with pride. "Both of 'em were born and raised in Sicily. They'd lived next door to each other their whole lives and got married when they were eighteen."

Andy sighed, pressing a hand over her heart. "That's so romantic."

"That was my old man, a real sucker for my ma. She was …" Pops pursed his lips, sucked at his teeth, and shook his head. "She ran a tight ship, let's just say that."

"Well, she kinda had to," Jen chimed in. Then, addressing Andy, she said, "She had ten kids, and all of them were boys."

"Ten boys!" Andy exclaimed, grinning widely. "Oh, my Lord. That poor woman."

"Right?" Jenna laughed, jabbing me in the ribs with an elbow. "I have to deal with him and Zach. I can't imagine putting up with eight more."

"Oh, please," I grumbled. "Like dealing with your crap was a walk in the park."

Jenna's jaw dropped with mock insult. "What did *I* do?"

"You think I liked finding your bras all over the damn place?"

"They wouldn't have been all over the place if you hadn't stolen them for yourself and your giant man-boobs."

I scoffed, grabbing at my chest. "You're just jealous 'cause I wouldn't have to stuff 'em."

Jenna rolled her eyes while Pops groaned. He turned his exhausted eyes on Andy and said, "My mother had to be a drill sergeant to keep all of us in line. I get why, lookin' back, but at the time, growin' up with her was, uh … it was a little tough."

Andy nodded slowly, her eyes softening. "You have a lot of resentment toward her."

My Nonna had been your quintessential grandma when I was growing up. She had always gifted us with baked goods and affection, and although she and Nonno couldn't afford much in the way of presents, what they could give was always more than enough. And while I had always known that the woman we knew, wasn't the mother my father grew up with, he had never talked openly about his youth. Yet, Andy made this statement, introduced it as a fact, and Pops pinched his lips, drew in a deep breath, and nodded once, revealing to Jenna and me a piece of a puzzle we never knew existed.

"You shouldn't hold onto those feelings," Andy replied gently. "You know she was only trying her best."

Pops didn't respond. He only glared at her, his lips still pinched, and to my horror, his eyes welled up. Andy seemed unfazed as she reached out, laid a hand over his, and looked him right in the eye.

"Ten kids was a lot to handle," she said quietly. "But she loved you all, you know that."

Rapidly, he nodded and cleared his throat, pulling his hand out from beneath hers. He hurried to stand, grabbed his cane, and looked toward the counter. "Junior, you better walk Andrea over to Penn before it gets too late," he said, his voice strained under his emotion.

I swallowed before saying, "Yep. Just grabbing my stuff now."

After collecting my phone, wallet, and keys and taking off my apron, I headed out with Andy, leaving Pops, Jen, and Moe to lock the place up. We walked with her arm wrapped around mine, casually strolling through the littered streets and avenues toward the train station. All the while, my mind was reeling. I was shaken by what had happened with Pops, the conversation and his reaction, and before long, I couldn't bite my tongue any longer.

"What the hell happened back there?" I asked, firing the question into the night without a second thought.

"What do you mean?" Andy replied innocently.

"That shit you were saying to my dad," I said, stifling my groan. She knew exactly what I meant. "How did you know that, about his mom?"

A siren blared through the night, adding a soundtrack to Andy's hesitation. I didn't like her silence or the way she chewed at her bottom lip, like she was hiding something.

Finally, she said, "Vinnie … this is all a part of my job."

"What is? Knowing random shit about some old guy's past?"

I glanced down at her face to see her tight mouth and the firm set of her eyes. Now, she looked more like she was offended and less like she was lying to me, and I felt like an asshole.

"Sorry," I said hastily, so scared of fucking up.

She sighed and rolled her eyes up to the lights, guiding our way. "No, it's fine. But you have to understand, I've been doing this for a long time, and I can read people. And when these people, my patients, are nearing the end of their life, it's my job to help them make that transition. If that means helping them talk through whatever past crap they're holding onto, then that's what I'm going to do. I'm sorry if that makes you feel weird, or if it bothers you, but I can't just turn it off just because you're my—" She stopped talking abruptly, clamping her lips shut.

"I'm your, what?" I teased, pulling her closer to my side.

"Nothing. Never mind."

"I'm your nothing?" Pressing a hand over my heart, I groaned in false agony. "Ouch."

Andy shoved against me. "Oh, God, stop. You know what I mean."

"Nope." I shook my head dramatically. "Don't have a clue. You gotta say it."

We had been seeing each other nearly every day for a few weeks, and there was nothing mysterious about what we were doing here. We were together, as a couple, in a relationship. Boyfriend and girlfriend. But still, even as adults, labels don't always come easy, slapping declarations of commitment onto things otherwise left to decide their own fate. And I was okay with the label, if she was. I just wasn't gonna be the one to say it first. I needed to hear it from her, my timid and courageous Andy.

She stopped abruptly on the sidewalk, pulled her arm from mine, and tore off her glasses, pressing a hand over her eyes. I took the moment to light a cigarette, and with pedestrians now dodging us with disgruntled glances, I watched her nerves unravel as smoke streamed through the air.

"Enjoy your cancer, asshole," some guy said, bumping his shoulder against mine, and with a wave of the cigarette pinned between two fingers, I tipped my chin and replied, "Thank you very much, sir. You have a fine day now."

Andy burst abruptly with a boisterous laugh, dropping her arms to her sides and throwing her head back. "Oh, my God," she exclaimed. "What the hell am I even doing with you?"

"I dunno." I shrugged. "Having the time of your life?"

She sighed, bringing her eyes back to mine. "I haven't had a boyfriend since I was in college."

"So?" I pulled the smoke from my lips and exhaled. "I've never had a serious girlfriend, and I didn't go to college. Why does it matter?"

"That's not …" Her brow furrowed as she shook her head, almost as though she was frustrated with me. Or maybe it was something else entirely.

"What?"

The shaking of her head slowed as her brow loosened and her lips curled into a smile. "I like this, and I'm just worried that it's not going to work out. So, I—"

"Oh, my God, get out of the way," a well-dressed woman groaned irritably, as she hurried around us with a little, hairy Chihuahua in tow.

"Yo, we're havin' a moment here!" I called after her, before turning back to Andy and saying pleasantly, "What were you sayin', sweetheart?"

Putting her glasses back on, she started to speak. "We should keep going—"

"Nah. These people don't matter. There's plenty of room for them to walk." I sucked heartily at the end of the cigarette before dropping it on the sidewalk and grinding it out with the heel of my boot. "If we're doin' this, we're doin' it here."

"Oh, God, I can't—"

"The sooner you say it, the sooner we can get movin'."

She rubbed her fingertips against her temples, pinching her eyes shut and pulling in deep breaths. In her glasses and scrubs, with her hair pulled back in a chaotic knot, she looked so cute, and I was the anxious asshole, practically bouncing on the spot, waiting for her to just say the damn thing.

"Fine," she said, before adjusting her glasses and looking me in the eye. "Vinnie, you're my boyfriend. Okay? Happy now?"

"Huh," I muttered, nodding slowly, as I glanced around at the crowded street. "That's funny."

"What's funny?"

"The world didn't explode."

Andy laughed and grabbed my arm, steering me around and continuing to walk toward Penn. "You're freakin' ridiculous."

"Hey. You're the one who acted like calling me your boyfriend would trigger the apocalypse."

We walked through the city in an almost-comfortable silence, allowing the chorus of cars and neighboring conversation to fill the air. But when I glanced down at her, to relish in the fact that this gorgeous, successful woman was somehow my girlfriend, I saw a look of trepidation on her face with pinched brows and her lip pinned between her teeth. And I couldn't shake the feeling that something was wrong, and I worried that something was me.

So, when we finally arrived at Penn and I had walked her down the stairs to wait for her train, I finally asked, "What's wrong, sweetheart?"

"Nothing's *wrong*," she insisted, not quite meeting my eye and keeping her gaze pinned on something behind me.

"Lemme tell you somethin' about me," I said. "I'm a horrible liar. And what's funny about that is, even though I know I suck, I've still been doin' it most of my life, ever since I was a kid. Except with you," I went on, poking her in the shoulder. Her lips curled into an apprehensive smile. "I have never lied to you, about anything. Not even about the stuff that maybe a sane guy would've lied about. So, all I'm askin', is that you return the favor. All right?"

She nodded gently. "All right."

"So, tell me what's goin' on."

"I … I wanted to invite you and your dad to my parents' house for the Fourth of July. So that you can meet my family."

Nodding, I crossed my arms over my chest. "You're nervous about me meeting your family?"

"A little," she said. "Yeah."

I let the invitation and her confession settle for a moment before nodding. "I'm nervous about that, too. But you know what?"

"What?"

"I'm not gonna worry about it. And do you know why?"

She wrapped her arms around my waist with a sigh, and I sighed back at the weight of her head pressed to my chest. "Why?"

"Because with all the other shit goin' on in my life, this is the one thing making me happy and keeping me away from doin' shit I shouldn't be doin'. And I'm not gonna let anything get in the way of that right now."

She hesitated before asking, "So, you'll come?"

"Yeah," I replied. "We'll come."

"*The train to Babylon has arrived on Track Thirteen.*" We both looked up at the sound of the announcement. She unwound her arms from my waist and stood on her toes to kiss my lips. I resisted the overwhelming urge to request that she not leave, to ask her to come back to my place and stay the night. It felt so ridiculous now, for her to go back to Long Island every damn day, when she'd just be back in the city the next morning. But the unspoken agreement had seemed to be that we were taking our time, and I was going to respect that.

Andy hoisted her bag up onto her shoulder. "I'll see you tomorrow?"

I nodded. "You know it."

Then, I watched her leave, keeping her eyes on the ground the way she always did. She disappeared through the door, and I imagined her descent on the metal staircase. I wondered what her house looked like, how big her bed was, and when I'd finally get to know what it was like to sleep with her. I wondered how much her family knew about me, if they'd treat me like shit, and if she'd allow their feelings to affect our relationship. And then, as I left Penn and felt the first drop of rain hit my shoulder, I wondered how it was a junkie like me could get so lucky with a good girl like her.

CHAPTER ELEVEN

ANDREA

"Would you stop looking at me like that?" I scolded Jamie, as I dug a pair of shorts from my dresser drawer. "It's just a barbeque. I don't need to dress to the nines for a freakin' barbeque."

Jamie planted her fists firmly at her hips and cocked her head, pursing her lips and rolling her eyes. She didn't need to speak for her attitude to still come across loud and clear. And even though I had insisted it wasn't, I knew she was right; this was a lot more than just a barbeque.

I had now been seeing Vinnie for a little over a month. The days and weeks had been filled with pizza and wings, walks to the train station, and the sweetest kisses any chance we got. It was pretty safe to say that I was swooning and enjoying every second of it. But now he was coming to Long Island with his father to meet my family, and what had initially felt like an innocent thing suddenly seemed serious.

And he still didn't know my closest friend was the ghost of a child.

Hell, he didn't know I could see ghosts, period.

"What do you think of this shirt?" I held up a flowy black top, and Jamie wrinkled her nose. "Seriously? It's nice!"

Jamie shook her head and walked to my closet. In my experience, the dead can't interact with physical objects, so she simply pointed at a pink, floral tank top. I plucked it from the rack and held it up, nodding my approval.

"Okay," I said, and Jamie turned around, allowing me to get dressed without her deep, brown eyes watching.

"You know," I began, as I pulled my pajama shirt over my head and grabbed for my bra, "you should come downstairs today and check him out."

She crossed her arms and shook her head.

"Oh, come on," I said, clasping the bra and pulling the tank top on. "Aren't you sick of being in here all the time?"

Jamie thrust a hand toward the window.

"I know you go outside sometimes, but I'm saying to come downstairs today, to see Vinnie."

She shot a resentful glance over her shoulder, with pouted lips and a furrowed brow. I had wondered if she was jealous, knowing that she had never been given a chance to have a boyfriend, and this was all the proof I needed.

"I'm sorry," I said quietly. She waved a dismissive hand at my apology, and I added, "I just thought you might wanna see the guy I'm with now. Just think about it, okay?" Jamie shrugged, then nodded, and I smiled, trying not to get too excited. "Good."

***

"Here you go," my father said, handing Vincent a cold beer, before sitting down on the brass love seat beside him. "Vinnie, you sure I can't get you one?"

Vinnie leaned forward in his chair, placing his elbows on his knees and clasping his hands, and then shook his head. "Nah, I'm good."

"Don't worry about impressing me by not drinking," Dad went on. "Help yourself to a beer. Or, if you want, I have a cabinet full of liquor, if you'd rather something harder. I can make you a—"

"Really, I'm good," Vinnie replied, and I couldn't help but notice his gritted teeth.

Dad clapped a hand against Vincent's shoulder. "Will you tell him he doesn't need to worry—"

"Daddy," I cut him off. "Vinnie doesn't drink, okay?"

"Ah, come on," he scoffed, then looked to Vinnie with a lighthearted grin. "You can't have *one* drink with your girlfriend's old man?"

I glanced in the direction of my sisters, tending to their kids but watching with glares of scrutiny. I was beginning to think that inviting Vinnie and his dad had been a horrible idea. My father, while well-intentioned, relied too much on alcohol to be social, and my sisters had snooped too much into Vinnie's past. My only saving grace was my mother, and she was still inside, finishing dinner and making iced tea.

"Hey, I'm gonna see if my mom needs help. You wanna come?" I asked, keeping my eyes on Vinnie and not on the older woman lingering behind his father.

He turned to me, gratitude in his eyes, and nodded. "Yeah, let's do it."

We walked quietly through the French doors and the living room, and into the kitchen. My mother moved quickly, bustling around to the sound of Devin O'Leary & the Blue Existence, and Vinnie immediately snickered. I looked up to him, a flash of warning in my eyes, with the assumption that he was about to say something uncouth about my mom.

When he noticed my glare, he shook his head, wide-eyed and apologetic. "No, no. It's just," he waved a finger toward the ceiling, "this band, my brother-in-law's dad is the drummer."

Mom whirled around on her heel, a dumbstruck expression on her face and a spoon, dirty with the makings of macaroni salad, in her hand. "Uh, what did you just say?"

Vinnie snorted. "Yeah, that guy, Sebastian Moore, is my brother's father-in-law. It's freakin' insane. He's a pretty chill guy."

I gawked unapologetically, momentarily forgetting why it was we had even come inside. "So, you've met the whole band?"

His cheeks flushed and his hand reached around to rub the back of his neck. "Nah," he replied, shaking his head. "I've only met Devin and the, uh, the piano player. Sebastian, though, I've hung out with a bunch of times. Greyson's really close with his old man, so he's around a lot when I head up there."

"I am totally coming upstate with you the next time you go," I blurted out on a burst of excitement. Then, immediately embarrassed and realizing how presumptive that was, I quickly added, "I mean, if that's okay. If it's not, then—"

"Nah, it's cool," he interjected, his lips curling in an easy half-smile that I was now desperate to kiss.

Vinnie then asked where the bathroom was and excused himself, leaving my mom and me to share a moment of quiet excitement over knowing someone with celebrity ties. She handed me the spoon with instructions to keep stirring the salad, while she cut tomatoes for the burgers.

"He seems okay," she commented quietly, lifting her gaze to watch for my reaction.

"Yeah," I agreed. "He is."

"You like him a lot." I felt my cheeks burn as I nodded. Then, she added, "He obviously likes you, too."

"I know," I said, pinching my lips between my teeth.

Mom came to stand closer beside me, bringing the knife and cutting board of tomatoes with her. "But?" she asked in a hushed voice.

"It's nothing. I just … I don't know. I just wish they'd lighten up a little."

"Who?" I gestured toward the back of the house. Mom nodded immediately, knowing exactly who I was referring to. "Well, you can't really blame your sisters for being a little worried."

"About what, though?"

Mom sighed, shame touching her cheeks with a hint of pink. "Andrea, they showed me that picture."

I released the spoon, letting it hit the side of the plastic bowl. "Oh, great. That's wonderful."

"They're just looking out for you, you know that."

"Yeah, I get it, but you can't hold an old picture against someone for the rest of their life, Mom. People change. I mean, you're really gonna tell me he seems like a freakin' drug addict to you?"

She let go of the knife and rubbed her fingertips against her forehead. "No, he doesn't. But, honey, people relapse. They—"

"You're forgetting what I do for a living, Mom. I *know*," I snapped heatedly. "I see that shit regularly. You don't have to tell me."

Mom's eyes clouded with sympathy as she reached out to rest her hand on my arm. "I'm not attacking him. I *said* I like him. I'm just explaining how I can see why your sisters might be a little more hesitant to trust him, that's all. There's nothing wrong with being aware."

Sense and clarity washed away my initial defensive reaction, and I nodded, taking a deep breath. "I just wish they'd stop giving him nasty looks. Like, they can watch out for me without being completely judgmental."

"That, I can agree with," Mom said, picking up the knife and resuming her chopping.

Moments later, Vinnie entered the kitchen and demanded to know what he could do to help. Mom gestured toward the vegetables on the island and asked if he could manage a garden salad. He scoffed and pretended to roll up his invisible sleeves.

"Can I manage a salad," he snickered, shaking his head. "Mrs. Bennett, I have been chopping and peeling since before I could spell my own name."

He then made himself at home, reaching for another cutting board and a knife from the counter. I resumed stirring the salad, periodically glancing over my shoulder at him, just to watch him work. He was quick with a knife, and took the job seriously, slicing cucumbers and carrots with meticulous care. I loved seeing him there, in his sleeveless shirt and with all his tattoos, adding a badass contrast to my parents' clean, country kitchen. I caught myself thinking, as I watched him work, *that's my boyfriend*, and I could feel my cheeks set aflame with butterflies and emotion.

To my surprise, Jamie wandered in at one point, to inspect the new guy in my life. She stood beside him and looked up with wondrous intrigue. I wanted to ask him if he could feel her there, and if he had any clue that there was someone else in the room. But then, I remembered, he still had no idea about the things I could do, so I kept my mouth shut, feeling more than a little sad that I held so much shame in something I couldn't help.

When we had finished our work and the food was ready to be served, Mom carried the salad outside, leaving us alone to clean up and wash our hands. Vinnie glanced at me to offer a small, adoring smile and said, "I like your mom. She's cool."

"Yeah, she's okay."

"She's a lot cooler than most moms would be, if they knew the shit I've done."

"She doesn't—"

"Andy, I heard you's talkin' in here."

Embarrassment curled around my neck, heating my skin. "What? How?"

He laughed. "The bathroom's right around the corner and, sweetheart, I ain't deaf."

I pressed my lips together and took a deep breath, releasing the guilt on my exhale. "I'm sorry."

"No, it's fine. I mean, really, I can't expect that people are just gonna put that shit on the back burner. I gotta earn their trust, I get it." He shrugged, stuffing his hands into his pockets. "I'm not even sure my own dad trusts me completely, so I can't expect your family to jump on board when they've barely met me."

From the corner of my eye, I saw Jamie. I saw her hands clasped against her chest and her smile, and I smiled back. She liked him, she approved, and that felt more important than getting the thumbs-up from my sisters.

***

My sisters might not have instantly fallen in love with Vinnie, but their kids certainly did. While at five, three, and two, they were pretty easily impressed, I was stunned by how easily Vinnie took to them. Walker had found a permanent spot in Vinnie's lap, while Clarke and Jordan busied themselves by admiring his tattoos. I sat back in silent speculation, watching and wondering what the old woman behind him was thinking.

"You're really good with kids," Willa commented, carrying a tray of watermelon wedges to the table.

Vinnie grinned, bouncing the toddler on his knee. "I lived with my sister's kids up until a few years ago."

"How many does she have?" Mer asked.

"Two little girls," Vincent chimed in, before sending himself into a coughing fit.

"Pops, take it easy," Vinnie muttered beneath his breath.

"Take it easy," his father mocked with a wheeze, scoffing and waving a hand through the air. "I wasn't *doing* anything."

Mom hurried to get up from the table. "Vincent, can I get you something? Some water maybe?"

The old man coughed again, holding a fist to his mouth and flattening his other hand to his chest. He began to shake his head, then thought better of it and nodded. Vinnie watched with wide-eyed worry, as if he thought his father would drop dead right here, in this backyard on Long Island. It wasn't his time yet though, I knew this and felt it, but I couldn't say it. Vinnie would ask how I knew, demanding some medical explanation, and that was a conversation I wasn't yet prepared to have.

I stood up, controlling my speed, not wanting to give Vinnie more reason to worry by showcasing any panic. I bent over his father, pressed a hand to his back, and said, "Take it easy, Mr. Marino. Try to focus on taking slow, deep breaths."

He listened and began with short, sputtered gusts of breath, but after several tries, he was breathing normally again, as normal as he could. He took a sip of water from the bottle my mother brought to him, then wiped the back of his hand over his mouth. When he noticed a streak of pink, brushed over his pale, spotted skin, he looked up at me with terror in his eyes.

"It's okay," I whispered, grabbing a napkin from the table and wiping the blood-tinged saliva away. "That's going to happen sometimes. But it's okay. You're going to be okay."

"Oh, yeah," he snickered morosely. "I feel really okay right now."

The old woman in the yard looked from her son to the dying man with sympathetic eyes. One hand reached out to cover Vincent's shoulder, and I watched his feathered brows lift. I didn't need to ask if he felt it, I knew he did. He turned his head slightly, to take a quick glance at his arm, to see if something was there. He couldn't see her hand laying there, of course, and he shook his head as he swallowed, probably assuming it was only the wind or maybe even his imagination. But he continued to feel it, I knew he did, and I hoped he found comfort in her touch.

"So, let me ask you a question," I said, pulling over a chair to sit beside him.

"Hm," he grunted, settling back in his chair and continuing to make quick glances toward his shoulder.

"How did you meet your wife?"

Vinnie leveled me with a steely glare I chose to ignore. He was my boyfriend, but this moment wasn't about him.

His father pulled in a deep breath and held tight to the arm of his chair. "Oh, that was a long time ago—"

"Yeah, but come on, you still remember."

Vincent pinched his lips and hesitated, shaking his head, but still he responded, "We met in high school."

"Ooh," I squealed, leaning forward in my chair. "High school sweethearts?"

He nodded. "Yeah, I guess you could call it that."

"That's so romantic."

He huffed a disgruntled laugh. "Sure."

Vinnie surprised me then by chiming in. "Oh, get outta here, Pops. You were head over heels and ready to marry her right after you graduated."

I gasped, looking between Vinnie and his father, and said, "Wow! Are you serious?"

It took Vincent a moment before nodding. "Not one of my prouder moments," he muttered.

Mrs. Marino scowled and pulled her hand back.

Vincent noticed immediately.

***

Vinnie and I sat on the front porch of my parents' house, while my family, his father, and the ghosts in both our lives watched the fireworks from the curb. Multicolored sparks streamed through the air and reflected off the Great South Bay, and although the night was sticky and humid, it was also beautiful, just to have this man by my side.

He blew into the air and hung his smoking hand between his knees. "He actually looks happy," he commented, and although he didn't say it, I knew he meant his father.

"I know you don't believe it now, but he *will* be okay," I insisted gently.

"It's just …" He stopped himself, pressing his lips shut and shaking his head. "Never mind."

"I told you, you can talk to me."

"Talkin' isn't gonna change shit, Andy," he said, gritting his teeth.

"But it might make you feel better."

He hung his head and sighed. "Here's the thing," he began, and sucked on his teeth before continuing, "there is no feelin' better about this. It's not just gonna go away by *talking*."

“No, maybe not, but you might be able to find some semblance of peace.”

“He’s my dad, Andy, and he’s fuckin’ dying. Where’s the fuckin’ peace in *that*?” His voice cracked and so did my heart. “It’s just … it’s just so hard to look at him and know that in a couple months, he’s not gonna be here. I can’t wrap my head around it. I don’t …” He blew out a breath and diverted his gaze from the old man across the street. “I don’t know how to cope with this shit. You know? Like, my brother and sister, they have their own lives to deal with and keep ‘em distracted. What the hell do I have? I’m with him all the time. I’m … I’m the one listening to him cough and struggle to breathe. *I’m* the one who’s just waitin’ to wake up one day and find him dead. They have shit to do, and I have—”

“Me,” I interrupted, trying to remind myself that he was just finally talking and not intending to hurt me. But it still stung.

His mouth stopped moving momentarily, frozen, before saying, “What?”

“You *have* me.”

He licked his lips and dropped his gaze to the cigarette, burning away and barely touched. He stamped it out in the ashtray my mom had found for him, buried in a kitchen drawer, then wiped a hand over his forehead.

“I didn’t mean—”

“I know,” I said. “I know you’re just venting and I’m glad that you are. But please don’t forget that I’m here, and that I want to help you get through this. Okay?”

Vinnie turned to face me. His eyes found mine and held me there, breathless and frozen, until his gaze dropped to my lips. His hand reached out, cupping my chin to lure me toward him, and I complied without hesitation. He stole my thoughts with a kiss, tearing me from the grey area between the lands of the living and the dead, and for a moment, I resided nowhere but in the taste of summer on his lips and cigarettes on his tongue. I knew that, if he was anybody else, I would've found reason to be disgusted, and if I were an outsider looking in, I would've judged. But this was Vinnie, and I was me, and I was falling for everything that made up the whole of us.

"I know I have you," he said, his voice rasped and whispered, as he moved his hand from my chin to my cheek. "I just wish I could keep him around, too."

"He'll always be around," I replied, sliding my hand over his.

"You don't know that, though."

Oh, this beautiful, broken man, I thought, as my heart ached. *Tell him. Tell him everything you know and release him from his torment.*

"Actually—"

"Shit, that reminds me," he said, abruptly, cutting me off.

"W-What?"

"Zach and Greyson are going to another one of those shows you like. They invited us to go with them. You interested?"

"A psychic medium?"

He nodded. “Yeah. I mean, I don’t love that shit, but I know you do. So, if you wanted to go, I’d tough it out.”

“Then, let’s do it,” I said, wondering if this could be the one to save my life, along with my sanity.

CHAPTER TWELVE

ANDREA

When I was sixteen, I discovered John Edward. One of my mom's friends had gone to see him live and was blown away by his ability to communicate with the dead. It was then that I'd developed an infatuation with him and an insatiable intrigue in his skill to harness his gift. I wanted to know how he did it, how he managed to balance life with the whispers of the dead, but I had never found the answer. So, I'd gone in search of others, with hopes that they'd be able to help me out, but always came up empty.

Now, sitting in the small, dark theater with Vinnie, his brother, and brother-in-law, my skepticism was on high alert. The stage lights flickered, imitating lightning, and a tin-canned rolling thunder echoed through the sound system. It was cheesy, reminding me of the low-budget school production of *The Telltale Heart* I'd seen when I was twelve, and it was a struggle to keep my eyes from rolling out of my head.

“I’m going to get something to drink before it starts,” Greyson said, standing from his seat. “Can I get you guys anything?”

“I’m good,” I replied with a smile, while also finding it very difficult to ignore the menagerie of spirits that swarmed in his vicinity.

They buzzed around him, three women and a man. They doted on him, fawning with adoring eyes and smiles. They showed me images of a time when they had been worried, concerned about his well-being and choices, but now, they felt nothing but contentment. It wasn’t his life that kept them here, but his questions and concerns about them and where they were. So, they were waiting to give him a message, telling him that they were okay. And I knew, with so much guilt in my heart, that I could pass it on, if it weren’t for my fear of being found out by these people I’d grown to care about.

“Ah, come on, you need *something*,” Vinnie said, wrapping an arm around my shoulders. He shifted in his seat and dug out his wallet. “Grab a root beer for us, will ya?”

“I’ll come with you, cupcake,” Vinnie’s brother, Zach, replied, as he stood up and took the cash from his brother’s hand.

The stage lights continued to flicker as they left, and once he was sure they were gone, Vinnie turned to me and rolled his eyes toward the front of the auditorium.

“Okay, but really, can we talk about how lame this is?”

I snorted, pressing a hand to my nose. "Oh, my God, I know, right?"

"Grey said this lady was a pretty big deal, so you'd think she'd have the budget for a little more, um …"

"Flair?" I offered, hiding my grin behind my fist.

He pointed his finger my way and nodded. "That's the word I'm lookin' for—*flair*. Like, I feel like I'm sittin' in on an elementary school's rendition of *Frankenstein* or some shit."

I laughed and relaxed into my seat. I already had a predetermined idea of how I'd feel about the show—disappointment and disgust—but I'd decided to at least have a good time. I was with Vinnie, and if I tried hard enough to ignore the constant static around me, I could enjoy my time with him. I always did.

But, after Greyson and Zach had returned to their seats and a louder crack of canned thunder announced the start of the show, my attention was no longer on Vinnie but the Stevie Nicks lookalike who just walked out onto the stage. The long-haired blonde was dressed in veils and a dress best suited for a woodland faerie, with several skirts and belled sleeves. She was barefoot, padding across the stage to the microphone with mystical grandeur, with her hands clasped together and her eyes soft. And I couldn't help the groan that escaped my lips.

Vinnie leaned into me, bringing his mouth close to my ear. "What the hell is this shit?" he muttered, keeping his voice low.

I shook my head, unable to speak. It still never ceased to amaze me, how gullible people are and how willing others are to take advantage of that. This woman before us, spreading her arms out and addressing the applauding audience with a wide, serene grin … there was no way she was the real deal. This was too showy, too much of a spectacle, to convince me of any genuine ability.

"Good evening!" she bellowed into the microphone and the crowd applauded. "Thank you all for joining me tonight. Spirit has been preparing for this occasion all day, and I am ready to pass along their messages," she extended her arms toward the audience, "to you."

Spirit. I snickered to myself, rolling my eyes. I hated that, always had. Having one all-encompassing, singular word to describe every soul to ever pass over, as if they had all combined to create just one entity on the other side of life. In my experience, the dead are just as unique and individual as they were alive, every one of them with their own personality.

"I will perform my readings first, and then I will allow a handful of questions. So, if you could all be very—" The woman stopped talking, her mouth hanging open and her hands frozen in mid-air. She turned soundlessly toward our section of the auditorium and pinned her eyes to where I sat, or so it seemed.

"I'm sorry," she said, urgency in her tone as she grabbed the mic from its stand. "I'm feeling a pull in this direction and I cannot ignore it."

I sat up straighter in my seat, while my heart pounded loudly in my ears, blending seamlessly with the static. She moved closer to the edge of the stage, until she was just a few rows away, and the closer she got, the louder their chatter became. Almost as if she were bringing more with her.

With a glance at Vinnie, I saw his curious trepidation, leaving its lines along his forehead and between his eyebrows. He didn't say anything, only watched as Tracey Lambert came to stand at the very edge of the stage, looking out at the rows before her.

"There's a woman coming through, a mother. She's here for her son." Her eyes bounced between every man sitting in those few rows. "Who here has lost a mother?"

"Um, my grandma—"

"No," Tracey abruptly cut the guy off. "A mother looking for her son. Someone right here." She made a circle with her hand. "Right in this area."

Every man turned to look at each other with an odd blend of accusation and hope. Every one of them wanted so badly for it to be them, while also knowing deep down that it wasn't.

Except for one.

"Raise your hand," I hissed at Vinnie, all of a sudden excited at the prospect of this woman being the real thing.

"What? Hell no. Greyson lost his mom. Maybe it's her—"

Tracey loudly sighed into the mic, putting a stop to Vinnie's words. "Someone *right here*. She's showing me pizza. Maybe someone loves pizza, someone owned a pizza place, or—"

"Our dad owns a pizza place," I heard Zach call out from beside Vinnie.

Tracey seemed to deflate with her relief. "You're brothers?" she asked, volleying a finger between Zach and Vinnie.

"Yes," Zach answered, nodding while Vinnie continued to scowl with skepticism, his jaw clenched tight and his eyes narrow.

"There's a sister, too. She's showing me a J name."

Zach looked at Greyson, wide-eyed and excited, before answering Tracey, "Yeah, our sister, Jenna."

Tracey nodded happily. "Yes. Your mother is nodding. She's very proud of the three of you and who you've become. Although ..." She pursed her lips, shaking her head. "You've been troubled, the two of you. You," she pointed to Zach, "have come to the other side, but you," her finger moved to Vinnie, "you continue to struggle."

All faces turned to Vinnie, including mine. He swallowed, then lifted his mouth in a forced half-smile. "Nah, I'm all good."

"Your mother wants you to know you're going to be fine, if you can fight temptation. That will be your downfall."

He scoffed. "Good thing she doesn't know anything about me."

Tracey wasn't perturbed by his snide comment. Instead, she smiled. "You will believe, sooner than you think." Then, her eyes flicked toward mine, as she said, "Your mother likes her, by the way."

My stomach twisted, hitting me with a relentless barrage of pangs. Not because she happened to elude to my secret, nearly leaving me uncovered and vulnerable. No, none of that was my reason for excusing myself and running to get some air.

This woman was the real deal, and she saw me.

***

We were nearly out of the theater, moving with a sea of new and old believers in the afterlife. Once we reached the door, I stopped abruptly, and Vinnie turned around.

"What's up?"

"I just remembered I forgot something at my seat."

He narrowed his eyes. "What?"

I released my lip that I'd been chewing from between my teeth, and was already turning around to head back into the theater, as I said, "I'll just be a few minutes."

He didn't have a chance to speak again as I hurried inside. A security guard stopped me, to ask where I was going, and I lied, saying I thought I had dropped a credit card at my seat. He let me go on the promise that I'd be quick. I raced along, moving down the aisle and straight to the stage, where a member of Tracey's crew was working.

"Excuse me?" I called to him.

He lifted his head from unplugging the microphone. "Yeah?"

"Is Tracey available to talk?"

He shook his head. “Sorry, she doesn't do autographs.”

“No, no,” I said hurriedly. “I don't want an autograph. I really just want to talk to her. I have questions and—”

“I'm sorry. She isn't available.” He stood up to wrap the cord, pretending I no longer existed.

“*Please*,” I begged, gripping my hands to the edge of the stage. “I just—”

“You the press?” he interrupted, now looking angry and menacing.

“What? No, I'm—”

“Tracey doesn't deal with the press.”

My desperation was slowly getting the better of me and tears began to sting the backs of my eyes. “I'm not a member of the press. Please. I just ... I just really need to talk to her. I-I need to—”

“Lady, in two seconds, I'm getting security in here. So, turn around and—”

“No, Chuck, it's okay.”

I looked up to see the whimsical frame of Tracey coming toward us. She had taken off her fairy tale dress, trading it for a skin-tight pencil skirt and blouse. She wore an expensive pair of heels, her lips were coated in a smooth, crystal pink gloss, and I realized she only played a part when she entered her stage life. Off stage, she was simply Tracey, gorgeous and with expensive taste.

“You sure?” Chuck asked, narrowing his eyes at me.

"Yeah," Tracey said, nodding as she waved a signal for me to follow her. "Come on, honey. Let's get a drink."

***

"Are you sure you don't want to invite your boyfriend?" Tracey asked on our way to the bar.

"No," I said. "He doesn't drink."

Tracey nodded as if she knew. I supposed maybe she did. I always assumed that people's abilities varied and I wasn't sure what hers consisted of. Maybe she could read minds or see the future, for all I knew, and I couldn't wait to find out.

After meeting Tracey, I had gone back to Vinnie and told him I had run into a friend and that we were going to grab a drink. It didn't make me proud to lie to him, but a little fib was easier than the whole truth. And I figured, maybe it wouldn't even be necessary to tell him the truth. Tracey might've held the secret to turning this thing off and I could be free forever.

Tracey and I entered The Thirsty Goose. I had made the suggestion, not knowing where else to go in the city, and Vinnie's friend recognized me right away with a broad, friendly grin.

"Andy, right?"

I smiled at the nickname Vinnie had given me. "Yeah, hi. Nice to see you again."

"You, too. Where's my boy tonight?"

Guilt washed over me as I forced myself to smile. "Home."

Goose was tall and reminded me of a Viking, with his long, reddish-blond beard and hair. He towered over Tracey and me, and when his bright, blue eyes swept over us, I felt the slightest bit intimidated. Like he saw me and my lies, and all I wanted to do was crawl beneath the bar and hide.

But then he smiled, wrinkling the corners of his eyes. "Ah, ladies' night, huh?"

"Yeah," I replied, relieved and ashamed.

"Well, then, what can I get for you?"

After I'd ordered my martini, I looked to Tracey expectantly, only to find her unabashedly transfixed on Goose, watching as he collected the ingredients, martini shaker, and glass. Glancing at her hand and not seeing a wedding ring, I wondered if her life had kept her from having a relationship, too.

She eventually ordered a gin and tonic, and with drinks in hand, we found a quiet table in the furthest corner, away from other customers. We silently sat and sipped from our glasses, as I mustered the strength to ask the first question and break the ice. But how the hell do you even start that conversation? I had waited so long for this opportunity, but I had never made it this far before. Now, sitting beneath the flickering bulb of a hanging lamp, I stared into my glass, feeling like an idiot.

Thankfully, Tracey saved me from my bumbling mind.

"So, what can you do?"

I laughed, suddenly feeling as if this was a job interview. “Um ... well, at the risk of sounding like Haley Joel Osment, I see dead people.”

Tracey nodded like it was nothing. “Anything else? Are you at all psychic?”

Pinching the toothpick speared through my olive and swirling it through my drink, I replied, “I'm psychic in that I can usually tell what's wrong with people and when they're going to die. I can't, like, see when someone's going to get a job promotion, or if they really should buy the house or anything like that. Everything I can do, is pretty much all revolved around death.”

Saying it out loud for the first time didn't make me feel better the way I thought it would. Instead, I felt horrible. Like some angel of darkness.

“Wow,” Tracey said, continuing to nod. “I can't do that. I can see when someone's health is in danger, but I'm not given the reason or an expiration date.”

“Consider yourself lucky,” I mumbled.

“Do they talk to you?”

“Who? The dead?” Tracey nodded eagerly and I replied, “They can't speak. Sometimes they move their mouths, like they can talk wherever *they* are—”

“The other side or something.”

“Yeah, exactly. But when they realize I can't hear them, they communicate through images. Like, transmitted to my brain.”

“I get that, too, but from Spirit. I can't *see* them here; I just get images of them, coming through in my mind.”

"The third eye or whatever," I offered, and she nodded. "Is it a constant thing?"

"What? The images or—"

"Everything."

Tracey seemed to consider the question, as she drank from her glass. I sat across from her, finding myself suddenly desperate and needing to know her answer right away. But she took her time, pulling her lips in and out from between her teeth, and taking small sips of her gin and tonic.

It felt like a half hour had gone by before finally she said, "When I was younger, I couldn't get it under control. I would tell my parents about the things I saw and the things I knew, and twice, they had me committed to try and figure out what was wrong with me."

My jaw dropped. "Oh, wow ... I'm so sorry."

She closed her eyes and shook her head. "Don't be. It wasn't malicious. They genuinely thought I was going crazy and just wanted to help. I was put on a lot of medications in my teens, for a number of issues the doctors thought I had. And even though I didn't really have schizophrenia or whatever they'd diagnosed me with at the time, the drugs *did* make it stop."

There was a finality in what she had said. Was she implying that pills were the only thing that had quieted the voices, or Spirit, as she called it?

I pressed my lips together, letting those words settle in, before asking, "So, what happened after that?"

"Well," she leaned back, folding her hands on the table, "the psych meds I was on had other side effects. I was sluggish, couldn't focus, and struggled in school. I barely made it through to my high school graduation, and after that, decided not to go to college."

It was hard for me to fathom that this put-together, successful, and beautiful woman had at one point been too doped up to thrive. I tried to imagine her struggling but it was difficult when before me sat someone I had quickly come to admire.

"I realized that I would never be able to function in society like that, so I decided to wean myself off the meds. And as my mind and energy went back to normal, so did Spirit. And it was crazy, because it almost seemed as though they'd been waiting for me to come back. I was all of a sudden bombarded with these images and messages everywhere I went, and it wasn't long before I turned to alcohol to make it stop."

"Jesus Christ."

Tracey nodded solemnly. "By the time I was twenty-five, I was a functioning alcoholic. There wasn't a second that went by in my day where I wasn't drunk. But," she sighed and shrugged, "I had a job at my uncle's law firm. I had my own apartment. I was working toward getting my GED. I knew what I was doing wasn't good, but I was also doing better than I had been, so I kept it up.

"But, the thing with that kind of lifestyle is, it's only okay for so long before it catches up with you. And when I was twenty-eight, I was on my way to work and got into a horrific car accident. I killed a man and his eight-year-old daughter on their way to school."

My gaze dropped to the table and her barely-touched gin and tonic. Vinnie had abused drugs and alcohol, and for that reason, he never touched it. How could she be drinking now?

"I was addicted to what the alcohol did for me, not the alcohol itself," she said gently, and I looked back to her, surprised and feeling like I'd been caught. The kindness in her smile wrapped around me like a warm hug and I relaxed. "A lot of people wonder how I can have a drink every once in a while, without feeling tempted, so I just thought I'd clear the air now. I can't read minds."

I snorted. "I was about to be really impressed."

Tracey laughed, shaking her head. "No, my thing isn't *that* cool."

Pulling in a deep breath, I glanced toward the bar and saw Goose. He had buried himself behind the bar, occasionally flicking his angry gaze toward the juke box, where a group of drunken girls were hovering. I smiled faintly, knowing he was struggling to hide his fuming assumption that they'd feel tempted by Lynyrd Skynyrd. The thought reminded me of my first date with Vinnie, which only reminded me of why I was here.

"So … what happened?" I asked, turning back to Tracey and wishing she'd just skip to the answers I was desperately searching for.

"Oh, right." She cleared her throat and sat up straight, as her smile faded with the memories of her past. "While I was in the hospital after the accident, I obviously couldn't drink and the only thing that they had me on was some very mild painkillers. I was bombarded with the messages again, but I felt I deserved it, like it was a punishment for what I had done. So, I dealt with it for weeks, just being harassed by this … *thing* I hated so much. Until I was visited by that man and his daughter."

My eyes grew wide at the shocking twist in her story. "Whoa."

She pursed her lips and nodded. "Up until that point, I had never taken the time to really pay attention to what they had to say. But when *they* came to me, I knew I needed to, if only for my peace of mind. And the amazing thing was, they had forgiven me. They had …" Tracey took a deep breath and shook her head, almost as though she couldn't quite believe it all herself. "They had understood that I was troubled, and that they had become a part of my story, as horrible as that is. But, they did have a message for their wife and mother, and for the first time, I did as Spirit wanted. I found that woman, let her yell at me and cry, and then, I gave her the message. Everybody was at peace, including me, and … I don't know, ever since then, I realized what good I could do for this world. I might not have asked for this ability, but it was given to me for a reason. So, I use it."

Her story was touching and inspirational, but she still hadn't answered my question.

"But," I began, moving gently back to the initial subject at hand, "how do you turn it off?"

Tracey leveled me with a soft glare and shook her head. "I don't," she said, and I deflated with a sorrowful exhale. "Honestly, I don't want to. Sure, it does get in the way sometimes, but I just accept it as a part of my life."

"How can you even have a life?" I asked, exasperated. "I can barely make it through a date with my boyfriend without them distracting me. They're always there."

"Well … does he know?"

I narrowed my eyes defensively. "What?"

"Does your boyfriend know you see ghosts?"

"God, no," I scoffed, shaking my head.

She cocked her head like a curious dog. "Why not?"

I rolled my eyes back to Goose and his angry glares toward the drunk girls, who had in fact chosen "Sweet Home Alabama."

"Because he would think I'm a freak. And he wouldn't want to be with me anymore." And just the thought of not being with Vinnie, the first guy I'd truly felt anything for, brought my throat to tighten and my eyes to water.

"But why would you want to be with someone who doesn't accept you for who you are? Don't you accept him for his past?"

"That's different."

"How?"

I narrowed my eyes at this woman's audacity. She might've been told about his past from the spirit of his dead mother, but that didn't mean she knew him, or us. It also didn't give her the right to throw these questions at me.

“Because that’s the *past,*” I spat at her. “*This,*” I jabbed a finger at my temple, “isn’t something I can go to rehab for and, and … *get rid of.*”

Tracey went quiet. She breathed evenly, calmly, as she watched me with a degree of wisdom that left me suddenly infuriated and fed up with this entire conversation. I had come here for answers, for solutions and remedies. Instead, I’d received nothing but a vat of fortune cookie wisdom and judgment. I didn’t have to put up with it. I didn’t have to sit there and take it. So, I stood up from the table, abruptly pushing the chair violently with the backs of my calves. The sound was loud, overpowering the second round of Lynyrd and his love for Alabama, and a few curious faces turned to us.

“Andrea,” Tracey said, keeping her cool while mine had clearly dissipated. “Please, sit down.”

“I have work in the morning. Thank you for your time.”

I snatched my bag from the table and turned toward the door, ignoring her pleas for me to come back and sit down. And I actually did think about it for just a moment before I could leave the bar. I thought about going back to her and talking, if for no other reason but to have someone who understood. But what was the point? She wanted me to accept this, to just settle for the bitter truth that there wasn’t a damn thing I could do about it, and I wasn’t ready for that.

Not now, and maybe not ever.

So, I left.

CHAPTER THIRTEEN

VINNIE

"You're doin' it wrong."

"No, I'm not, Pops."

"Yes. You are." Pops got up from his chair and with his oxygen tank in tow, he hurried over to the counter. He pointed at the wad of dough, sitting in the center of a swirled mess of flour, and shook his head, a sour look on his face. "You need more flour. You're gonna screw it up and waste all that dough."

I set my jaw firm and furrowed my brow, glaring hard at my father. "Funny 'cause this is how I've been doin' it forever."

Pops spat a puff of air at me, waving a hand. "I never would've taught you like that."

Throwing my hands in the air, I shouted, "Yes! You did!"

Jabbing a finger at me, my father narrowed his eyes. "You lie."

It was too early in the day for this. I was too tired, and he was way too infuriating. I left the dough and stormed out from behind the counter, walking past him, while digging for my cigarettes.

"Where do you think you're goin'? We open in an hour!"

"Havin' a smoke," I grumbled, about to unlock the door.

"Don't you think you do that enough?"

My hand paused and my teeth gritted, as it took every bit of willpower I had to not spin around and scream in his face. But, with a deep breath, I turned the lock to open the door, and silently stepped out into another humid, summer day. Leaning back against the brick building, I lit a cigarette and pulled in a deep breath. My eyes pinched shut, a forceful demand to feel the burning in my lungs and the warmth in my chest, and then, I exhaled until there wasn't any breath left in my body.

The weeks had gone by slowly, but time was flying, killing my father and driving me crazy in the process. His temper had heightened, his patience was nonexistent, and shamefully, I was on my last nerve. I wanted to yell at him. I wanted to say, "I'm sorry you're dying, I'm sorry you're mad, but what about the ones you're leaving behind, huh? What about *us*?" But I wouldn't say it. I couldn't bring myself to. Instead, I smoked. I smoked and I hoped things would get better, even just a little.

Later that day, around lunchtime, I told Pops I was heading out to grab some food with Andy. He glowered in my direction and asked if our pizza was too good for her. Flabbergasted, I pulled a pair of sunglasses from the pocket of my open button-down and shook my head.

"Pops, knock it off."

"It's an honest question. The two of you's have gone out twice this week. Why not save money and eat here?"

"Because—" I caught myself, as I slid the sunglasses on, and shook my head. "Never mind. I'll be back in a little while, okay?"

"Why won't you answer my question? You think you're gonna hurt my feelings?"

Moe hauled a garbage bag out of a can, tied it up, and threw it over his shoulder. "Lay off him, Mr. Marino, come on," he said on his way to the front of the shop.

I patted myself down, making sure I had everything I needed, just as the door chimed open and Pops said, "What, you need Moe to fight your battles, huh? You can't stand up to your old man yourself?"

Behind my glasses, I shot Pops with an angry look. "You're really testin' my patience, you know that?"

Although I knew he was sick and frail and dying, Pops all but flattened me with an infuriated look, reminding me of when he was healthy, and I was about twenty years younger. "You will *not* talk to me like that, boy."

Despite the residual chill from my youth trickling down my spine, I kept my steely glare unfaltering as I replied, "What the hell do you think—"

"Hey." Andy rushed to my side and wrapped her arms around one of mine. "You ready to go?"

Without a word, I watched Pops, as if I needed his permission. He slashed his hand through the air and turned away from me. “Get the hell outta here,” he grumbled, and so I did.

***

“So ... you wanna tell me what happened?”

Unblinking, I stared off in the direction of the hot dog vendor. I hadn't chewed the bite in my mouth for what was probably minutes, and the bread was now soggy, the hot dog and sauerkraut blending together to create a taste I suddenly found unpleasant. I squashed the remaining half of my lunch in a napkin and tossed it into the garbage can beside the bench we sat on.

Finally swallowing, I said, “I dunno.”

Andy sighed, keeping her eyes on the sidewalk and her hands. I pulled my white Famiglia Bella hat off and scratched my hairline, knowing I should talk to her. It's what people in relationships do. They vent, they complain. They talk things out until they're better. It's what Jenna did with Nicky, what Zach did with Greyson, and I knew, if I wanted to make things work with Andy, I had to do it with her, too. But our relationship wasn't the same. She was Pops's nurse and I feared she would take his side, if there were sides to take, and all I wanted was for her to simply listen.

So, I asked, “If I tell you what happened, can you promise to keep the nurse in you quiet?”

She snorted. “That's kinda hard for me to do.”

"Well, I need you to try. 'Cause I don't wanna talk to Andy the Nurse. I just wanna talk to my girlfriend."

"Okay. I'll try."

I pulled in a deep, refreshing breath. There had been a break in the heatwave, a welcome reprieve that promised fall was coming, and I enjoyed the feeling of crisp air in my lungs before exhaling.

"I dunno how to deal with him anymore. We fight about literally everything. I can't even breathe without him sayin' somethin' about it. And it makes me feel bad, you know? 'Cause I know he's gonna die. But no matter how many times I try to remind myself of that, he goes and does somethin' else to piss me off." I swallowed, knowing what I wanted to say and what I wanted to elude to. I wanted to tell her about the whispering devil on my shoulder and how he was tempting me more and more with every passing day, but I wouldn't let myself say the words. I wouldn't admit that I could be that weak. "It's just hard," I settled on, letting my secrets settle uncomfortably inside my brain.

Andy nodded. I could see how hard it was for her not to be a nurse. I knew she wanted to use her medical advice on me, separating herself from what we were to revert to something more comfortable for her. She took her time replying, allowing a few seconds to go by before she answered.

"Could you get your brother or sister to stay with him?"

I sniffed a bitter laugh. "And what, disrupt their perfect little lives?"

It was the first time she had heard about my growing resentment toward my siblings. She looked up to me, surprised, then I watched her concern take over.

"I thought you got along with them."

I groaned, wishing I hadn't said anything at all. "I *do*," I pressed firmly. "I'm just sayin', they got their own lives to deal with. Jen's got the girls, she's got the house ... Zach has his business, and he and Grey are talkin' about kids. I can't expect either of them to take care of the old man when they got all this other shit goin' on."

"But do they not care about what *you* have going on?"

"And what is it that I have going on? It's not like I have all this important stuff happening."

It was the wrong thing to say. I saw that in the way she clamped her lips together and looked the other way. But that wasn't to say I hadn't meant what I said. Sure, our relationship was important to me. I was enjoying myself and we were having fun. But when I held what we had next to the lives of my brother and sister, I couldn't deny that we seemed to pale in comparison.

"They're still his kids," she finally said, keeping her voice low.

"Sure."

"So, they should do their part."

"And is that your professional opinion?"

She turned back to me, her jaw taut and her glare hard. "It's my opinion as your *girlfriend* after watching you get more and more stressed over the past few weeks."

"I can't make them do anything," I replied, feeling myself slowly seeing her side of things.

"Well, what if you went upstate and visited Zach? Stay with him for a weekend and recharge. Have Jenna stay with your dad."

God, that sounded nice, just to get away for a little while. But how could I leave him? Even if he was making me angry and stressing me out. He was still Pops and he was still dying.

"I don't know ..."

"You being here isn't going to stop anything from happening," she replied gently, as if she knew exactly what I was thinking.

"I'll think about it," I said brusquely, knowing my decision had already been made.

***

"I'm takin' off this weekend," I announced to Moe. "Jen's gonna be here."

He looked up from washing the dishes, his eyebrows lifting with intrigue. "You and your lady friend going away?"

"Nah, she's gotta work. I'm just gonna go upstate and chill with Zach and Grey. I gotta get away from Pops for a couple days."

Moe nodded, his eyes turning a solemn shade of brown. His sympathy was thick and evident and I turned away, not wanting to acknowledge the sadness I knew I'd soon be forced to feel.

"It's just gonna be an overnight thing," I went on, stacking pans and opening a cabinet to put them away.

"I think it's a good idea."

"Yeah, Andy suggested it."

We worked quietly, side by side. He washed the dishes and I put them away, while Pops's old radio played some Notorious B.I.G. in the background. The silence felt uncomfortable at times and I realized how little I knew about him. We'd known Moe for years, keeping him fed when he was homeless, then giving him a job when we had the means. For all intents and purposes, we had turned his life around without any demand for compensation. Seeing him clean, healthy, and happy was more than enough. But every now and then, I couldn't help but wonder, who was he? Who had he been before we'd really gotten to know him?

"So."

"So," I repeated, keeping my eyes on the plates in my hand.

"I, uh, I wanted to talk to you about something."

My brow furrowed. "Sure, man, what's up?"

Moe shut the tap off and grabbed for a dish rag to dry his hands. There were still plates and utensils in the sink, but this conversation obviously required his full attention. So, I decided to give him mine.

"I know you and your dad've been bumpin' heads a lot lately."

"That's an understatement," I grumbled, crossing my arms.

"I know, brother, I know," he replied, so sympathetic and sincere. "I feel for you. It's rough and he has been dealt a terrible hand, that's for sure. All of you have. You're good people and you've dealt with enough as it is. So why you gotta go through this, too …" He shook his head, making his thick, dreadlocked hair sway. "I just don't know. I don't know why bad things happen to good people. I really don't."

I shrugged. "It is what it is, man. It's just life."

"Isn't that the truth," he said somberly. "But you know, my man, you can't do nothin' about the hard times you're going through. But you *can* do somethin' about how you react to them. And you and Mr. Marino, man … you are both actin' like fools."

I pursed my lips and cast my gaze downward, teetering between the need to get defensive and the desperation to agree and demand how to make it better.

"You know, my ex-wife and I—"

"You were married?" I looked up to him, unable to understand why I felt so surprised.

Moe smiled, a hint of sorrow flickering in the golden specks in his brown eyes. "I was. And man, did we fight. I mean, things were good in the beginning, real good. We had it all, man. Good money, good kids, a nice house. But then, one of my kids, my daughter, she passed away. And lemme tell you, it's truly amazing how quick one horrible thing can take all the good things away."

"Fuck, Moe," I muttered, swallowing hard. "I had no fuckin' idea."

“Of course you didn’t,” he said good-naturedly. “It’s not exactly something I advertise, you know what I mean? But I’m just sayin’, that one horrible thing made me and my wife fight a lot. I started drinkin’ and shootin’ up. I lost my job, I lost my wife, and I lost my other daughter—man, I lost my whole fuckin’ *life*. And I know you and the old man are hurtin’, brother, I know. But if the two of you don’t start fixin’ this shit before it’s too late, I’m worried you’re gonna lose a lot, too.”

CHAPTER FOURTEEN

ANDREA

"So, what are you and the boyfriend doing this weekend?" Elle asked, twirling a long strand of hair around her finger.

"Nothing," I laughed, taking a bite of a taco.

"Nothing? Well, that's boring."

I shrugged, swallowing. "He's going upstate to visit his brother."

"You could've gone with him," Elle said, lilting her voice in sing-song fashion.

"I have to work!"

Elle rolled her eyes. "Girl, please. You could've called out sick."

"Whatever, it's fine."

"Except it's not, but like you said," she shrugged, popping a tortilla chip into her mouth, "whatever."

I knew it wasn't necessary, but I felt the need to add, "Vinnie just needed some time away. I'll see him on Monday."

"Time away from you, though?"

I shook my head. "No. I'm just—"

"Andrea, I'm just giving you a hard time, relax. But seriously, you should've gone. You could use some time away, too. Like, you're always here. Play hooky once in a while and spend a day in bed with your hot boyfriend. Nobody would judge you, believe me."

The mention of sex left me with an increasingly uncomfortable gnaw in my gut. In the weeks we'd been seeing each other, we hadn't found ourselves in a position to even think about it. I guess that was just the nature of us both living at home with our parents. At what point would the opportunity arise without us feeling like teenagers trying to sneak in a quickie? That didn't mean I didn't want to though, and I was fairly certain Vinnie felt the same. But how could we, given our circumstances? And how the hell was I supposed to bring it up to him without sounding like a horny adolescent?

After lunch, Vinnie texted me when he arrived at Zach's house. He told me he missed me and asked if I'd call the next chance I could. So, I told my patient and the two silent men lingering in her room that I'd be back to check up on her after my break. I went downstairs and headed outside to sit in the atrium.

"Hey," I said after he'd answered the phone.

"Hey, Andy." I closed my eyes at the sound of his name for me. "How you doin'?"

The way he said it would've made me laugh months ago, with visions of *Friends*' Joey Tribianni in my head. But now, I only smiled, biting my lip and enjoying the warmth that coursed through my veins and settled in the lowest part of my belly.

"I'm okay," I answered quietly, almost shy. "How are you?"

"Good, good. No. You know what? I'm fuckin' *great*. It's beautiful up here. And my brother just had this gorgeous in-ground pool put in, so you know where I'm gonna be."

Images of Vinnie in a pair of trunks, wet, shirtless, and bathed in sunlight, clouded the cluster of landscaping before me. I wondered exactly what he looked like shirtless. I wondered if he had a thick blanket of chest hair or if he shaved. I wondered what his skin smelled like, tasted like, looked like in the sun. I closed my eyes, ignored the two other hospital personnel occupying the other benches in the atrium, and envisioned his hands in my hair, his tongue in my mouth, and his body pressed against mine.

"Sounds nice," I replied.

"What are you doin'?"

Swallowing at the dryness in my mouth and throat, I said, "Sitting outside. Why?"

"Oh ... you just sound out of breath. Thought you were running or somethin'."

My cheeks singed with embarrassment. "No, I'm just," I cleared my throat and shoved a hand into my pulled-back hair. "It's hot, so ..."

"Hm. Yeah, I'm dyin' up here. Z and Grey went to grab some burgers and dogs to throw on the grill, but they're comin' back soon. Otherwise I'd go skinny dipping."

How cruel, I thought, shifting on the stone bench, and wiping a hand over my face. I laughed awkwardly, too awkwardly, then answered without composure, "Yeah, I wish."

The words were out before I could stop them from dropping from my lips and I laid a hand over my eyes, wishing I also possessed the ability to disappear.

Vinnie was momentarily quiet, allowing my flickering humility to build until my face and gut were both ablaze. I wasn't smooth. I wasn't skilled in the art of wooing. I could respond with enough tact, but making that first move? That wasn't typically my thing, with the exception of our first kiss, and I was suffering the aftereffects of that now, scorched cheeks and all.

"You wish, huh?" he finally responded, his voice low and gruff.

"Um ..." It was too late. I couldn't rewind and erase. I could only accept and own. So, I replied, "Yeah. I-I wish I was there."

"I wish you were, too."

I was suddenly sixteen and on the brink of a major breakthrough with my biggest crush. Here it was, that big confession, the big turning point in what seemed like a fling of innocent sweet nothings and sweeter kisses. The bench I sat on was my bed, the slim phone in my hand was thicker and heavier, and the ghosts were nothing but curious illusions.

"God, I just saw you yesterday, but I miss you. How fuckin' ridiculous is that?" He laughed, deep and rough, and I said I missed him, too. His laughter faded gently, and he said, "You should come by my place tomorrow."

The knots in my gut tightened as my excitement piqued. "I should, huh?"

"Yeah, you should."

"What about your dad?" God, it felt ridiculous to ask.

"I can be quiet if you can."

I bit my bottom lip with the promise that this was happening, before replying, "I can try."

Vinnie groaned in a way that made my entire body feel filthy and my mind even filthier. Immediately I envisioned us, alone and in bed, and I wished so badly I was at home, behind my closed bedroom door and not in this atrium.

"God, you shouldn't do that," I whispered into the phone, glancing at a doctor about six feet away. "I'm still at work."

"Dammit. So, I guess phone sex is out of the question, then, huh?"

"What? Seriously?"

His laugh bubbled through the phone, bordering on a giggle, and the butterflies in my heart joined those fluttering in my stomach. "Nah, I'm kiddin'. I can't do that shit. Makes me feel weird. And besides, the first time we do anything like that, it's gonna be you and me. That's it."

My stomach dropped with a swoop of nervous anticipation. "Tomorrow night," I said by way of confirmation, chewing on my lower lip and glancing away from the doctor.

"Tomorrow night."

***

The prospect of intimacy had me wired with copious amounts of nerves throughout the rest of my workday and on the train home. It had been years since I'd slept with someone. I could remember who it was with—a guy named Theo, who I'd been seeing for a few weeks in my mid-twenties—and I could remember how it had been—decent, satisfying, but not earth shattering. But I couldn't recall feeling this rattled beforehand. Surely, I had known that we would sleep together, but had I felt like *this*? So certain and so *assured* that the first time we had sex would be a pinnacle of certainty that this was *it*? I shook my head to the passing trees, buildings, and a neighboring train, because no, I had never felt like this before. Not ever, not once. And that was terrifying. And, he still didn't know. What if he found out after we slept together, after we both knew, with clarity, what we were to each other?

It would be cataclysmic.

"I have to tell him," I muttered to the silent woman sitting beside me.

She belonged to the melancholy man across the aisle, who had been mourning her sudden and tragic passing for three long and lonely years. Caught in the middle of an avoidable turning point in their relationship, an argument he'd started, neither of them had seen the car as it ran through a red light. Neither of them had said goodbye, not realizing that they had to, not so soon, and he'd blamed himself ever since.

"What? Are you talking to me?" he asked, turning from the window across from mine.

Startled, I shook my head. I'd never learned to not talk to them. "N-No, sorry. Just thinking out loud."

"Oh," he muttered, nodding. "Okay."

He turned back to the window with a forlorn sigh and I felt the push to say something, to make him feel the slightest bit better. It weighed me down, pressing against my shoulders with an invisible grip, and I wished for it to go away. I had my own problems to deal with, my own life, but the longer I willed it away, the more force was added. By the time he had reached his stop, I was sweating and drowning under the pressure, while her merciful eyes pleaded and begged amid the images of their sweet and happy relationship that had ended far, far too soon.

"Wait."

The man paused, frozen with his hand on the back of his seat. "Huh?"

"She forgives you."

His brow furrowed, his lips frowned. "What—"

"The argument and the accident. You were having a bad day, and she forgives you for that."

Against the seat, his fist clenched and beneath the layer of stubble along his jaw, his muscles tightened. "Who the fuck are—"

"She loves you, she always will, but she wants you to be happy. She worries about you, and if that woman from the office will put a smile back on your face, she wants you to go for it."

His eyes flooded, then blinked rapidly as he furiously tried to keep himself from crying in front of a mysteriously meddling stranger. "How the hell do you—"

"You're keeping her here." I gestured toward the seat beside mine. He couldn't see her, but it was occupied. "When you feel the bed move late at night? When you're trying to sleep but can't? That's her laying down, trying to comfort you."

His broken face crumpled and the battle against his tears was lost. They spilled over his cheeks and onto the dirty train floor. I hated this part, when people realized I was telling the truth, when they knew I had *it*; the sixth sense, the third eye, *something* they were desperate to possess themselves. They always had more questions I couldn't answer, always wanting more from me than I could give. And this man was now preparing to miss his stop, but I had my own life to deal with.

"What is she—"

"You have to go."

He made a move to sit down. "I can miss my—"

"Please, I have nothing else for you."

The broken heart he unsuccessfully tried to hide, was displayed in the never-ending stream of tears on his face and the defeat was reflected in the shallow sigh that passed through his nose. He nodded once and thanked me profusely as he collected his things and ran for the door. The woman across from me smiled and bowed her head, grateful that I had done what I did, probably assuming, like him, that there was nothing more I could do. But the truth was, I had lied to them both. It was simply that I hadn't wanted to. Because for once, my life had been more important to me.

CHAPTER FIFTEEN

VINNIE

"It should be illegal for a sky to look like that," I commented, shaking my head in utter amazement at the sheer volume of stars speckling the backdrop of crisp darkness.

"Beautiful, isn't it?" Greyson's dad, Sebastian, agreed. "I don't even miss the city most of the time."

"You're full of crap," Greyson laughed, pointing across the pool at his lookalike father, his other arm wrapped around my brother's shoulders. Then, he turned to me and said, "He's always talking about how much he hates being up here in this shit-hole town."

Sebastian sent a splash of water in his son's direction. "I said *most* of the time."

"It's true," I corroborated, laughing. "He did say that."

A wet hand clapped against my shoulder. "And I didn't even have to bribe you to back me up." Sebastian shook me gently as I continued to laugh. "I *knew* I liked you."

"Stop encouraging him," Greyson's aunt and Sebastian's wife, Tabitha, groaned, walking past the pool with Greyson's little sister, Izzy, on her heels. "You'll be his best friend and he'll harass you for the rest of your life."

"Nah, Thumbelina," Sebastian said, reaching out of the water to wrap a hand around her ankle. "That's just you."

We all laughed together, the five of us in Zach's starlit backyard. The scent of the grill still lingered in the air, reminding me of dinner, as it blended pleasantly with citronella from the candles bordering the fence. The humidity was minimal and for the first time in weeks, I could breathe, pulling in nothing but the lazy comfort of summer. But despite being surrounded by people I cared for and loved, my heart was hollow, and I missed Andy. I stared across the pool at my brother and the man he'd committed his life to, watching with a jealous glint in my eye as they cuddled close and shared a sweet kiss when they thought nobody was looking. I wondered if I could bring Andy up here soon. I wondered what her wet skin would feel like, and if she'd be daring enough to do more than just kiss in the deep end. I bit the inside of my cheek and turned toward the house, trying to think about anything but her wet, warm body against mine.

"So, Vinnie," Tabitha said, sitting at the end of a lounge chair.

"Yeah," I blurted, quickly looking from the house to her.

"When are we going to meet your girlfriend?"

I smiled. "I was just thinking about that."

"Oh, I'm sure you were," Zach chided, splashing me from across the pool.

I splashed him back. "Shut up, dick."

"Don't worry, we'll soundproof the guest room before you guys come up," he jabbed playfully, winking.

"Good," I fired back. "'Cause the last thing I want is to listen to you guys goin' at it all night."

"Vin, if you're jealous, all you gotta do is say somethin'. I'm sure Greyson wouldn't mind if you wanted to join—"

"Yo, man, knock it off." I squeezed my eyes shut, shaking my head.

"Too far?" Zach laughed.

"Way too far." I opened my eyes and addressed Greyson, smiling apologetically. "I mean, I love you, man, but not enough to experiment like that."

"It's all good," he answered, chuckling.

"Anyway," I said, looking back to Tabitha, "I dunno. Her hours are kinda crazy at the hospital, but I'm sure we can come up for a couple days soon."

"Let us know," she replied, pulling the sleepy Izzy into her lap. "Sebastian will make his ribs and I'll throw together my macaroni salad."

"Oh, man, you know Aunt Tabs means business when she starts throwing around Dad's ribs," Grey commented. Then, he groaned, laying a hand over his stomach. "You better bring Andy up here soon, Vin. I wanna eat those damn things now."

I promised I'd talk to her and set aside time to visit. Zach, Greyson, and I climbed out of the pool, blew out the candles, and said goodnight to Greyson's family, before retiring inside to lay out on their plush living room furniture. The air conditioning goose-pimpled my drying skin and I wrapped myself in one of their fluffy throw blankets, sighing at the comfortable warmth.

"Okay, I'm just gonna pass out right here," I said, closing my eyes and kicking my feet up on a leather ottoman.

"Nice, right?" Zach laughed from beside me on the couch.

"Hell yeah, man. I wish we had the space in the apartment for furniture like this." The large sectional sofa was too big for Pops's and my kitchen and living room combined.

While I did like our modest couch and recliner set, there was no denying it didn't hold a candle to this type of luxury.

"You guys gotta get outta the city. You could buy such a bigger, nicer place if you did."

I shook my head. "Pops would never go for it, and you know that."

"I don't wanna say it, but Pops isn't gonna be in the picture much longer—"

"Stop, Z."

Zach sighed. "I know you don't wanna talk about it, but man, you gotta start thinkin' about what you're gonna—"

"Cut it out," I interrupted, raising my voice. "I know what I gotta do, but I don't gotta do it yet, so knock it the fuck off."

The room was blanketed in tense silence. Long, painful moments passed before Greyson quietly excused himself to head upstairs and get ready for bed, leaving my brother and me to marinate in the looming darkness that hung over both our heads. Except, Zach would never feel the pressure the way I did. He would never know what it was like to live his life for the man, to have put everything on hold, only to lose him and be left not knowing where the hell to go next. He had escaped that fate years ago, and good for him, but that meant he was the last person who could lecture me. Not even Jenna had experienced the type of freedom from our father that Zach had, and so I braced myself for an argument, because there was no way I was going to put up with it.

"Vin, I know it's hard, but—"

"You don't know shit," I fired at him, immediately on the defense.

He huffed, teetering on irritated, and scrubbed a hand over his face. "Fine. Don't talk to me. I'm just sayin', if you need someone—"

"I get it. You're there, thanks, now drop it."

Zach pressed his lips together, eyeing me with an annoying amount of concern. I was concerned, too. I didn't trust myself and didn't want to know how I was going to cope with our father's passing. I hoped and hoped that I'd never have to find out, but I wasn't an idiot and knew that was pointless. I looked at myself in the mirror, the way Zach was looking at me now, worried and afraid. I didn't want him to look at me like that. The concern on his face, made it all the more real, and fucking hell, I didn't want it to be.

"I think you need help, Vin."

"Here we go," I growled.

"For real, listen to me. I'm worried about you, and so is Jenna."

"Oh, so you agreed to me comin' up here to, what? Have a fuckin' intervention or something?"

"No, why? Do we have to intervene with something?"

I knew what he was asking and I hated him for it. "Fuck you."

"You're gettin' defensive."

"Yeah, 'cause you're accusing me of doin' somethin' I'm not fuckin' doing!"

Zach shook his head, the worry in his eyes deepened. "You jumped to that conclusion on your own, bro."

"Oh, go fuck your—"

My irate comeback was cut off abruptly by my cellphone ringing from the coffee table. It was Andy and I considered letting it go to voicemail. She didn't need to talk to me when I was feeling this livid. But answering the phone meant having a valid excuse to walk away from my brother without him following on my heels. So, I snatched it from the table, answering it without a word to Zach, as I pressed it against my ear.

"Hey," I grunted.

"Vinnie, have you heard from Jenna?"

I narrowed my eyes, not sure I had heard her correctly. "What? No, I haven't gotten any—"

"Okay, I guess she hasn't been able to yet," she replied quietly, almost as though she was talking to herself. Then, she said, "You need to come home. Now. Zach, too."

"What? Why?"

The urgency in her voice was enough to scare me and I bolted up from the couch, leaving the security of the blanket behind. Zach watched, his eyes wide and spine rigid, as I shoved my bare feet into my sneakers before I could hear her reply.

"It's your dad," she said shakily.

I stopped before I could grab the keys to the old car Zach had given me. "W-what? What happened? Is he—"

"He's alive," she said. "But Vinnie ... he doesn't have a lot of time, and I can only hold things off for so long. You need to hurry."

I snapped my fingers at Zach, signaling for him to get his shoes on. He ran upstairs quickly as I replied, steadier than I felt, "We're on our way."

***

Zach tried to drive as quickly as he could, but his house in Hog Hill was still three hours away from the city and there was still traffic. It also didn't help that he was skeptical of Andy's urgent call, especially after Jenna had gotten a hold of us.

"He fainted," she had said. "Dr. Singh isn't worried, but she's going to keep him overnight just in case."

She and Zach were convinced that Andy was being unnecessarily alarmist, telling me there probably wasn't much reason to rush back home. Maybe they were right, and we'd get there only to find it was nothing at all. But either way, wasn't it better to be there for him? I thought so. But something told me that wasn't the case. Something told me that Andy was right, the way she'd been right about his disease, and I was scared. I was more scared than I'd ever been in my life.

I just hoped we made it in time to say goodbye.

CHAPTER SIXTEEN

ANDREA

"Go grab yourself a cup of coffee," Vincent told his daughter.

Dr. Singh had told them that Vincent had just fainted and it was nothing to worry about. But, although Jenna didn't seem too concerned, she still hesitated at his demand. She eyed him with fearful trepidation, like leaving would allow him to take a turn for the worse. Yet he remained firm in his insistence that she take a break.

"Andrea is here," he said, gesturing in my direction. "You think she's gonna let anything happen to me? Come on."

Jenna turned to me, worry and apology in her eyes. "Do you mind?"

"Why would I mind?" I asked, reaching out to lay a hand over her knee.

"Because you're not on the clock and you have to work in the morning and—"

"Jen, stop. I wouldn't have come if I didn't want to be here, okay? Now, go get a cup of coffee. Get some air. He's going to be fine."

Her eyes searched mine, as if to determine whether I'd just told a lie or not. But I must have been more convincing than I thought because she believed me. She grabbed her purse from the floor and turned toward the bed as she stood from the chair. Looking her father in the eye, she held his gaze for a few seconds longer than normal. She probably didn't know why, she probably didn't even realize, but her soul did.

"You're my favorite daughter, you know that?" Vincent said, reaching out for her hand.

"Oh, knock it off," she grumbled, her voice tight with emotion. Then, she added, "You're my favorite daddy."

"I love you."

She looked away, lifting her eyes to the ceiling and blinking rapidly. "God, Pops, you're gonna make me cry."

"I know, but I gotta say it. I love you, Jenna."

Swiping a finger under her eye, she replied, "I love you, too, Daddy."

Mrs. Marino watched from the corner, allowing her husband and daughter to have their moment. Her hands remained folded at her waist, as she waited her turn.

She'd been waiting a long time.

"I'll be back soon," Jenna said, squeezing her father's hand.

"I'll be here," he said, then pulled her fingers to his lips, kissing her knuckles one, two, three times before letting go.

She hurried out the door without another word, leaving us alone. I had been dreading this. I was fine in the day-to-day monotony of my life and this part of the job was just another piece of the routine. But tonight, wasn't a part of that usual grind. This was a man I'd grown attached to. A man I'd now built a relationship with. He was my boyfriend's father and no longer just another patient, and for the first time, I felt a sadness I'd never experienced with the others. I wanted to tell him to hold on. I wanted to tell him to stick around, for just a little longer, but the light in his soul was dimming. I could see it—a hazy glow, flickering like a dying bulb—and I knew it was almost over.

So, I pulled up a chair and asked, "Will you tell me a story?"

Vincent regarded me with an exhaustion he'd hidden well from his daughter. It was my job that made him comfortable around me and I couldn't stand it.

"About what?"

"Your wife."

He spat a puff of breath into the air. "Nothing to tell."

"But there is. It's why you still love her so much."

His jaw tightened and he shook his head. "Andrea ..."

"Please?"

His eyes met mine, and as his brow furrowed, he said, “You’re pretty special, aren’t you?”

I swallowed and asked, “What do you mean?”

He never answered my question. He just simply smiled, sighed, and said, “We were high school sweethearts. We loved each other so much, maybe even too much, and right after graduation, we were married. We had all these plans of travellin' the world, seein' things, doin' things. But, those were the plans of kids who didn't understand that life doesn't always happen the way you want it. We needed money, we needed jobs, and so, for several years, we both worked our asses off to build our savings account. Then, we had Jenna.

“After she was born, we realized that we couldn't just travel the world with a baby, that wasn't gonna happen. Luckily, in the time that we'd been married and buildin’ up our savings, I started having a new dream. I wanted my own pizza place. And I told her, whatever I take outta savings, I'll be able to put back. We'd save up again, and then, when Jenna was older, we'd go do the things we always wanted to do but as a family.

“So, I bought Famiglia Bella, and I dumped every last penny from our savings account into it. Then, we had Zach, and a year later, we had Vinnie. And my wife, she ... she wasn't right after that, after havin' two babies so close together. I dunno if it was her hormones or if everything just suddenly felt like too much, but whatever it was, she changed. Or at least, that's when I noticed it.

“We, um ... we tried to make things work for a while. But I was always workin', while she was at home with the kids. I worried about that sometimes, 'cause she was alone so much and she'd have these episodes. Like ... like she was a pot of boilin' water and sometimes she just bubbled over, you know? But as far as I know, she never hurt them, so I thought it was okay.

"But then, one day, I came home from work late—I usually did—and as soon as I got inside, everything felt off. Like, I didn't know what was goin' on yet, but I could tell somethin' was wrong. You know what I'm sayin'? And it didn't take me too long to realize her purse was gone. I thought, hmm, okay, maybe she had to run out for somethin'. But when I went to our bedroom, I saw that the suitcases were gone, too."

My widened eyes flicked toward the woman now standing beside the bed. The regret in her eyes and the sorrowful downturn of her lips. There was so much guilt there, written in the lines on her face, and now I understood why.

She had abandoned her husband and left her three kids motherless.

"She had left me a note," Vincent went on. "It said that she loved me, and that she loved the kids, but she couldn't continue to wait for her life to begin. And I couldn't understand that. 'Cause, yeah, maybe life wasn't what we had dreamed it would be when we were kids, and maybe we were hurtin' bad for money and things were tough, but it was *our* life and we were livin' it, or so I thought."

I nodded somberly. "Did you ever see her again?"

He shook his head. "Never in person but always in my dreams."

And there it was, his broken heart, displayed proudly in his eyes and the gruffness of his weakening voice. I didn't need to ask if he'd ever been remarried, or if he'd at least seen other women. I knew the answers to those questions. Vincent Marino had remained faithful to the woman who had abandoned him and their children. With a glance at his wife, tears now trickling slowly down her cheeks, I knew her heart had never left him, even if she had. And then, I was mad. I wanted to ask her if it was worth it. I wanted to ask if she was happy with the way her life had turned out, while her husband and kids had struggled. I wanted to ask if she'd do it again if she could. But this moment was about Vincent, not her, and I kept my mouth shut.

"You still love her," I said.

He nodded. "I made a promise to her when we were kids, and I kept it."

"So did she," I replied. Then, I rolled my eyes to the ceiling and added, "Well, I mean, she left you, but she had always remained faithful."

He didn't look surprised. Not by the statement, or the certainty in which I said it. Instead, he nodded and asked, "She's here, isn't she?"

"She is."

"I've been feelin' her around for a while now. I just didn't know for sure if ... if it was really her or just my mind playin' tricks on me."

That was a typical reaction. The heart always knows but the brain struggles to let go of what we've been told about science and logic. I smiled at the part of him that was still so innocently human, even as his soul readied itself to leave.

"She came to get you," I said.

"I thought so." He nodded, smiling in the very direction in which she stood.

Then, he said, "I'm not scared, you know. I'm tired and I'm ready. But I worry about Vinnie. Jenna and Zach, they're gonna be fine, I know it. But Vinnie ..." Vincent shook his head, frowning. "Vinnie's gonna need some help."

"I'll be there for him," I promised. "I'm not going anywhere."

He turned to face me, lifting a brow. "You love my boy, don't you?"

I hadn't said it, neither of us had, but his father already knew the things my heart cautiously whispered. There was no point in lying, so I nodded and whispered, "I do."

Vincent sighed, bobbing his head slowly in a tired nod. He outstretched a hand toward the furthest corner of the bed, where Mrs. Marino stood, smiling. His lips curled upward, his eyes closed, and then he whispered, "Okay."

***

I remained by his bedside in the minutes after he'd passed. The monitors he was hooked up to ran in a low, monotonous beep that I'd fallen deaf to the second he'd left. The on-duty nurse hurried in, asking me what had happened, and I told her the truth.

He had fallen asleep and died.

She sighed sorrowfully and nodded, saying she would get the doctor, as she walked out of the room. There was no need to hurry; the man was dead.

I had been answering Vinnie's texts all night. Giving him regular updates and reassurances that he was still alive. But now, I didn't know what to say, and so, I said nothing. I couldn't tell him his father had passed away through text, and even a phone call felt too impersonal. So, I continued to wait there in the room, until the Marino siblings' loud voices filled the hallway.

"It was the scariest thing," I heard Jenna say. "We were just watchin' *Breaking Bad* like it was just a normal Sunday, and then, he just went limp. I thought he was already dead."

"This is why you're not a doctor," Zach chided.

"Oh, don't act like you wouldn't have been scared shitless, Zachary," she fired back. "I've never been so—oh, my God."

The trio turned the corner into the room, hurrying faster with every step they took toward their father's bedside. Vincent was gone, and so was their mother, but they grabbed his hands and held his face, calling his name. Calling him back.

"Pops, Pops," Zach repeated, clapping a hand to his father's cheek. Then, he turned to me. "Andy! Get the doctor!"

I went to Vinnie, standing at the foot of the bed. I slipped my hand into his and squeezed, noting that his fingers never wrapped around mine.

"Guys, he's—"

"*No*," Jenna said, shaking her head as she gripped the fingers of her father's lifeless hand. "I was gone for a half hour. That wasn't a long time. He said he'd be here when I got back. He said he'd be here. Daddy ... you *said* you'd be here!" Her voice cracked in her throat as she brought his hand to her lips, kissing his knuckles. "Oh, goddammit."

"I'm sorry," I said, my voice strangled by my own emotion.

I held firm to Vinnie's unmoving hand while Zach took one, two big steps away from the bed, thrusting his hands into his hair and gripping tight, before hurrying around to Jenna's side of the bed. He caught her in his arms before she fell apart, sobbing against his chest as he sobbed into her hair. I choked back the tears as the doctor came in to definitively pronounce him dead. He asked the Marinos if they'd like a minute to say goodbye, and while Zach and Jenna said yes, Vinnie remained silent. Emotionless. Still as stone.

And I worried that I wouldn't be able to keep my promise to Vincent.

CHAPTER SEVENTEEN

VINNIE

Standing at the front of the funeral parlor, I shook the hands of sympathetic friends and family members that I couldn't remember ever meeting before in my life. They forcefully offered their condolences and shared their stories about my father. As if I cared to hear them. As if I needed it. As if, somehow, in their convoluted minds, that would make everything better.

But it didn't.

It felt wrong; everything did. This—Pops being dead, and me being at his wake, standing in front of his open casket—all felt wrong. Living, breathing, eating, just carrying on felt *wrong*, and I was slowly starting to sink. Drowning in the harrowing seconds that continued to pass since he had died.

I didn't know what to do without him.

So, I did nothing.

"I remember your father bringing a dozen pizzas down to the station after 9/11," Jason, a retired NYPD officer, said. "He was always supportive, always there for the community. This city won't be the same without him."

I nodded, keeping the painful smile plastered to my face. "He was a great guy."

"He really was. I'm just so sorry for your loss, man. If you need anything, you let us know, all right? We got your back."

"Thanks a lot. I appreciate it."

I shook his hand and he moved along, offering a hug to my red-eyed sister. Zach stood on the other side of me, engaging in emotional conversation, and I began to wonder if maybe I should've mustered up a few tears.

"Hey," Andy said, squeezing my hand. I peeled my eyes away from Jason and my sister to look at my girlfriend, and she asked, "How are you holding up?"

I shrugged, trying to buy some time to decide what was appropriate to say. "Hangin' in there, I guess."

She searched my eyes with concern. "Are you sure?"

"Yeah," I told her, nodding a little too profusely. "It's all good."

I tucked my thumbnail between my teeth and began to chew. Because the truth was, it wasn't all good. I could look at my brother and sister and clearly see how I should act and feel. How I should be holding it together. But I was so far from feeling that way, I was practically on another planet.

The next morning, at the cemetery, we laid roses on our father's casket. First, Jenna, then Zach. They cried unabashedly, whispering their final goodbyes to the wooden box, before hurrying off to cry in the arms of their waiting significant others. I kept a watchful eye over them, so acutely aware of my jealousy and anger as it took control. I imagined the homes they were retreating to. The distractions and all the fucking hope they would find within those walls, and all I could think was, *what the hell do I have*? I hadn't been to the apartment since Pops had died. I'd been staying at Jenna's house, for no other reason than to avoid the inevitable. But now, I knew I needed to go home. I needed to throw out the rotten milk. I needed clean clothes. I needed to face the loneliness I was sure to find there and the reality that he wasn't coming home.

"Vinnie?" It was Andy and she was pulling me gently to lay the clenched and crumpled rose in my hand on the casket. "Come on, I'll go with you."

The tiniest bit of emotion tugged at my throat. This woman had stayed by my side ever since that night in the hospital. She had only left to sleep at her house, just a few miles away from Jenna's place on Long Island, and then, she would return in the morning. She had called out of work and put her own life on hold and what had I ever done to deserve that? This type of affection and devotion? I hadn't tried, I hadn't done anything, but there she was, and I hated myself for not being more grateful.

I took the rose and with more care than I thought I could muster, laid it gently against the enameled mahogany. The white petals were a stark contrast on the dark wood, and I stared as one wrinkled petal dropped away from the others to lay alone on the glossy surface. And that hurt. All at once, it hurt so fucking much that the last thing I'd ever give to my father, had broken, right at the moment I gave it to him. I felt that hurt so deep in my chest, pressed firm and unrelenting against my heart, that I struggled to breathe as Andy gently lured me away.

We came to stand with my siblings, a couple of feet away from the casket, suspended over his final resting place. They had decided to open Famiglia Bella for lunch, free for anybody who wanted to attend and honor our father.

"Moe's over there now, getting things ready," Jenna said, red-eyed and snotty.

I nodded. "Cool."

"Are you up for this?" Andy whispered, as we walked back to her car.

"Why wouldn't I be?" I glared at her across the top of the silver sedan.

"I mean, if you just wanted to relax or, I dunno ..."

"I'm fine," I insisted, and climbed in.

***

Famiglia Bella had never been so packed. Not even when Devin O'Leary and a few of his band members came to draw attention to the place several years ago. It was heartwarming, to see how many people our father had touched in his lifetime and how many people cared.

Or maybe they just wanted free pizza.

Andy had taken quite a liking to Moe. While I cooked and kept my mind off of the empty apartment awaiting me, she busied herself with asking him questions, things I had never even thought to wonder.

"Where did you used to live?"

"Well, before I lost everything, my wife and I had a house on Long Island," he said.

"Oh, I live on Long Island! Where were you?"

He grinned with pride for what he'd lost. "I lived in Islip."

She nodded slowly. "Me, too."

Moe grinned over his shoulder at me. "Your girl and I are findin' common ground over here, my brother. Better watch out. I might steal her away if we keep this up."

"Yeah, my ass," I grunted in reply, offering my first genuine smile since leaving Zach's house days before.

Then, Moe said to Andy, "I'm just messin' with you, girl. I'd never do that to my boy. And besides, you're a little too white and skinny for my tastes."

"Moe likes some cushion for the pushin'," Zach threw in matter-of-factly.

Andy's laugh bubbled up from her belly and she held her arms around her middle. "Wow, okay. Too much info."

"It's true," Moe said, nodding sincerely. "My ex-wife, boy, she had these thighs I just loved sinkin' my teeth into. And that ass—"

"Guys, guys," Jenna interjected, gesturing toward her kids sitting at a table. "Can we remember the little ears? Please?"

I enjoyed the brief reprieve from the cloud hanging over my head, but like all moments, it was fleeting, and before long, we were once again quiet and doling out slices of pizza in solidarity. I didn't want to be doing this. I didn't want to be there. The pictures of Pops displayed proudly on the wall, that were once a hanging scrapbook of memories, were now a memorial. But what I wanted even less, was to go home, and every second that passed, was another second bringing me closer to the moment I didn't want to face.

That moment was inevitable though, and before I knew it, we were closing up shop and putting an end to the day. It felt so final. Like this was it, the official end to my father's life, and now, the world as I knew it, would continue on without him.

Zach locked the shop, tossed the keys at Jenna, and said, "I'll call you guys when I get home."

"You sure you don't wanna come stay at the house?" she asked. "Nicky already has the girls in bed, but if you're quiet, you're welcome to the guest room."

Greyson regrettably shook his head. "We have an appointment with an adoption agency in the morning. We could reschedule if—"

"Oh, Jesus, why would you do that?" Jenna asked, flabbergasted.

"Well, because ... you know ..."

Jenna reached out and laid a hand over Greyson's mouth. "Stop it. Pops never would've wanted you's to put your life on hold for him. Give him more grandkids. That's what he would've wanted."

She pulled her hand away, revealing Grey's reluctant smile, as he said, “We're gonna try.”

I loved my brother and the man in his life. But at that moment, as I stared at their optimistic smiles, I hated them both for having something, anything, to give them hope for the near future.

After hugs and promises to call were given, I took Andy by the hand and began to walk. I didn't want to take her to her car and allow her to drive home, because I didn't want to be left alone. I didn't trust myself to be left to my own devices, not when my heart was so vulnerable to the emotions threatening to rip me to shreds. So, without announcing the destination, I walked her to the apartment I once shared with my father.

She looked at the ground level coffee shop where neither Pops or I ever bought anything and asked, “You want coffee?”

I shook my head. “Nope.”

“Then ...” She turned and looked up into my eyes, raising a brow in question.

I pointed up. “I live on the fifteenth floor.”

Andy didn't smile. Her mouth formed a little O and she slowly nodded. “Oh,” she whispered, reminding me then of how shy she could be. I hadn't seen that side of her in weeks. I'd missed it, that part of her that seemed so innocent and pure, it felt almost sinful to even look at her.

“I don't have any expectations,” I told her, and that was the truth. “I just ...” I pulled in a deep breath and continued, “I don't want to go up there by myself. I ... I don't know if I can do it.”

Then she seemed to relax, blowing out a sigh that left her shoulders sagging, and she nodded. “Okay. Let's go.”

***

My overnight bag was in the living room, Zach had dropped it off over the weekend, but other than that, nothing seemed to have changed. The shoes Pops wore to work, were still beside the door. His meds were still on the counter. The clock on the wall ticked the time away, in the exact way it always had, and although everything felt the same, there was a stillness in the air that told me everything would never be the same again.

I stepped inside and grabbed my bag in a hurry. “I have to put this shit away,” I said brusquely, wrenching my hand from Andy's grasp and moving quickly through to the living room and down the hall.

“Vinnie, wait,” she called after me, following as quickly as her heels would allow. “Give yourself a minute.”

But I wouldn't. I passed the open doorway of Pops's room, daring to take a peek inside, to see the streetlights illuminating the room in an ethereal glow. His bed had been left unmade. The remote to his TV was on the floor, presumably dropped in the rush to get him to the hospital after he'd passed out. A bowl of popcorn sat on the nightstand, and I froze, focused on the kernels that had escaped their confinement.

"Seriously?" I grunted angrily, dropping my bag on the floor.

"What?" Andy asked, peering into the room.

I moved quickly inside, focusing only on those kernels of popcorn. "He bitches at me all the time about leaving food around and look at this shit." I grabbed the bowl and swept the rogue pieces into it. "Un-fuckin'-believable."

"It's not a big deal," she said, as I angrily walked from the bedroom to the kitchen. "Vinnie, just clean it up later."

"And what?" I asked, my voice loud and furious. "And let ants take over the goddamn apartment?" I dumped the popcorn into the trash and threw the bowl into the sink. "That's the last fucking thing I need right now, to deal with fucking ants."

I smacked my hand against the knob, turning on the faucet and thinking about my father, getting so pissed at us for leaving food out and around our old house. I soaped up the sponge and remembered his nightly ritual of TV and a bowl of freshly popped corn, the scent of it wafting throughout the house. I picked up the bowl and scrubbed it vigorously, replaying his laugh in my mind. And then, I dropped the soapy thing back into the sink, realizing that soon, so, so soon, I would no longer remember the sound of his voice. He was already fading from my mind and this place. The process had already begun the second he died, and I could acutely feel the bottom of my heart drop out. Pain swept over me, filling my chest and my stomach, and it took every ounce of effort to remember to breathe.

"Fuck," I uttered, my voice unrecognizable as my own.

Andy was at my back, pressing her hands to the dress shirt I had borrowed from Jenna's husband. "Vinnie, it's okay."

I shook my head as the torrential downpour of tears finally ensued. "No, it's not. This isn't okay. None of this shit is okay."

"I know you don't think it now, but you're going to be fine."

Turning around on my heel, I pinned her to the spot with a fiery glare. "Don't you fucking pretend to know what I think. You have no idea what's going on in my head. You, you have no fucking *clue* what it's like."

She blinked, startled, and I knew I should've felt bad, but I didn't. "Okay," she said, nodding. "You're right. I don't know. I've never lost a parent—"

"I've lost two parents!" I shouted. "Did you know that? I'm a fuckin' orphan now."

"—but I do deal with death every day of my life," she continued without answering my question. "Everybody copes with it differently, so if you're mad or upset or-or ... whatever you're feeling, you're not wrong. Just tell me what I can do to help. I *want* to help."

There was one thing that I knew without a doubt would help me. One thing I knew would take the pain away. The impossible itch was tickling at my veins and whispering its sweet nothings into my ear. It fed me it's delicious, empty promises, and I wanted it. I *needed* it so badly, yet I knew I couldn't have it. And that very act of slapping myself with a big, fat *no,* was in and of itself torture.

"You can't help me."

Tears sprung to her eyes at the cold slash of my words. "Tell me what I can do. *Please*," she begged, reaching out and pressing her hands over my stupid beating heart.

Her insistence was infuriating, but her hands were so warm, so soft and gentle. I melted just slightly under her affection and was reminded of something else I hadn't had in a long time. Something not as numbing as cocaine but just as temporary and almost as good. And Andy could give it to me.

"You wanna help?" I asked, laying a hand over hers, as my brief stint with tears dried sticky on my face.

She nodded. "Yes."

I took a step forward, then another, slowly backing her into the table and staring at her with impure, carnal intent. Then, I smiled at the sharp inhale of breath she took at the impact of wood against the top of her thighs. She had worn a dress to my father's funeral, and while I knew it hadn't been chosen for sexual convenience, it certainly was convenient now.

"Turn around," I instructed, calm and cold.

"W-what?"

Her fingers clenched at the fabric against my chest, her eyes searching mine frantically, looking for the guy she'd been dating for the past couple of months. The guy who was crass but romantic, sarcastic but kind. She wanted that guy to carry her to his room, lay her down, and make love to her. But right now, on the precipice of grief and weakness, I wasn't that guy. I couldn't be. I could respect her, I would never hurt her, and if she told me to stop, I would without hesitation. But she wanted to help me and all I had known was to fuck, and so, in that moment, that's what she'd be.

An easy fuck.

"I said, turn around."

I waited for her to tell me no. I think, somewhere deep down, I hoped she would. But after pausing for just a moment, she stood on her toes, pressed her lips to mine for the smallest fraction of a second, then nodded.

And some part of me still tried. Tried to show that I appreciated her, as I bent her over the table and lifted her dress. I tried to show that I genuinely wanted this, wanted *her*, as I unzipped my pants and pulled her panties to the side, putting her on full display—eager and trembling. I tried to be gentle, as I repeatedly thrust into her body, holding on tightly to her hips. But all I did was destroy and wreck everything within reach, as we moved from the table, to the wall, to the counter, breaking picture frames and shattering salt and pepper shakers. Mugs crashed to the floor and the toaster fell with a metallic clatter. The kitchen I had shared with my father was all but burnt to the ground as I fucked her, trying so hard to reach a point within her body that would take me to a place of numb euphoria, while also trying to show her I cared.

I succeeded at neither.

CHAPTER EIGHTEEN

ANDREA

Someone so angry and sad shouldn't have been so beautiful, but that's exactly what Vinnie was—angry, sad, and so devastatingly beautiful. He had used my body so thoroughly, it was a wonder I could even walk from his bedroom to the bathroom the next morning.

And I should've been mad, I knew that. I should've felt disrespected and betrayed. But even as I stared at myself in the mirror, smudged makeup and all, I only felt sorry for him. And glad I hadn't left him alone.

Splashing cold water on my face, I recalled the seemingly endless night of animalistic sex that took place in the kitchen, living room, and finally, his bedroom. Decorations had been shattered, appliances had been broken, and not once had he said my name. There had been no cuddling afterward. No romantic moments of sated euphoria. We had simply rolled in opposite directions on a bed too small for two people and laid there silently until sleep took us both. I had stared at the wall for hours, listening to the change in his breathing as he fell asleep, wondering how I should confront him, or if I should confront him at all. After all, I had given him permission. I hadn't said no. And it wasn't as though the sex wasn't good, because oh, God, it was. But I couldn't help but be disappointed that our first time hadn't been more meaningful, more romantic, more … more … Just more.

And so much less of what it was.

Now, the moment of confrontation was here, and bloated butterflies moved sluggishly around my stomach. Still in my dress from the day before, I exited the bathroom and walked through the small apartment, stepping over strewn papers and broken glass, until I reached the kitchen. There I found Vinnie, shirtless and picking the Keurig up off the floor.

Not yet knowing what to say, I reached down to pick up the salt and pepper shakers, cooking utensils, and the plastic container they'd been kept in, until Vinnie cleared his throat and asked, "So, um … coffee?"

"Sure," I replied in an awkward whisper.

After plugging the machine in and grabbing a couple of mugs from the cabinet, he set to work, silently brewing, and pouring, before handing me one steaming cup.

"Thanks."

"Yeah. Sure."

He walked past me, and I followed him with my eyes as he moved into the living room, shoving some things out of the way before sitting on the couch with an agitated groan. Slowly, I trailed behind, approaching him with caution like he was a wild animal. Unpredictable and formidable. I hated feeling like this. I couldn't stand that I loved him and feared him all at the same time. I couldn't stand not knowing what he was thinking and not knowing what to say or do, when all I wanted was to hug him and tell him it would all be okay. But really, what the hell did I know? What I do in my life had never taken me this far. I didn't know what happened to the families, after the funeral and the dead were buried and had crossed over.

I felt helpless.

Sitting down at the edge of an overstuffed recliner, I clutched my mug between both hands and said, "Do you—"

"Andy."

I swallowed. "Yeah?"

His eyes, ringed in dark circles and trouble, lifted to meet mine. "I'm so fuckin' sorry."

It felt like enough that he began the conversation and not me. So, I shook my head to force a smile. "Don't worry about it. It's fine."

"No," he replied, firm and sincere. "Do not tell me that this," he gestured out toward the living room and its disheveled state, "is fine. What happened last night wasn't fuckin' *fine*. I'm not …" He groaned, shaking his head and shoving a hand forcefully into his hair. "I don't do that type of shit, okay? I'm not that kinda asshole. I shouldn't …" Sighing, ragged and defeated, he dropped his hand between his spread knees. "I *never* should've done that to you, Andy. And I'm so fuckin' sorry."

“You were upset.”

Furrowing his brow, he shook his head. “That doesn’t give me the fuckin’ right to be a piece of shit!”

Tearing my gaze from his, I shrugged halfheartedly, not knowing what to say.

Then, he asked, “Did I hurt you?”

I shook my head. “No, I’m … I’m okay.”

He was quiet. Breathing evenly and biting his thumbnail as he looked out into the living room. I wanted to know what he was thinking but I didn't think I should ask, when he said, “I gotta clean this shit up.”

Without another word, he stood up and began to pick things up from off the floor, and I helped. Picture frames, floor lamps, throw pillows. It was amazing that such a mess could be made in such a relatively short period of time, almost as if it had been done intentionally. And Vinnie confirmed just as much when he said, “Pops would've been so pissed if he was here to see this.”

I managed a smile. “He didn't like things messy?”

“Hell no.” He surprised me with a laugh. “We didn't have a whole lot growin' up but he was a firm believer in taking pride in what we did have.”

“Smart man,” I commented quietly, and Vinnie's smile faded as he replied, “Yeah, he was.”

***

Together, we cleaned the place up, and while it was tense, I found a comfort I wasn't quite used to in that apartment. It was quiet, free of ghosts and static, and I was given the freedom to focus on us.

Vinnie was sad, of course he was, but he could also laugh. He cracked jokes, we had fun, and even though the road would be long, I saw the future in his smile, and it was bright.

"So," he said, after the last of the debris had been swept from the floor, "what should we eat tonight?"

He dropped the dustpan to the floor and wrapped an arm around my waist, pulling me into him and kissing my neck, as I replied, "I don't know. What's good around here?"

"Sweetheart, whatever you want, I can get."

As his whiskered chin tickled my skin, I laughed, wrapping my arms around his neck. "Oh, so you're like my own personal genie?"

"If that's what you want me to be, then yeah, your wish is my command," he muttered, moving his kisses lower until he reached my collar bone.

"Well," I said, tipping my head back and giving him better access, "I could eat Italian—"

He groaned, sliding his hands from my back to my hips. "I got your Italian right here. What else you want?"

Giggling and pressing my waist to his, I ran my hands through his hair and said, "How about Chinese?"

"Hm," he hummed contemplatively, moving his fingers to the hem of my wrinkled dress, "I could have that. But, first," he clenched the fabric and slid it up over my thighs and waist, "I'm havin' this."

His raspy tone and wandering hands tripped my heart and stuttered my breath. "Oh, yeah?"

"Yeah," he replied, nodding. "I need a do-over."

He pulled the dress over my head and threw it to the side, before slowly, carefully backing me into the couch and laying me down. This, his hands and lips gently caressing my skin and paying tribute to my body … *this* felt like everything I'd wished our first time had been. And while I wouldn't hold the night before against him, I wished I could replace the memory of our actual first time with this.

"You're fuckin' beautiful," he said, settling between my hips and fitting into place.

"So are you," I replied, keeping my gaze pinned to his.

He hadn't once looked at me when we first had sex. I wasn't sure if he could, with the way he'd been feeling at the time—angry, upset, and desperate for release and distraction. But now, in this moment, he never tore his eyes away, never daring to look anywhere but at me, and I saw in them everything I felt but hadn't yet said. I *wanted* to say it, I needed to, and although I wasn't always the one to take the first step, with this, I couldn't resist.

"Vinnie."

His forehead pressed to mine. "Yeah?"

"I love you."

The words felt so light, so airy, on my tongue, like the sweetest cotton candy. They dripped from my mouth, floating on my breath to dissolve somewhere between our beating hearts.

His hips froze and his brow furrowed. “You're serious?”

I nodded, suddenly afraid that he wouldn't say it back. “Yeah. I am.”

Vinnie bit his bottom lip, searching my eyes with a growing intensity. Then, he said, “Say it again.”

I felt my cheeks burn with embarrassment. “Why?”

“Because I wasn't prepared the first time,” he replied, unleashing his smile. “Say it again.”

Pulling in a deep breath, I whispered, “I love you,” on my exhale. And Vinnie thrust his lips against mine, kissing me deep and thoroughly, before muttering, “I fuckin' love you, too, sweetheart.”

It wasn't a perfect moment, but it was us. Vinnie and Andy, with all our secrets, darkness, and troubled minds. And I cherished it deeply and held onto it as we made love on the couch. But all moments, good and bad, always end, and this one was no exception.

After we were sated and finished, he held me close in his arms and said, “I need you to promise me somethin', okay?”

“What?” I asked, pressing my grinning cheek to his chest.

“If I ever do hurt you, you'll leave. You got me? You won't stick around for any reason.”

Taken aback, I sat up and shook my head, because that's not how love and commitment works. You stand by each other, for better or worse, yet here he was, telling me to leave.

"No, I can't—"

"Andy. If I hurt you, you will leave. Promise me."

And looking back, that should have been my warning. I should have taken that, the very possibility that he could hurt me, and ran far away. But I couldn't. I loved him, and right now, he was the one hurting. I needed to help him, not leave him, so all I did was nod.

I got up from the couch to find a more comfortable spot on his lap, and kissed him to maybe, hopefully, unlikely take the pain away, and whispered, "I promise."

CHAPTER NINETEEN

VINNIE

I stumbled into work two hours late with my clothes wrinkled and my hair a wreck. My excuse was, I hadn't heard the alarm go off. That was a minor human error, as far as I was concerned, and I strolled behind the counter and into the kitchen, hoping my older sister would agree.

Judging from the look on her face, though, she didn't.

"So, what's the story today?" she muttered, not looking up from the pot of sauce she was making.

"Didn't hear the alarm," I replied, grabbing an apron and tying it around my waist.

"This is the third day in a row that you *didn't hear the alarm*." She parroted my words with a hint of condescension, like she didn't quite believe me.

"Yeah, I dunno what's up with my alarm clock. Maybe I need to get one of those ones that sound like a friggin' bomb's goin' off or somethin'. You know, they make 'em where they'll shake your bed and—"

"I don't know why this is a joke to you," she snapped, cutting me off. She looked up from the pot, slicing through my attempt to keep things light-hearted with a steely glare. "It's just you and me now, Vin, and we have a business to run. *We*. That means we *both* come in at six o'clock in the morning and get shit ready to open at nine. Six o'clock. Not eight, not eight-thirty. *Six*. That's when the big hand—"

"I know when six is, Jen. You don't gotta talk to me like I'm a little kid."

Dropping the ladle onto the spoon rest beside the stove, she said, "Then, stop actin' like a little kid."

I bit the inside of my cheek hard enough to feel the pain. She held my glare in a staring contest I was determined to not let her win, and with every second that went by, the more annoyed I became. So what if I was late a few days this week? I still always came in before opening and did what needed to get done. So, what was her problem?

"So," she said, finally looking away and making me the victor, "you gonna tell me why you've been so late every day this week?"

Shaking my head and rolling my eyes, I grumbled, "I already told—"

"Yeah, I know what you told me. Now I'm askin' why you've been sleeping through the alarm. You never had a problem before this week, so what's goin' on with you?"

To anybody else, this would've been an innocent question. Simple curiosity. But I knew better. It was an accusation. A dig to find out if I was up to no good and up to old habits. But who the hell was she to think so poorly of me? Did she really think I was that weak, that *stupid*, to slide down that dark and dirty spiral again so easily?

"The hell you askin' me that for?"

At the belligerence in my tone, she turned to me, brow furrowed. "I'm allowed to ask you a question, Vin. Why the hell are *you* gettin' so defensive?"

"Maybe because it's none of your damn business why I'm late. I'm here, okay? So, drop it."

Crossing her arms over her chest, she shook her head defiantly. "I'm not droppin' nothin'. You're gonna tell me why—"

"Because Andy's been stayin' over every night this week. You wanna know what we've been doin'? Want me to give you the play-by-play?"

Her rosy cheeks brightened under the florescent lights as she quickly looked back at the pot of sauce, now bubbling and spitting against its lid. "Oh," she replied, swallowing. Then, she nodded, relenting with a noisy exhale. "I guess it's, uh, been a little nice to have your privacy, huh?"

My heart sank a little deeper in my chest as I crossed my arms and shrugged. "Pops was kinda cock-blockin' me, yeah."

Then, to my relief, she smiled. "I get it. I mean, I did manage to have two kids while livin' under his roof, but I'm still not entirely sure when we managed to actually do the deed. It was tough having him right across the hall."

Snorting, I said, "Yeah, try sharin' a room with him until you were thirty years old. Gettin' my own room was the highlight of my fuckin' life."

Jenna laughed gently, not bothering to hide the undertone of sadness as it misted her eyes. She nodded and stepped toward me, wrapping her arms around my waist and squeezing until I relented and hugged her back.

"I'm sorry," she said. "It's just been a rough week for all of us and I started to feel like I was in this alone."

"You're not alone, Jen."

She nodded against my chest. "I know. Just ... just try to get here on time, okay? Stop makin' me worry about you."

I made a promise to try harder and that was good enough for her. She gave my waist another squeeze and set back to work, finishing the sauce and pulling together the ingredients for meatballs. I excused myself, leaving the kitchen to start the first batch of pizzas.

I'd been making pizza since I was a kid. Pops had wasted no time putting us to work as soon as we legally could, and it'd always been a love-hate relationship for me. The end result was glorious. I enjoyed the pride I felt, seeing the happy looks on customers' faces and hearing their sounds of satisfaction, but making the pies themselves was tedious busywork that I didn't love. I needed music, I needed conversation—I needed something to keep my thoughts from getting the best of me. Before Pops had died, I'd made sure of it. I'd pop my earbuds in or turn the radio on. I'd reel Jen in for some banter or call Zach, knowing he was also getting ready for his workday at Famiglia Bella II. But Pops's death had done something to me and I'd become a glutton for punishment. In near silence, I let the thoughts slip in, to eat away at me as I kneaded the dough and spun it on my hands.

Jen was wrong in thinking she was alone. She was fine. She had her husband to go home to, she had her kids. If I wasn't here, she'd still have Moe and Nicky to rely on and keep the restaurant going. She could always keep her head above water without any problem because she had never known what it was like to lose her footing and drown. Me, though? I wasn't fine, and I knew I wasn't by the fact that I wouldn't allow Andy to leave.

In the days that had passed since Pops's funeral, Andy had spent her several days off work at the apartment. She did what she had to do during the day, while I was at work, and was there, waiting for me when I came back. She cooked us dinner. She gave me someone to talk to and sleep with. I loved her, and I loved having her around, but above that, I was scared of what could happen if she wasn't.

***

"Vin, what the hell do you call this?" Jen asked, holding up a slice. Melted mozzarella cheese only covered half, while the other side was oversaturated in marinara. "I can't give this to anyone."

"So, don't."

She peeked inside the case and groaned. "This entire pie is bad. How the hell did you manage to do this?"

I glanced over my shoulder from the pie I was making. The pizza in question looked like crap and I knew it, but my pride wouldn't let me admit it. "It's not that bad," I insisted before quickly diverting my attention.

Moe snorted. "Man, that thing looks like a damn bullseye."

"I can't serve this," Jenna groused, pulling the pie from the case and hurrying into the kitchen to shove it in the fridge.

"I can't believe she's gonna waste that whole pie," I mumbled, shaking my head.

"You'd have her serve that to someone?" Moe asked doubtfully.

"Sure."

"You're so full of shit," he laughed, shaking his head.

"I don't understand what the big deal is," I lied.

Jenna emerged from the kitchen, wiping her hands on her apron. "The big deal, baby brother, is that Pops had dreams of you taking over the place and you are, for some reason, slacking miserably."

I swallowed, recalling the conversation we'd had with Pops's attorney the day before. Zach had come down for the reading of the will, for us to find that Pops had divvied his savings in three ways but wanted to put Famiglia Bella in my name with Jenna as co-owner.

I couldn't have thought of a worse idea.

"I'll put it in your name," I said to Jenna, dusting a pie with oregano. "I can't handle this shit."

"You could," she said. "You just need to get your head out of your ass."

It's something I could imagine Pops saying. I could almost hear his voice. And it made me so angry that everything—his heart disease, his death, his dying wish—had all come as a surprise. I hated that he hadn't spent more time preparing us. I hated that he hadn't told us. Fuck, sometimes I just hated him, and I hated that more than anything.

"I know how to make pizza, Jen, and I'm good at it," I practically whined. "But I don't know the first thing about running a business."

She came to stand beside me, gawking. "Uh, how long have you worked here?"

Laughing, I shook my head. "You know what I'm sayin'. The business shit, you and Pops handled. You know, keepin' the books, orderin' shit ..."

Crossing her arms, she considered what I was saying. It was an excuse, but it wasn't a lie. "Okay," she said, nodding her agreement, "but I could teach you."

"*Or*," I went on slyly, "you could just do it, right? I mean, why do I need to learn if you're here?"

Jen furrowed her brow. "Well, I guess I could, but—"

"For now," I quickly added without any plans of following through.

CHAPTER TWENTY

VINNIE

Over the next few days, I did the right thing. I woke up when I was supposed to, and once, I even came into work early. After spending my nights with Andy, having sex and staying up late, keeping my promise to Jen wasn't easy, but I managed. I kept her off my back, and it was fine. I was tired and I was sad, but I had Andy and the distraction of her being at the apartment.

But on Saturday, a week after Pops had died, Andy's week off had come to an end and she needed to go back to work. Additionally, she broke it to me that she really had to get home.

"Why?" I asked, taken aback.

"Why?" she repeated, stifling her laugh. "Vinnie ..." She shook her head and ran her fingers through disheveled hair. "I don't live here."

I shrugged, pouring a cup of coffee for her and myself. "I mean, you *could*."

She sighed, taking one of the mugs and sitting at the table. “I know I could,” she said. “And it's not that I don't want to—”

I cut her off with a laugh. “You're kinda sounding like you don't want to.”

“No, I don't mean it like that,” she insisted, reaching out a hand and luring me to sit beside her. “I don't think it's a bad idea. I love being here with you, and I really think we should talk about it. But I still have responsibilities at home ...”

I took her hand in mine. “I'm just bustin' your balls, sweetheart. I get it.” And I really did. But that didn't stop me from worrying about being alone. “Just come back to me, okay?”

Andy laughed, squeezing my hand. “Obviously.”

But after going our separate ways and knowing she wouldn't be waiting for me when I got home from work, it didn't feel so obvious to me. I felt abandoned and deserted. And throughout the workday, I found it hard to stay focused. I kept envisioning that apartment, empty and silent, save for my own footsteps, and I would stand there, frozen, with the dough sticking to my fingers.

I decided then that I couldn't go home. It was still too soon after my father had died to face it alone. Eventually, I'd be ready, but ... not now, not today.

So, with too much on my mind, I told Jenna I was leaving work early. She and Moe stared at me, with narrowed eyes and parted lips.

“You feelin' okay?” Moe asked, scrutiny in his tone.

I nodded assuredly. “Yeah, I'm just tired. I got here early and I didn't get much sleep last night.”

While Moe settled for the excuse and went back to wiping down the countertops, Jenna wasn't as easily convinced. She crossed her arms over her chest and tipped her head back, studying my face and looking for clues. Looking for those telltale signs she wouldn't find.

“What?” I laughed, taking off my apron.

“Nothin'.”

Throwing the sauce-stained apron into the laundry bin, I continued chuckling, laying the nonchalance down a little too thick. “You're not lookin' at me like it's nothin'!”

Jen pursed her lips and shook her head. “Nope. Just makin' sure.”

“Makin' sure of what?” I challenged.

“You know what.”

I did know what. I knew exactly what. But she wasn't going to find it. So, I kissed her cheek, told her I was fine, and hurried out before my thumbnail could find itself between my teeth.

***

“Goose!”

At the sound of my bellowing voice, my friend looked up from his work at the taps. “Yo, Vin. Haven't seen you around in a while. What's goin' on?”

"Well," I sidled up to the bar, resting my elbow on its surface, "my old man died and my girlfriend's been hangin' at my place, so I haven't had much time to—"

"Whoa, hold up." He handed the full glass of beer to a customer at the other end of the bar, thanked him, and headed my way. "You said your dad died?"

I shrugged, like it wasn't a big deal. Like it wasn't eating me alive. "Yeah. He was really sick, so—"

"Man, I'm sorry to hear that. You holdin' up okay?"

He was talking about this too much. I bit my lip and shrugged again, tapping my fingers against the glossy wood. "Yeah, I'm good. I mean, my, uh, my girlfriend's been hanging around, so she's been keepin' my mind off shit, you know? She's been a good distraction, if you catch my drift." It was a feeble attempt at a chauvinistic diversion, luring him toward brutish discussion about sex and women.

But he wasn't biting.

"You were so close to your dad, man." Without another word, I nodded, moving my eyes away from his. "How've you been doin' with ... you know, resisting temptation?"

This is what happens when you make friends in rehab. They know shit about you. They understand shit you wish they didn't. They can sense your triggers without asking, and they can see straight through the bullshit you try to lay on too thick. I felt vulnerable. I felt truly seen for the first time in weeks, and suddenly, home didn't feel so bad. But I couldn't run now, and this is what happens when you make friends in rehab; you can tell them things you wouldn't dare say to anyone else.

"I gotta be honest, it hasn't been easy."

He nodded sympathetically. "I bet."

"Sometimes, I just wanna get completely wasted, just to turn this shit off."

He winced and asked, "You really think you should be here, then?"

I laughed and raked a hand through my hair. "I dunno, man. It's always helped to watch other people drink, so I thought ..." I shrugged, glancing at a guy, sipping at his beer. The condensation on the glass drew my attention first, then the bubbling brew inside, and my mouth watered.

"You thought wrong, huh?"

I nodded, unable to look away. "Yeah."

I felt his knuckles against my shoulder and I tore my eyes away from the man and his beer to face my friend and the concern written on his face. He offered a compassionate smile but I wished it was a hug. I wished he'd open up his big, Viking arms and tuck me inside. To comfort me and make me feel better. To protect me from the storm relentlessly beating against my heart. But what kind of man would I be to ask for that? And what kind of man would give it?

"Go home, man."

"I'm okay," I lied. "Just get me a Coke and some wings and I'll be good."

And I sort of was, after three glasses and two rounds of the best BBQ wings New York City had to offer. I chatted with Goose, telling him about how things were going at the restaurant. He laughed when I asked what he was up to, spreading his arms wide.

"You're lookin' at it, man. Same shit, different day."

"You need a woman," I said, dropping another bone into the bowl.

He sighed, shrugging as he went back to work polishing the bar. "I don't have time for a woman."

"That's what I thought, too, until I met Andy." I smiled at the taste of her name, remembering the way she felt this morning, naked and wrapped in my arms. "I dunno what I'd do without her right now. I'd probably go insane."

"Well, you're already insane, so that's not sayin' much," Goose jabbed, smirking.

"Yeah, maybe, but at least I got a girl who finds it endearing. You got nothin' but Mrs. Right," I teased back, holding up my right hand and waggling my fingers.

"Joke's on you, fucker," he laughed, lifting his other hand, with the middle finger raised. "I'm a lefty."

It felt good to joke around, like I was free from temptation and turmoil. But then, Goose said, "Speaking of women, I actually saw yours in here recently," and I was reminded that I wouldn't be seeing her later that night.

"Oh, yeah?"

He nodded. "She came in with this really hot chick. A friend, I guess, but she seemed to leave pretty pissed off."

"Hot chick?" I screwed up my face, trying to think. Andy didn't have many friends. There was Elle, a nurse she hung out with on occasion, and she mentioned a Jamie every now and then. But while Elle wasn't unattractive, I wouldn't have described her as really hot, and Jamie, she said, lived close to her house on Long Island. I couldn't think of a reason why she'd come all the way here. "What did she look like?"

"Dude, this was a few weeks ago, I don't remember." I leveled him with a knowing glare and he easily relented. "Okay, fine. She was tall, blonde, curly hair. She looked like a fuckin' model."

I nodded as my curiosity got the better of me. So, later on, when I'd finally had enough Coke and wings and conversation, I dared to go home, calling Andy before I had to face the silence alone.

"Hey," she answered on the first ring, just as I turned the knob.

"Hey, sweetheart."

"How are you doing tonight? You okay?"

I braced myself as I pushed the door open and stepped into the apartment for the first time by myself. "Yeah, I'm fine," I muttered, peering across the living room and into the kitchen, not knowing exactly what I expected to see.

"What have you been up to?"

"Went and saw Goose after work," I said, closing the door. The sound seemed to echo off the walls. "Ate some wings and shot the shit for a while. What about you?"

She sighed into the phone, a sad, lonely sound. "I just did some laundry and hung out with Jamie."

"Hey, what does Jamie look like?" I asked, walking quickly to the bathroom.

"Um ..." Andy hesitated, allowing several seconds to go by before answering, "She's, um ... Well, she's got dark eyes and hair and skin. Um, I mean, she's a kid, so she looks like a kid, I guess."

"A kid?" I narrowed my eyes as I stood in front of the toilet and unzipped my pants. "You hang out with kids?"

"She, um, she lives in the neighborhood and I've been babysitting her for a long time. So, she's really attached to me."

"Oh." I nodded, trying to remember if she ever mentioned being a babysitter. "Okay. That's sweet."

Andy was silent for a moment, until she asked, "Why do you ask?"

"Oh, Goose just mentioned tonight that he saw you at the bar a few weeks ago with a friend. So, I was just wondering—"

"I told you, I bumped into an old friend after that show and I went out with her afterward. Remember?"

There was a hint of defensiveness in her tone that I found slightly irritating and curious. But I took a deep breath and considered that maybe it was simply because I had forgotten something that she'd clearly told me.

"Oh, right," I said, nodding to myself. "I forgot."

"I went to Goose's place because it was the first bar I thought of. I wasn't hiding anything from you."

Narrowing my eyes at the frantic sound in her voice, I said, "Sweetheart, you don't have to explain anything to me. I was just wonderin'."

She took a deep breath and exhaled against the phone. "Okay. I'm sorry. It's just ..." She sighed again. "It's just been a long day."

"Tell me about it," I muttered sympathetically. I felt my shoulders sag and relax as I left the bathroom and hurried past my father's room, foolishly afraid that the door could swing open at any second. I had never been afraid of ghosts, and I was never afraid when Andy was here. But now, I was absolutely petrified. "I miss you."

"I know, I miss you, too. But I'll see you tomorrow."

"Will you stay here tomorrow?"

Andy was quiet and I feared she'd say no. "Vinnie, I have stuff I really need to get done here. I'll try to do as much as I can tonight, but I might have to stay home tomorrow, too."

I closed my door behind me and raked my fingers through my hair. I wouldn't beg her and sound as weak as I felt. But dammit, I was slipping and the one person I had to hold onto wasn't here. She was only an hour away, but right now, that hour felt like an eternity.

"Maybe I should come and stay with you. You know, to christen your bed," I threw in, keeping my tone coy and rough. Acting as though sex was my motive instead of the temptation to silence the little devil on my shoulder.

"I wish," she muttered. "My parents would kill me."

Desperate, I groaned out of frustration. “Andy, you're like, thirty fuckin' years old.”

“Right. But I still live under my parents' roof. You can't tell me you don't understand that.”

I did understand it. And fuck, I missed my dad.

“No, I know.”

“I'm sorry,” she added quietly, as if she knew.

“It's all good, sweetheart.”

“Is it, though?”

I smiled weakly to my quiet room, acutely aware of my father's untouched things on the other side of the wall. “Yeah, you don't gotta worry about me,” I replied, wishing so badly I was better at lying.

Especially to myself.

CHAPTER TWENTY-ONE

ANDREA

"So, what's been going on with you?" Mer asked, pouring a glass of iced tea from the pitcher. "I feel like we haven't seen you in forever."

"It feels that way because we haven't," Willa jabbed, waggling her brows. "She's too busy shacking up with her hot, bad boy boyfriend."

"Oh, yeah, he's a real bad boy," I grumbled, rolling my eyes. "He works all day in a pizza place, then goes home to the apartment he shared with his dad. What a rebel."

"Ooh, someone's getting defensive," my oldest sister teased, smirking as she put the pitcher back into the fridge and closed the door.

I followed my sisters outside onto the deck. Fall should have been right around the corner but summer was still thick in the air. Mom lounged lazily in the bright sun, while my nieces and nephews ran wildly through the thick grass. Dad had gone out golfing with my sisters' husbands, with the promise that they would be back early enough to throw the burgers and dogs on the grill.

"Speaking of your hot boyfriend, what's he doing today?" Willa asked, pulling out a chair from the table.

"Working," I mumbled half-heartedly.

Mer dropped onto the couch. "You didn't invite him?"

"What, are you worried we'll interrogate him again?" Willa teased.

"No," I fired back, sitting beside her at the iron table. "And just so you know, I did invite him. But his sister is out on Fire Island with her in-laws, so someone needs to be at the restaurant."

"He couldn't take off for *one* day?" Mer looked at Willa and the two shared a smirk. "I mean, it's one day, and how often do you really hang out with us?"

"Yeah, seriously," Willa agreed. "He could be here golfing with Daddy, Eric, and Tim."

I snorted and shook my head. Mer raised her brows, asking what was so funny, and I replied, "Oh, it's just that, I can't imagine Vinnie golfing. I don't think he even knows how to be that lame."

Neither of my sisters were amused. They pursed their lips and looked off toward their frolicking kids, clearly insulted by the unintentional jab at their husbands and our father. It wasn't that I looked down on golf or the men who enjoyed the game, but nobody could deny that it wasn't the most thrilling sport and that it typically attracted a certain kind of guy. And nobody could tell me that Vinnie fit the bill.

"So, if he doesn't like golf, what *does* he do?" Willa asked, taking our originally playful, albeit irritating, conversation to a more hostile level.

I shrugged, because the truth was, I didn't really know. He worked so much and so often I didn't know if he really had time for any hobbies. Apart from smoking and hanging out at Goose's bar. "Normal guy stuff, I guess," I replied, knowing it was a cop out, and so did they.

"You mean in between getting high and snorting coke, right?" Mer commented snidely.

I loved my sisters, and all things considered, we had a good relationship. But their care for me was occasionally represented in a catty manner. These underhanded, snarky comments, the jabs at Vinnie's troubled past ... I knew they all came from a place of genuine concern. But I wished so badly they could express themselves in a kinder, gentler way. I wished they could do it without hurting my feelings or distrusting my judgment.

"He doesn't do that stuff anymore," I said, dropping my gaze to my lap.

"Here's the thing, though, Andrea," Willa said, crossing her legs and pointing a finger in my direction. "I don't know how you can trust him, period. Drug addicts fight those demons for a long, long time, sometimes forever, and—"

"I'm really sick of you thinking that I don't know this," I interrupted defensively.

"We're not saying you don't. But you have to consider that you might be blinded to the shit that's right in front of you, you know?" Mer threw in, keeping her voice irritatingly gentle.

"Plenty of women are oblivious to their husbands' drug addictions, even when it's happening in their own house," Willa corroborated, nodding.

"Like Felicia's husband," Mer said, sitting up straighter. "Oh, my God, remember that?"

Willa nodded enthusiastically, widening her eyes. "Yes! Ugh, God, that asshole wiped out their entire savings account to buy drugs."

"He stole her engagement ring!"

I laid a hand over my eyes, feeling suddenly sick and exhausted. "Can you guys just stop?"

Willa laid a hand over my bare knee. "Seriously, we're not trying to make you upset. But you love him, and sometimes, when you love someone, you become blinded by your feelings and—"

"Oh, my God, I'm not a child!" I jerked my knee away from her hand. "And yeah. I do love him. So, stop talking shit about him. I don't want to hear it anymore."

Willa swallowed and glanced in Mer's direction, looking for backup. But Mer only shook her head and gestured toward me, as if to say, "*What can you do? We've lost her already.*" I busied my brain with every possible thing I could say, every pointless jab I could make at their lives and husbands, but what would be the point? What would it accomplish? Truthfully, there wasn't much to say about their husbands. They were successful, Ivy League graduates, working as a surgeon and a defense attorney, and each made money to support their families on one income. Their records were clean, their lives were otherwise boring, and I'd have to really try to dig up any dirt on them. Vinnie was filthy in comparison, and they had plenty of ammo to fire at me if I dared to open my mouth. So, I remained silent throughout the rest of the afternoon and into the night, right up until they left and I was alone with my parents at the house.

"So, what happened today?" Mom asked, rinsing the dirty dishes, and handing them to me to put in the dishwasher.

"What do you mean?" I replied, playing stupid.

"You girls got into a fight?" Her innocent tone told me she knew exactly what had happened, and I groaned in response, shaking my head.

"What did they tell you?"

"They didn't tell me anything," she insisted. "I overheard a couple of things when I was sitting in the yard."

Dad walked into the room and stood at the kitchen island, then also asked, "You girls had a fight?"

"Oh, God," I grumbled, shaking my head. "It wasn't a *fight*. Willa and Meredith just like to stick their noses into stuff that has nothing to do with them. That's all it was."

"About Vinnie?" Dad asked. Sighing, I responded with a firm nod, and he said, "They're just worried about you, honey pie. And if I'm being honest, we all kinda are."

I shot him a sour, hurt look over my shoulder. "Seriously? Come on, Daddy."

Holding his palms out in front of his chest, he offered a sympathetic smile. "I'm not attacking you, or him. But ... can you really blame us? You never talk about him, you spent the past week over there and never once talked to any of us—"

"His father *died*!" I shouted, throwing a spoon into the rack and backing away from the dishwasher to stare him down. "And by the way, it was so nice of you all to not come to the funeral. I *really* appreciated that."

"Andrea," Mom muttered, shaking her head and shutting off the faucet. "Nobody is attacking you, and like I've said to you before, I like him. But we're just concerned about—"

"About what? About his past?"

Dad winced apologetically. "Well ..."

Throwing my hands in the air, I shouted, "What the hell do you really think I'm doing? Do you seriously think I'd be over there with him, getting high and risking everything I've worked hard for? How stupid do you think I am?"

"Nobody called you stupid," Mom answered, her tone teetering on her own anger. "But you cannot expect any of us to trust this guy when you have only brought him around once in the however many months you've been seeing him. We don't know him—"

"He's always busy!"

"Busy doing what? You're going to tell me he's working twenty-four hours a day? You don't want us to treat you like you're stupid, Andrea, but stop treating us like we are, too. And you can't get mad at us for caring about you and being concerned. We're your family, we're supposed to care."

I looked at my mother, and then my father, as hot rage boiled the blood in my veins. I heard my heartbeat, pounding in my ears, and tempting me to detonate right there in the kitchen. But I forced myself to stay calm and pulled in a deep breath.

"I'm not mad at you for caring," I said, my voice eerily controlled. "I'm mad that you all saw one stupid picture on his Facebook page, from *years* ago, and have decided that's how he's going to be forever. None of you would be treating him like this if he was wealthy or if he was a Harvard graduate—"

"You're being ridiculous. We didn't—"

"Let me finish," I shot at my mother, and she clamped her lips shut. "I've been over at his apartment all week because he's heartbroken, and that's what you do when you love someone. You don't abandon them when they need you. And I'm sorry that I haven't thought to call you in the middle of helping him mourn. I'm sorry you haven't been the first thing on my mind while I've been washing dishes and making sure he eats. I thought you'd understand all of that, but I guess not."

With that final word, I hurried from the kitchen and went up the stairs to my bedroom, where I closed the door behind me and threw myself on the bed. Jamie was there, of course she was. Sitting on the chair at my desk. I ignored her and wished I was at Vinnie's place, where there weren't any ghost or static. Where I could live my life and just focus on us, on him and our relationship, without them getting in the way.

I closed my eyes and pretended she didn't exist. But when I opened them again, there she was, standing in front of me, with a look of curiosity and concern on her face.

“Leave me alone, Jamie.”

But she wouldn’t leave me alone. She stood there, standing over me and watching with her deep brown eyes.

“What?” I asked, abruptly sitting up. “What do you want?”

She pointed at my face, at the tears welling in my eyes.

“You want to know why I’m pissed off and sad?”

She nodded.

“Fine. I’m pissed off because my family treats me like a child. They treat me like … like I’m incapable of making an educated judgment about someone.”

She cocked her head.

I sighed frustratedly. “I’m talking about Vinnie. They hate him. They don’t trust him. But they hardly even know him, so how the hell can they judge?”

She pressed her lips in a firm line and looked off to the side, shrugging. The look said, “Well, maybe they have a point,” and it only fueled the flame in my gut.

"Oh, stop," I groused, rolling my eyes. "You have no idea either. You've only seen him once."

Looking back to me, she raised her brows and pursed her lips. "You're getting defensive," the look said, and I shook my head.

"You know what? I don't even know why I'm talking to you about this. You've never even been in a relationship. You have no experience to speak of. You're just a jealous little girl living vicariously through me, so just … just drop it and leave me the hell alone."

The words came too quickly for me to stop my stupid mouth from saying them, and by the time they were out, it was too late. The damage had been done, and I saw the hurt written plainly on her face.

"Jamie," I began, wishing I could pull her into my arms and give her a hug, "I'm so sorry. I didn't mean it."

But she wasn't listening. She moved from the side of the bed, out of my line of sight, and when I turned to find her and beg her to stay, she had already disappeared.

CHAPTER TWENTY-TWO

VINNIE

Two weeks.

That's how long it had been since Pops died.

It's incredible how quickly two weeks can float by when you're busy trying to keep yourself from diving off the deep end.

It's incredible how everybody else just seems to keep going, as if nothing had happened, as if they'd never even existed, while you're struggling just to get out of bed.

Zach hadn't been back to the city since the funeral. He and Greyson had their appointment at the adoption agency, and while it had gone well, they had made a definitive decision with Jenna to use her as a surrogate. Now, as she excitedly prepared to carry their baby, she was also putting the finishing touches on her new bathroom and getting ready to redesign the basement apartment in her house. And while it might have been a big distraction for them all, it was one they shared in together, and one that left me standing alone on the sidelines.

Andy was my saving grace. The combination of love and sex gave me something to wake up for and come home to. But when she needed to go home, no matter how few and far between the days were, I dreaded it and the nights they eventually brought.

"I have to get ready for work," she mumbled sleepily, moving away from my tightening arms.

"No, you don't."

"Vinnie," she whined, smiling and pressing her lips to mine. "You know I have to work the next three days. Come on, let me up."

I groaned in protest, but I did let her go. I watched her naked body climb out of bed and run for the bathroom, and I listened for the shower with the intent that I'd climb in after and give her something to remember throughout the workday. But before I heard the water beating against the tile wall, I heard her voice, talking to someone, presumably on the phone.

"Hey, yeah, I was going to stay here tonight," she said. "Uh, really? I thought that wasn't until tomorrow? Can't we—fine, okay, yeah, I'll grab the train after work. Yep. It's okay. Yeah, I'll talk to him. Okay. Okay. Bye."

I didn't move from the bed as I listened to her footsteps coming back into the bedroom.

"Baby, I just got off the phone with my mom. I completely forgot that my parents are having a party at their house, for their fortieth anniversary, this weekend, and I need to go home tonight to help them with some stuff."

"It's Thursday," I pointed out, as the dread crept in swiftly. "Why wouldn't you do this tomorrow?"

"I know, but Mer has something going on tomorrow, so we're apparently doing it tonight."

It was obvious I wasn't going to talk her out of going, so I nodded. "Okay, yeah, then do what you gotta do."

"Mom wanted me to invite you. The party is on Saturday. I'll probably stay here tomorrow night, so we can go together, if you wanted to come." She presented the invitation like it was an option, but there was hope in her eyes and a plea in her voice.

So, once again, I nodded. "Obviously, I'll be there, sweetheart."

She sighed a breath of relief. "You sure it's not a problem with work?"

I shook my head. "Nah. I'll tell Jenna and Moe I won't be able to. It's all good."

Then, she leaned over me and pressed a kiss once again to my lips, the taste of joy and relief on her tongue. "I love you," she whispered, as if to not let the ghosts in the apartment hear.

Andy left the room and disappeared behind the bathroom door, and while I wondered how I was going to get through the night, she showered alone.

***

"So, we're supposed to be going to the fertility clinic in the next few weeks to get things started," Jenna said, pulling a pie from the oven. “It's crazy, you know? Thinkin' about havin' another baby. But, I mean, the baby wouldn't *really* be mine, so I guess it's not *exactly* the same, but still ...”

“Well, like ... where's the egg coming from?”

She slid the pie into the case and said, “Mine, obviously.”

“So, then ... the baby would be kind of yours, wouldn't it?”

She sighed, tipping her head back with exasperation. “Vin, it's not the same.”

Looking to Moe, I said, “Is this makin' sense to you? 'Cause I'm failing to understand how this kid isn't also hers.”

He glanced at Jenna and muttered, “You're on your own with this one, girl.”

Jenna groaned, cocking her hip and raking a hand through her wild, curly hair. “Okay. Let me try to explain this in simple words for you to understand. Zach and Greyson want a baby with both of their genes, so it's like, both of theirs, right? But two men can't make a baby—”

“I'm not an idiot, Jen,” I grumbled, laughing as I shook my head.

She smiled and went on, “Anyway, normally they would have to just get an egg donor to merge with their swimmers, but as luck would have it, Zach has a sister from the same gene pool. I offered my eggs to create an embryo with Greyson's sperm. So, that way, it's as close as they can possibly get to having biological children.”

Nodding, I replied, "No, I get it, but," I wrinkled my nose, "don't you feel like you're gonna have a baby with your brother's husband?"

She shoved my arm. "We're not like, sleeping together, you moron."

"I know, but ..." I shrugged. "I mean, whatever, I'm glad you can do this for them, but like, what kinda family tree is that? Greyson's dad married his aunt, and now, he's having a baby with his sister-in-law. So, that kid's gonna be his son *and* his nephew, or—"

"Can you stop?" Jenna snapped, clearly unamused. "You don't have to be so mean, you know that?"

"I'm not bein' mean," I insisted. "I'm makin' a joke."

"Well, you're not funny," she threw at me before storming off and disappearing behind the kitchen door.

Moe and I were left to handle the impending lunchtime crowd and my sister's anger toward me wasn't helping the already fragile state of my mind. I leaned against the cool, butcher block counter and crossed my arms.

"What the hell did I say?" I asked him.

Moe shrugged, playing stupid. "I dunno, man ..."

"I just don't understand what she's so upset about."

He sighed, turning from the register to say, "Vin, man, it's not really *what* you said, even though that in itself was pretty fuckin' ignorant and insensitive, if I'm bein' honest—"

"Whatever," I mumbled, rolling my eyes while also knowing how right he was.

"You sound really jealous," he said, cutting to the chase. "All this stuff you're sayin' and doin', man, you just sound resentful and it's rubbin' us all the wrong way."

"Us?"

He shrugged, then nodded apologetically. "I love you, man, but ... the way you've been ..." He grimaced. "We don't like it, and if I'm bein' real here, we're worried."

"Worried because I made a joke about my sister having my brother's baby?" I snickered as the smallest part of me—the one unaffected by grief and depression and nagging addiction—begged to ask him for help.

"Goddammit, man, no! You know exactly what I'm talkin' about!" He stared at me, wide-eyed and bewildered, as he shook his head. "You gotta get your head outta your ass, Vinnie. Before it's too late."

I pulled my pack of smokes from my apron pocket and clapped a hand over his shoulder. "Well, I'm gonna go have a cigarette. Good talk." Then, I hurried from behind the counter and rushed outside before he could say anything.

Guilt was a heavy burden to carry and my shoulders were sagging with the load. I couldn't understand how I could be so desperate for their care and affection, while simultaneously pushing them further away. I hated myself. I hated my stupid mouth and stupider brain. I was losing my control and the more I tried to hold on, the more slippery it became.

Cigarettes weren't cutting it.

I groaned, pushing my head back against the building and sucking hard on the cigarette in my mouth. It was tasteless, useless, and worthless, but I sucked and sucked anyway. Filling my lungs with so much smoke that my chest burned.

"Hey, my brother." I opened my eyes to see an older man in tattered clothes, a guy I remembered seeing Moe with years ago. When he saw he had my attention, he smiled with Jack-o'-lantern teeth and asked, "You got any change?"

I shook my head and gruffly replied, "No, I'm sorry."

He nodded, bobbing the dirty dreadlocks that framed his pale, weathered face. "No problem, man, it's all good."

He wiped under his nose, sniffling loudly. One might've thought he was sick, and I suppose in a way he was, but it wasn't with a cold. I'd seen the length of his dirt-crusted pinkie nail and the wild look in his eyes. I swallowed at the temptation and itching need, over and over again, but fuck, it was thick and suffocating.

"Can I bum one of those?" he asked, pointing a finger at the nub of a cigarette in my mouth and wordlessly I nodded, fishing the pack out and handing him a smoke. "Thank you very much," he said, grinning and putting it behind his ear.

Don't let him walk away, temptation whispered. *He's right there, don't let him leave*. But I didn't stop him from walking away. I let him walk down the block until the voice in my head screamed too loud and I couldn't take it anymore.

So, I ran.

***

I had given him a hundred bucks for a dime bag full of blow.

The shame was extreme as I carried out the rest of the day without so much as looking at my sister or Moe, afraid they'd sense the cocaine in my pocket. And it was pathetic. The anticipation I felt was like a kid waiting for Christmas morning and the promise of Santa and presents. Except, there was nothing pure about the snow awaiting me and there was nothing jolly or good about the devil on my shoulder, telling me to sneak off to the bathroom to do it now.

Still, it felt better just to have it, to have options. Nothing said I ever had to get high. I'd just hold onto it, like an old security blanket. It would be fine, I told myself, and I held tightly to the comfort in those lies.

But that comfort was rapidly depleting and by the time I got home to the haunting emptiness of the apartment, I felt nothing but desperation zipping through my bones.

Old habits die hard and my body was on autopilot as I quickly moved into the living room and emptied my pockets on the coffee table. Keys, smokes, and lighter. Wallet. And then, the star of the show: my little plastic baggie of pristine, white powder. I laid it down carefully, giving it a place of honor away from the pile of everyday stuff. I hurried to the bathroom, found Pops's old hand mirror, and quickly went back to the coffee table, to sit down at the couch and pull a card from my wallet. It all came to me as second nature, in the way you never forget how to swim or ride a bike, and I laid out my tools beside the baggie.

For a moment, I sat back and stared.

"What the fuck am I doin'?" I muttered, reeling away from the old rituals and habits.

I didn't expect tears to spring to my eyes and for my vision to blur the sight of coke on the coffee table. Shame and guilt spilled over, wetting my cheeks and dripping off my chin, and I missed my dad. I missed him so much that the cavern in my chest echoed with a silent howl of pain.

"Fuck you," I muttered to the walls. "Fuck you for leaving me."

I was deflecting, putting the blame on him for the weakness in my actions. But, really, fuck him. Fuck him for not telling us he was sick. Fuck him for abandoning us, just like she did. Fuck him for all the responsibility he dropped on me without showing me what to do.

"God, I hate this," I muttered through gritted teeth, wiping a hand over my sodden face.

Quickly, the anger toward my father manifested into a desperate rage toward Andy. She made me forget. She calmed my mind and eased my pain, but where the hell was she now? Andy had left. Just like he did. And just like *her*. They all did. They all leave me, and now I was left with nothing but this bag of blow.

"Call her," I said aloud. "Just call her. Tell her you need her now." And I really did; I needed her. I needed her *right now* and if she could come, I wouldn't need the coke. But if she couldn't ...

Well, I wasn't sure.

"Hey, baby," she answered on the first ring.

I wanted to smile at the sound of her voice. I loved her. God, I really did love her. But right now, in this moment, love wasn't enough and there was nothing to smile about. Not even her voice.

"Hey."

"What are you up to?"

"Nothin'," I answered, making a feeble attempt at sounding calm. "I, uh, I wanted to see if you wanted to come back tonight."

Andy was quiet for a moment before answering, "Vinnie, I told you ..."

A frantic frenzy erupted in my heart. "N-No, no, I know, but I was just seein' if maybe anything had changed."

"No, we're making centerpieces right now, so I can't leave. But I'll be back tomorrow. Okay?"

The urge to cry was overwhelming. I hated feeling like this, so weak and unable to control myself.

I rubbed a hand beneath my nose, stifling the sniffle that threatened to give me away. "Yeah. Yeah, okay."

"Baby," she said, then dropped her voice to a whisper. "Are you okay?"

All I could see now was the bag of coke. All I could feel was the desperation to tell her I wasn't okay, that I wasn't fine or hanging in there. And all I wanted to do was line it all up into neat little rows and snort it, fast and easy. I was torn up, ripped apart, conflicted and crawling out of my skin. And she was so far away, and I was so alone.

"I just, um," I cleared my throat and sniffed back the tears, "I miss you."

"I miss you, too," she answered quietly. "But I'll see you tomorrow. Okay? I love you."

"I love you, too."

She hung up first. I wondered if she would've been able to, if she knew what was happening to me. I wondered if she would've hopped on the next train, if she knew what I was about to do, as I slowly opened the bag and poured the smallest bit of powder out onto the mirror. But I'd never know, and that was fine, actually, because this was a one-off. A one-time thing, to get me through the night and to make it to tomorrow. That was the lie I told myself, as I made a perfect little line, leaned forward, and in one smooth inhale, pulled it into my body.

And I believed it.

CHAPTER TWENTY-THREE

ANDREA

The train ride back into the city was long and exhausting, despite getting a good night's sleep in my comfortable bed at home. This split life I was now living was wearing on me and I noticed it more with every trip back and forth. Between the secret I was keeping from Vinnie, and the disapproval of my relationship from my family, I could sense an inevitable breaking point coming. Things would be said, people would be hurt, and I, without a doubt, would suffer the most.

I had spent the night sprinkling glitter on silk flowers and assembling favors. Mer and Willa had their own duties and together, we had transformed my parents' backyard into something that would've made Martha Stewart proud. It had been a good night, full of white wine, Chinese food, and good company. Until Vinnie had called. And then, the conversation had been geared strictly toward how toxic our relationship was.

"He can't even let you have a night with your sisters," Mer had said, shaking her head as she cut another strip of tulle to wrap around a glass vase. "How the hell are you even okay with that?"

"He was just calling to see what I was up to," I'd replied, defending him while finding it difficult to get the sound of his voice out of my head. He'd sounded so troubled, so desperate, and it had left me feeling worried and guilty. "What's the problem with that?"

"If Eric ever did that to me, I'd tell him to get a freakin' life," Willa had muttered, sipping from her glass. "You need to set your boundaries, Andrea. Otherwise, he's never going to know what's okay and what isn't. He's just gonna control your life and do you really want that?"

I'd spent the night after they'd left lying in bed and wondering if they were right. When I was with Vinnie, I never once thought he was stealing the reins and calling the shots in my life. But how could I judge our entire relationship, over the past couple of weeks since his father had died? He was hurt and mourning. It was only natural to cling to the people you love during troubled times, and he loved me.

I'd fallen asleep assured that we were good, that our relationship was fine and that the only problem was with me and the secrets I was too afraid to divulge. But now on the train, I was trapped again inside my head and unsure.

"I need to relax," I muttered to myself and the young man beside me.

"What?" the middle-aged woman he belonged to replied, looking up from her book.

"Sorry," I said, smiling. "I'm just having a bad day."

"You and me both, hon."

The young man begged me with his eyes, clasping his hands in his lap and leaning toward the woman's side. Something about him was familiar and reminded me so much of a younger Vinnie. The familiar, desperate longing in his eyes irked me, raising the hair on my arms in a train car that was otherwise warm and humid. But it was because of that familiarity that I succumbed to the urge to help him.

"You were never going to save him," I said, reading the images of his overdose and premature death. "He was going to get his hands on the heroin, one way or another, and he was always going to die. Nothing was going to change that."

The woman gasped, holding a hand over her mouth. "How did you … who, who are you …"

"He's sorry for stealing," I said, looking ahead at the nodding head of the young man. "He put the rest of your money in the mattress. He didn't spend it all."

She turned her head toward where he sat. "He's here?"

I nodded. "He's sitting beside you. He goes to work with you every day. He wants you to know he admires what you're doing for other addicts, but he doesn't want you to think that you could've done something different for him. It was never going to be different."

She turned to me and offered a weak smile. "I know. I mean, deep down, I know. But … it's hard for me, as a mother, to accept that there was nothing I could do to save my son. I was …" Her lips pressed together, she shook her head, and her eyes filled with tears. "I was never going to be okay with burying my baby boy."

The young man reached out and laid a hand over his mother's shoulder, and I said, "He wants you to know how sorry he is for all the pain he caused you."

She turned to face her invisible son and I wondered for a foolish moment if she could see him, and if she knew that she was staring directly into his eyes. My heart clenched at the sight. He looked so much like Vinnie, too much like him, and I envisioned him, dead and gone. I imagined him somewhere not here, somewhere not with me. I wondered if my sisters were right, whether it was too late for him and if I was doomed to get hurt in the end.

"It's okay," she whispered to the air. "Calling you mine was worth it, baby boy. It was always worth it, even when it hurt the most."

***

"Hey, baby," I said, walking into the apartment.

"Hey, Andy, get in here!"

"In where?" I asked, peering into the living room to find it neat and empty.

"Bedroom!"

I followed his voice and entered the room, where he lay in bed, bright-eyed and lively. It had been weeks since I'd seen him like this and weeks since I'd seen him genuinely smile, but there it was.

He pulled back the blanket, revealing his nudity and the empty spot beside him. “Get those clothes off and get in here,” he ordered, and I couldn’t help but laugh as I dropped my bags on the floor.

“You’re in a good mood today,” I noted, slowly unbuttoning my dress.

“I had a good night,” he said, watching my fingers as they moved.

“What’d you do without me?” I asked, opening the front of my dress with painstaking care, finally letting it slide off my shoulders and onto the floor.

“Missed you.” He reached out with wiggling fingers to grab the hem of my lace underwear and pulled me into bed.

“That’s a good answer,” I muttered, finding my lips pressed to his and his body over mine.

“It’s the only answer,” he replied, speaking into my open mouth and tugging my underwear down my thighs.

I was ready for the intrusion and we moaned in unison the moment we fit together. We made love then and it was vigorous, aggressive, and mind-bending. He touched me thoroughly, making sure that every part of my body knew it was wanted and appreciated, until all of my nerve endings sang in pleasurable chorus. And when it was over and he’d collapsed at my side, I couldn't help but grin stupidly at the ceiling.

“Oh, my God,” I sighed, snuggling my back against his chest. “That was amazing.”

“Mm-hmm,” he moaned, nodding into my neck.

“What's gotten into you?”

His arms tightened around my waist and his lips kissed my neck, before he asked, "What do you mean?"

I closed my eyes, smiling at the touch of his gentle lips against my skin. "It's just ... you've been so sad, and I dunno, you just seem ... better, I guess."

"Well, maybe I feel better."

I laughed, holding his arms tighter to me. "Oh, so you're saying, since I was gone last night, that made you feel better, huh?"

"No, sweetheart," he muttered, his voice gruff against my neck. "There's lots of shit I wish would go away, but you ... you'll never be one of 'em."

I breathed into the romance of the moment as his fingertips trickled with feathery touches over my stomach and to the apex of my thighs. I giggled, tipping my head back against his shoulder, as his hand covered me in calloused warmth, dipping in with skilled fingers and luring me again toward climax.

"You're never letting me leave this bed today, huh?" I groaned before gasping as he entered my body from behind in one smooth thrust.

"I told you last night, Andy," his teeth sank into my shoulder and then he kissed the pain away, "I missed you. I feel like I've been missin' you for weeks, and now, I'm makin' up for lost time."

***

Three times, he made love to me, and after losing count of the orgasms, we passed out sometime after feasting on each other and leftovers from Famiglia Bella.

In his arms, I had forgotten about the night with my sisters and the woman on the train. I had pushed the concerns and eerie signs from my mind, because they were wrong, and that's all there was to it. I was happy, we both were, and there was absolutely no sense in allowing outside forces to weasel in and ruin it all.

So, I slept comfortably with him in a deep, dreamless slumber, tangled up in a mess of sweaty limbs and soiled sheets that barely clung to the mattress. Hours later, when I woke up to darkness and an aching bladder, I kissed his chest, licking the salt from his skin, before climbing out of bed with a promise to come back and go for round four.

I walked to the bathroom, surprised by how quickly my arousal was returning. I giggled, thinking of what my sisters had said about him corrupting me. It wasn't as though I'd been innocent before meeting him, but my experience with men had always been bland and very vanilla. Missionary was the norm, and it was a really wild time if I ever found myself on top. But Vinnie had somehow uncovered the vixen inside me, with cigarettes and sex appeal. And while Mer and Willa seemed to think there was something wrong in being adventurous, I couldn't get enough.

After using the toilet, I looked in the mirror over the sink. Smudged makeup ringed my eyes and my tousled, knotted hair seemed to have a mind of its own. I looked like a mess. Disheveled and oversexed. And yet, I had never felt more beautiful or more confident. And what exactly was so bad about that?

I smiled at my reflection, jittering with excitement at the thought of what awaited me in bed, in this apartment where my mind could switch off and my worries left themselves at the door. I splashed water on my face, took a deep breath, and pointed at the girl in the mirror.

"You deserve this," I told her. "Now, go get yourself thoroughly fucked."

I giggled at my own absurdity, shaking my head and rolling my eyes. I took another deep breath before turning off the light and opening the door. Immediately, I gasped, stifling my scream behind a hand as my heart pounded wildly in my chest. Because standing on the other side of the door, as if he was waiting for me to emerge, was Vincent.

CHAPTER TWENTY-FOUR

VINNIE

At the sound of her muffled scream, I bolted out of bed and hurried to the doorway. I found Andy with her back pressed to the wall beside the bathroom door and hands clutched tightly over her heart. Her already-pale skin gleamed like paper under the hallway light, stark white and chalky, while her eyes remained wide and transfixed on the wall across from her.

"What happened?" I asked, reaching out to grab her shoulders and pulling her into my protective arms. "Andy, what's wrong?"

She blinked rapidly, shaking her head. "N-Nothing, it's nothing," she stammered, breathing in long, labored pushes and pulls.

"You're shaking," I stated, trying to see what she was looking at. "Tell me what happened."

"I'm, I'm okay. I thought I saw a spider."

"You're scared of spiders?" I asked, squinting my eyes at the wall to find the offending eight-legged fucker. "I don't see anything."

Her lungs calmed and her breathing slowed. “I don't know if it was really there. I just ... I just came out of the bathroom and thought I saw something. I'm okay, though.”

“Are you sure?”

She nodded against my chest. “Yeah, yeah, I'm sure. Let's just go back to bed, okay?”

“O-kay,” I drawled slowly, holding her away from me and studying her face.

The color had returned to her face and now she stared back at me with amusement twinkling in her eyes. One might've thought she was laughing at her own expense, embarrassed by her reaction to a little spider on the wall. But while her eyes displayed mirth, she also worried her bottom lip between her teeth. A liar knows a lie when he sees it, and that little tell always gave her away.

I quickly tried to remember if I had thoroughly cleaned the hand mirror. Had I put it back where it was supposed to go? Was it possible she had found the half-empty bag of cocaine, taped securely to the top of the medicine cabinet? I didn't think so, but still, after leading her back to bed, I told her I needed to pee and quickly returned to the bathroom to make sure. Just to be safe. And as luck would have it, nothing had been touched. The mirror shined pristinely without a trace of white and the bag was where I'd left it. I didn't even see how she could've reached it without a step stool, and what reason would she have had to find it in the first place, without knowing to look?

I gripped the edge of the porcelain sink and stared deep into the reflection of my eyes. I didn't appear strung out and I wasn't high anymore, but I wasn't thinking clearly. I was rattled from the secrecy, from going back on my pledge to remain forever sober. But ... it had done the job, hadn't it? I'd gotten myself through until Andy got back. I had gotten a good night's sleep, and with that refreshed burst of energy, I had satisfied her thoroughly with a handful of orgasms that had left her shaking and gasping for air. So, if a one-off hit of coke could accomplish that, then where was the harm, really? And why the hell did I feel so guilty about it?

"Chill," I muttered through gritted teeth. "It's all good, man. Just chill."

But even though I'd given the order, I couldn't chill, as I went back to the bedroom to find Andy wide awake and waiting. I saw the trepidation in her eyes and her bitten bottom lip. I hated to admit it, but I was scared. She knew something, or at the very least sensed something, and I was terrified that this, who we were at this very moment, was the beginning of the end.

***

"Why are you so nervous?" she asked, as I stomped on the half-smoked cigarette.

"I'm not nervous," I insisted, grinding my heel against the asphalt.

“Vinnie,” she cocked her head, with a knowing glint in her eye, “that's the third time you've smoked since we got off the train.”

“Smoking's got nothin' to do with my nerves,” I said, telling only half of the truth. “And besides, you'd be smoking too if you were about to willingly jump into the lion's den.”

I peered up the steps to the large, wrap-around porch. The big and beautiful stained glass doors were a gorgeous disguise for this lair of mean-spirited, judgmental women and a guy who couldn't wrap his head around the concept of not having a drink.

“Oh, stop,” Andy hissed. “Come on, we gotta get inside. Oh, and pick that up,” she pointed at the crushed cigarette butt, “before my dad sees it.”

Sighing, I bent over and snatched it up, stuffing it into the pocket of my slacks.

“We do have garbage cans, you know,” Andy said, her tone edging on a giggle.

I feigned a gasp, clapping a hand over my chest. “Garbage cans? Really? I've never seen one of those before!”

She groaned, shaking her head as she took my hand. “Come on.”

“Where I come from, we just dump our trash in the streets,” I went on, forcing an air of amazement. I gripped her hand with both of mine and jumped excitedly. “Tell me, miss, do you have indoor plumbing, too? Golly, it sure would be swell to use a toilet for the first time!”

"Oh, my God," Andy grumbled, her lips twitching. "I hate you."

I laughed, allowing her to lead me up the steps to that big, solid, mahogany door. "No, you don't. You fuckin' love me."

"Yeah, well," she dug her keys from her purse, "I'm starting to wonder why."

"Oh, I know why," I said coyly, and when she looked up at me expectantly, I added, "It's the earth-shattering orgasms, isn't it?"

Andy quickly glanced toward the door, eyes wide at the muffled sounds of voices inside. "Vinnie, they'll hear you—"

"Come on, sweetheart," I said, wrapping an arm around her waist. "You're tellin' me you don't want your family to know about my magic cock?"

And of course, that was the moment her mother threw open the door, in a dress that I would guess cost more than my rent. "So nice to see you again, Vinnie," she snickered, offering a pinched smile. "And thank you for wearing pants. Some of us have no interest in seeing your, how did you put it?"

"Magic cock," Andy's father muttered from just inside the door, and if I could've ceased to exist in that moment, I would've been grateful.

"Sorry about that," I muttered, smiling sheepishly.

"Ah, it's fine, relax," her dad said, laughing and offering a hand. I accepted and we shook for a brief moment, before he waved into the house. "Come in, come in."

Andy's mother stepped out of the way, allowing us entrance. I noticed that she hadn't laughed or smiled, and while I felt like I was in her father's good graces, I knew I was officially on her shit list. I didn't expect to ever be off of it, and that hurt.

"Happy anniversary," I said to them, standing awkwardly in the foyer, while Andy abandoned me to hurry off toward the kitchen. I watched the fabric of her flowing dress trail behind her and silently begged her to come back before her mother had a chance to castrate me.

"Thank you," she replied, standing tall.

"So, forty years, huh? That's great."

"Long time," her father replied, wrapping an arm around his wife and kissing her cheek. "But it's been worth every second."

"I hope we're all that lucky," I complimented, smiling at the genuine curl of her lips.

Her smile faded as she asked, "Do you plan on getting married one day?"

"Uh ..." I glanced toward the kitchen, wishing Andy would rescue me at that very second. "I mean ..."

"Don't put him on the spot like that," Andy's dad said, reaching out to clap a hand against my shoulder. "When he's ready to marry Andrea, he'll let us know. Right, Vin?"

The corner of my mouth ticked, twitching into a half-smile at the thought of marrying Andy and the idea of making her my wife. Could a future like that really be in the cards for a guy like me?

"Well, we'll see," her mother quickly added, narrowing her eyes at her husband and then at me. "That wouldn't be happening for a long, long time. And who knows what'll happen before then, right, Vinnie?"

I could only imagine what she was implying, and none of it could be good. But, as much as I didn't want to admit it, she was also right. Who really knew? There was plenty of room for me to fuck things up, for Andy to find out about my little secret stash and leave. And then, what? Depression? Rock bottom? Overdose?

The possibilities were endless.

"Yeah," I replied, my voice gruff. "Right."

***

I learned something about Andy's family—both immediate and extended—that night.

They were all wealthy, and they were all, for the most part, assholes.

As one of her parents' three daughters, she had deserted me on more than one occasion to help with the party, leaving me to stand alone in the middle of the decorated yard, a ruffed-up mutt surrounded by wolves. I felt their eyes on me, curious and questioning as they picked apart my bargain bin button-up and hand-me-down slacks, as they wondered why I held a bottle of water and not a glass of champagne. They didn't know I had worn the very same clothes to my father's funeral, just a couple of weeks before, but I did. They didn't know that one of their cars cost more than what I made in a year, but I did. They didn't know I had snuck a glance at the little bag of cocaine right before leaving the apartment, but I did. And with every comparison I made, the more I wished for a drink, or better yet, the coke that I'd left taped to the medicine cabinet.

"So, what do you do?" her cousin, Brad, asked, sipping slowly from an etched tumbler.

"I work at my family's pizza place."

He nodded. "Is it just the one or do they own a chain?"

That was what he asked, but what he really wanted to know was, *how successful are you?* So, I replied, "Just the one. But that's intentional." Which wasn't a lie. After the restaurant took a turn toward success several years ago, Pops could have afforded to open up another Famiglia Bella in a different part of Manhattan, or maybe in Brooklyn, my old stomping grounds. But he decided against it, realizing how thin he'd have to spread himself.

Brad's preppy face wrinkled with disbelief. He couldn't understand why someone wouldn't want to expand and make more money, even if it meant sacrificing the quality of the product. But I knew it wasn't something I could explain in a way he'd understand, so I didn't try.

"How'd you meet Andrea?" he asked, changing the subject.

"Well, we kinda met twice. Once outside of a show in the city, and the second time, in the hospital."

"Ah, right. She said your father was a patient." He nodded. "Makes sense."

I narrowed my eyes at the remark. “Makes sense? What do you mean?”

Brad laughed and I could smell the bourbon on his breath. My mouth watered as desperation slowly crept in.

“Oh, I didn't mean anything by it. It's just, well, you know. I can't imagine where else she would have met you.”

“Hm,” I grunted, pursing my lips. “Well, I better go find her. Nice chat, Brad.”

I walked away before he could reply and I could once again catch a whiff of the booze on his breath. I searched the yard, peeking into clusters of well-dressed people. Nobody said a word to me or acknowledged my intrusion. It felt like being invisible, and I didn't like it.

I found Andy in a garden, with a glass of wine in her hands. She never drank alcohol around me until now, and while it had never been a stipulation of mine, I was surprised to find that it hurt me, just a little, to see her take a sip.

“What are you doin' over here all by yourself?” I asked, approaching with my hands stuffed in my pockets.

I startled her, as I emerged from the shadows to stand in the glow of well-placed lights. She smiled bashfully, holding up her glass.

“I'm sorry,” she said. “I-I figured you wouldn’t like me to drink around you, but I had to. This party is ...” She shook her head, casting her gaze toward the large gathering only feet from where we stood. “It's a freakin' chore.”

"Then," I took a step forward to stand beside her, "why are we here?"

She laughed, raising her glass and gesturing with it toward the party. "They're my family! I have to be here!"

"What does family have to do with it?" I challenged, narrowing my eyes. "My mom walked out when I was five years old and never came back. You think she gave a shit about family?"

Andy's glass lowered, hovering over her heart, as her eyes filled with sympathy. "Vinnie, you know—"

"Sweetheart," I said, pulling the pack of Marlboros from a pocket along with my lighter. "Don't look at me like that. I want nothin' to do with your pity."

"I'm not saying I pity you," she insisted. "I'm saying, you know it's not the same thing. You can't compare. I have a good relationship with my family. We get along and I love being with them."

Holding a cigarette between my teeth, I lit it with a flick of the lighter, then said, "You don't gotta justify anything to me."

"I know," she said, nodding and wrapping an arm around herself. "I know that."

"Then, what's wrong?"

"Nothing," she insisted, sipping on her wine.

I imagined the way it washed over her mouth, sliding down her throat and diving deep to warm her belly. That one sip relaxed her, I saw it in the sag of her shoulders and the drop of her chest. Every drink she took left her a little more unraveled as it stained her tongue with its flavor, and I craved its taste.

“Nothin', huh?” I inhaled the tobacco and nicotine and exhaled a plume of smoke into the air. “You know I know when you're lying to me, right?”

She released her lip from between her teeth. “I'm not lying.”

“No?” I turned to step in front her, blocking her view of the party. “Tell me why you're really over here.”

A flame ignited in her eyes as she stepped backward and pressed her body against a tree. She lured me with her eyes, daring me to acknowledge the line she had cast. Daring me to bite.

“I told you, to have a drink.”

“You could've had a drink inside with your sisters,” I pointed out, taking another puff from the cigarette as I stepped forward, assuring her that I'd taken the bait.

“I don't want to be with my sisters right now,” she admitted, speaking lower and huskier, as my body pressed against hers.

“Oh, no? And why is that?”

One of her dress straps had slid down, leaving her shoulder bare. I couldn't resist the sight of her skin, tempting me with memories of having her naked, and I bowed my head, sinking my teeth into her flesh and smiling wickedly at her moan wrapped in a gasp.

“They ... God,” she groaned, moving her hips against mine. “They can't keep their mouths shut and I'm sick of it.”

I licked my way from her collarbone to behind her ear. “Keep their mouths shut about what?”

Andy tipped her head involuntarily, exposing more of her neck to my wandering mouth. "Just ... everything."

"You gotta be more specific, sweetheart. I can't make you feel better if you don't tell me."

She raised her glass and downed the rest of its contents before dropping it to the ground at our feet. Her hands reached out, tangling her fingers in my hair and pulling, maneuvering my head until my lips hovered over hers.

"You're making me feel pretty good right now," she said, and I dove in. Sucking the wine from her tongue and relishing in the taste of her mouth.

We made out like two misbehaving teenagers, mere feet from her family and the ongoing party. I heard someone announcing that it was time for cake, as my hand inched its way up Andy's dress, and then someone else, one of her sisters, asked where she was just as my fingers disappeared beneath her underwear.

"Oh, God, this is so bad," she groaned.

"Then, tell me to stop," I said, both a request and a dare.

But her only answer was to spread her legs wider, to grant me better access, and I wouldn't deny her. Maybe a better man would have, the type of man she deserved, but that wasn't going to be me, not then. I wanted her to feel good, I wanted her happy, and if getting off on my hand while I finished my cigarette would do the job, then that was fine with me.

Her arms hooked around my neck and her forehead dipped to touch my chest. She worked her hips against my fingers until she was whimpering and begging me to keep going. As if I'd stop. I could tell she was close, as her thighs shook and her head fell back against the tree trunk, but she never reached the peak of orgasm. We never got that far. Because the next thing I knew, a guttural "oh, my God" came from behind me and I was backing away from Andy so fast I nearly tripped over my own feet.

"Are you *kidding* me?!"

Andy smoothed her dress out as she said, "Willa! What are you—"

"Do not ask me what *I'm* doing right now, Andrea. What the hell do you think *you're* doing?!"

Her other sister, Meredith, must've heard the commotion and hurried over, arms crossed and already scowling. "What's going on over here?"

"Our little sister was just having sex over here, while we were having cake," Willa said, sneering at Andy and never once allowing her eyes to pass over mine.

Andy gasped. "I was not having—"

"Oh, would you prefer I say you were getting fingered? Is that better?"

Meredith narrowed her eyes at their little sister. "What the hell is happening to you? I mean, Christ, Andrea. Just because you've chosen to date trash doesn't mean you have to act like it, too."

The cigarette between my fingers was now nothing but a smoking filter and ash, and I threw it to the ground, crushing it beneath the heel of my grease-stained boot. I immediately pulled another from the pack, placing it between my lips, and lit up. All while Hell broke loose around me.

"Who the hell do you think you are?" Andy hissed, her voice choked.

"I don't know who you think *you* are," Meredith retorted, "but this shit, what you two are doing over here, is *not* fucking okay."

"I'm thirty years old! I'm an adult, dammit!"

Willa snorted, shaking her head. "Then act like it, instead of sneaking off during your parents' anniversary party to fuck your boyfriend—"

"Where anybody can see you!" Meredith threw in. "Jesus, Andrea ..."

With a smirk, Andy crossed her arms and said, "I think you're both jealous. I think you wish you were in my shoes. I think you're so fucking tired of your boring lives, that you need to dig into mine. You wish your husbands would get the sticks out of their asses and—"

"Sweetheart," I interrupted gently, pulling the cigarette out from between my lips.

"What?" She shouted at me, breathless and furious.

"Stop," I said, reaching out and laying a hand on her arm. "Calm down a little before you say somethin' stupid."

Meredith uttered a sound of disgust. "Don't tell her what to do."

I shook my head, holding out my palm and surrendering. "I'm not. I'm just—"

Willa shook her head, pinching her eyes shut and slashing her hands in the air. "You know what? I'm sorry, but no. You don't get to talk right now. *You're* the problem here. *You're* the reason she's never around. *You're* the reason she doesn't talk to us anymore, and *you're* the reason she's doing God knows what when she's supposed to be celebrating her parents' anniversary."

Taking a long drag from the cigarette, I shook my head. "Listen to me—"

"No, *you* listen to *me*," Willa went on, jabbing a finger in my direction. "You—"

"What's going on over here?" Andy's mother asked, coming into the garden that, only ten minutes earlier, I'd thought was so secluded and private.

This was their chance to throw us under the bus. This was their chance to tattle and I fully expected for them to grab at it. But they didn't.

"We caught Vinnie smoking and told him to stop," Meredith said, voice flat and eyes pinned on me.

Andy's mom saw the lit cigarette pinched between my fingers. "Please put that out," she commanded, and without a single protest, I did as I was told. She nodded with approval, then said, "There's cake if you guys want it. And Vinnie?"

"Yeah?"

"You have lipstick on your shirt."

With that, she walked away and I was left clearing my throat and feeling like I was thirteen again. Caught in the middle of a make out session I never should have been in, with an old friend's seventeen-year-old sister. That had been just as embarrassing, and just as wrong, as this. I had known then, just as I had known now, that it was a bad idea. But I had done it anyway. For the thrill of it, I guess. But, back then, I'd had the excuse of foolish immaturity to defend my decision. What the hell could I say for myself now, other than I simply wanted to do something stupid with my girlfriend? And at what cost?

Willa never did finish her thought and we never did have cake. Andy and I quickly said goodbye to her parents and called an Uber, despite her father's insistence that he drive us to the train. I don't think Andy wanted to be in a car alone with him, and if I'm being honest, neither did I. But I felt the rift growing between her and her family, that I knew she'd always been close to, and I wondered how truthful her sister had been. Was I really the cause for the newfound distance between them? Or had it been a long time coming and our relationship was simply the final straw to break the camel's back?

I was teetering on the edge of a mental breakdown the whole ride into Penn, while Andy sat beside me in uncomfortable silence. I wished she'd talk to me. I wished she'd save me from the bullshit in my head. But she didn't. She just kept her eyes down and her lip pinned between her teeth, and I guessed maybe I deserved that.

My brother and sister had both grown up in the same household as me. We'd had the same childhood, the same parents, the same misfortune. Yet, we all had coped in our own way; Jenna had busied herself with boys and an active social life, while Zach and I discovered drugs and alcohol. We'd done it together, as our own little dysfunctional team, and later, we'd gone to rehab. Much like our descent into addiction, we had also begun the journey to recovery by each other's side, and our dysfunctional team became a support system. But then, Zach met Greyson. He had fallen in love and moved away, no longer needing the support I could offer.

He'd gotten out. He'd broken free. And not once had he looked back to see if I was still shackled or if there was any part of me still holding on.

But, I guess that's the way things go, isn't it? You win some, you lose some, and Zach had won. I guess that left me in the position to lose. And that's exactly what I was: a loser. Pops saw it. Andy's family saw it. And there was a part of me that wished she'd see it, too—hell, maybe she already did, and that was the reason for the silent treatment the whole way back to the apartment.

The second we walked through the door, her entire body went rigid and she headed straight to bed, with the excuse that she was tired. I didn't doubt she was, but there was something else. Something that stopped her from kissing me goodnight. Something that kept her eyes on the floor and not on me. That type of emotional and physical rejection hurt me in a way it shouldn't have, and the second she closed the door to the bedroom, I headed straight to the bathroom.

As I reached up to the top of the medicine cabinet, my hand landing immediately on the prize, I looked into the eyes of my reflection and whispered, “Fuckin' loser.”

CHAPTER TWENTY-FIVE

ANDREA

When I was twenty-three, my parents and I went out to the movies, leaving Willa at home with her then-boyfriend, Eric. We were gone four hours and when we returned home, my dad walked in on Willa having sex—in my parents' bedroom.

I laid in bed at Vinnie's apartment, festering in that memory and the things that had happened at the anniversary party. I wanted to call my sister up and demand she apologize to us for her judgments and accusations. I wanted to remind her of the way her first born had been conceived and ask her how she would've felt if Mer and I had assaulted her with insults and names. But I knew I wouldn't do those things, because I also knew that two wrongs never made a right.

What had I been thinking? I never should've let Vinnie put his hand up my dress. I never should have let things go as far as they had. But I had been tipsy, after drinking a couple glasses of red wine, and the anger I felt toward my family had coupled with the thrill of being caught by them. And yes, it had been exciting in the moment, and yes, it had been good, but at what cost? Would my sisters ever be able to look at us again? Would they ever be able to respect him as the man I chose to be with?

Amid the torture of my self-loathing, there was the perpetual hum of the spirit world, something I had successfully escaped in this apartment for two weeks, until now. Vincent was here, Vincent was watching. He wanted something and needed to pass along a message, but I wouldn't let myself listen. I couldn't. I had issues of my own to handle right now, and maybe that was wrong and selfish of me, but after so many years of making time for the ghosts, I felt I deserved this.

If only he would go away.

I opened my eyes to find him standing at the side of the bed, looming over me. I rolled over to face the other wall, and he followed, moving to the other side. I hated the way he stared at me, unblinking. I hated the way he kept his mouth in a taut line. Other spirits sometimes tried to talk. They tried to hold onto the part of them that was still human. But not Vincent, and it creeped me out.

"Please," I groaned, rolling my face into the pillow. "Please, go away."

But, just as I suspected, he remained where he stood and continued to syphon the static into my brain, begging me to listen.

Finally, I couldn't take it anymore. I needed to watch TV, listen to music, fuck Vinnie—something to distract me from the ever-persistent buzzing in my head. I rolled out of bed quickly, still in the dress I had spent way too much money on to sleep in and moved hurriedly for the door. Vincent didn't follow the way I thought he would but instead watched me leave with those unblinking eyes.

"Please, please, please, go away," I muttered with my back to him. "I'm sorry. I'm so sorry. Just ... please, leave me alone."

I opened the door, praying he wouldn't follow and praying he'd be gone by the time I came back. I moved quickly down the hallway and turned the corner into the living room, to find Vinnie sitting on the couch and leaning over the coffee table.

"Hey, what are you—" I didn't have the question out of my mouth before realizing very quickly what exactly he was doing. "Oh, my God."

He sputtered as he sat up, rubbing frantically beneath his nose as he coughed. "A-Andy," he stammered, simultaneously trying to look at me while also scrambling to wipe away the evidence of his actions. Like I hadn't already just seen him snort a line.

I backed into the kitchen, seeing him then as a doped-up monster and not the boyfriend I loved. "Don't. Just ... just don't."

He stood up and held his palms out. I could see, even from where I stood, that his pupils were already dilated, creating two black holes where his beautiful, brown eyes once were.

"Andy. It's not what it—"

"Oh, give me a fucking break, Vinnie. It's *exactly* what it looks like. Don't treat me like I'm an idiot!"

“I know,” he said, nodding rapidly and taking a step forward. I took a step back. “I know. But, but listen to me, okay? Listen. I only did it one other time, okay? Just one other time, the other night when you weren't here. That's it. And now, obviously. But that's *it*.”

He was already riding the buzz. Erratic movements of his eyes and hands showcased the energy from his high and it felt so wrong, all of it. How could he still look and sound like the man I loved and wanted to be with, when there was now something inside him, making him act like a complete stranger? And I realized in that moment, why some people stay with their addicted spouses.

“You were high ... the other night,” I reiterated, trying to wrap my head around the sequence of events. As if it mattered or changed a thing. “When you called me and asked me to come back, you were fucking high.”

“Yes,” he said, then quickly shook his head and waved his hands with the motion. “Wait, wait. No, no, no. That's not what happened. I hadn't cut the line yet, Andy. I called you up to get you back so I wouldn't do it. I didn't want to be here by myself. I fuckin' hate this place. I hate how it feels like, like, like a freakin' morgue with all this dead guy's stuff around and all the quiet. And I just needed you back, to make me feel alive again. 'Cause when it's just me here, I feel dead, too.”

“So, you're blaming me,” I answered quietly, clutching my hands to my chest and slowly shaking my head. “I can't believe ... I can't believe you're blaming me.”

"No!" he shouted, startling me. "No. Sweetheart, no, I'm not blamin' you for nothin', okay? 'Cause all of this shit," he moved his hand in a wide circle, "is all me, okay? But I was weak the other night and you make me strong, but since you weren't here, I ..." He nodded to himself. "I gave in. I tried not to, but I did."

He claimed he wasn't blaming me for his actions and I believe he thought he was being sincere. But then, I felt weight of his addiction fall on my shoulders, breaking my back and snapping my bones. I sagged with a ragged sigh, dropping into a chair at the kitchen table and covering my face with my hands. I didn't want to look at him, still so sexy and attractive, despite the black holes that were once his eyes. And I didn't want to see his dead father, standing in the entrance of the hallway, mere feet from where Vinnie stood.

It was toxic. There was no doubting that now. This, my relationship with him and what he was doing to himself and me, it was dangerous and scary and so, so unhealthy in every sense of the word. An outsider might look at the situation and think me insane for still being inside that apartment, sitting at that table. An onlooker might say they'd never put themselves in this situation to begin with. But it was my reality now, and no, it wasn't good, but somehow, in the moment, it didn't seem as bad as one might think it should.

I cleared my throat and scrubbed my hands over my face, not giving a single shit about my makeup. "This isn't good," I muttered behind my palms.

"I know," he said.

"I shouldn't be here, Vinnie. I shouldn't ..." I swallowed at the bitter taste of the words in my mouth, before saying, "I shouldn't be with you."

"No. Definitely not. I told you, I'm no fuckin' good. Your sisters are right. I'm—"

Dropping my hands to the table, I asked, "Why do you do it?"

He cocked his head curiously. "Why did I get high? I-I told you, I—"

"But why? Why did you start in the first place? What is so *amazing* about this shit that you just *had* to start doing it again? Why?"

His breathing was so controlled for someone so high. He nodded slowly and came toward me, and this time, I didn't retreat.

"Pops asked me that a while before he died," he said.

"What did you tell him?" I asked as he sat beside me.

"Nothin'. 'Cause I couldn't just ... I dunno, tell him the reason was him."

I narrowed my eyes, trying to wrap my head around his answer. "But you were so close with him. You loved him. Why ... why would he be your reason for using drugs?"

Vinnie shook his head. "It wasn't him but life with him. Growin' up in his house was hard, with him workin' all the fuckin' time. He was hardly ever around and when he was, he was always stressed. And I always thought, if Ma hadn't run away, shit wouldn't have been like that, you know? But he drove her away, he did that, and we suffered for it."

His energetic buzz faded away to reveal the thick blanket of sadness and years of hurt beneath. "I guess I ... we, Zach and me, used to go somewhere else. You know? Somewhere not ... here."

"An escape from reality," I whispered, understanding more than I would've liked.

"Yeah, exactly. An escape from reality."

Drugs are bad, drugs are wrong, and I shouldn't have understood as much as I did. But I couldn't help that I empathized with the need for an escape. I couldn't help sympathizing with the young kid he once was, desperate to shut himself off from his own life, and how the hell do you do that when you're stuck?

In that moment, I thought about Tracey. About what she had said about the pills and alcohol and how it kept the ghosts at bay—or Spirit, as she called it. Sure, she had nearly thrown her life away because of it, but maybe, just maybe, I could be different. Maybe I could find a balance, and maybe Vinnie could help me.

"Show me how to do it," I found myself saying, relenting way too easily as I lifted my eyes to his.

"No," he told me, point blank. "No fuckin' way."

"Please," I begged him, forcefully ignoring his lingering, unblinking father and the worry in his eyes. "I want you to show me. I want to escape, too. Let me go with you."

He surprised me by tearing up and clenching a fist, raising it to his forehead, and holding it there. "Fuck," he muttered, teeth gritted and throat choked. "Fucking hell, Andy. Don't make me do it."

"Fine. I'll figure it out myself." I stood from the table and moved swiftly toward the living room. "How hard can it be?"

Vinnie pushed himself up from the table and shouted, "Dammit, Andy! Fine!"

He rushed past me and sat down on the couch. He laid his palms over his face, groaning and cursing. I should've felt guilty for putting him through this, but my need to turn off and feel good outweighed any guilt.

I stood by as he shook out his hands and resigned himself to playing the teacher role. He grabbed the little baggie of snow-white powder and emptied its contents onto the mirror. Then, he picked up the Dunkin Donuts gift card.

"Moe gave this to me for Christmas," he needlessly explained, as he pushed the cocaine into two neat, even lines. "It was good for a couple cups of coffee and I guess it's good for somethin' else now, too."

He chuckled humorlessly and dropped the card back on the table. "Okay, watch me carefully." And I did, paying close attention to the way he pressed a finger to one nostril and bent over the table, close to the little white rows. Then, it went so fast, his noisy inhale and the swift motion of his head. He sat up, gasping and pushing his hands through his hair. It didn't take long for his smile to return, bright and euphoric. I wanted that, I wanted that type of numb happiness.

So, I followed his example, sucking up as much as I could, unsure if I was doing it right. After, I sat up, throwing my head back and waiting for it to feel good. Waiting for the disappointed ghost at my side to disappear. When I eventually heard nothing but the sound of my own heart beating in my ears, I opened my eyes to find Vinnie, and only Vinnie, in the apartment.

"How do you feel?" he asked, arms stretched out over the back of the couch.

"Quiet," I replied, and I stood up, certain I was floating on footless legs as I rounded the coffee table and climbed into his lap.

"Is quiet good? I hate quiet."

I cupped his perfect face in my palms, feeling like I was seeing the bright, beautiful colors of his rosy cheeks for the very, very first time. "I only hear you when it's quiet," I whispered, as he wrapped his arms tight around my waist. "Quiet is good."

CHAPTER TWENTY-SIX

VINNIE

The morning greeted me with sunshine and an insatiable craving for a cigarette. Andy was still asleep, naked and tangled in the throw blanket Pops had left draped over the couch. I lifted her arm, in an attempt to carefully slide my way out from her hold, but she stirred and opened her bleary eyes.

"Hey," she whispered groggily, her lips full and puffy.

"Hey, sweetheart, I'm just getting up to smoke. Go back to sleep."

She smiled, reaching out to graze her fingertips over my morning erection. "Well, hurry up. I want this when you get back."

I laughed, bending over to press my lips to hers. "I'll see what I can do," I said, before pulling my underwear on and grabbing my smokes and black Zippo from the coffee table, purposely diverting my eyes from the leftover cocaine mess.

I climbed out the window and onto the fire escape, grateful for the dirty, humid air as I filled my lungs. With a cigarette in my mouth and the flick of the lighter, I set myself up for a thorough thinking session, despite my resistance to think at all.

We'd had a lot of fun, Andy and I. Doped-up and diving into a sweet abyss, we fucked on the couch until the high faded and we fell asleep. I could have looked back on the night wearing a fond smile, but as sweet as the memory might have been, what we had done, and what I had taught her to do, wasn't.

Her family was right about me; I was toxic. If I hadn't believed it before, I did now, and that truth left a sick, hollow feeling in my gut.

I loved her. God, I loved her so much. But if I loved her so damn much, how could I have allowed this to happen? How could I have allowed her to talk me into getting her high, and so easily? This isn't what love does. Love protects. It wraps itself around you like an impenetrable shield and stops the bad shit from infiltrating the fortress you've built. Yet we had seen that bad shit knocking on the door and chose to invite it in.

But, wasn't she also a grown woman, capable of making her own decisions? She had made up her mind and would have done it whether I showed her or not. What if she had screwed up? What if she had hurt herself? When I thought of it like that, I wondered if I had actually done the right thing. Maybe, in some twisted way, I had actually protected her. Because that's what love does, and I loved her.

***

We both had work to return to, and I was glad for it. As much as I would have loved to sit in the apartment and make lazy love to her all day, I also felt that a taste of normalcy would be good. Andy needed to see the hospital, she needed the distraction of her patients, and I needed pizza, just to take our minds off her family and the things we had done together. To reassess and figure things out.

So, we went our separate ways and both walked into work late. It had been expected by her colleagues, Jenna, and Moe, because of the party, but they all had no idea what the real reason was and, as far as I was concerned, they never would. Because the coke was gone now, and there wouldn't be any more.

"How did it go yesterday?" Jenna asked, as I pulled my cap on.

"What? The party?"

"Obviously," she laughed.

I hesitated. In the moment, what had happened at the party was hot and I'd loved every second of it. But now, in hindsight, I was embarrassed. A secret tryst in a bedroom during a party was one thing, but what I had instigated had been reckless and disrespectful.

"It was okay," I settled on, hoping she'd drop it.

"Oh, come on," she groaned, dropping the ladle and turning to face me. "You gotta give me more than that."

"O-kay," I drawled. "How 'bout, I fingered her in the backyard to get a rise out of her family and now they more or less hate me?"

She let her jaw drop open, before saying, “You, *what*? Vinnie, what the hell!”

I shook my head, chuckling brusquely. “It wasn't *exactly* like that, but ... yeah, it was, uh, not one of my finer moments.”

“You have to apologize to them!”

Leveling her with a hard glare, I said, “No way. I mean, maybe one day, when this shit blows over, but not now. Her sisters are ...” I rubbed my fingers over my bristled chin, searching for the words. “They're ... difficult, I guess is the best way I can put it. They're judgmental as fuck and they've been sayin' shit about me since before I even met them. So, like, I'm not sayin' that what we did was okay, 'cause it wasn't, but if I owe them an apology, they owe me one, too. And until they're ready to give it to me, I ain't giving them shit.”

Jenna crossed her arms, considering what I'd said, then nodded. “What don't they like about you?”

“Honestly?” She nodded. “It feels like everything, but I'm thinkin' it's more along the lines of, I don't meet their standards. I have a shitty past, I wasn't born with a silver spoon in my mouth, and I dunno, I'm not going off and playin’ golf with Daddy to impress him or some shit. I think that rubs them the wrong way.”

“And Andy's a good girl,” Jenna pointed out.

Snickering, I shook my head. The events from the day before were proof of how wrong she was. “Well, maybe at one point ...”

“Right. Before she met you.”

I pursed my lips, letting that sink in. Then, I nodded. "So, you think I corrupted her, too."

Jenna groaned and rolled her eyes. "I didn't say that. I'm sayin', maybe she lived a sheltered life or she always played it safe or ... I dunno, whatever. But then, you come along and you ..." She snorted. "Well, let's just say you've never played it safe, and you've introduced her to a whole new world."

"Okay, Aladdin," I laughed, shaking my head.

She groaned again and grabbed the ladle, stirring the sauce. "I'm just sayin', it might've been a long time comin' for her. Everything she's doing with you, maybe she was always destined to do it and you were just, uh, there to open the door to rebellion or somethin'. Her family might blame you for it, when really, her bad girl side has always been begging to come out."

I laughed, reaching out to grip her shoulders. "Sis, just say I corrupted her."

She laughed as I shook her gently. "Fine. You're the devil and she signed her soul over to you."

"Thank you. That's all I wanted, just a little bit of credit," I said, laughing, as my phone buzzed with a text.

I pulled it from my pocket and saw it was from Andy.

Andy: So, I don't know how to say this but ... what we did last night, I want to do it again. Can you get more? Like, I don't know how you go about doing that but I figured you do. Obviously.

Andy: Also, I'm being vague in case anybody else sees this, haha. You know what I'm talking about. Okay,

I'll see you later and hopefully we can do that stuff again. Love you so much.

I stared at the screen, not knowing what to say or what to do. This wasn't supposed to happen. This wasn't how it was supposed to go. But why hadn't I assumed she'd enjoy it and want to do it again? I knew how this story went, I had lived it before, so why hadn't I suspected it would happen to her, too?

Because she's a good girl, the devil on my shoulder whispered, *or was. But you've ruined that, haven't you?*

It struck me then that there was no devil, sitting on my shoulder and whispering his sweet nothings into my ear. There was only me. A devil in disguise.

"What's up?" Jenna asked, reminding me I wasn't alone.

"Oh," I forced a smile and stuffed the phone back into my pocket, "just my favorite client."

She laughed. "She beggin' you to corrupt her a little more?"

"Yeah," I muttered, as I headed out of the kitchen, while a sickening feeling twisted in my guts. "Somethin' like that."

CHAPTER TWENTY-SEVEN

VINNIE

It had been a couple of weeks since the party at her parents' place, a couple of weeks after she'd been introduced to the beautiful tragedy that is cocaine, and we'd fallen into a routine.

Every day, after I got out of work, I went home to her and cut a couple of lines for us. It wasn't good and it wasn't healthy, but I'd convinced myself after a few days, that at least it was contained. I was holding the reins and the control, and I figured, as long as I could hold onto that, things couldn't get too out of hand.

I tried not to consider how that was just another lie I was telling myself.

One Friday night, after getting home from work and getting high, I rolled out of bed in a just-fucked stupor and grabbed my overnight bag.

“Shit,” I groaned, opening the bag and heading to my dresser.

“What are you doing, baby?” Andy asked, spreading her arms and legs wide, as she rolled her head lazily from side to side against the pillow.

“I forgot we’re going upstate this weekend,” I said, throwing in a few shirts, some jeans, and half the contents of my underwear drawer.

Andy laughed wildly at the ceiling. “How many butts do you have?”

“I don’t know. You think that’s too much? It’s too much.” I returned some of the underwear to the drawer, then said, “You need to pack. You want me to do it? I’ll do it.”

She began to move her arms and legs, like she was making a snow angel on the mattress. I stood back, transfixed by the movement and the smooth glide of her limbs, and she laughed at my stare.

“You’re freaking me out.”

“You’re fuckin’ beautiful.”

“No, I’m not. I’m plain. And crazy.”

“Not plain,” I shook my head, “just crazy fuckin’ beautiful.”

“And you’re stoned.”

I laughed, raking my hands through my hair. “Crazy fuckin’ stoned,” I agreed wholeheartedly.

“So, why are we going?”

I spread my arms and shrugged. “Zach wants us all up there for a barbeque or somethin’. I dunno. I said yes, so that’s what we’re doin’.”

“Why can’t we just stay here? ‘Cause I wanna stay here and do all the coke.” She laughed, clapping her hands over her crazy beautiful face. “Oh, my God, can you imagine if we did *all* the coke? Oh, my God, would that be bad?”

“It’d be *so* bad,” I said, shaking my head. “God, we’d probably fuckin’ die.”

Andy abruptly sat up in bed, her eyes wide. “Are we going to die? Oh, my God, Vinnie, I don’t want to die. I’m not ready.”

She looked so scared, so sad, as her eyes quickly filled with tears. I dropped to my knees at the edge of the bed and took her face in my hands. I pressed kisses to her cheeks, forehead, and lips, then said, “I won’t let us die, sweetheart. Okay? Don’t worry, we’re gonna be fine. I’ll make sure we’re fine.”

With a smile and a nod, her face took on another look of serenity. She grabbed my wrists and pulled me down to the mattress to lay beside her. I protested, telling her we needed to pack, but she shook her head and started to press kisses to my lips and cheeks.

“Not yet. We have to do something else right now.”

I nodded, keeping my eyes on her full lips. “Okay. What are we gonna do?”

“Let's pretend we *are* dead, okay? Let's pretend we did all the coke and died.”

“No.” I shook my head and pulled from her grasp. “I don't want to do that.”

“Why? Come on,” she giggled, grabbing at my arms and keeping me from leaving. “It's just pretend. We're gonna pretend we're dead, but we're not really, okay? It's fine.”

I wasn't sure if it was fine. I wasn't sure if it was fine at all. But I tried to relax, lying still beside her, staring at her face and the mischievous smile she wore. She laid on her back, instructing me to do the same; our hands clasped between us. She kept her eyes trained on the ceiling, and said, "Okay. Now, close your eyes and hold your breath."

I did as I was told and trapped the air in my lungs as my eyes shut. The world was still and quiet around me and for one second, exactly one, I was calm. But that second quickly passed and then I thought about my father. Dead. Cold. So still and quiet in the ground. Trapped. That's what he was and so was I. Trapped in my own head. Trapped in my fear of being alone and of being left behind.

I opened my eyes and gasped for air, wrenching my hand from hers and clutching at my bare chest. I felt for my beating heart. I felt for the expansion of my lungs. Then, relieved, I laid my hands over my face and felt the wetness of my tears.

"Baby," Andy said, reminding me that she was also still alive. She sat up and ran her fingers through my hair. Soothing. Calming. "Baby, you're okay. We're okay."

"No." I shook my head. "It's not okay."

"But death *is* okay," she insisted, pressing her hand to my cheek. "When you let go of your body, you're free."

"Andy!" I shouted, my voice sharp with panic. "Stop!"

I looked at her naked body. Long, blonde hair draped over her breasts. Legs bent at the knees, crossed at the ankles. She looked like an innocent woodland faerie, with her pert nose and big, round eyes. The only things that gave away her innocence were those eyes. Devious, black pupils, surrounded by a thin, icy ring of blue. She was so crazy, fucking beautiful. And she gave me the chills.

"You're afraid," she whispered.

I nodded slowly. "Yeah, I'm fuckin' afraid. I don't like this shit."

"Are you afraid of ghosts?"

I looked away from her, acutely aware that my high was fading. "I don't believe in that shit. You know that."

"But what if you're wrong?"

"I'm not."

She sighed, curling her lips in a small, sad smile. "Oh, Vinnie ... you don't know how wrong you are. You're so wrong. The world is so loud, all the time, with all their noise and faces. You can't hear it, not you, but baby, I—"

"Andy!" I bolted from the bed and grabbed for my sweatpants.

"You're mad at me," she stated quietly.

"No," I said, shaking my head. "I'm not mad at you, sweetheart. But I told you, I don't like this shit and I don't wanna talk about it. So, I," I bent over her to press a kiss to her forehead, "am going to take another hit, while you," I moved my lips to her mouth and kissed her there, "are gonna pack your shit."

She smiled and nodded, but that touch of sadness moved to her eyes and there it stayed. “Okay, baby. Cut one for me, too.”

***

“I know I've met your family before but I'm so nervous,” Andy said, sitting behind the wheel. “This feels more serious.”

“Hate to break it to you, sweetheart, but we're pretty serious.”

She rolled her eyes toward me for a split second. “I know that. But like, spending a weekend at your brother's house ... That's practically a commitment.”

“It's not that big of a deal,” I laughed, reaching out to mess with the radio controls.

“Oh, really?”

“Nope.”

“Okay,” she said, challenge in her voice. “Then, tell me. How many women have you taken to stay with your family?”

“Oh, come on. I can count on two fingers the amount of women who have ever met members of my family, and you're one of 'em.”

“And I'm the only one you've ever invited to stay overnight, right?”

“Yep.”

She reached across the car and swatted my arm. “See! This is like, really serious! We might as well be getting married!”

I chuckled quietly, while also imagining the two of us, standing together at an altar. Warmth spread across my chest and nestled in my belly. "You're ridiculous," I commented softly, as I wondered how she'd feel if we were, actually, getting married.

"I'm so nervous," she complained, gripping the wheel. "God, I really wanna get high."

I snapped out of the reverie of wedding bells and faced her. "Andy, I told you, we cannot do that shit at Zach's place. He can't know about it, do you understand? We can't make him suspect a fuckin' thing."

"I know, I know," she said, tapping her fingers against the wheel erratically. "I'm just saying, I wish I could, you know? Just to take the edge off a little."

I hadn't thought about it before, but now I realized that I was afraid of why my brother wanted us to come up to his place. Our weekends together were usually so informal and casual, and nobody needed an invitation to come hang. But this had been a phone call from Zach, cordially inviting us to his place for a barbecue, along with his in-laws and our sister's family. My imagination was pretty set on what this was all about, assuming it had something to do with fertility clinics and babies, and I found that I was anxious, too.

"Yeah, sweetheart," I muttered, reaching out to take her hand in mine. "I know."

***

"Hey, bro!" Zach shouted from the porch.

I briefly offered him my attention, throwing a half-hearted wave as I climbed out of the car, before diverting my eyes to the driveway. There were more cars than I had anticipated. At least five of them were lined up in two rows, with another half dozen parked along the curb. Andy glanced at me over the car, her brows pinching with nervous worry. I returned the expression with a little shrug, before shutting my door and heading around the car to take her hand.

We walked up the steps and the second we were within arm's length, Zach pulled me in for a hug.

"Holy shit, I've missed the fuck out of you," he said, clapping his hand against my back. "You need to stop bein' such a stranger, man. What the hell's been up with you?"

"Been a little distracted," I said, stepping out of his grasp to place a hand at the small of Andy's back.

"I'll settle for that excuse," he replied with a grin, then extended an arm toward Andy. "Get over here, gorgeous. Thanks so much for coming."

They hugged tightly and for a moment, all feelings of trepidation disappeared. I watched her, grinning against my big brother's chest, and I was overwhelmed with the need to thrust my lips against hers. She fit in with my family like a long-lost missing piece and I wanted so much to glue her into place, to ensure she'd never break free. But I also knew the two of us were playing with fire, and anybody dancing in the flames, was destined to burn.

And just like that, the worry returned.

“So, uh, what the hell is with all the cars?” I asked, jabbing a thumb over my shoulder toward the street.

Zach rolled his eyes and wrapped an arm around Andy's shoulders, steering her toward the front door. “Greyson insisted on turning a little thing into something way bigger. He invited some of his relatives and Devin drove up to chill with his dad.”

Andy’s eyes grew wide. “Devin O’Leary? He’s *here*?”

My brother grinned. “Yep.”

She muttered an “oh, my God” beneath her breath, as I jabbed, “And, how many of these people are stayin' in the guest room with us? 'Cause I mean, I'm not opposed to an orgy, but I'm gonna be picky. I got standards, you know.”

“Just you, dick,” he laughed. “Now, go get your shit from the car. I'm stealin' your girl.”

Andy looked back at me, eyes dancing with insecurity and nerves. Her anxiety was evident in the way she stiffened beneath his draped arm, and I tried to relax her with a grin.

“I'll be in there in a minute, sweetheart,” I said. “And don't worry, you're not his type.”

And as I jogged back down the porch steps to the car, I thought, *but she is mine, and I don't know yet if that's a good thing.*

CHAPTER TWENTY-EIGHT

ANDREA

The yard was enormous. Greyson said they only lived on two acres of land, like it wasn't that impressive, but if I took off my glasses, their piece of property seemed to trail on forever.

I wished I could appreciate it and all of its natural glory. I wanted to stop and smell the literal roses, planted in the flower garden surrounding the deck, and admire the expansive vegetable garden that Zach said took him two years to perfect. But it was hard to appreciate the peaceful joy of this beautiful backyard when, dotted among the flowers, there were ghosts. So many ghosts.

And they wouldn't shut up.

I desperately wished I was high, and I hated that almost as much as I hated the ghosts.

But, amongst the distractions of my life's burden and my new addiction, I found that I really loved Vinnie's family. They were warm, welcoming, and absolutely wonderful in every sense of the word, accepting me and my quirks. They didn't ask questions about my financial situation or upbringing. And what melted my heart even more, was that I wasn't special. They all treated each other the same way, with sharp wit and kind smiles. And I never wanted to leave.

"You're looking good, man," Sebastian, Greyson's dad, said to Vinnie. "You losing weight?"

Vinnie was a professional at feigning cluelessness. He shrugged nonchalantly and said, "I haven't really noticed, but you know, I've been walkin' to work a lot lately, so maybe it's payin' off." But he was also a bad liar, and immediately afterward, his thumbnail was clamped between his teeth.

"I need to get moving more," Sebastian said, patting his flat stomach. "I'm getting huge."

"Yeah, Dad. Real big," Greyson grumbled from behind us.

"Yeah, well, you know why that happened, right?"

Greyson sighed exhaustedly. "Nope, but I'm sure you're gonna tell us all."

"It's because your little sister has decided she's never leaving my bedroom. So, instead of getting laid every night, I'm trying to sleep with three million stuffed animals and a little girl's feet jammed into my ass."

I tried to fight the laugh bubbling up quickly from my stomach but couldn't. I grabbed Vinnie's arm and doubled over in a fit of giggles.

"I'm totally failing to see what's so funny about this," Sebastian continued. "I mean, not only am I suffering from the world's worst case of blue balls and I'm not getting my nightly exercise, but I'm also really fucking tired. Like, I could totally lean right here," he draped an arm around Vinnie's shoulders and tipped his head, "and go the fuck to sleep."

His tone was so serious, so sincere, that I immediately stopped laughing and apologized. Sebastian responded with a boisterous laugh that left me feeling momentarily confused.

"Beautiful, I was put onto this planet to be laughed at. It's part of my charm." He pulled me under his arm and said to Vinnie, "How the fuck does she manage to put up with you?"

"I'm still figuring that one out," he replied as he stared at me with eyes full of hunger and question.

I tried to relax a little more in their company and ignore the lingering spirits, but God, they were abundant. There were the women who crowded around Greyson. A man that never left the side of Devin's wife, Kylie. Tabby, Greyson's aunt, was followed by a couple of older people. And, of course, there was Vincent. And while the others meandered about, like they themselves were guests at the party, Vincent stood in the background. Staring.

Their presence was so loud, and the interference of the land of the living clashing with the land of the dead was deafening to my ears. But nothing had ever been as loud as Vincent. And I refused to listen.

It's funny how I never stopped to question if that was maybe the point.

We ate dinner—a spread of barbequed meats, salads, baked potatoes, and roasted corn—and I tried engaging in as much conversation as I could, before being distracted by the dead. The way the man at Kylie's side smiled with fatherly pride. The way the woman at Greyson's shoulder looked fondly at Zach. The images of their lives that they presented to me, the love they felt, and all the things they missed. I wished I could've known these people, and I wished they would go away.

"Come on," Vinnie said, taking my hand and pulling me from the long bench seat at the table.

"Where are we going?"

He led me to the pool, stripping off his shirt and throwing it to the ground. "Your head is somewhere else. I need you to come back to me."

"I can't help it," I said, fixing my gaze on his muscular physique, while noting that Sebastian had been right. Vinnie was getting thinner. The skin stretching across his rib cage nearly gave them away. Just a little longer and I'd be able to count them.

"I know it's hard," he whispered, his hushed voice breaking through the static. "But you gotta try. Okay? I need you."

Nodding, I agreed to do my best and pulled my oversized t-shirt off, to expose my bikini to this backyard of absurdly attractive people. Jenna, who had given birth to two kids, had the body meant for a swimsuit edition, while Kylie and Tabby, also both mothers, belonged on the runway. And they all had personalities to match. They were a fiery, outgoing group of women, and I knew I paled in comparison, with my average body and antisocial, wallflower personality.

I covered my breasts with my arms, but before I could tighten my hold, Vinnie took my wrists and pried them away from my body.

"Don't do that," he said.

"But I don't look like ..." My words trailed off as my eyes flitted toward Kylie and Tabby, sitting together and chatting.

Vinnie followed my gaze, then cupped my chin in his palm and turned my eyes back to him. "Why do you care?"

"Because they're pretty."

"Yeah, and?"

"Well, I mean," I gestured down at my body, that was also maybe showcasing a few more ribs than usual, "look at me."

"Oh, believe me, sweetheart; I'm lookin'. I always am."

My laugh was laced with every insecurity I had. "You're only saying that because you're with me and not them."

I expected a snicker or a chuckle, but he didn't show any sign of amusement at all. Instead, he nodded and said, "That's right. If I wanted someone like them, I'd have it. But I don't." He took one step closer and I could feel the heat radiating from his body, as he placed my hand discreetly over the front of his trunks. "You feel that? That's from lookin' at *you*. *You* do that. Nobody else. Okay?"

I bobbed my head in a slight nod, both flustered and turned on. He dropped my hand and made a sardonic crack about not wanting to recreate the scene at my parents' house, then without warning, dove unceremoniously into the pool.

The crystal water shimmered beneath the late summer sun as it rippled from the impact, then broke around his body as he resurfaced. He sucked in a gulp of air, then grinned, his olive skin wet and glittering. His hair hung in his eyes, dripping, before he raked it back, smoothing it over the crown of his head, and I thought, *this is the stuff fantasies are made of.*

"Get in here, Andy," he demanded, crooking his finger and beckoning me to him.

I laughed, knowing my cheeks were glowing with a magnetic flush. He wasn't the only one in the pool. A couple of Greyson's cousins were batting a beach ball back and forth in the shallow end, while his grandma, Sebastian's mom, lounged on the steps leading into the water. But my attention was only on Vinnie, and for a moment, not even the white noise could distract me.

I didn't jump in, not like him. I sat at the edge of the pool, dangling my legs in the water first, before sliding in. It was amazing to be surrounded by the warm water and I closed my eyes to the feeling of weightlessness. Vinnie swam up to me, pressing his wet chest to mine, and with my eyes still closed, he kissed me. Open-mouthed, his tongue swept against mine and our bodies took on a mind of their own, moving against each other and rippling the water around us. Without even realizing, I had ended my own resolve to not recreate that moment at my parents' anniversary party. But when I felt Vinnie's fingers tracing the edge of my swimsuit bottoms, I unlocked my mouth from his.

"No," I said, shaking my head.

He nodded, pulling his hand from the water. "Sorry. I didn't mean—"

"Your family would hate me," I whispered.

Chuckling, he shook his head, wrapping his arms around me. "Sweetheart, they might tell us to get a room, but they would never hate you."

"You don't know—"

"Whoa, man!" Greyson shouted from beside the pool, looking directly at us and smirking. "We gave you guys a freakin' room. Go use it."

I was speechless, as Zach knelt down to whisper, "Yo, if you guys wanna do shit, at least wait until the kids are gone, you know what I'm sayin'? Don't scar anybody for life. But, I mean, if you came out here later, I wouldn't stop you." And he reached out, clapping Vinnie on the shoulder as he winked, while my cheeks burned with embarrassment.

Vinnie leaned in, brushing his cheek against mine, and whispered, "See?"

I brought my forehead down to his shoulder and groaned. "God, I wish I was high right now." He grunted in response, a disapproving sound, and taken aback, I reared my head back to ask, "You don't feel the same way?"

He glanced around us, to make sure the coast was clear, before answering, "Don't get me wrong; I love bein' wasted. But sometimes, I love bein' in the moment more. And this, right now, is one of those."

***

The sky was dark and the yard was lit by what must've been a million little faerie lights, wrapped around the deck railing and decorating the surrounding bushes and trees. The pool was lit from within, glowing in a blue ethereal splendor. Vinnie and I had found ourselves a floating lounge, big enough for two people, and that's where we were when Zach clinked a spatula against his bottle of root beer.

"Okay, so you're probably wonderin' why we wanted all of you's up here today," he said to the crowd of us, speaking loudly for everyone to hear. "Well, I'm sorry to say it wasn't 'cause we just love all your company."

I cuddled my cheek to Vinnie's drying chest, trying hard to keep my attention on the deck, where Greyson came to stand next to his husband.

"What do you think they're gonna say?" I whispered.

Vinnie grunted beneath my ear. "Gonna be somethin' having to do with kids."

"They're having kids?"

Another bitter grunt in response.

"Okay, so as most of you know, we've been explorin' our options when it comes to having a family, and well, we decided to have my lovely sister as our surrogate."

Jenna stood and bowed flamboyantly. Zach chuckled. "Thanks for that, Jen. Anyway, uh, well … I guess in about seven months, we're gonna be parents."

Friends and family erupted in a chorus of whoops and cheers for Vinnie's older brother and his husband. They rushed to the deck, offering hugs and congratulations to the happy couple and squeezed Jenna for her loving sacrifice. Everybody was so happy and excited. Everybody but Vinnie.

He wore an expression of sincere dread. I caught the corners of his mouth trying to smile and show his brother support, but the attempts were feeble.

"Baby, what's wrong?"

He shook his head and lifted the side of his mouth in a somber half-smile. "I'm okay."

"No, you're not."

Sighing, he pushed a hand through his damp hair. "I'm happy for them, seriously. It's a great thing. But, I dunno, I guess maybe I'm jealous or some shit."

Warmth nipped at my heart and ovaries, as I asked, "You want babies?"

He shrugged. "I love kids. I always have. But that shit isn't in the cards for me. I'm, you know, me. No kid would deserve me as a parent."

The warmth I'd begun to feel was put out with a brisk chill. "That's really … final. And sad."

"That's life, sweetheart. We make our choices, you know? Zach chose to get his shit together and have a family. I chose to buy some coke after bein' sober for a long time. Now, our lives are in different places, and there's no disputing who the fuck-up is." He winked and tapped a finger to his chest. "Spoiler alert, it's me."

I knew he was talking strictly about himself. I knew it wasn't meant to be a jab at me. But it still felt like a slap to my face, and I displayed as much by shaking my head.

"You didn't make that choice. You *needed* it. You can't help that you're—"

"Do not say I can't help that I'm addicted, Andy," he growled quietly, so nobody would hear. "I *did* make a choice, and I fuckin' own it. But you're right about one thing; I did need it. And right or wrong, that's the way it is for now. Maybe one day, if I don't end up dead in a ditch somewhere—"

"Okay, stop," I squeezed my eyes shut, shaking my head as the float moved lazily over the water's surface. "I don't want to think about that, okay?"

"I'm just speakin' the truth, sweetheart."

Choked up, I nodded and blinked rapidly, turning back to him. "I-I know, but …" I pulled in a deep breath, glancing back at the happy crowd on the deck. "I love you. And I can't think about you not being there, okay? If you die, I'll die."

His expression was flat, studying my face for a minute, before saying, "I love you, too. And I'm not goin' anywhere. I was just sayin'."

We climbed out of the pool, to congratulate Zach and Greyson, and to tell Jenna to call if she ever needed anything. Then, in somber fashion, we headed upstairs to our room to dry off and fall asleep after a long, emotional night that had ended on a far heavier note than either of us would've liked. And all the while, with every move, Vincent stood, watching and waiting.

All I hoped was that he was here to give his son a message and not to take him away.

CHAPTER TWENTY-NINE

ANDREA

I used to see the junkies stumbling into the hospital or being wheeled in after an overdose. I would wonder how they got themselves into that situation, and how they could function in the real world while being a slave to a substance. I'd look down on them, with the belief that I was above that sort of lifestyle. Like it could never, ever, in a million years happen to someone like me.

Now, cutting my own lines on our coffee table covered in Chinese food cartons, it occurred to me, with startling clarity, that it had, in fact, happened. Because drug addiction doesn't care where you're from, what color your skin is, or how much money you have. It doesn't care if you're living in the slums of Brooklyn or in a cushy house in suburban Long Island.

If it wants you, it'll grab you. Now, it had me, and it was holding on tight.

Vinnie was slumped on the couch beside me, his head tipped back and his eyes closed. I checked his chest to make sure he was breathing, and released a sigh of relief when I realized he was only sleeping. Sometimes his depression won out and it didn't matter how high he was; he still fell asleep. Because sometimes, it was better to be asleep, than it was to be sad and stoned.

My buzz had begun to wear off and there was no way I was going through the rest of the night with his father's somber expression keeping me on edge. So, with Vinnie's old gift card, I finished lining it up, nice and neat, just the way he did. I got to my knees, and before I took the hit, I glanced at his father.

"Please go away," I whispered, hoping he'd listen. "Whatever you have to say to him, you'll have to go to someone else. It won't be me. I can't do it."

He didn't listen, he never did. But in the past, he'd simply stand there, staring vacantly at his youngest son, until I was too high to notice his presence. Tonight, however, I was presented with an image through the static; a still picture of Vinnie, laying on the floor of the apartment. Motionless and breathless.

Lifeless.

I gasped, as tears immediately sprung to my eyes. The image faded and my vision focused entirely on Vincent and his firm stare, still aimed directly at Vinnie.

"I-Is he going to die?" I asked, my voice small and weak. But I was answered with silence, of course I was, and I wasn't in the mood. "What the hell is the point of doing this to me if you can't even fucking talk? Huh?"

Vincent's gaze shifted to meet mine. There was no other movement, no other acknowledgement, and my frantic agony only escalated.

“Oh, God, fuck you. Fuck all of you. If you're not going to help, then just go the fuck away!” My eyes dropped to the rows of white powder and driven by determination, I said, “You know what? I'll just *make* you go away.”

I snorted one line, two lines, and then, I waited, watching as the drugs took over and took him away. The apartment was quiet again, with no more static and visions, but that sight of Vinnie, laying on the floor, remained. And the despair I felt in that moment was so much greater than the high I was desperately trying to reach.

The problem with this ability, other than the inability to control it, is that I can only read whatever they show me. I don’t always know what it means, or what they want, and that was very much the case in this situation.

“Fuck,” I cried, throwing my head back against the couch.

Vinnie stirred beside me. “Andy,” he rasped, and I imagined not hearing that name again. The name only he called me. A quick pinch of death tore violently at my heart and my body shook with a sob.

“Sweetheart,” he said with urgency, sliding off the couch to sit beside me on the floor. He gathered my face in his hands and kissed the salty tears from my cheeks. “Andy, sweetheart, why are you crying? What happened?”

“If y-you die, I'll die,” I cried, pressing my forehead to his and grasping his t-shirt in my fists. “I don't want to die. Not yet. So, you can't die, baby. P-Please, don't die.”

His eyes, so full of life, found mine. “Sweetheart, why ... why do you keep saying this shit?”

“I'm just so, s-so scared,” I whispered, sobbing and squeezing my eyes shut against another torrent of tears.

“Stop, okay? Just stop,” he said, soothing me with his voice and gentle fingers through my hair. “We're okay. We're always going to be okay.”

I forced myself to nod. “I just l-love you s-so fucking much,” I said, moving my hands from his shirt to his cheeks. “I want this forever. I want you forever.”

“You got me, sweetheart,” he replied, pressing kiss after kiss to my lips and cheeks.

“Then ...” I grasped his face, his hair, his neck, and I looked into his eyes, remembering so vividly the image of him dead. I didn't know what it meant. If it meant he had to die, I didn't know if I could save him. But what I could do, was love him and love him hard, for however long we had together. “Then ... then, let's get married.”

“Wait,” he said, pulling back. His brows drew together, as he narrowed his eyes. “Are you serious right now?”

“I've never been more serious about anything in my life,” I said, wrapping my arms around his neck and moving into his lap. “Please, baby, marry me.”

His arms circled my waist as the bright, rosy hue of happiness pinched at his cheeks. “I don't think your family would approve,” he said, his voice gruff as laughter filled his tone.

"I don't care. I don't care about them. All that matters is *we* approve. You and me. We don't need anyone else."

Vinnie pulled in a deep inhale, then very slowly exhaled and I relished in knowing that he was still here with me—alive. When he nodded his reply, I tightened my hold on his neck and buried my face against his shoulder.

"You and me, baby," I said, my voice muffled by his skin.

"Yeah," he said, kissing my neck, ear, and hair. "Let's do this."

***

"You're, *what*?" Mom exclaimed into the phone.

I had called my parents the next day to invite them to our wedding--a casual, impromptu thing at an arboretum on Long Island. I didn't expect them to attend but Vinnie had convinced me to extend the invitation. I knew it was the right thing to do but that didn't help how difficult it was to have the conversation.

"Um," I chewed my bottom lip, staring at the cracked sidewalk. "We're getting married this weekend."

Her moment of hesitation spoke volumes. "Andrea ... don't you think you're rushing things right now?"

"You were with Daddy for only two months before he asked you to marry him," I pointed out quickly.

“But we waited a year to get married after he proposed,” she replied, her voice shrill. “Why not wait a while to be sure?”

“I'm thirty years old, and he's thirty-four. How long would you really like us to wait?

“Well, let me ask you this, then: what's the rush? Are you—wait, are you pregnant?”

I groaned, massaging my temple with my fingertips. “No, Mom,” I sighed. “Not pregnant. We're just sure this is what we want, that's all. So, can we expect you there?”

She sighed, her exasperation evident. “Well, I don't know. I mean, I guess so. But I just really wish you'd think about this—”

“Okay. I'll text you the details. Love you, bye.”

And just like that, I hung up, before she could keep trying to talk me out of it. Then, I smiled, because I was getting married to the man I loved, and my parents would be there.

***

Vinnie said he wouldn’t wear the same shirt and slacks he’d worn to his father’s funeral to our wedding, so he rented a tux that fit him well. I didn’t think it was possible for him to look any better than he already did, but as we drove to the arboretum, I could only stare at him from across the car and think, *how lucky am I.*

We met my parents, his siblings, and their respective partners at the entrance of the arboretum to take a few quick pictures. The moment I stepped out of the car in my new dress, my father approached with a teary-eyed grin.

"You look beautiful, honey pie," he said, wrapping his arms around me in a tight embrace. His mouth dipped closer to my ear and he whispered, "I always knew you'd do things your way, Andrea. You were never meant to be ordinary."

The sweet sentiment was enough to make me flutter my eyes shut as tears gathered in my inky lashes. I thanked God for waterproof mascara and swiped at the moisture before it could trickle down my cheeks.

"Thanks, Daddy," I whispered in reply, and then, stepped back to allow Vinnie to come forward.

"Thank you for coming, sir," he said, extending a hand.

"I wouldn't have missed it," Dad replied, accepting. Then, stilling the movement of their arms, he said, "I gotta be honest with you; I wasn't thrilled about this. And it's not that I don't like you; it's that I don't *know* you."

"I understand."

"But I have to trust that my daughter does, so I'm also trusting that this is a good decision," Dad continued, leveling my recent fiancé with a warning glare. "I'm telling you now, though; you will not hurt my daughter, or there will be hell to pay. You understand what I'm saying? You better take care of her."

Vinnie hesitated in his response and I could only imagine what he was thinking, likely reminiscing on the high we reached the night before. The rough, animalistic sex we had over the coffee table, to ride out our buzz before collapsing on the floor. I wondered if he wished he was high right now, while in the face of my father's dubious approval and if he regretted insisting they be invited.

But after pulling in a deep breath, he nodded. "I'll hurt myself before I ever do anything to intentionally hurt your daughter."

Dad pursed his lips and nodded. "I'll settle for that."

We accepted the excited congratulations from his brother and sister, along with their husbands. It was a wonderful feeling, to have their acceptance and encouragement, but the persistent expression of discontent on my mother's face was slowly burning a hole through my joy.

But she never said a word, as we took pictures among the trees and flowers, alongside a quiet creek leading down to the Great South Bay. She silently smiled and stood with us, playing the parts of doting mother and mother-in-law for the photo album. But as the photographer was changing his lens, in preparation for the judge's arrival, she approached me, arms crossed, and head tipped to the ground.

"Andrea," she said quietly. "Can I talk to you for a second?"

I looked up to Vinnie, silently asking if I should. He nudged his chin toward my mom and said, "Go ahead, the judge'll be here in a few minutes. You got time."

So, I walked with her, allowing her to lead me to the creek's bank. I sighed in preparation and watched the babbling water as it shimmered in an amber glow from the sun's rays. She pulled in a deep breath beside me and then shook her head.

"I'm trying to think of the right way to say this," she began, and I remained silent, allowing her the time to put together whatever stream of nonsense I was already resigned to ignore. "I think you're making a mistake."

"Is that a message from Mer and Willa?" I asked, bitter that my sisters had refused to witness me getting married.

"They told me about what happened at the party," she confirmed, nodding slowly. "And I'd be lying if I said I wasn't disappointed—or disgusted, if I'm really being honest. But that's not why I think this is a mistake."

"Oh, good."

Then, she jabbed my shoulder with a gentle finger. "I don't think he's good for you. He can barely take care of himself. How the hell is he going to take care of you, too?"

"You have no idea what you're—"

"You might not want to see it, and that's why I'm telling you now. He's … troubled. You can see it in his eyes, and I don't know what exactly it is. You can make excuses for it all you want, but the bottom line is, I'm afraid that whatever's going on with him, he's just going to drag you down there with him."

Tears stung the backs of my eyes at the agonizing despair in her tone, at how clueless she really was to what was going on and the fact that I didn't think I'd ever be able to tell her. She and my sisters had accused me of being blind, but it was them who refused to see. They had all put the blame on Vinnie, when so much of it came down to the one person they'd never point a finger at: *me*.

"I wish you'd believe that I love him," I whispered past the emotion rising in my throat.

"I do," she insisted. "But sometimes, love isn't enough."

"Yeah," I said, sniffing and turning to head back. "And sometimes, it's all that matters."

***

I was grateful when the judge had agreed to meet us at the arboretum. Vinnie and I both liked the privacy of it, surrounded by a natural hush, and I thought I could avoid the fuzzy sounds of spirits. Apart from Vincent, forever staring, I'd been right, and for the first time, I didn't want him to disappear.

I wanted to watch him watch his youngest son get married.

I wanted him to see Vinnie happy.

Standing beneath the sagging bows of a weeping willow, the judge instructed us on where to stand. I took my place, facing Vinnie and grinning at the euphoric expression on his face. That was his stoned face, the one he made just as the buzz really took hold. But there weren't any substances influencing him here. This was just Vinnie, high on his love for me, and an unexpected sob burst past my lips.

"Come on, Andy," he whispered, using his thumb to brush away a rogue tear. "Don't be sad."

"She's not sad, you moron," Jen muttered, and I laughed, nodding in agreement.

"I'm just," my breath caught in my throat, "I'm just so happy."

Pulling his lips between his teeth, he took my hand and nodded. "Me, too, sweetheart."

The judge coached us through the vows, and I'm really not sure that I paid much attention to what was said. I know I promised my life to him. I know I promised to stay by his side. But all I cared about, all that truly mattered, was that I was committing my heart and soul, fully and completely, to this beautifully broken man.

For better or worse.

Until death do us part, to then be reunited somewhere else.

If you die, I'll die.

"Vinnie," the judge said, smiling kindly. "Go ahead and kiss your wife."

"Holy shit," he gasped, as he pulled me into his arms to cover my mouth with his in a deep kiss better suited for the bedroom. And even though my mother groaned and his sister coughed awkwardly, I didn't care.

Because he was alive and we were together.

I loved him and he loved me.

And that was all that mattered.

CHAPTER THIRTY

VINNIE

Our honeymoon was an overnight stay in a ritzy hotel with a bottle of vodka and an eight ball of blow. I didn't expect to go through it all, being just the two of us, but a party of two is still a party and we spent the night fucking and maintaining a high that I knew teetered on the edge of too far.

But there was something about the way she did lines that turned me on. Previously, I'd been with girls who used, before rehab and temporary sobriety, but they all did it like a junkie. They had lacked control and poise. Andy, though ... She was addicted and needed her fix as much as anybody dependent on drugs. But she seduced it. She took her time. Snorting it quickly before slowly throwing her head back, no different than when we made love. Maybe that was all it was. I thought of sex when I watched her take a hit, and thoughts of sex always led to, well, sex. And we traveled that endless circuit until the sun streamed through the veil of curtains.

"Dance with me," she demanded, clambering to her feet and wearing nothing but my t-shirt.

"Oh, man," I groaned, raking my fingers through my hair, damp with sweat.

"Come on, on your feet, Mr. Marino. You need to dance with your wife. Those are the rules."

I slumped on the velveteen couch, looking up at her and her crazy, beautiful eyes. "Don't make me get up. I'm crashin' fuckin' hard right now, sweetheart."

"Nobody told you to drink all the booze." She was giggling, grabbing at my hands, and tugging. "Dance with me, baby. Please? I need to dance."

She tugged and tugged with little success but she wouldn't quit trying. So, I eventually submitted, standing up with a sigh. "Okay," I relented. "I'll dance with you one time. And then, I'm takin' my wife to bed, because we need to sleep."

"God, you're such a lightweight," she grumbled, laughing. "Okay, okay, okay. I have the song we're gonna dance to. Okay? You ready?"

I nodded and she tapped through her phone until she found what she was looking for. The opening notes were vaguely familiar, like they came from a time in another life. I could hardly pinpoint where I'd heard them before, too inebriated and tired, but I tried hard to place them in my memory.

"Do you remember?" She stepped into my embrace, looping her arms around my neck, and pressing her body flush with mine.

"Kinda," I replied, squinting and peering into the hazy moments that cluttered my mind.

"I'll help you, husband. This was the first song we ever danced to, on the street outside the restaurant. Remember it now?"

The alternative sound of the guitar instantly sparked a crystal-clear memory from that night which otherwise seemed too faded to recall. She'd been so impressed with my dance skills, so taken with the guy she never should have gotten tangled up with in the first place. It was only months ago but it felt like a lifetime. So much had happened and changed since then. I remembered the innocent look in her eyes from all those months ago. Then, I was punched in the gut with the memory of our first time together, the time I'd taken her rough and hard, with too little regard for her feelings. I remembered the first time she got high, the first time she said she loved me. And finally, in a more recent memory, I heard her say 'I do.'

It felt so wrong. I felt like a thief, the robber of her potential and life, and I hung my head in shame.

"What's wrong, baby?"

"You never should have been with me," I whispered, swaying with her lazily.

She pressed her fingertips to my lips. "Shhhh. Don't say that."

"No," I disputed, moving my lips against her fingers. "I'm a fuckin' wreck and I pulled you down with me."

"Shhhh," she repeated, tracing my bottom lip with her fingernail. "We're not talking about the bad stuff right now. There's too much bad in the world, too much to think about, and right now, I'm going to pretend that all of life is good. Because you and I are perfect, we are meant to be, however long we're meant to be for, and I don't want to waste a second of our wedding night on thinking about anything other than that. Okay?"

I agreed to not talk, but I never promised that I wouldn't think. And so, as we danced and as she hiked her leg up around my waist, drawing me closer and, eventually, drawing me in, my thoughts circled in an endless loop.

I was never perfect, but she was.

And I ruined her.

***

We stayed past check-out and slept off the drugs and booze. I awoke with a skull-splitting ache pounding in my brain, caught somewhere between starving and never wanting to look at food again. Andy was already awake, laying beside me with her hands tangled in her wild nest of blonde hair, and when I offered to order some aspirin and food, she shook her head.

"I don't need food. I just need drugs," she whined, squeezing her eyes shut tight.

Andy had always been thin, but I couldn't recall her wrists ever being so pronounced. I reached for one of them, capturing it in my grip, and ran my thumb over the protruding knob of bone.

"You need to eat something," I said quietly. "I'll order food and you just eat what you want, okay?"

"Yeah," she agreed, sniffling and wiping a hand over her eyes. "Sure. But will you get more coke later?"

I didn't want to be sober any more than she did. I wanted to shut out the world, and I was just as addicted. Yet she was scaring the hell out of me, and still, I couldn't say no.

"Yeah. Later."

And I kept my promise. I found Moe's old friend, bought another eight ball, and when I got back to the apartment, I made Andy promise we'd make this one last. A line or two every night didn't freak me out as much as it probably should have, but a whole eighth of an ounce in one night wasn't okay. Never had I ever done that much, sharing or otherwise, and I was dead set on never doing it again. Especially with her.

After all, I had promised to protect her as best as I could.

We headed to work the following morning, two days after we'd been married, and although I stumbled in late, I felt it was better than not coming in at all. But the constant nights of using had begun to screw with my body and mind, and I had to drag my weary, jittering bones to get through the day.

Jenna approached me outside after I'd finished my tenth cigarette since clocking in.

"Long night?"

I dropped the ash-ridden butt onto the ground and crushed it beneath my boot. "Yeah."

She offered a pinch-lipped nod, keeping her arms crossed tightly over her chest. "What, uh, what were you guys up to?"

Snorting, I replied, "Are you askin' seriously? Or just makin' conversation?"

She shrugged. "I'm just wonderin'."

"Why?"

"Why can't I ask my little brother what he's been doing?"

"Because you're askin' me what I'm doing with my wife. That ain't okay. It's fuckin' weird. What's next, Jen? You wanna sit in and watch?"

"Wow," she huffed, rolling her eyes and shaking her head. "Defensive much?"

I groaned, pushing the hair from my eyes. "We ate dinner, watched some shit on TV, and fucked until we went to sleep. Okay? Do you approve?"

"What shit did you watch?"

"I don't know!" I shouted, exasperated at the very thought of coming up with another lie. "Uh … *Breaking Bad*, I think," I stammered, naming the first show that came to mind.

"Hm." Jenna pursed her lips again and nodded. "Pops and I were watchin' *Breaking Bad* the last night he went into the hospital. Did you know that?"

I sighed exhaustedly and shook my head. "No, but yeah, that makes sense. He was bingeing that shit for a while."

"Yeah," she said. "He told me that Jesse reminded him of you."

I grunted, stuffing my hands into my pockets and tipping my head toward the sidewalk. “Oh, that’s awesome. I reminded him of a skinny, weaselly, loser. Nice.”

“He said it was because you both really try to make your lives better, but trouble just … finds you, I guess.”

I snickered, hoping I was successfully hiding the shock I so abundantly felt. “He really talked about that shit like I haven’t been sober for fuckin’ years?”

“Have you, though?”

The question left me gaping at her, shaking my head, and frantically thinking of how I could convincingly deny the accusation. Was it that obvious? How the hell had she known?

“What the fuck, Jen?” I spat out, while wondering if Moe’s former buddy had said something to him. Or whether Moe had seen a transaction? It had to have been him. How else would she have known?

“I’m just askin’,” she said, keeping her voice light and innocent.

“I haven’t done shit,” I insisted, turning away from her and storming back into the restaurant.

Moe stood at the register, waiting for the lunchtime crowd to show and give him something to do. I headed straight toward him, leaned my forearms against the counter, and said, “Jenna just asked me if I’m usin’ again. How fuckin’ nice is that?”

He shrugged. “Family worries, man. You should know that better than anyone.”

"Yeah, yeah, I get that. But what would give her the idea that I'm doin' shit?"

His deep brown eyes looked from the screen of his phone to my face. "Oh, I dunno, maybe it's just a vibe she's getting." There was insincerity in his tone, I could sense it, but I wouldn't push it. I couldn't, not without making myself look guilty.

"Yeah. Maybe."

Jenna came back in and said, "Anyway, Vin, I just wanted to talk to you about the way things have been. Like, I know you have your own thing going on, but you gotta work on getting here on time. You have to. I'm gonna be going on maternity leave before you know it and I need to be sure you can hold down the fort. Either that or you gotta hire someone you can work with."

In a split second, I went from angry to understanding her point. She was right. The pregnancy was still new, but time flies, and before I knew it, she'd be out of work and I'd be all alone at the restaurant. There was no way I was going to get my shit together if things kept going the way they were, and I found myself wedged tightly between responsibility and addiction.

I told Jenna I would make it a point to do better, and she responded by saying, "Yeah, well, I've heard that before. I'll believe it when I see it." The jab flicked at my nerves and tested my anger, but there was no denying that she, once again, had made a fair point.

After work, I headed home with it all weighing heavily on my mind. Walking down the streets and avenues, I recalled my time in high school, when addiction had been new and exciting. I'd struggled then, trying to balance schoolwork with the never-ending desire to get high, and eventually, I dropped out at seventeen. Looking back, it really was such a stupid thing. I'd only had one year left until graduation, but my dependency on cocaine didn't care about things like diplomas.

Zach had been lucky, though. He'd already gotten his diploma. He had the privilege of calling himself a high school graduate.

Zach always got lucky, though. All things considered.

I resigned myself to talking to Andy. We needed to reel things in. I was struggling to balance life with leisure, and I could only begin to imagine how she was coping at work. She never talked about the hospital anymore, and that alone was worrisome.

Before entering the apartment, I braced myself. It was funny that I still had to do that, all those weeks after Pops's death. But it wasn't until after I'd collected my bearings, that I unlocked the door and went inside.

"Hey, sweetheart," I called, emptying my pockets on the kitchen table.

"Hey, baby."

"I wanna talk to you about somethin'."

I headed into the living room, and there I found her, sitting in front of the coffee table. Her head was thrown back against the couch, with that telltale smile on her face. My eyes were drawn to the mirror, sprinkled with white powder, with that stupid gift card beside it.

"You are … the most beautiful husband, you know that?" she said, opening her eyes to reveal two rich black holes where her bright blue irises once were.

"Fuckin' hell, Andy," I muttered in reply, feeling all at once jealous and defeated. I dropped to my knees across from her and, on autopilot, began to set up a few lines. Then, before I bent over to pull them into my system and chase her into nirvana, I shook my head and repeated, "Fuckin' hell."

CHAPTER THIRTY-ONE

VINNIE

I watched her slip the dress on, jealous of its flimsy fabric, clinging to her curves. She caught my eyes in the mirror and grinned before swiping on a coat of lip gloss.

"Stop, you're making me self-conscious," she giggled.

"What?" I laughed, kicking one ankle over the other and folding my arms behind my head. "I'm not allowed to watch my wife get dressed?"

Andy shook her head, grabbing her hairbrush from off the dresser. "Nope. You're allowed to watch me get naked, not when I'm putting on clothes and makeup."

"Why not?" I asked, my mouth twitching into a lopsided smile.

She shrugged, dropping her gaze, and I thought, *there she is, that shy girl who always knew exactly what she wanted.*

I missed her.

"I was never good with fashion and stuff," she told me, pulling the brush through her long, blonde hair.

"Before our first date, my sisters actually helped me get dressed."

I smiled, remembering fondly. "The sparkly purple shirt."

She sniffed a soft laugh. "Yes. That was actually Mer's."

"Still my favorite color," I commented gently, hoping that maybe we could go back there someday, to the people we once were.

She flashed a smile over her shoulder before tying her hair back into a messy bun. Having the long, blanketing lengths up off her shoulders, I could see the sharp definition of her shoulder and collar bones. Looking at her now, I saw her as a skeleton, frail and sickly. I'd been debating with myself for days now, since that chat with Jenna, and now I knew for sure; I needed to get that shit away from our lives before it killed us. Mustering the willpower to do so though, was another issue entirely.

"Anyway," she went on, coming to sit beside me on the bed, "I just feel a little self-conscious about it, that's all. I don't have great taste in clothes."

Furrowing my brows, I let my eyes sweep over her and the lavender sundress. It was simple, sure, but there was nothing wrong with that. I wrapped my hand around her thin arm and pulled her toward me.

"Well, I think you're perfect," I said, my breath tickling her lips before I gently kissed her.

“That's just because we're perfect together. I'm not perfect alone,” she argued, pressing her hands flat against my chest.

I smiled, making an effort to keep my mouth shut. We had been, at one point, perfect together, and I believed we could get there again with time and effort. But I couldn't consider this, what we were doing now, to be anything other than toxic.

Andy stood from the bed and slipped her feet into a pair of white heels. I whistled at the sight of her long, lean legs, accentuated by the extra height, and she blushed.

“You really think I look okay?”

I nodded. “Sweetheart, if you weren't running out the door, I'd be pulling you onto my dick right now.”

She laughed and, on her way out of the room, said, “I hope you take rainchecks.”

***

Andy had gone out to spend the evening with Elle. She hadn't wanted to, but for the sake of keeping those close to her from getting suspicious, she went. It was only for dinner and drinks, she'd said, which was fine, and I had encouraged it. She needed to get the hell out of that apartment, away from bad habits, and so did I.

I took the opportunity to see Goose, as I hadn't gone to his bar since before I'd succumbed to my demons. I found that I missed him and apparently, he'd missed me, too.

“Well, holy shit,” he shouted over the jukebox. “Vinnie! How've you been, man?”

“Well,” I sauntered over to the bar and flashed him my left hand, showing off the ring I now wore proudly, “I've been taken off the market.”

Goose peered at the titanium band, like he couldn't quite believe it, brows pinched and eyes narrowed. “You for real?”

“For real.”

His expression softened as he nodded. “Andy?”

“Yep.” I grinned. I still wasn't tired of calling her my wife.

“She's a good one, dude. I'm happy for you.”

He offered a hand and we shook as I gave him thanks, appreciating that he hadn't commented on how little time we'd known each other before tying the knot.

Goose poured me a Coke and grabbed a basket of wings from the kitchen. I would've preferred something stronger to drink, something like whiskey or tequila, but I kept my mouth shut. He could read me well enough without my stupid mouth helping him along.

“How's shit with you?” I asked him, monopolizing the conversation before he could steer it toward me.

He shrugged. “Ah, you know. Same shit, different day.” He folded his thick, tree trunk arms on the bar's surface. “Been seein' this chick, actually. It's nothing serious right now but it's been kinda nice to be monogamous for once, you know?”

Goose and I had once upon a time shared a certain taste for casual sex and no strings attached. Now, to hear him say he'd been exclusively seeing someone made me wonder if my relationship with Andy had inspired the change.

"Nice," I said, nodding before sipping at my drink. "That's awesome, man. Where'd you meet?"

He chuckled, a deep, jovial rumble. "Here, actually."

I feigned shock, pressing a hand to my chest and gasping. "I thought you said you'd never get involved with a girl who came in here."

"Yeah, well," he grumbled, tipping his head down to hide his pinking cheeks, "if you saw her, you wouldn't have said no, either."

"Hot, huh?"

He closed his eyes and nodded slowly. "Smokin'."

We shot the shit for a while, making casual conversation while he tended to the occasional customer. It was a quiet Thursday night and I was grateful for the time spent with my friend.

Until he said, "So, hey, can I ask you a question?"

"'Sup?"

Goose pulled in a deep breath and dropped his gaze to the dirty glass in his hand. "So, uh, the last time you were here, you had said shit was getting pretty hard for you."

My heart began to jitter with anxiety as I nodded. "Yeah."

"So, uh ... what happened with that?"

I lifted my shoulders high, too high, and shook my head. "Nothin', man. Nothin' happened." Then, my shoulders dropped heavily as I quickly added, "Why do you ask?"

He slowly placed the glass in the sink, then said, "Nah, I was just wonderin', you know? You were in a real bad way last time, so I was just making sure you were all good."

"All good, man," I said on a deep sigh of relief.

I felt uplifted and triumphant, convinced that I'd dodged a bullet. And then, he had to ask, "So, how come you've lost so much weight?" Accusatory eyes found mine and, in an instant, I saw red.

"The fuck you gettin' at, Goose?"

He ran his tongue along his upper teeth as he shrugged one shoulder in an infuriating display of false nonchalance. "Oh, nothin', man. I'm just wondering why it is you came in here tonight, looking like you've spent the last month strung out on some heavy shit."

And this is what happens when you make friends in rehab.

They know too much.

"Fuck off."

"Oh, you're really helping your case now," he retorted coolly.

"There is no fuckin' *case*," I argued, flattening my hands against the bar.

"Then, why the hell are you yelling at me, huh?"

"Because I don't appreciate *you*," I jabbed a finger into his wide, barreled chest, "makin' bullshit comments and accusing me of shit that isn't true!"

"So, what is it? Coke?"

“Oh, Jesus Christ,” I grumbled, shaking my head as I got down from the stool. “I'm not dealing with this shit.”

“Don't let it get the best of you, Vinnie,” Goose went on. “I'm here for you, man. Okay? Whatever you need—a place to stay, a ride somewhere, whatever. I'm there. Just—”

“Shut the fuck up!” I shouted, grabbing my empty glass off the bar and throwing it onto the floor where it shattered into a hundred glittering shards of crystal. Through gritted teeth, I repeated, “Shut the fuck up. You have no fuckin' idea what you're talking about. So, stay the fuck out of my business. Got it?”

Goose never flinched in reaction to my outburst. He stood behind the bar, looking completely unmoved and unamused, while his eyes gave away the true magnitude of his hurt and concern.

“Sure, man,” he answered quietly. “Whatever you say.”

I didn't stick around after that. I hurried out of there before he could say something else, before he could coax a confession out of me. Because deep down, beneath the need to chase the next high and disappear, was the part of me that didn't want this. The part that wanted to go back and be better. But there was no way in hell that he could rely on the rest of me.

And as I hurried away from the bar and the neon signs glowing in its windows, it was that small, nearly undetectable part of me that teared up and wanted desperately to cry and beg my friend for help.

CHAPTER THIRTY-TWO

ANDREA

"How'd it go with Elle?" Vinnie asked as I entered the living room.

"It was okay."

I knelt in front of the coffee table and opened one of the dime bags, while also reading my husband's body language. He wasn't rushing to join me in our nightly routine. Instead, he remained seated on the couch, his arms folded over his chest and a stony look on his face.

Tapping some of the powder onto the mirror, I casually asked, "So, what's up?"

He hugged an incoherent sound, then said, "Went and saw Goose tonight."

"How's he doing?"

His lips pinched and he slid his eyes, full of contempt, toward me. "He knows what we're doing."

I stopped mid-pour. "What? You told him?"

"No, I didn't *tell him*," he snapped, dropping his head back against the couch. "He fuckin' guessed, and I didn't really do much to prove him wrong."

He was wound so tight, so full of stress, and I wanted him to feel good. *And*, I thought, as I resumed my task, *I need his father to go away*.

As per usual, Vincent was there to greet me the moment I got home. I couldn't stand the look on his face, or that he was still here and hadn't moved on. Over time, my desperation to make him go away had strengthened, as did my dependence on the drugs.

I hated how good it felt.

I hated that I felt I needed it.

Really, I just hated *it*.

But Vinnie was with me. And as long as he and I were together, everything felt okay, on the surface at least.

"Here," I said, cutting him a line and making it neat. "Do this."

"Andy," he groaned. "I'm fuckin' tired, okay? I'm tired and I'm stressed. So, just ... not tonight."

My jaw dropped at the chill in his voice. He sounded like he couldn't stand me and like he was disgusted by my presence.

"Fine," I said, leaning over and doing it myself. Sitting up I rubbed at my sniffling nose and looked back at Vinnie, to find that he wouldn't look at me. "What is your problem?"

He slouched forward and rested his forearms over his knees. "My problem is that I have this shit with Goose to worry about now, on top of everything else. And all I want is to catch a fuckin' break."

My heart pounded with sympathy toward my husband and I crawled to him on my hands and knees. I let my fingers wander from his knees to his inner thighs as I said, "Let me make it better."

"Christ, Andy," he groaned, head falling back as my fingertips ran the length of his hardening erection, moving upward to skirt the waistband of his gym shorts. "I'm not in—"

"Not in the mood?" I teased, pulling the shorts down to expose him to my eager mouth. "What's this, then?"

I took him in to the back of my throat in one smooth, languorous swallow. Vinnie groaned again, this time out of pleasure, and I responded with a moan. His fingers threaded through my hair, gripping and pulling, as I worked him with my tongue and lips. I sucked and hummed my personal approval as he came closer and closer to climax, his groans escalating as his hold on the back of my head tightened.

And then ...

"No."

He gently pushed me away, to stand from the couch and pull up his shorts. He shook his head in adamant protest as I sat there on the floor, stunned and utterly rejected.

"W-What's wrong?" I asked, now acutely aware of the persistent buzzing in my nerves.

"I can't right now. I just ... I can't. I have too much shit on my mind. I have to ..." He sighed loudly, pushing his hair back with both hands and cursing under his breath. “I have to just clear my head, okay, sweetheart? I just ... I just wanna go to bed.”

Everything had happened so quickly and the ease in which he went from hot to freezing was startling. I stood on shaky legs as a flood of tears sprung to my eyes. He noticed and the cold demeanor was stripped away, revealing his compassion underneath.

“Andy,” he said, coming to me as the tears began to fall.

I slumped against his chest and laid my hands against the defined structure of his sternum. “You're mad at me. I don't want you to be mad at me. Was it the blowjob? I can do better, I swear I'll do—”

“Stop, no,” he said, running his fingers through my hair. “It's not that. It's not even you. I swear, I'm just too fuckin' distracted tonight.”

I nodded against him and said, “Yeah, okay, yeah. I understand, baby. Um, maybe ... maybe we should go out to my parents' house? You know, go swimming and hang out, just to relax and get a, uh, a grip on things. You know? What do you think, baby? Do you want to do that?”

I hadn't seen my parents since the wedding. And although I knew they weren't thrilled with my decision to marry Vinnie, they were still my parents and, up until just a few months ago, I'd been with them constantly. I missed them and I hoped he'd agree to see them with me.

His sigh was heavy with guilt. “I can't. I need to step up my game at the pizza place. Jenna's getting suspicious and she'd only have more fuel for the fire if I took off.

But you should go, sweetheart. Get the hell away from here for a while. It'll do you good."

"Being away from you could never be good," I said, holding on tightly to the fabric of his shirt.

"Well, I guess you don't know until you really try," he replied in jest, as my heart ached at the possibility of what was to come.

***

"Anybody home?" I called into the house, closing the front door behind me.

It was strange, as I stepped into the living room and surveyed my childhood home. I remembered sitting on that couch, watching Saturday morning cartoons, while waiting for my dad to cook breakfast. I remembered birthday parties and running through the house with the few friends I'd made. I remembered hide and seek, Easter egg hunts, and sparkling Christmas trees. Then, I remembered the dreams I had once, of growing up and getting married, of everything little Andrea Bennett wanted for her adult life.

She had never wanted this.

I was still that girl, the last time I had set foot in this house. But everything was different now, and I no longer felt that I belonged here. It no longer felt like mine.

But that was my father, coming down the stairs and that was my mother, walking into the living room from the kitchen. They both smiled like they recognized me. Like I was still the daughter they knew.

"Hey, honey pie!" Dad exclaimed, approaching with wide-spread arms and a grin. "We weren't expecting you today."

"Yeah, I thought I'd surprise you guys," I said, relaxing into his hug.

"Where's Vinnie?" Mom asked, eyeing me warily over Dad's shoulder.

"Working."

"Everything okay?"

Dad released me but kept his arm around my shoulders, as I replied, "Yeah, everything's fine." She let out a short contemplative sound and I sighed, rolling my eyes. "Seriously, Mom. We're good."

"Have you been getting enough sleep?"

I nodded, forcing a smile. "Oh, yeah."

She stepped toward me, reaching out, to lay her hand against my cheek. "You have such dark circles under your eyes," she commented softly, brushing the pad of her thumb over the top of my cheek in a gentle, caring embrace.

I fought the ache of emotion as I turned from her touch. "Mom, I'm fine," I insisted, faking a laugh. "Stop worrying so much!"

"I'm your mother," she said, crossing her arms over her chest. "I'd be worrying even if there wasn't a reason to."

"There isn't a reason to," I muttered, slipping out from under my father's arm to head for the stairs.

Then, as I made my way upstairs, I heard her mumbled reply, "You'll have to work harder than that to convince me."

***

My disdain toward the ghosts had only increased since discovering I could turn them off while under the influence. They were more of a nuisance now—at work, on the train, along the sidewalks, at home, and, apparently, at my parents' house, too.

I walked into my room to find Jamie sitting on the bed, as though she'd been waiting for me to return all this time. I was struck with a horrible bout of guilt, knowing she had nobody else, but still lingering among that guilt, was the desperation to hide away from this aspect of my life.

After being around Jamie for so many years, I often forgot that she was just a little girl. She had always been my friend and the age she had achieved in life never mattered. But now, I saw that little girl, with her beaded pigtails and missing front tooth, as she grinned from ear to ear. The look on her face and the way she jumped up from the bed to greet me ... It made me feel like she'd chosen me as not her friend but her adopted parent. And when had I ever agreed to take on that responsibility?

"I can't hang out, Jamie," I muttered, as I headed for the closet door.

She followed, rotating her arms, telling me to tell her what I've been up to.

"Nothing," I lied. "Just hanging out with Vinnie. I, uh, I moved in with him."

She furrowed her brow with curiosity and pointed at her chest.

"No," I said firmly, opening the door to pull out some clothes to bring to the apartment. "We're not coming here to live with you. We have our own place."

She frowned, her eyes filling with disappointment and rejection, but I couldn't let myself care. I was living my own life now, one free of ghosts, and I couldn't let her in without giving them all a free pass.

"I'm sorry."

Ghosts couldn't produce tears, but like a newborn baby, they could display the emotion. They could cry, albeit soundlessly, and at that moment, Jamie's bottom lip began to quiver.

I tried to ignore her as best as I could, pulling clothes out of the closet to decide what to keep and what to get rid of. I kept my eyes down and my mind busy as best as I could, but she was always there. Always pouting and always staring. Driving the guilt home, like a stake through my heart.

"Jamie, stop."

She dropped facedown onto the bed, shielding her head with her arms. But I didn't need to see her face to know she was crying and hurt.

"Knock it off," I growled from between gritted teeth. "Stop it."

I hated myself as I scolded and tried to get rid of her, my constant friend. But this was all a part of life, wasn't it? You move on, and your friends do, too. Sometimes you catch up at the local Starbucks, chatting while your kids argue over cookies, and then, you don't see each other again for another year—sometimes never. But you still have something in common with those friends: you all embrace and respect the changes in your lives.

Not Jamie, though.

I took a deep, controlled breath to collect my resolve, and said, "You need to leave me alone now."

Jamie lifted her head, revealing the heartbreak in her eyes.

I shook my head, fighting off the annoying prick of emotion. "I don't know what to do for you anymore, Jamie. I can't help you. Just ... just leave."

But no matter what I said or did, Jamie was here for a reason, and because I could never figure out what that reason was, she was stuck. She was here forever it seemed. But even so, I didn't have to deal with it. I had options now. And in a rush of determination, I dropped down at my desk and fished the snow-filled baggie from my pocket.

Jamie peered over my shoulder, innocent curiosity on her face, as I dug through my desk drawer to find an old compact disc and Blockbuster Video membership card. I couldn't stand to look at her, as I poured the coke from the bag and cut a couple of lines. She didn't know what I was doing, there was no way she could, but I did. I knew I was wiping the slate clean and making her disappear, and my heart snapped with every tap and push of the plastic card.

“I'm sorry, Jamie,” I said, as I took my position. “I really fucking am. I just ... I just can't do this anymore. I'm sorry.”

It went so fast, it always did. But, as much as I liked Vincent, he was never my best friend. I hadn't grown up with him. We hadn't binged movies and danced around to music together. So, each time I took a hit in the apartment, I never cried when I opened my eyes to find him gone. I didn't ache at the sight of him no longer being there.

But I did now.

“I'm sorry, Jamie,” I repeated to the empty room. “I'm so, so, so sorry.”

“Hey, Andrea?”

It was Dad, right outside my door. He was there, so close, and how much had he heard? Could he hear the cocaine? Could he hear it, so loud and electric, plucking at my veins and drumming against my heart?

“Yeah?” I called out, breathless as I frantically set to cleaning up.

“Can I come in?”

My hand bumped the open bag of cocaine and some of the remaining powder spilled in a white cascade over the black walnut desktop. With my heart racing wildly, I scrambled, brushing the powder into my palm, as I shouted, “Yeah, just give me—”

The door creaked open and in an agonizing panic, I rubbed a dab of the remaining coke against my gums, not wanting to waste it all, as I reluctantly brushed the rest against my jeans.

Dad stood in the doorway, surveying the room, and I watched him, trying hard to remain calm while my nerves grabbed a hold of the high and began to run, run, run away.

His eyes landed on me and an apologetic smile spread across his face. “Sorry,” he said. “It's just kinda weird, you know? We've lived here since you were a little girl and this has always been your room. But now, I guess,” his smile shifted, now sad and sentimental, “I guess it's not.”

“I-It's not a big deal, Daddy,” I stammered, as my racing anxiety heightened.

“Well, I dunno. It sort of is,” he said with a melancholic shrug. “I guess I just thought there'd be more warning, you know? Like, it wouldn't be so ... sudden.”

A wave of nausea nearly knocked me over, and I gripped the back of the chair. “Did you ... Did you want something?”

“Oh,” he snapped his fingers, as though remembering what it was he was there for. “Right. Your mother wanted me to ask if you were staying for dinner.”

“I can't,” I hurried, reminding myself that I needed to breathe to stay alive and that if I held my breath, I would die.

Was I dying?

Oh, God, I didn't want to die.

Dad's disappointment was clearly evident as his smile transformed into a frown. “Oh. Well, that's okay. Some other time, right?”

I nodded erratically. “Y-Yeah, Daddy, sure.”

His tone shifted then, as he stared at me. His eyes narrowed suspiciously and I knew, I just knew, that he suspected something. He had to. You don't witness your daughter's death, just moments after she snorted a couple of lines, and not have a single clue.

“Andrea,” he began, his tone full of caution, “are you okay? You don't look good. Should I—”

“No,” I interjected roughly, shaking my head. “I'm fine, I'm okay. I'm just--”

“Are you pregnant?”

I gawked at my father, shocked, and realized I wished that's all it was.

“No,” I answered, shaking my head. “Vinnie and I ... we had some sushi last night and I don't think it's sitting well,” I lied.

He nodded with understanding. “That'll do it. Okay, well, I'll let you finish up in here. But, honey pie,” his worried gaze dropping to my trembling hands, “if there's ever anything you need, if you ever need help ... We're always here, okay? I'm always here.”

There were still traces of that innocent little girl, trapped somewhere beneath the sins I'd committed over the past several months, and she cried. She screamed out now, urging my legs to run toward him, pleading to beg him for salvation. But I remained still while the anxious high ate away at me, corroding my blood and guts, as my stupid, numb lips said, “Thanks, Daddy. But I'm fine. Really. Everything's fine.”

CHAPTER THIRTY-THREE

VINNIE

"What the hell do you call this?"

I glanced up from the pie I was making to look in Jenna's direction. "What?"

She thrust her hands toward a different pizza, fresh out of the oven. "Look at this!"

"I'm lookin'."

My older sister gawked at me before aiming pinched fingers at the pie, to peel a used cigarette butt out of the mess of cheese and sauce. I grimaced, not knowing how it got there or when, and then flinched when she threw it at my shoulder.

"I don't know—"

"You don't know a lot, do you?" she accused, her face red with anger.

"I'm sorry. I've been so—"

"Distracted, tired, busy," she rattled off. "Yeah, I know. We both do." She looked over her shoulder at Moe, standing at the register. "And we're sick of the excuses, Vinnie. We're done."

The fury was quick to strike as I narrowed my eyes. “Are you *firing* me?”

“No,” she groaned, closing her eyes and planting her hands on her hips. “But I'm sendin' you home today. You need a break, you need to ... I dunno, reassess and think, and I can't have you poisoning customers.”

I didn't want to go home. Andy wouldn't be there yet and all I'd have to keep me company, would be the ghost of my father, lurking around every corner and door. That was the last thing I needed. So, I shook my head, ready to plead with my sister. But she held up a finger and sharpened her stern glare.

“I'm not negotiating, Vin. Get the hell out of here. Zach's comin' by later for a sonogram appointment, so you can come back to see him. But I don't want you here now.”

Jenna was a stubborn woman—she'd inherited the trait from our father—and there was no point in arguing when her mind was already made up. So, I collected my stuff and stormed out, ignoring the curious faces of a few diners.

I wandered the streets for a while, enjoying a cool bite in the late summer air. This had been one hell of a summer, but fall was coming soon, and I couldn't wait, as I occasionally tipped my head back to breathe deep and fill my lungs.

Eventually, I grew tired of walking and knew I had to go home. And it wasn't all that bad, walking through the door into the empty kitchen. I saw Andy's hospital shoes by the door, her sweatshirt hanging over the back of a chair, and a book she'd brought home from work on the table. All these little traces of her seemed to mask what was really in this place, and I could live with that.

I sat on the couch and watched TV, doing my best to ignore the stockpile of cocaine on the coffee table. I didn't like to get high without Andy, but I was also exhausted, unable to stay awake without its influence keeping me energized. Before long I'd fallen asleep, only to be woken up by someone knocking at the door.

"Yo, Vin! You in there?"

It was Zach. Fucking Zach, showing up unannounced. I instantly flew into a panic, grabbing the bags of coke off the coffee table and shoving them under the couch cushions, before rushing to answer the door.

"Hey," I said, breathlessly. "Sorry, I was sleeping."

"Yeah, Jen told me you've been tired and shit," he said, brushing past me and inviting himself in. He slowly surveyed the place—the floor, table, walls—then said, "Holy shit ... the hell is goin' on here?"

My entire nervous system took a jolt as I asked, "What do you mean?"

My brother shook his head. "Vin," he bent over and picked up a used paper plate, "this place is a fuckin' mess. Don't you guys clean?"

I didn't have an answer for him. The truth was, I couldn't remember the last time the apartment was swept. I couldn't remember the last time I'd even thought about it. Not when all of my time at home was spent getting high and having sex. It was a miracle that I managed to do laundry every once in a while.

Zach slowly walked through the apartment, shaking his head and sighing, probably thinking about what Pops would've said if he was alive. I bit my tongue, watching warily as he got closer to the couch. Hoping that he wouldn't have a sudden urge to lift the cushions, hoping that I had hidden it all, and hoping he'd turn around and get the hell out.

"Yo," I said, as he got closer to the couch, "I wanna smoke. You wanna go outside with me?"

He glanced over his shoulder, then nodded. "Yeah, sure."

Relieved, I snatched my cigarettes and lighter off the table in a hurry. I made a beeline for the window, urging him with my mind to follow, and thank Christ, he did. He was close behind me and I opened the window, ready to step over the ledge and onto the fire escape.

"Wait a second."

I squeezed my eyes shut. "What's up?"

Zach was still for a moment, just staring in the direction of the couch. I had hidden the cocaine, though. I was sure of it. But he kept staring, and then he slowly walked over. Until, just as my palms began to sweat, he bent over.

"What the hell is this?"

I didn't want to look.

I had to look.

Turning, I saw him checking out the mirror and gift card still on the coffee table. It wasn't coke, and my heart calmed just a little. But Zach and I had walked that path together. He knew things, he saw things, and right now, he saw something.

Why the hell hadn't I tucked those away with everything else?

“I dunno,” I said, playing stupid. “Just some crap.”

“Some crap,” he mocked, picking the mirror up and inspecting it closely. “Some crap, huh?”

“Yeah.”

His glare turned on me as he held the mirror up. “Then, what the fuck is *this* shit, Vinnie?” he shouted.

“It's a fuckin' mirror, Zach,” I muttered sardonically, then swallowed as he licked a finger.

“So, this white shit all over it, is just dust, right? Nothin's gonna happen when I do this, right?” He swiped his wet fingertip along the reflective surface and I instinctively stepped forward. He raised a brow. “What?”

“N-Nothin',” I stammered. “Just, that's fuckin' gross.”

“It's just dust, though, right?” he challenged, before rubbing his fingertip against his gums, and I began to pray.

First, I prayed it really was dust. I prayed he'd feel like an asshole and leave. But then, as his lip began to curl and his head began to shake, I prayed that he'd take it easy on me. I prayed he'd realize that I'm not him, and that I'm not strong. That I'm not able to just break free from the demons that still have me shackled to their bed.

“Zach, listen—”

“Shut the fuck up.”

My lips pressed together, before I tried again. “Zach, you gotta—”

I was interrupted by a whistling sound passing my ear, as the mirror flew by, and then shattered on the wall behind me.

“Where the fuck is it?”

I shook my head. “W-What—”

“Do not play stupid with me, you fuckin' asshole. Don't you fuckin' dare play stupid,” he said, stepping forward and pointing his stern finger at my face. “Now, tell me where the fuck it is before I tear this place apart.”

“I-I don't—”

Hard knuckles met soft flesh with a sickening *thwack* as Zach's fist came in contact with my cheek. A blinding throb began only seconds after impact, along with a sharp sting and trickling heat. Stunned, I brought my hand to my face and came away with blood.

“Where is it, Vinnie?” he asked again in a frighteningly calm tone. But when I didn't answer, he just snickered. “Fine. Don't tell me. I'll find it myself.”

The pain in my face was nothing compared to the shame I felt, as I watched my older brother head straight toward the couch. He never needed to hunt for it. He just wanted to hear it from me, and I’d failed him, again. He tore the cushions away, revealing the bags of coke. And I wondered then, as he stood over the pile, chest puffed and heaving with anger, if he felt the temptation at all. If his own little devil had come out of hibernation at the kiss of blow numbing his gums.

I took a timid step closer and said, “You can do some, if you want.”

Zach squeezed his eyes shut and pinched the bridge of his nose. “Shut up, Vin.”

“Seriously,” I said in a rush, hurrying to the couch and picking one of the bags up. “I'll cut some lines. I can—”

I choked on the words as my back was slammed against the wall. My eyes closed against the impact as the air was thrust from my lungs. When I opened them again, I saw the face of my big brother, red-cheeked and fiery-eyed.

“What the fuck happened to you, man?” he asked. “We were good, Vinnie. We were clean. So, what the fuck *happened*?”

I couldn't run from this. I couldn't hide. He had me cornered, with his hands at my collar, and for once, I decided to tell someone the truth.

“I couldn't do it anymore,” I admitted quietly, dropping my gaze to his fists, gripping my t-shirt. “I-I couldn't fuckin' stand bein' alone.”

“You could've said somethin'!” he shouted, thrusting my back against the wall once more. “Goddamn, Vinnie, you were supposed to say somethin'!”

I rolled my eyes to the ceiling, shaking my head and fighting the emotion as it clogged my throat and bit at my nose. “Yeah, okay,” I snickered, “and then what? Get in the middle of the shit you got goin' on with Greyson and Jen? Or make you miss work and fuck up your business? I don't think so.”

"I would've helped you. I want to help you *now*."

He put his guard down, loosening his hold on my neck, and I grasped at the chance to have the upper hand. I pulled away and shoved him back.

"I don't need your fuckin' help," I fired at him. "I got this shit under control."

Zach stared at me, breaking my heart with a glare that said he no longer recognized me. I was still his brother, the kid he'd grown up with, the guy he fucked up with, but he had changed since then and I was now a stranger. Someone that he used to know.

"You got it under control?" He shook his head, slapping a hand against his thigh, then gestured back toward the couch. "You call this under control? What the fuck happens when Jen finds out? Or, hey, what about Andy? What happens when your *wife* finds out about this?" And I guess my silence spoke volumes because he said, "Oh, so you're doin' it *together*. Well, that's just great."

I wanted to remind him that he was once no better than me. I wanted him to remember how he'd use his mouth in exchange for a dime bag. I could still vividly recall guarding a door, with my back turned, while I listened to my brother use his body to score us some blow. I could've said all of this shit to him and done it in vivid detail. But I remained silent, afraid of how he'd reply, as I watched him push the hair out of his eyes and shake his head.

"I don't want you anywhere near me," he said, as he backed out of the living room.

He felt it, that old, nagging itch, and I knew I could've persuaded him to stay. But I didn't have it in me to tear him down, too. Not when he had a kid on the way. He was better than this. He was better than me.

"Do you understand me, Vinnie?"

I snapped my eyes to his and said, "You don't want me near you, I get it."

"No. I don't think you do. As long as you're doin' this shit, I want *nothing* to do with you. You won't come to my house. You won't come near my kid. You get me?"

My brows drew together and I saw red. "Wait, what the fuck? You're writing me off?"

He thrust his hands into his hair, gripping the strands between his fingers. "I've been down this fuckin' road before, Vinnie! I know where it goes. And if you're around and you're doin' this shit, I don't trust myself to stay away from it, and I can't do that. I *won't*."

"So, you're punishin' me for being weak? You're weak, too, asshole!"

"Yes! I am! And that's why I gotta stay far, far away from you. 'Cause *you* might wanna throw your life away, *you* might not give a fuck, but I like the shit I have goin' on, and I don't wanna lose it."

"Oh, how fuckin' nice for you," I spat, cutting my hand through the air. "You and your perfect life. What a goddamn success story," I snickered bitterly, shaking my head. "I'd hate for you to lose your nice, big house or your cushy job or—"

“Or *you*!” he yelled over me, bringing his fist down on the dining table. “You fuckin' idiot, I don't wanna watch you die!”

His voice caught in his throat and his eyes dropped to stare at the floor. And I had nothing to say, to reassure him that I wasn't going to die, because, the truth is, I'd been lying to Andy. I knew that, if I didn't stop this now, I wouldn't see the other side of it. I wasn't going to be okay. I knew this, and Zach knew it, too. But Andy didn't. She didn't want to see the truth that she too was barreling toward the end at lightning speed. That’s why she so easily believed my bullshit.

Turns out I'm a pretty good liar after all.

The apartment fell thick with silence. Zach rubbed at the back of his neck, warding off the emotion that kept biting at his quivering bottom lip. And that broke my heart, that it was so hard for him to say goodbye.

“If you're ever ready to get help,” he finally said, his voice low and tight, “I want you to come to me. But until that point, you stay the hell away.”

I nodded. “Okay.”

A quiet sob escaped his lips. “I love you, man. I fuckin' love you and I ... I wish that was enough. I just ... I wish that was enough.”

He didn't wait for me to reply because he knew I wouldn't. He also didn't wait for me to change my mind because he knew I wouldn't. He just rapped his knuckles against the table, where we'd shared countless dinners in Brooklyn, and then, he left.

CHAPTER THIRTY-FOUR

VINNIE

When Pops had died, I thought the world as I'd known it had fallen apart. I thought that was the absolute worst I could ever feel, the absolute lowest I could go.

But I'd been wrong.

Zach had punched me in the face, then written me off. My big brother. My best friend. My partner in crime. And he had done it to protect himself and the life he had created. I couldn't help but wonder, if he'd never gotten lucky, would he have still walked away? Would it have been so easy?

I was sure he had already told Jenna. I knew she'd already had some inkling as to what was going on, and I was sure she'd stand by him in the decision to give up on me. And why not? She was pregnant. She was carrying my brother's baby, to give him and Greyson a family. She also had her own kids, her husband, her house ...

And what did I contribute to all of that? Someone else to worry about? Someone else to take care of? It occurred to me that maybe it wasn't me who had been taking care of Pops, but the other way around. And now that he was gone, really fucking gone, who was going to take care of me now? Andy?

I sniggered at the thought. I loved Andy, truly, but I had been right about our relationship from the start. She was too good, I was too bad, and I was always destined to ruin her.

I *did* ruin her.

As I sat on the couch, beside the pile of coke, the door opened and in walked my wife. Looking beautiful and so much like something I never should've called mine in the first place.

"Hey," she said cheerfully, dropping a heavy-looking garbage bag on the floor.

"What's in the bag?"

"I told you, remember? I was grabbing clothes from my parents' place."

"Oh," I nodded, recalling our conversation from the morning, "right."

It was then that she noticed my face. The cut on my cheek, the blood I hadn't yet washed off, and the ugly bruise that threatened to seal my eye shut. Zach had hit me hard and the evidence of the beating, had Andy rushing to me and dropping at my side.

"Oh, my God, baby! What happened?" The nurse I'd originally known came out then, touching areas of my face with a delicate touch.

"Zach punched me."

“What? Why?” She stood up and rushed into the bathroom, returning with a first aid kit I hadn't been aware we owned.

“To teach me a lesson.”

Her eyes jumped from me to beside the couch and I followed her widened gaze to find nothing there. When I asked, she shook her head hurriedly and insisted, as always, that she thought she'd seen a spider.

There were never any spiders.

Returning her attention to my face, she soaked a cotton ball in rubbing alcohol before dabbing at my cheek and saying, “What kind of lesson?”

“Drugs are bad.”

She stopped her ministrations and stared at me, frozen. “He knows?”

Nodding, I replied, “Yep.”

“What is he going to do about it?”

I could tell from the look in her eyes that she was worried of being caught, of being found out, and I shook my head reassuringly. “Nothin',” I said. “Well, except for cutting me outta his life.”

Her momentary relief was wiped away with heart wrenching sympathy. “Baby, I'm sorry.”

I shrugged. “Whatever.”

Andy finished tending to my wound with a few butterfly stitches and a frozen bag of peas held to my cheek. She didn't think it was broken but said that it'd look worse before it got better, and that was just fine with me. I deserved it.

Afterward, she declared we needed to get high and run away for a while. The red flags waved wildly, but what the hell was the point in listening now? So, I agreed, and then watched as she ran to her purse.

"I already opened this one, so we should finish it up," she told me, hurrying over with a baggie that looked to be about half empty. She looked at the coffee table and asked, "Where's the mirror?"

I pointed at the opposite wall. "Over there in about a thousand pieces."

"Oh. Okay." She was unfazed and ran again for her purse, while something peculiar, something different, began to nag at my mind.

"Hey, sweetheart," I began, as she came back with a compact in hand, "did you get that shit from your bag?"

"What? This?" She held up the coke, dangling it from her fingertips, and I nodded. "Yeah, I brought some to my parents' house."

"You, *what*?" I asked, raising my voice.

Andy was surprised by my tone and stammered, "I-I-I brought it to my—"

"I heard you." I stood up, thrusting my hands into my hair and beginning to pace. "Oh, fuckin' God ..."

This wasn't supposed to happen. We always did this shit *here*, in the apartment, where I could oversee things and maintain some semblance of control. But the control I thought I'd had was nothing but an illusion, just something I'd told myself to make it seem like I was handling it. But I now realized, it was just another lie that

I'd been holding onto. The only one that I had actually believed.

"You weren't supposed to do that," I muttered, scrubbing a hand over my face. "Goddammit, you weren't supposed to do that ..."

What had I really thought would happen? Did I really think I could introduce her to this shit and expect we'd always be on the same page? I had always been very disciplined in my drug usage, even in my youth, but why had I ever been stupid enough to expect she would be the same way? Why hadn't I known better?

"Vinnie," Andy said, rushing over to take my hands in hers, "it's okay, just relax."

"I can't fuckin' relax!" My anger was explosive and I pulled my hands from her grasp. "Jesus Christ, Andy! What if someone saw you?"

She lowered her gaze and worried her bottom lip. "Nobody saw me, but ..."

"But?"

"My dad did walk in but I don't think he saw—"

"Jesus fuckin' Christ! This is why we only do this shit here! This is why we don't ever take it out! Goddammit!" I was pacing, gripping my hair in a white-knuckled grasp and thinking of every possible worst-case scenario.

"I don't understand what the big deal is. I—"

"And *that*," I pointed at her, "is the problem. Do you understand how many people I've known who've ended up in prison over this shit?"

She shook her head, keeping her rapidly blinking gaze on the floor. "I don't—"

"A lot, Andy. I've known a lot of people who've had the cops called on them. What if your old man had called the cops on *you*? What if, right now, you were sittin' in a precinct somewhere while the police raided this apartment? Huh? And that's the least of the problems that could've happened. Do you even realize that?"

She didn't, and that was an issue. Maybe the biggest one of all.

"Fuck ..." I turned away from her quiet, blank stare, to face the couch and pile of coke. Then, I asked, "Why are you here?"

"What? Because I live here—"

"No," I spun on my heel to face her, "why are you *here*, with me?"

Her jaw flapped several times before she responded. "I-I love—"

"I know, you love me. But *why*? Why did you let this get that far? Why didn't you turn around when you found out about this shit and run far away?"

She began to cry. I didn't take pride in her tears, but I did feel relief. They meant she still had a conscience, that she could still feel.

"I don't know," she admitted. "I just ... I didn't want to leave you, and I wanted to see—"

"Wanted to see *what*?"

"I-If it really does help you escape. Baby, why ... why are you asking me—"

I stared off toward the wall and asked myself more than her, “What the hell could've been so bad you needed to escape?”

Suddenly, none of it made any sense, none of *her*, none of *us*. What the hell was I even doing with her? I could still remember the initial spark and what I had found so appealing. It had been the anomaly of her innocent confidence and her brazen reluctance. She had been intriguing to me and I'd gone for it, not realistically thinking that this good, sweet woman would want anything to do with a low-life like me.

But that had all changed somewhere along the way. *She* had changed. And it had been me to change her, I knew that, but was there something else? Something I had missed?

“Why did you need to escape?” I asked her, turning around to face the tears streaming from her eyes.

“You wouldn't understand.”

“No,” I said, shaking my head. “You don't get to play that game with me. I am ruining my life for the shit we're doin’ together and I need to know if it's at least worth it.”

“You have your reasons and I have mine,” she offered with a weak shrug.

“Why, Andy? Just tell me why.”

She closed her eyes and pressed her hands over her temples. “Because I needed it to stop. I needed it to be quiet, in order to be happy.”

I narrowed my eyes and watched her as the tears continued to fall. She was shrinking before me, wilting in on herself as the truth finally blossomed from the lies.

"What?"

Her eyes opened and she looked off to somewhere beside me. "I, um ... I don't know how to even tell you this. I never wanted you to know. But I hear this sound all the time, like TV static or, um, radio interference. It's always there, and it's so annoying. But there's something else ..."

"Okay. What is it?"

"I ... I see, um," she swallowed hard against the war she was fighting, "I see ... spirits."

I was sure I hadn't heard her correctly. I was also sure I was going crazy, if I wasn't there already.

"Andy," I groaned, pressing my fingertips to my forehead. "Come on."

"No!" she shouted, a fresh air of determination taking over. "It ... It's been happening my whole life, but I didn't realize it until my imaginary friend, Jamie, didn't go away. My family thought I was insane, and so, I've had to pretend that it's not there anymore, but it *is*. It never went away. And this is why I've been single forever, because it's so distracting to hear this, this *shit* all the damn time, and to see them, and all the shit they need me to—what?"

I could only shrug and shake my head, but when I didn't speak, she pressed harder. "What, Vinnie? Tell me exactly what you're thinking right now and justify every one of my reasons for doing this crap with you, instead of just being honest with you in the first place. Go ahead."

I pulled in a deep breath and lifted my shoulders. "I'm thinkin' that I really fucked you up. I-I-I fuckin' drove you crazy."

"No," she insisted, shaking her head fervently. "No, I swear to God, this is the truth."

"Your family was right," I went on. "You didn't wanna listen but ... fuck ..."

"Your father!" she shouted, desperation making her shrill, as she thrust a hand out toward the area beside me. "He's right there!"

A wave of anger swept me away from my concern at the mention of Pops. "Don't you dare go there with me."

But Andy wouldn't listen. "He's been here for months. I needed to make him leave—"

"Enough!"

"—so I tried getting high and it worked. For the first time ever, something actually worked. But then, I get sober, and there he is, just staring—"

"God, Andy, shut the fuck up!"

She shook her head, stepping toward me without caution. "He's so worried about you, baby. He won't go away, not until—"

Thwack!

Her hand immediately flew to touch the spot on her cheek where I had slapped her, now hot and bright red. Fresh tears formed in her eyes and I faltered before pulling her against my chest.

“I'm sorry,” I whispered, shaking and appalled with myself. “I'm so sorry. I shouldn't have done that, I just ... I just couldn't listen to it anymore.”

Andy sniffled noisily, soaking my t-shirt with her tears. “I knew I sh-shouldn't ha-have told you,” she sobbed. “I knew y-y-you wouldn't be able to handle it.”

There was a hollow ache building in my chest that came along with my reluctant acceptance. Andy was sick. She was mentally unstable, and whether I had made her that way or not, I didn't know. But what I did know was, I was hurting her, physically and psychologically, and that it would only get worse. I knew that the best thing I could do, the best way to show my love for her, was to let her go.

“Sweetheart,” I said, pulling her away from my chest.

Her cheek wore the mark of my palm and I swore I couldn't hate myself more than I did in that moment, and I knew that I deserved the pain I was about to suffer. Every last drop of it.

“What?” she asked, wiping her tears with the sleeve of her shirt.

“I want you to go back home to your parents, okay?”

Realization drew her brows together tight. “What? No.” She shook her head. “I'm not ... If it has to do with, with ...” She lifted her hand to delicately touch her tender cheek. “I understand w-why you did it. I don't—”

“I fucked up, okay?” I cut her off. “I fucked up and I accept that, 'cause I'm used to it. But I won't keep draggin' you down with me. I would rather fuckin' die than watch you kill yourself with this shit, and I know that if you stay with me, that's exactly what's gonna happen. I love you too much to wanna do that. I *can't* do that."

I pushed past her with determination charging my bones, and began to collect her things. Anything I could find, I gathered into a pile on the table, all while she followed at my heels, grappling at my arms and begging for me to stop. But I wouldn't stop. I couldn't. Not when her life was on the line.

"I'm gonna call you an Uber," I told her, surprised by the calmness in my tone. "You can take all this stuff with you now, or I'll have it sent to your parents' place, but either way—"

"You just need time to adjust," she tried to reason as I took my phone out. "You, you need to wrap your head around it, I get it. S-So, I'll go back and stay overnight and give you some space, okay? But tomorrow, I'll—"

"No," I interrupted gently.

"Yes! I'll come back and we can talk about everything, okay? W-We can get help together. We'll go to rehab, we'll go to therapy, we'll ... we'll ..."

Her eyes roamed the apartment, searching for the thing that would convince me to back away from my resolve. She was panicking and I understood why, because sometimes the hardest things are the right things to do. And this, letting her go, was the rightest thing I'd ever done.

"Andy," I said, pocketing my phone and knowing the car was on its way. "Listen. I don't want—"

"What about what *I* want?" she cried, her face a mess of tears and snot. "When the fuck do I get to choose what I want?"

"You can choose whatever you want, sweetheart," I said, reaching out to pull her against me one last time. "But you don't get to choose me."

***

When the car arrived, I didn't have to drag her from the apartment building. I had thought I might need to, but she went willingly, with the promise that she would be back—or was it a threat? But what she hadn't realized, when she stormed out like a kid being forced onto the school bus, was there would be nothing to come back to.

"So, this is rock bottom," I said to the empty apartment later on, as I sat down in front of the pile of coke, now back on the coffee table.

After Andy left, I'd had the sense to clean up a bit, because Zach had been right. The place was a fucking mess, and if there'd been any truth to Andy's psychobabble and Pops really was here, I could only imagine how pissed he was.

"Zach hates me," I said, opening five of the bags and dumping them together on the largest shard of mirror I could find. "Jenna will, too, if she doesn't already." I cut the lines thick, using more than I normally did. "I can't run the restaurant. I'm too irresponsible, or fucked up, or somethin'."

I clasped my hands together to hover over the three, fat lines, like I was praying over my last supper, and tipped my head back to look at the ceiling. I wasn't sure if I needed to, in order for Pops to hear me, if what Andy said was true, but I did it anyway.

"You asked me why I did it," I said. "You wanted to know, but I wouldn't tell you then, 'cause I didn't want you to feel bad. But now, I got nothin' to feel bad for. It's just the truth, nothin' more than that."

I pointed a finger at a splotchy, old water stain. "*You* did this. And look," I shrugged, "I made my choices, that's all on me, but none of this ever would've happened if it weren't for you. *You* drove Ma away. *You* were never there for us. *You* gave us the need to run away from our shitty problems. And yeah, okay, sure. You did get us into rehab, so go ahead and pat yourself on the back for that one. But what the fuck does it all even matter when I'm where I'm at now, because *you* didn't think we needed to know you were fuckin' dyin'?"

I choked on my own voice and wiped a hand over my mouth. "Fuck. I swore I was gonna hold my shit together here," I muttered, before continuing.

"You let me build my life around you," I said, dropping my gaze from the ceiling to the empty room around me. "You never prepared me for this, and maybe that's on me, too, you know? Maybe I should've been more realistic. But you were my *dad*. Wasn't that your fuckin' job, to prepare me for this shit?" I swiped my arm beneath my nose as I sniffled. "I'm fucked up because *you* fucked up, and I just can't deal with it anymore. I'm all alone here, and man, I'm not gonna let myself go through another day of this, this *pain*." I laid a hand over my chest and tried to rub the ache away. "I can't do it. And I don't have to, so I won't. Sorry if that disappoints you, Pops, but you disappointed me, too, man. So, consider us even."

Then, clearing my throat, I leaned over the coffee table and looked forward to never feeling this way ever again.

CHAPTER THIRTY-FIVE

ANDREA

As he collected my stuff and ignored my pleas, he claimed to have ruined my life. Never once willing to stop and understand how he had actually made my life better.

He had given me love. He had given me hope. And as wrong as everything we had done together was, he had given me happiness. Isn't that all any of us can hope for in this life, just to be happy, whatever it takes to get there?

But now, as I sat on the bed in my room at home, I ached with the last thing he had given me: my first broken heart.

Of course, my parents hadn't been expecting me when the Uber dropped me off. It had only been hours since I'd last been there, declining their dinner invitation, but there I was, walking in just as they were cleaning up the meal. On the way over, between bouts of tears, and as the nerves wormed themselves in and out of my intestines, I'd wondered what I'd say to them once I got there. How could I explain another surprise visit? And how was I going to explain that I was, apparently, going to be staying for at least a few days until I made up with Vinnie? I had my doubts, but by the time I got to the house, it was all planned out. I had felt confident and prepared, but the moment I stepped through the door I realized, you can never be prepared for when you're crawling home with your tail between your legs and a man-sized handprint on your cheek.

"Oh, my God, Andrea!" Mom had cried out the second I stepped through the door. "Oh, honey, what happened?"

She had rushed to me while Dad hung back, silently observing with murderous intent flaring in his eyes. I allowed Mom to lead me to the couch, where she instructed me to sit and wait while she got me some ice and something to eat.

Alone with my father, I looked at him and said, "Daddy ... I need help."

He hadn't wanted to talk to me then, not wanting my mother to hear everything just yet. And so, now I waited, laying in my old bedroom and wondering how I was supposed to confess to my father, that everything my mother and sisters were afraid of had, in fact, come true.

There was a soft knock and I told him to come in. He did, closing the door behind him, before coming to sit at the edge of my bed.

"So, before you say anything, I have to know," he began, "did Vinnie hit you?"

I stalled before nodding, but when his breath hitched under the weight of his anger, I said, "It's not what you think."

"I don't care what it is," he snapped, keeping his tone calm and controlled. "No man should ever raise a hand to a woman, ever. End of story."

"You don't even know the story," I answered quietly.

"Don't make excuses for him," he countered, glaring in my direction.

"I'm not." I sighed and sat up, wrapping my arms around my knees. "He slapped me because he thought he needed to shock me."

"Shock you, why?"

"Because ..." I licked my lips, discomforted by the dryness in my mouth. "I ... I have a, um ..." I found I couldn't say the words while looking at him, unsure that I could even say them at all. So, I laid my hands over my face and said, "I, um ... I have a ... a drug problem."

Dad's exhale was slow and pained. "Oh, God," he muttered quietly, and I dropped my hands to find him scrubbing his palm against his lips. "This is ... This is Vinnie's influence?"

The last thing I wanted was for my entire family to villainize my husband, and while I could never control the way they felt, the least I could do in his honor was defend him by telling the whole story.

And so, I did. I laid it all out for my dad. The spirits that had never stopped haunting me, and the depression and old habits that had eaten away at Vinnie until they could no longer be ignored. I told him about that first time, when I'd caught Vinnie succumbing to his demons on the couch and how my curiosity had gotten away from me, and then, all the times after. I left no detail hidden, not even the ones best left private, simply because this was a story I needed to tell, to give it away, to get over it. And when it was all done and out in the open, Dad sighed sadly and nodded as his palm cupped my knee.

"I'm glad that, when it was time to leave, you came home," he said, his voice gruff with sorrow and disappointment.

"I wasn't going to leave," I confessed, "but Vinnie made me. He sent me here."

Dad absorbed the information for a quiet moment, before he nodded and said, "Well, maybe there's some hope for him after all."

"Maybe," I muttered, remembering the vivid image given to me by Vincent.

"You have a long road ahead of you," Dad replied, with another nod. "You will go to rehab, and you will go to therapy, and ... whatever you need to sort out your, um ... issue. I'll make sure you get the absolute best care you can get—"

"Thank you," I croaked, swiping my hand beneath my nose.

Then, Dad held up a single finger and said, "But, you will *not* be in contact with Vinnie."

My jaw dropped with immediate distress. "What? I can't do that! He's my—"

"I don't care what he is to you, Andrea," he replied, his tone soft but unforgiving. "He's the one that got you into this mess and if I'm the one helping you get better, I won't put up with him ruining your progress."

It was all so final and I was far from being okay with it. But I could see the logic in what my father said, and my heart and shoulders sank with heavy defeat. I wished I had known that would be the last time I would see Vinnie. I wished I had said more, I wished I had at least said goodbye.

And, as if he could read my mind, my father offered a small, encouraging smile. "I can't tell you what's in the future, honey pie. I don't know if you'll be able to work things out with him one day, or if you were only meant to know him for a few months. None of us ever really know how long someone we love will be in our lives, but we can hope that no matter how long we have, we love them enough."

I struggled with my emotions, as I asked in a whisper, "Enough for what?"

He squeezed my knee in a loving grasp. "To make a difference."

I didn't know how to decipher those words at first, and all I could do was nod in reply. Then, I lost the battle against a long, wide yawn and Dad took the hint. He tucked me in, the way he used to when I was a little girl, and as he kissed my cheek, I settled into the fact that I still was his little girl. She was still in there, alive and well, and begging the damaged, adult me to remember and bring her back. It was my father's unconditional love that did that. He loved me enough to make that difference, and then, I understood.

Vinnie had put me in that car and sent me home, where he knew I would get the help I needed.

He had loved me enough, but what had I done for him?

The vision of his lifeless body, laying cold on the floor, filled my exhausted mind. I hadn't told him about it and I hadn't taken the time to know if it was a premonition or a warning. But I was afraid, and I used that fear to pick up the phone.

I hoped that would be enough.

CHAPTER THIRTY-SIX

ANDREA

Dad had talked to Mom, because like a coward, I couldn't face her myself. I couldn't stand to see the look of blatant disapproval and disappointment on her face. I couldn't handle hearing the horrible things she'd have to say about Vinnie. I was grateful for my father, who carried more of my burden than he ever should have, and when he dropped me off at the rehab facility the next day, I had hugged him tighter than I ever had before.

I didn't want him to leave. I didn't want to be left alone with all of these strange people and ghosts, in a place I was unfamiliar with. It was the first day of school jitters at their finest, but I managed to check myself in while holding my head high, and my father said he had never been more proud of me.

The withdrawal had been the worst.

Just hours after I'd checked into Hope Meadows Rehabilitation Center, the anxiety and agitation had begun. I worried about Vinnie, about the damage I'd done to my body, family, and future. The ghosts—all loved ones of the other patients—came to me in droves, and when the aches in my muscles and bones began, I couldn't take it anymore. Detox had begun, with a cocktail of medications, and so had the dreams.

Vinnie was in them, and he was always dead.

I always awoke unconvinced that he was truly gone. He would have come to me, I knew that in my heart, but that never stopped the tears from coming. It also never stopped the crack in my chest from widening, allowing for more of the good to spill out while all the bad and despair rushed in to fill me up.

I hadn't wanted to use more than I did then. Because, although I found I could handle the ghosts, I couldn't handle the despair of not having Vinnie there to hold the pieces of my heart together.

My therapist said it was just the withdrawal and that, with time and medical intervention, it would go away overtime. And after two months, the paranoia, anxiety, dreams, and insatiable cravings had faded. But the broken heart hadn't.

After my ninety days were over, I was released from Hope Meadows with a prescription for anti-anxiety meds and a new lease on life. My therapist was optimistic that, with a bit of positive direction, I could control the so-called visions I experienced without the urge to run back to the drugs. I was never sure if she had believed I saw the spirits, but it didn't matter. It was enough that I'd been honest with her, and that she hadn't called me crazy.

Dad picked me up in his Lexus and asked if I had made any friends. I snickered and rolled my eyes before saying, “I wasn't there to make friends, Daddy.”

“I just thought it'd be nice to have friends who understand what you're going through.”

I wanted to tell him that I did have someone who understood—my husband. But I had kept my promise and hadn't spoken to Vinnie in three months. I didn't know what he was doing, or if he was okay, and so, I said nothing.

The ride from Hope Meadows was long and when we finally got home, I found my sisters' cars in the driveway. I turned to Dad, horror and betrayal written all over my face. I hadn't spoken to my sisters since the night of their anniversary party and the last thing I wanted now, was to face their *I told you so* bullshit.

“They insisted,” he explained with a weak smile. “You don't have to talk with them. Just thank them for thinking of you and eat some dinner.”

“I really just want to go to bed,” I replied.

“I know, honey pie.” He reached out and tucked my hair behind my ear, treating me the way I felt—like a child, helpless and so painfully dependent. “If you want, I'll just tell them you're exhausted.”

I shook my head. “No, it's fine,” I said, taking a deep breath before opening the car door and heading inside.

Sitting on the couch, Willa and Meredith turned their heads the moment I walked in. Their expressions were of transparent judgment, staring at me as though they had never really known me, and I had to wonder why the hell they had bothered coming.

"Hey, Andrea," Willa spoke up first.

"Hey."

Meredith stood from the couch and walked around, slowly at first, to come to me with her arms outstretched and tears leaking from her eyes. "Oh, my God," she sobbed against my ear. "You're going to be okay. We got you."

I couldn't help shedding a couple of tears as Willa hurried over to wrap her arms around both of us. They whispered their tearful declarations of protection and support, and I slumped exhaustedly into their embrace. I don't know if they would've supported me as much if I'd walked through the door with my husband, instead of our father. I don't think they'd support Vinnie this much in the battle against his own demons. But still, I welcomed their love. I found I had needed it, that I had needed *them*, and I didn't need for them to love my husband to admit that I'd missed them.

I had missed them a lot.

And I found they weren't all that I'd missed, as I climbed the stairs to my room after dinner. I hesitated before opening the door, unsure of what I'd find on the other side. I hadn't seen Jamie since the day I told her to leave, not even after I'd returned home, rejected and sober. I was scared she was gone for good and that I'd thrown away my unconditional friend. But, after opening the door a crack, I found her there. Sitting on my bed, where she always was.

She was startled to see me there and jumped up from the bed, acting in a hurry, like she'd been caught doing something naughty. My heart ached, realizing she was going out of her way to not look at me. I wished so much that I could hug her, and the ache in my heart intensified with the realization that I had never once known what it was like to feel her in my arms.

"Jamie." My voice tripped along in my throat as I stepped into the room and closed the door.

She stilled in the center of the room, bowing her head to divert her eyes from me.

I moved closer as I said, "Jamie ... I'm sorry. I'm, I'm so sorry."

By the time I realized I was crying, the tears were already dripping from my chin. She looked so small. She was just a child in this big world, all by herself, and I'd tried to send her away. How could she ever forgive me for that when I couldn't forgive myself?

"I'm sorry," I repeated. "I was so messed up. I had gotten into some bad shit with Vinnie and I wasn't thinking. Please, look at me."

Reluctantly, Jamie raised her eyes to mine, as she twisted her fingers. She looked at me curiously, working her bottom lip between her teeth, then turned her head toward the desk. The memory of using drugs in my childhood bedroom came back to me, as vivid as if it'd just happened, and I nodded.

"Yeah," I answered, swallowing and fighting the battle against my cravings. "I did some bad stuff. But I'm done with it. No more. I don't want you to go away, okay? Please stay. Stay forever."

Jamie held up her pinkie finger and I tried to take it, watching as my pinkie passed through hers.

"Yes," I said with a nod. "I promise."

***

"Andrea!"

I turned at the sound of the familiar voice. Elle ran toward me in her scrubs and pink sneakers, blonde hair bopping wildly from side to side. My mouth dried down to sandpaper at the thought of talking to her. I had tried to avoid this, even using the guest elevator and sneaking in between shifts. But I had spent so much time thinking of a sneaky plan, that I'd forgotten Elle liked to come in a few minutes early for breakfast.

And now, I had to face her.

She stopped in front of me, cheeks red from the nipping wind. "Hey, did you not hear me calling you back there?"

I had.

"Oh, uh, no ... I don't think so. Sorry."

"Where the hell have you been, girl? I feel like it's been forever."

It hadn't been forever.

"Yeah, I know. I've been, um ..."

I stopped myself from continuing, as I thought about what I was about to do. Did I really want to make something up, when I now knew that a lie will always be uncovered, no matter how deep it's been buried? Was I prepared to lose another friend, another person who had always had my back? No. The answer was, no, I wasn't. But what damage would my truth do to our friendship? Did it even matter? Was a friend who was unwilling to accept the ugly truth, really a friend at all?

Elle cocked her head. “Yeah?”

I smiled and asked, “Do you have a few minutes?”

***

We sat in the atrium, with paper cups of coffee in hand. Elle was stiff with trepidation, as she sat at the edge of the stone bench. It was my fault for making her so nervous, with the anxious chewing of my bottom lip and the incessant tapping against the sides of my coffee. But I couldn't help it, as I recalled my sisters' initial reaction to Vinnie's past. They had written him off before they'd even gotten to know him, and while Elle knew me, this side of me had been kept a secret. What if she decided every part of me was better left as someone she once knew?

“So ...” She fidgeted with the plastic lid, flicking its thin edges with one, long nail.

I wetted my lips and decided this was it. I had enough problems to deal with; her opinion of me didn't have to be one of them.

“I turned in my badge today,” I admitted, keeping my eyes on the ground.

“Oh, my God, are you serious?”

I nodded. "Yeah ..."

"But," she shook her head with confusion, "*why*? You love this job!"

I took a deep breath and said, "No, I know. It's just ... I can't work here anymore. I, um ..." I rapidly wondered why I had thought this was a good idea, just before I said, "I have a history of substance abuse and I ... I can't handle the job anymore."

Elle was quiet, and when I finally looked at her, I found an expression of inquisitive suspicion. "Substance abuse? Is that," she gasped quietly, "is that why you've been forgetting things lately?"

My cheeks reddened, remembering the last few weeks I'd been at work. The medication mishaps, the days I showed up late, and the days I forgot to show up at all.

"Yeah, um ... it got pretty bad at the end, and Vinnie and I—"

"Wait. Was he using, too?"

I bit my lip before nodding. "He, um ... he was clean for years, but after his father died—"

"I get it," Elle interjected lightly, without the slightest hint of judgment tainting her tone. I found it surprising, and I guess my expression said as much because then she added, "My brother, Rob, is a recovering drug addict."

"Really?"

She nodded. "Yeah. He was in a hiking accident years ago that destroyed his leg, and long story short, he really enjoyed the pain meds. He's relapsed a few times over the years, but for now, he's doing okay."

My lips parted slightly, and I closed them immediately. I wasn't allowed to be shocked, not after what I'd just told her. But I couldn't help but think, *I've met Rob*. He'd never given me the impression of being troubled, or addicted to anything other than Diet Coke and Yankee games. But addiction doesn't have one face, does it? Sometimes it hides behind the guy down on his luck, just looking for an escape, and sometimes, it grabs ahold of a guy trying to recover from a broken leg … or a nurse just desperate to escape the ghosts.

"I'm sorry," I felt the need to say.

Elle offered a sad smile. "I am, too. I'm really gonna miss you."

Sighing, I nodded and stared out into the atrium, spotting the ghost of a young man following a doctor. "I'll miss you, too. I'm going to miss everything about this place, but ..." I turned back to her and smiled. "I really need to focus on getting my head on straight, you know?"

"I get it. I do. It's just ..." She released a deep, melancholic sigh. "Lunchtime isn't going to be the same."

I laughed, choking back the threat of emotion. "I'll come and visit."

She laughed with me, dabbing beneath her eyes with the hem of her sleeve. "Girl, you better!"

Then, she asked, "What made you do it, if you don't mind me asking?"

Looking down at the cold cup of coffee in my hand, I shrugged and said, “I was just looking for an escape.”

“But ... from what?” She laughed again, a bit uneasily this time, and added, “I’m sorry. It’s none of my business, and I am not judging you, I swear. It’s just ... you seem like you have it all together, you know? You live in a gorgeous house, and yeah, you live with your parents, but that’s not so bad. You’re beautiful. You’re smart. You’re funny. You recently married this guy who is absolutely gorgeous, and he has his demons, I get that now, but ... I just don’t understand, and I wish I did.”

For years, I had kept myself in the dark with my secret and its burdening static, out of fear of what others might think. But now, after my brief and harrowing stint with addiction, I knew what a true burden was. I now understood what it was truly like to be controlled by something against my will, and this ability wasn’t it. After years of living in the dark, I was suddenly ready to turn on the light.

So, I turned to my friend and asked, “Do you believe in ghosts?”

CHAPTER THIRTY-SEVEN

ANDREA

Too many months had passed since I'd last seen or heard from Vinnie. Now, it was winter and just a week before Christmas.

I was sad.

I thought about the apartment and wondered if he had decorated. I thought about what our tree might have looked like and wondered who's house we would have celebrated at. But mostly, I just thought about him and wondered if he was okay.

My father had been right in insisting I keep my distance from him. We were fire and gasoline, and together, we could set our world ablaze. There would be no recovery while even one of us was still using, but knowing this didn't stop the crack in my chest from pulsing with the ache of missing him. His voice. His laugh. The taste of nicotine on his tongue. God, how I ached, knowing for certain that this was the worst withdrawal I could ever experience. Knowing that he was the drug I would never recover from. And I didn't even know if he was still alive.

“She's killing me,” Mer muttered, as she rolled out the cookie dough.

“Come on, Andrea. Smile.” Willa poked me in the cheek with the end of a spoon, covered in sticky, gooey dough.

I batted her away and wiped at my cheek. “Get out of here.” Mer threw a sprinkle of flour my way, dusting my hair and red sweater. “Mom! Make them stop!”

Mom didn't even bother to glance up from her cookie sheet as she mumbled, “Girls, stop trying to make your sister smile.”

Sticking my tongue out defiantly, I set back to work, balling up the sugar cookie dough and dropping the little mounds onto my tray. I thought about Vinnie and how much I would have loved having him here, with his arms around my waist and his breath against my ear, as he watched me partake in the annual tradition of baking Christmas cookies.

“Seriously though, Andrea,” Willa whined, pressing candies into her batch of oatmeal butterscotch chip. “We know you're sad and you're going through a lot, and really, we sympathize with it. But sometimes, the best thing you can do is just to decide that, you know what, today, I'm going to have a good day.”

“People who choose to be sad will never find the power to choose happiness,” Mer chimed in, sounding like she was reading from a cue card. Willa, Mom, and I all turned to look at her and she shrugged. “I dunno, I saw it on Instagram.”

“Well, it's freakin' lame,” Willa murmured. “But, you know, there is some truth to it.”

My mouth remained shut as I went to the oven with my full sheet of cookies-to-be and slid it in. As I closed the door and set the timer, I wished they'd just let me fantasize about my husband and the Christmas we should've had in peace.

“Maybe you should go on a date,” Mer suggested slyly.

That had my attention. “Uh, what?”

She shrugged. “I'm just saying—”

“I'm married!”

She and Willa exchanged a look that could only mean one thing: they didn't take my marriage seriously. And that hurt.

“Thanks,” I muttered under my breath, wiping my dirty hands on my apron and noticing flour on my leggings and grasping at the opportunity to step out. “I'm just gonna change—”

Guilt washed over Mer's face. “Andrea, I wasn't saying you have to—”

“It's fine, really. I just gotta change these pants and I'll be right back,” I cut her off, leaving the kitchen and heading for the stairs, when Mom stopped me.

Our relationship had been strained ever since the wedding, but not from a lack of trying. It’s just that, sometimes pushing for a relationship to work, is more damaging than simply letting it be. I felt that was very much the case for us and I hated it. I hated feeling that I was to blame, just for falling in love with a guy my family didn't approve of. I hated feeling like I'd thrust a wedge between us with every poor decision I had made. It was crippling and enough to make me cry if I let myself think about it too much.

Now, she stood next to me at the bottom of the stairs with a soft and sympathetic gaze, as she asked to talk to me. I shrugged like it didn't make a difference to me either way, while also desperately wanting that connection we once had to reattach itself.

“What's up?” I asked, when we were behind the closed door of my bedroom.

Mom moseyed around, like she was wandering through a museum. Her hands stayed clasped behind her back, as her eyes surveyed the scrapbook of memories, tacked to the walls and closet doors. Pictures of the past. Posters of bands I doubted were still together. Things I never thought to take down.

“I can't believe you still have these,” she commented, pointing at my pyramid of Beanie Babies.

“They're worth something on eBay,” I reasoned with an I-don't-care shrug.

She touched the edge of my four-poster bed and asked, “What did you ever see in him?”

I froze on my way to the dresser and stared ahead at the chipped white paint and crystal drawer pulls. Without asking for clarification, I turned to her and replied, “I-I don't know. We don't always choose—”

"Humor me," she said quietly, as she lowered herself to sit on the bed. "I get that he's a good-looking guy, and he's funny and ... well, I'm assuming the sex is—"

"Mom," I groaned, turning and shaking my head as I resumed the walk to the dresser.

"Anyway, I'm just saying, I get it on the surface. But ... after everything else ..." She sighed noisily. "I guess I'm just confused about what the appeal is there. I don't understand it, Andrea, but I want to. I want to get it."

Keeping my mouth shut, I rifled through my drawer for another pair of leggings. My mind was caught somewhere between wanting to scream at her to leave and laying it all out on the table, in its purest, grittiest detail. But what good would it do either way? It wouldn't change anything. Nothing could bring him back to me or change the opinions of my family. It would serve only as wasted breath and nothing more.

"I don't want—"

The doorbell interrupted my protest. I looked over my shoulder at my mother, silently asking if she'd been expecting anybody and she only shrugged. Together, we strained to listen through the closed door as Willa answered the door.

"Um ... yes, I'll just go get her ..." There was uncertainty in her tone, and then there was the sound of footsteps against the stair treads. "Andrea?"

My stomach performed somersaults as I called out, "Yeah?"

"Someone's here for you."

Fidgeting with the leggings held in my grasp, I hoped with every hope I could muster that it was my lost husband, coming to reclaim the heart that was rightfully his. "Who is it?" I asked, all but crossing my fingers.

"Some guy named Moe?"

All hope was washed away with a nauseating tidal wave of dread. My mouth flooded with the taste of bile as every possible horrible reason for him being here flooded my mind. Mom watched me curiously, asking what was wrong and who was Moe.

"Tell him," I swallowed at the sour taste on my tongue, "tell him I'll be right there."

Ignoring my mother, I pulled in a deep breath, pressing a hand to my stomach and begging the rumbling organ to stay calm until I knew exactly why Moe had come for a visit. Then, I left the room, still in my dirty leggings, with my mother following close behind.

He stood on the other side of the door, his long, thin dreadlocks pulled back and half-hidden beneath a grey knitted cap. The look of disdain on his face was warning enough and I said a silent prayer as I took the last few steps to the door, promising that I would never ask for anything else, as long as Vinnie was okay.

Please, please, please, let him be okay.

"Hey, Moe," I greeted him through the glass storm door, before opening it and saying, "Come in. It's freakin' cold out there."

He shook his head, putting on a painfully forced smile. "I'm good out here, honey. Thanks, though." Then, as I stepped outside to join him in the cold, he took a moment, taking me in with kind, somber eyes. “You look good, girl. You been takin' care of yourself?”

I nodded, crossing my arms against the bitter chill. “Trying, anyway.”

“Good. That's ... that's good ...” He turned to look through the door, his eyes vacant of all emotion. All but sorrow.

I followed his gaze and there, at the bottom of the stairs, was Jamie. Her eyes widened with childish joy and excitement, jittering from one foot to the other and waving her hands wildly. As if she was trying to get someone's attention.

And the visions struck like lightning. Quick and powerful.

Jamie on her father's lap in front of the fireplace.

Jamie in her bedroom—my room—with the dollhouse her father built.

Jamie in the pool, struggling, and then, no longer breathing. All while her father took a quick phone call inside.

Her father. Jamie's father.

I turned to him, nearly crippled by the thundering anguish that crushed against my heart. I couldn't believe I hadn't noticed before and that I hadn't put the pieces together. They had the same eyes, the same nose, and the same grin that could brighten the most dismal of moments.

Except this one.

“Sorry,” Moe said, turning from the door to brighten the moment with his daughter's identical smile. “I thought I could do this, but ... damn, I just ... I just can't believe you actually live in *this* house."

"You lived here," I whispered, choking out the words between the chipped pieces of my forever breaking heart.

He took a deep breath before nodding. "I did," he said, tipping his head back to look at the slatted porch ceiling. "The place looks a little different, but ... it still looks like home." Then, he looked back to me, eyes narrowed with curiosity. "How did you know that?"

I pushed myself to smile, as I ignored Jamie and her deafening static, telling me to tell him. Telling me to set her free and finally, finally, *finally* let her go. But, letting her go would mean losing my best friend and being alone, and goddammit, hadn't I been through enough? Hadn't I hurt enough?

"What are you doing here?" I asked, changing the subject while keeping my eyes on Moe and only Moe.

"Oh, right," he said, snapping himself out of what was sure to be a heartbreaking trip down memory lane. He reached into his coat pocket and continued, "So, I dunno if you heard about anything that went down."

With a quick shake of my head, I replied, "I haven't. I, um ... I haven't talked to Vinnie, or anyone for that matter, in months."

His eyes glazed with sadness and sympathy as he stated, "Vinnie tried to kill himself."

In all my years of dealing with the dead and dying, I've had to deliver some horrible news to people who never deserved to hear it. And I've tried to imagine what it would be like to be on the receiving end, thinking of how I'd want it said and where I'd want to be. I've even tried to imagine how I'd react. How quickly the tears would come, and how deep the pain would seep into my chest.

Hearing that my husband, the man I loved most despite it all, had tried to end his life, was the worst piece of news I could imagine, or that I'd ever been given. Moe's pointed delivery was more blunt than I would have preferred. I reasoned that it probably made it easier for him, to say that his friend, his brother, had wanted to die, in the same way you might tell someone that you had a baked potato with dinner. And the pain of those words, as calm as they might've been delivered, pierced my heart and traveled beyond flesh, bone, and muscle, until they touched my soul. My hands clutched tight to my chest, afraid that if I let go, the essence of my own life would spill from the hole that was surely there and puddle at our feet.

But the tears didn't come. I was already beyond frivolous emotion and headed straight toward shock, as my mind zeroed in on the image of him, sprawled out and lifeless on the floor.

"H-How?" It was the only thing I could think of to say, as if I didn't already know.

"Overdose."

I nodded, unblinking and hoping he would fill the air with something other than the buzz of my silent best friend and the sickening crack of my breaking heart.

"After you called me," Moe continued, "I ran over to his place, just to check on him. I knew he'd been using again; he thinks he hides his shit well, but I always knew. But I didn't think shit was that bad, you know? And, I know, drugs are always bad, they're never good, but I have seen some guys reach the end of their rope and Vinnie never gave me those vibes, you know?

"Anyway, I ran over and banged on the door. I got no answer. I was gonna call him, tell him to let me in, but I just had this feelin', you know? This horrible, deep down feelin' in my gut. So, I kicked the door in and found him on the floor."

The tears still hadn't come as I nodded, keeping my hands pressed to my chest. "But, but, but you weren't too late," I said mostly to myself. "I called you in time. You got to him before ... before ..."

Moe laid a hand over his beanie-covered forehead. "I have run all the possibilities through my head so many times and it always boggles my damn mind. I hate thinkin' about it. I, I don't know what I'd do if he had, uh ..." He cupped a hand over his mouth and shook his head, peering through the glass door at my curious family. "I told him I've lost enough and I never wanna have to bury his dumb ass."

I laughed beside myself. "I bet he appreciated that," I muttered sarcastically.

"No," Moe laughed, and Jamie smiled warmly. "He definitely did not."

"So, um ... what happened?"

"Well, after I called 9-1-1 and the paramedics came, I called Zach and Jenna. We were at the hospital for a longass time before they finally let us see him. And that was ..." He shook his head, still disbelieving that new reality. "It was crazy. They had him strapped to the bed, tellin' us he was a danger to himself. And, I guess, at the time, he was."

Vinnie. Suicidal. It was difficult to grasp, but looking back, hadn't there been signs all along of his depression and anger?

And I had missed them all.

"So, he was in the psychiatric ward," I croaked.

Moe nodded solemnly. "For a week. Then, he was upstate with Zach for a while, before heading up to Boston."

"Boston?"

Exhaling heavily, Moe turned and took a seat on a rocking chair that once belonged to my grandfather. He pulled out a pack of cigarettes and held them up. "Mind if I smoke?" I didn't, and so, he lit one before continuing.

"Vin didn't think he could handle going to rehab in New York. He thought it was the best idea to get away for a while and really separate himself from the shit goin' on here. So, he and Zach found this really nice place in Boston." He took a long drag from the cigarette and left a silvery cloud in the frozen air. "He found this really great doctor up there, who had him write all these letters to everyone he hurt or, I dunno, had somethin' to say to." That was when he pulled an envelope from his pocket and handed it over to me. "And this one is for you."

I took the white envelope from him to look at the big, bold **ANDY** scrawled across the front in black marker. Seeing his handwriting and the creases in the crisp paper where his hands might've been, made me realize that this was the only piece of my husband I physically had in my possession. There was nothing else. No threadbare t-shirt that smelled of his skin. No photographs or simple mementos from past holidays. Up until just seconds ago, he might as well had been nothing more than a ghost of my past. But whatever this might have been, it was now the most precious thing I owned.

It was proof that he'd once existed in my life.

I slid my finger beneath the sealed flap and began to rip it open when Moe protested with a frantic wave of his hands.

"Oh, hell no, girl. You are not opening that right now. It's takin' everything in me to keep my shit together as it is, and—"

His eyes locked on something in the front yard, his mouth frozen around what he had meant to say. Beside him, was Jamie, jumping ecstatically, as Moe stood up with the cigarette between his fingers.

"I can't believe it's still here," he muttered, walking down the porch steps and across the winter brown grass, to the bird bath in the center of the yard.

Jamie was on his heels the whole time.

Curiously, I watched him, not daring to follow father and daughter, as he crouched to the circle of rocks surrounding the old stone bath. It had been right where it stood ever since my parents bought the house twenty-four years ago and wore its age gracefully. Not a chip or stain marred its etched surface and the same could be said about the rocks that surrounded it. Our parents had forbidden us from touching it as kids and not a single rock had been turned in over two decades. Until now, as Moe knelt beside the circle and lifted one specific stone.

He turned it over in his hands, brushing away the dirt from its surface. A single tear trickled down his cheek and he hastily swatted it away, leaving a smudge of soil in its wake. Then, he smiled and came back to the porch.

"My Jamie gave me this rock for my last Father's Day," he said, using her name for the first time, giving me all the confirmation I no longer needed. He turned the rock over and showed me the message written in worn, but still legible, marker.

I love you, Daddy. Love, Jamie

My heart sat heavy, weighing against my lungs and gut, and making it so difficult to breathe. I was trapped. Caught between wanting to do the right thing and wanting to keep her to myself forever. What if I never left? Couldn't she and I live happily together, until I died? *But then*, reason asked, *what happens to her after Moe dies, or hell, after* you *die?* I didn't know the answer. Would she be trapped here for all eternity, or would she, by default, be set free once her tether to this earth was severed? Was I really willing to find out? Was I truly that selfish, to ignore her silent pleas and keep her here, when I had set so many others free? Hadn't she waited long enough?

The battle against my emotions was lost as I looked at the pleading eyes of my friend and released a sob.

"Andy?" Moe's hand drooped to his side, still clutching the rock. "Baby, what's wrong?"

I closed my eyes to his concern and let the images speak. "She found that rock in the woods across the street, before they tore them down and built the houses. It reminded her of you, of when you'd take her camping by the lake. She saw it and brought it home."

Moe remained as silent as his daughter, and I continued, pulling at another image, another piece of proof.

"It was you that did her hair, not your wife. Jamie thought it was funny, how you were more like the mommy and your wife was more like the daddy, with the good job and all the money."

That brought a hushed chuckle. "My wife was a surgeon, and when we had our first daughter, we decided I'd be a stay-at-home dad."

I nodded, opening my eyes to find his stare pinned on me with a cocktail of astonishment, sadness, and speculation swirling around in his misty eyes. Jamie stood beside him, smiling with so much warmth and just a dash of sadness and I knew that smile was for me.

"You have blamed yourself for too long for what happened," I stated, holding Moe's unrelenting gaze. "She has never, ever blamed you. But she has always felt sad for what happened after. She hates that she was the reason you and your wife divorced. She hates that you ruined your life, because of her."

There was no attempt to stop the tears as they began to fall from his big, brown eyes. His gaze left mine as he searched the ground, the sky, anywhere she might have been. I smiled at his attempt to catch any glimpse of the daughter he thought he'd failed, and I reached out, touching his hand.

"She's beside you," I informed him gently, and he looked at me, bewildered, as he nodded.

These moments never failed to amaze me. The ease in believing. The willingness. Moe turned to look in the direction of his daughter, and while I knew he couldn't see her, I also knew he imagined that he could.

"Oh, baby girl," he whispered tearfully. "You are not the reason my life was ruined. That's all on me. I did that. You hear me? You had absolutely nothin' to do with that."

He glanced at me and asked, "She can hear me, right?"

Swallowing at my watery laugh, I bobbed my head. "She can. She's listening and she's," I exhaled against a sob, "she's so happy. She's so happy you're finally here."

He turned back to where Jamie stood. "You could've come to me, baby girl. I've always been out there."

Jamie shook her head and I interpreted, "She didn't know where to go or how to get there. So, she's just ... been here."

Moe's eyes slid reluctantly from the blank spot in front of him to look at me. Realization spread across his face, as his lips parted and his eyes grew wide.

"And you've been with her."

I nodded, dropping my gaze to the porch floor. “Yeah ...”

“You've been her friend.”

The best.

“Yeah.”

He exhaled, cocking his head and loosening his shoulders. “She wasn't alone, because of you.”

I didn't know what to do, or what to say. I could only shrug and swallow again, in an act of desperation to keep from losing it, as I knew this was it. She would never be there again, waiting for my return, or listening to my troubles, or helping me decide on an outfit. She would be gone soon, no longer hanging on, and I would be truly alone.

I began to cry.

“She's my best friend,” I told him, needing him to know that I wasn't only there for her but her for me as well. “She's been my best friend since I was six years old.” I looked at her, my oldest and closest friend, wondering how I had any heart left to break, and added, “She was my only friend.”

Moe blew out a breath. “She'll leave now, won't she?”

My eyes closed, searing her smile against my brain. “Yes.”

The wind blew harsh against my skin, and then I felt the warmth of his arms, enveloping me in a cocoon of comfort and mutual sadness. I settled against his chest, and sighed to the peaceful thrumming of his heart, and together, we wept on the porch of the house where his daughter had died and become my friend.

"Thank you, Andy," he whispered into my hair. "Thank you. You've made me happier than you can ever know. I dunno what's in the cards for you and my boy, but you're so special, baby, and you deserve to be happy, too."

I could only nod, as I pulled away from his comforting embrace. And when I finally opened my eyes, Jamie was gone.

CHAPTER THIRTY-EIGHT

ANDREA

Mom had insisted I invite Moe in for dinner, and to my surprise, he'd accepted.

"We never met the owners when we bought the house," Dad explained, passing the potatoes.

My friend nodded, helping himself to a heaping spoonful. "My wife walked away from the place after the accident."

"What about you?" Mer asked, popping a piece of pot roast into her mouth. "What did you do?"

"I became addicted to drugs and bounced from couch to couch, until I found my home on the streets," Moe replied, so matter-of-factly my mother's chewing slowed and Willa dropped her fork. Moe chuckled at their shock. "My daughter's death made my wife angry and hateful, and it made me stupid."

"Understandable, though," Dad commented, nodding somberly. "On both accounts. Everybody copes with grief differently."

Willa shook her head and pursed her lips. "I don't think there's any excuse. I mean, I'm sorry, but a coping mechanism or not, drugs are never okay."

I opened my mouth to speak, in defense of myself and my friend, when Moe spoke first.

"You're absolutely right," he said, nodding. "I'm not proud of what I've done, and I thank God every single day of my life that I have the Marinos. If it weren't for them, I'd still be out there, sleepin' in the gutter and bummin' cigarettes."

His smile turned nostalgic as he said, "Those guys, Zach and Vinnie ... they always took care of me. Made sure I was fed, and eventually, they got me a job."

Mom's eyes flitted quickly toward mine before saying, "They're good friends."

"They are," Moe agreed. "They're great guys."

My sisters exchanged a pointed look. I could only imagine what they were thinking and I knew I was better off not knowing. Their judgment didn't shock me, but it was my father who turned my head.

"Well, I've only met Zach the one time, but I know Vinnie is a good man. Troubled, sure, but I've never known troubled to mean bad."

Moe grabbed his glass of soda and raised it up to my father. "Truer words have never been spoken."

The meal continued, with utensils clattering and dishes passing, and amidst it all, my mother looked over the table at me and said, "I get it, now."

***

I said goodbye to Moe, and although he insisted it wouldn't be forever, I argued that he couldn't know for sure. Nothing is guaranteed, and I knew that to be true, more than ever, the moment I stepped into my room.

God, the silence had never been so loud.

My bones begged to be free of the ache in my chest, while knowing there was no escape. It had been six months since I last took a hit, and for the first time since the initial withdrawal had subsided, the itch to escape filled my mind. Lying in bed, the craving was so insatiable I began to wonder how it was someone went about finding a drug dealer, and I smacked a hand against my forehead.

"Stop it," I scolded through gritted teeth. "Just stop it." And I climbed out of bed.

In my months of recovery, I had searched for something else, something to grasp my attention and help me battle against the cravings. The only thing that had come close was exercise. The endorphins from working out always offered enough of a high to distract me. So, I grabbed my workout clothes, hanging over my closet door, and dropped my sweatshirt in the process. I cursed out of frustration as I picked it up, when something fell out of the pocket.

There, on the floor, was the envelope from Vinnie.

Somehow, between losing Jamie and having dinner, I had managed to push the letter to the back of my mind, but now, it stood front and center and I no longer craved the escape of cocaine.

I chose his words instead.

***

Hey, Sweetheart.

So, in case you haven't noticed, I've never been great at communicating. I'd rather smoke and get high than talk through my problems, and apparently, according to my shrink, this is a problem. My biggest issue though, is that I never know where to begin. But Dr. Travetti says a story should always start at the beginning, so buckle up, baby. It's gonna be a long one.

I was only five years old when my mom left us, and I watched her leave. I had been sick as hell the night she went, puking and with explosive diarrhea. It's crazy because I still remember it all so clearly. Like, I was only five, but I can remember the way her hand felt against my back. Her palm was cold on my clammy neck and I remember crying and asking her to make it stop, I was so fucking hot and tired, and she just kept saying, "Where the hell is your father?" I couldn't tell time yet, but I knew he was late, and there wasn't much that made her more angry than him being late. And finally, just as I Love Lucy *came on, I puked all over the fucking couch, and she said, "I can't do this anymore." So, she packed her shit, kissed me on the cheek, and told me she loved me. I cried so fucking much I threw up again, and I begged her not to go. She told me she had to, like she didn't have a choice, and then, she walked out the door and never came back.*

Just like that.

Fuck. I've never told anyone that before.

I lied to everyone and told them I saw nothing. I said I had fallen asleep on the couch and didn't know she had gone. I was scared to tell the truth, because I thought they'd be mad at me for letting her leave, as if I could have stopped her or something. It's the first lie I can remember ever telling and I think it's the only one anyone has ever believed. It's like I got all my lying mojo out on that big one.

Anyway, it fucked me up big time. I mean, that would fuck anybody up, but I was really mad. I got into fights a lot. I was a fucking bully and picked on anyone weaker than me. Like, I remember this one kid from elementary school, Robert, who wore these glasses that looked like he stole them from an 80's housewife. I ripped the shit out of this poor kid, and then I would go home and cry because I hated being so fucking mean. I just couldn't let them get the better of me, you know? Because if I didn't tease them first, they would've teased me for being the kid without a mom. And I couldn't fucking deal with that.

So, then I got mixed up with the wrong crowd, as the story goes. Zach and me, we were partners in crime by that point, and we'd crash parties we had no business being at. I lost my virginity when I was fourteen to get us booze from a chick I never knew the name of. We moved onto weed, and then, we went to this party where some guy way older than us showed up with a bag of coke. Zach was more interested than I was, but I was down to try anything. So, this dude told him that if we wanted some, we'd have to pay. Of course, we didn't have any money at the time, so he said, "I'm not just talking about cash." Zach agreed to suck this asshole's dick for two lines, one for him and one for me. I was fucking horrified that he'd bend so easily, but afterward, he told me he was gay and that it wasn't a big deal.

But, Andy, it was a big fucking deal. Because that was how my brother came out to me. By whoring himself out for drugs. And, as if that wasn't bad enough, we liked the high—no, we loved it, a lot. So, Zach did more "favors" and we spent whatever money we had to get our fix, and this went on for a long time before we got stupid.

We scored some blow one day from a neighbor and couldn't wait to get high. So, we brought it home, even though we had never done that shit at home before, and that was the one day Pops came home early. He told us if we didn't go to rehab, he'd kick us out, because he couldn't stand to lose anyone else, so we went. And while we were there, Zach got himself a boyfriend (who ended up being a fucking loser but that's a story for another day) and a new addiction to his video game, and I picked up cigarettes and the decision to never leave my father.

After that, I devoted my life to him. Pops was my world. He was my best friend and my hero. I gave up all ambition to live on my own and to have sex anywhere but in the bathroom at Goose's bar. And, I guess that was all well and good, but the problem with heroes is that they're not immune to mortality. I think I actually convinced myself that my father was incapable of dying, so when we got the news that his heart was giving out, I immediately began to spiral. And the further I fell, the angrier I got, and so much of that was taken out on you.

You have to believe me when I say I tried.

I tried not to be an asshole.

I tried not to put you in the middle of my rage.

I tried not to give in to temptation, and when I eventually did, I tried not to get you involved.

You have to believe that. PLEASE, believe that. I never wanted to drag you down with me. I never wanted to prove your family right. But I did. I did all the things I tried not to do and all I can say is, I'm so sorry. I'm so fucking sorry, and I wished we lived in a world where that was enough to take it all back, but we don't.

No. You know what? Fuck that. I wouldn't take it all back. I'd take back the bad parts. I'd take back the parts that hurt you. I'd take back everything that made you go crazy. But I wouldn't take back the part where you asked me to marry you. I wouldn't take back our wedding. I would keep all those moments that made me want to devote my life to you instead of my father. I wouldn't give those up for anything in the world.

But every bit of good is always contrasted by something bad. That's the beauty of being alive, and my addiction to you was so beautiful. But it was still an addiction and that type of obsession has always been my downfall. I couldn't handle being left alone again, I couldn't handle being your *downfall, and so that night I made you leave, I decided the world would be a better place without me. So, I tried to off myself and apparently, I can't even do that right.*

Dr. Travetti says that's not funny, but I think it's hilarious. Because someone out there clearly loves me enough to keep me around, and I can't for the life of me figure out why.

Anyway, I think that's everything. I'm scared to end this, though. I'm scared this will be the last time I have any contact with you. But I need to learn to be alone. I need to teach the devil in me to keep his big mouth shut. I need to, I dunno, love myself enough to see those reasons to be alive before I can even think about being in your life again...if you'd even still want me.

I hope you will.

Love you, sweetheart.

-V

P.S. I don't expect you to wait for me. I wouldn't ever ask that of you. But there's no harm in hoping, so that's what I'm gonna do.

CHAPTER THIRTY-NINE

VINNIE

"You sure you're ready for this?" Zach asked, his hand on the doorknob.

"I wouldn't be here if I wasn't," I muttered in reply, shifting my gaze toward my sister.

She looked back at me, her brows lifting gently with doubt and concern. This was my new norm. The looks and constant questions asking if I was okay. I guess that was my own fault, and I'd done it to myself, but that didn't mean I wasn't tired of reassuring them.

"Okay," Zach drawled doubtfully, as he opened the door.

The last time I had crossed that threshold, I'd been strapped to a gurney. Bits of memory pelted against my guts in fragments of something that fell somewhere between reality and a dream. I could remember the decision to overdose, but I couldn't remember setting up the lines. I could remember Moe, slapping my face and shouting my name, but I couldn't remember waking up, or passing out, or how I ended up with a two-inch-long gash on my forehead. I wished I could remember, yet I'd do anything to forget.

And I wished to God my brother and sister would stop watching me like I could spontaneously combust at any second.

"How are you doing?" Jenna asked cautiously, as I slowly walked through the dining room and into the living room.

"I'm fine, Jen," I grumbled, as my eyes fixated on the coffee table.

Somewhere during the time I'd been away, at Zach's place and in the Boston rehabilitation center, my brother-in-law, Nicky, had come by and cleaned up the mess I'd made. But he'd missed a spot, and I leaned down to scratch my thumbnail against the blood stain on one of the corners.

"Fucker got me pretty good," I commented, chuckling humorlessly.

"You're lucky that's all that happened," Jen replied, her voice reflecting all the hurt I'd inflicted on them.

"Lucky," I snickered, shaking my head and standing to survey the room. "Not sure that's the word I'd use."

"You *are* lucky," Zach said with a stern furrow of his brow. "I mean, for some reason, you keep getting more chances at life. Someone obviously wants you around."

"Yeah, well," I muttered, as I grabbed a garbage bag from the box I held, "I'll let you know if I ever figure out why."

***

While I was in rehab, I'd spent a lot of time with this shrink, Dr. Vanessa Travetti. She had talked to me a lot about the past, my relationship with family, my fear of being left alone, and the reluctance I felt about letting go. She never once shamed me for my methods of coping, but she taught me that, sometimes the best way to deal with those fears is to do the very thing I was afraid of. And even though it might have been a very basic approach, I had never had it laid out so simply before.

So, I had returned home with just one goal in mind: to get the apartment cleaned and packed up. And that was exactly what the three of us did one rainy day in January. The kitchen was scrubbed, and the appliances were stuffed neatly into boxes. Pictures were wrapped in newspaper and handled with care, while the couch and dining room set were dragged out to the street. None of the furniture held any value and I wanted nothing to do with any of it, especially that damn coffee table, which I not-so-accidentally dropped off the fire escape.

When it came time to tackle our father's room, we did so with care and respect, knowing we would keep nothing but a few sentimental belongings from his closet.

Jenna, now very pregnant with Zach and Greyson's twins, was in charge of unpacking his dresser, and bagging up his old clothes to be donated. She wrinkled her nose, emptying his underwear drawer into a garbage bag, before gasping.

"You okay?" I asked, flipping through some ancient receipts the old man had held onto for reasons I couldn't imagine.

She held up a small bundle of envelopes bound together by a thin, dirty rubber band. "They're from Ma. And they've never been opened."

Zach and I both dropped what we were doing to look at the crinkled, old envelopes. The rubber band broke as Jenna tried to slide it away, and as she read who the letters were addressed to, her surprise was washed away with an expression of sorrow.

"What is it?" Zach asked, reaching out for the yellowed envelopes.

She swallowed before whispering, "They're addressed to us."

My jaw locked around the anger I'd been holding onto for far too long, and from the looks of it, Zach's did, too. I shook my head and told Jen to burn them, before I returned to the tedious task of rifling through Pops's desk. But Jenna protested with a firm "hell no" and came to drop the envelope addressed to me on the desk, right beneath my eyes.

"We're gonna read these," she declared. "We don't have to share 'em with each other, but we need this. We owe it to ourselves, and to Pops. I mean, he held onto them for a reason."

We agreed that we'd keep the letters until we were ready, and in near silence, we finished packing everything that Pops had held onto throughout the years. The day left me heavy with an ache in my chest, so great

I thought my own heart was about to give out on me. My brain struggled to understand how a life so full and loved could be amounted to just a few boxes and bags full of stuff to be tossed and donated. But then, at the end of the night, as I stood in the kitchen with my siblings, our shoulders sagging with grief and despair in witnessing the end of this chapter of our lives, something dawned on me. That maybe what makes a life full isn't the stuff we fill it with, but the love and memories we accumulate throughout the years. And here, in the empty apartment, the heat of that love for Pops was insurmountable.

That's what made it so hard.

"I can't believe this is it," Jenna said, staring into the dark living room.

"It's not like this is the place we grew up in," Zach reasoned, while fighting his own emotional battle.

"No, I know," she replied, wrapping her arms around her big belly. "But this was the last place he lived. Like, this was the last place that was his. It just feels so, I dunno, final."

"*Death* is final," I grunted, itching for the cigarettes I was no longer smoking.

"You know, I don't believe that," Zach said, as his eyes swept over the ceiling. "I mean, I feel like that's what should make sense, 'cause he's not here anymore. Like, I can't see him, so he must be gone. But ... I dunno." He shrugged, looking back to Jen and me. "I still feel him. And I dunno if that's just some bullshit I'm tellin' myself to feel better or whatever, but I do."

"So, you think death is more like a new beginning," Jenna mused, an air of mysticism in her voice.

Zach shook his head. "Nah. I don't see it as an ending or a beginning. More of a, uh ... continuation, I think."

"Well," I said, slapping him on the shoulder, "I think you're crazy as fuck, and I think I'm exhausted. So, I'm gonna head out."

The two of them nodded with the resignation that it was time. Zach and I hoisted what was left of the bags and boxes into our arms, while Jenna pulled her purse further onto her shoulder.

"So, I'll take this stuff back to my place for now," Zach said, "and when you guys are ready, we'll just, I dunno, divvy it up or whatever."

I nodded. "Sounds good."

We had already discussed this but we were hesitating and stalling, grasping for more time. We didn't want this to be the last time we ever stood in our father's home. And for them, that's all it was, but for me, it was also mine. This was me also letting go of my old life and habits, and I was scared. I had never known how scared of the world I was, until I was forced to face it alone, but there was no other way around it. Everything in life is a temporary blip in the universe, and this moment was no exception.

"You ready, man?"

Zach drew my attention with a soft tone, and I took a deep breath before nodding toward the darkness.

"Yeah, I'm good."

And as the three of us left the empty apartment and closed the door, I repeated those words to myself, hoping one day soon I'd believe them.

I'm good.

CHAPTER FORTY

VINNIE

Vinnie,

You're ten today. I can't believe it. My baby is double digits! How did that happen? They're really not kidding when they say that time flies—whoever 'they' are.

I don't know when you're going to read this. I don't know if your father would ever allow it at all. Hell, maybe you're reading this when we're both dead, after you've found it stuffed in one of his drawers somewhere. Maybe you're a man right now, with a wife and a little ten-year-old boy of your own. Whoever you are now, I just hope you're better than me. I guess that's all any parent can hope for, but I hope in my case, it's the truth.

Can you believe it's been five years since I've seen you? I know I can't. I replay those last moments with you over and over again in my mind, trying to understand how I could be such an awful person to someone I love so much. You were so sick, and you were only five, just a few short years after I'd rocked you in my arms, swearing to God I would never hurt you. And while I know I can't ever take it back and make it better, I want you to at least understand why I did it. I want you to at least see it from my end, even if you never forgive me. But God, I hope you do.

Simply put, I was suffocating. I had dreams for my life that weren't coming true, and I was living a life that felt all wrong. I never wanted to be a mother. I never wanted to remain tied down to one place. I never wanted the pizzeria, either. These were all things your father decided he wanted and he dragged me along for the ride. But I resented him for forcing me into it. Sure, I could have walked away at the beginning, but I loved him and I wasn't ready to leave—oh, the irony.

I'd been seeing a therapist for a while and she had said I was suffering from depression. I didn't need a doctor to tell me that, but she gave me some pills which did help to make it a little better. The problem was that I became so dependent on the fog I was living in and not enough on what would truly make me happy. And I was sick of it. I hated how much I resented your father. I hated how much I yelled at you kids. I was a monster, and after a while, I felt we'd all be better off if I just wasn't in the picture.

But deciding to leave that night had absolutely nothing to do with you. I know it probably didn't seem like it at the time, you were just a little boy, but I hope you understand that now.

I was only doing what I thought was best for everyone.

If you are a man now, I wonder how you turned out. I've thought about that a lot these last five years. I wonder about your brother and sister, too, but I mostly wonder about you. You were my clingiest baby and could never be left alone without screaming. I hope your father was able to love you enough for the both of us and I hope you grew up fine. I hope you met someone special and that you don't give up when things get hard. But above everything else, I hope you're happy and capable of giving the love I could never give.

God, I hope you're not like me.

But if you are, I hope you can let that go and change. Before it's too late.

Whether you believe it or not ... I love you.

Mom

***

I leaned back against the couch and wiped a hand over my face. I hadn't been crying but I felt like I could, with tears prickling my eyes and burning my nose. I wanted to call Zach and Jenna to compare notes but stopped myself from grabbing the phone.

This was too personal.

The rage I contained in my heart was intense and I grabbed at whatever my hand landed upon. I reeled back and chucked a marble ashtray against the wall, leaving a dent. Within seconds, Goose ran from his bedroom to the living room.

“What the fuck is—” He stopped when he caught a glimpse of the ashtray on the floor. “Why you takin' shit out on my stuff, man? And,” he pointed at the cracked wall and looked back at me, “why the hell are you wrecking the place?”

I shrugged apologetically. “Because my mom's face isn't here.”

“You got mommy issues, too?”

Laughing, I stood from the couch and tucked the letter into my pocket. “I told you, man. I'm a real shit show.”

“You belong on *Dr. Phil.*”

“Yeah, right?”

He spread his arms out slowly with flourish. “Ex-junkie with mommy and daddy issues dates girl who sees dead people, marries her after two months.”

Laughing and walking into the kitchen, I shook my head. “Yo, people would pay to read that book.”

“I'd see the movie,” Goose agreed, following.

I needed this. After the day and night I'd had at the old apartment, I knew I could use a little time with my friend before getting back to business the next day.

The *old* apartment.

God, I don't know when I'd ever be used to saying that.

After leaving Zach and Jenna, I had called Goose and asked what he was up to. I hadn't expected much, as it had been late, but he was so surprised to hear from me after months of silence, that he invited me to crash at his apartment for the night.

He sealed the deal by mentioning his case of Coca-Cola.

I reached into the fridge for a can. “Nothin' like a nice, cold can of Coke.”

“Might wanna pick a new drink of choice,” Goose grumbled. “It was ironic before, but being a repeat offender makes it weird.”

Popping the tab, I pursed my lips and nodded thoughtfully. “You’ve got a point there.”

We returned to the living room and sat down. Goose was exhausted after a long night at the bar, but he seemed determined to give me some time. And that's what happens when you make friends in rehab. They understand the loneliness and they get that desperation for a connection.

He was a good guy.

“So, you gonna win the wife back?” he asked, stretching his arms out along the back of the couch.

Nodding, I slurped the first sip and smacked my lips. “Fuck yes. But … I dunno, man. I'm hoping we can make it work. I *want* to make it work. But my shrink in Boston really stressed how toxic a relationship between two recovering addicts can be. She thinks we'd be destined to relapse because we'd associate the relationship itself with gettin' high.”

His eyes hooded as he nodded. “Smart lady.”

I sighed, plunking the can down on the coffee table. “Yeah. So ... I don’t wanna even say it, but I kinda think she should just, you know, move on. Find someone better for her.”

Goose scoffed, shaking his head. “You really believe there's someone better out there?”

Flattening my hand to my chest, I feigned bashfulness. “Aw, Goosey. I had no idea you felt like that about me. Too bad you're not my type.”

“You're an ass,” he chuckled. “For real. You think there's better?”

“For her?” I put my entire body into the shrug, slapping my hands against my thighs. “I don't know, man. I wanna say no. Like, I fuckin' love her and we're good, you know what I mean? Like, without the drugs, we're *really* good. But ...” I shook my head, shrugging again. “She had no business gettin' with me in the first place. That was my fault. I had too much shit goin' on and I took her down with me. So, now I feel like, I gotta get my crap in order before I can even think about tryin' to make things work with her.”

Goose raised a brow. “You think she doesn't have shit to deal with?”

“She does, but—”

“Let me tell you something,” he said, leaning forward to rest his elbows on his knees. “I had a lot of shit to get through when Krystal got pregnant. I was completely blasted by the time she woke up the next morning and she knew we could never make that relationship work. We were never gonna be okay together. But she gave me an ultimatum. She told me that, if I wanted a relationship with my daughter, I needed to get my shit together. And you know what I did?”

My gaze dropped to my hands. “I know what you did.”

“Right. I went to rehab and I got myself cleaned up. It was fuckin' hard, it *still* is! But guess what, buttercup? Life *is* hard. We gotta work at the things that are worth having 'cause otherwise, we'd never appreciate them.”

Goose was a big lumberjack of a man, but he had the heart of a teddy bear and the soul of a lion. He was fierce and soft, kind and hard-working, and if there was ever a guy to admire, it was him. He had taken himself one notch away from rock bottom and climbed his way to a healthy, enviable relationship with his ex-wife and daughter. And I knew it hadn't been easy to earn his way back into the family. But that was Goose and we weren't talking about him.

“Things are just a little different for me,” I muttered, tapping the tips of my fingers together. “And she and I both have issues.”

“Yeah, you might have to work harder, but if you love her that much, then I think she's worth fighting for. So, make up your mind to let go of the stuff holding you back, turn shit around, and prove it.”

Goose concluded the conversation with a slap of his hand against my knee. “All right, I gotta get to bed. Gotta wake up early and sign for some deliveries. You can hang as long as you want, but just lock up before you leave tomorrow, okay?”

“You got it,” I replied with a nod.

“Awesome. 'Night, man.”

“'Night.” Then, as he left the room, I stopped him. “Hey, Goose?”

“'Sup?”

I tipped my chin and said, “Thanks. You know, for bein' a good friend. I'll pay for the wall.” I gestured toward the dent where the ashtray had made its impact.

His beard-framed lips lifted in a smile. “Don't worry about it. But, hey, remember what I said. Let shit go. You deserve to be happy, too.”

Goose turned off the kitchen light and headed to bed, leaving me in the soft glow of a single lamp in the living room. Alone again, I studied the perfect circle indented into the wall. It was a minor incident, not a big deal in the long run, but that spot on the wall spoke volumes.

Dr. Travetti had said it before but now I saw it, too, clear as the streetlights from Goose's living room window. I was damaged. Ever since that one life altering moment, when my mother ignored my tears and shut the door on her responsibilities as a parent. I'd been on a path of destruction ever since, and I had known it all along. Truthfully, I'd been aware of my toxicity for a long time.

But there was one thing I had overlooked.

Damaged does not equate unworthy.

I was hurt and rough around the edges. But I also wasn't doomed to be a prisoner of the past if I didn't want to be, and I was so tired of being locked up.

I stood from the couch and headed into the kitchen. I found the garbage can and pulled the letter from my pocket. With one final look at my mother's handwriting, I dropped it in and went to bed.

Tomorrow was a new day, I would face the morning as a free man, with determination and strength. Because Andy was absolutely worth fighting for. And with that knowledge, I knew that I was nothing like my mother, and thank God for that.

CHAPTER FORTY-ONE

ANDREA

"Thank you so much for having me. You have no idea how much I appreciate it," I said, desperately trying not to lay it on too thick.

Dressed in a floor-length, gauzy, blue dress, Tracey smiled graciously and outstretched her arms to me. "Don't thank me, Andrea. I'm just glad you're finally ready to accept the gift that's been given to you."

I walked into her embrace and welcomed the soul-soothing hug. She smelled of flowers and earth, like springtime in the rain. It was the scent of a new beginning, and I thought, *how fitting*.

It had taken weeks of soul-searching, therapy, and NA meetings to finally decide what I really wanted to do with my life at this point in time. It was funny when I really thought about it. Because, it turned out what I wanted to do, was the very thing I'd been running from my entire life.

I wanted to give people closure and ensure that the spirits of their loved ones were granted safe passage to whatever comes next. So, I dug around the internet until I found the contact information for Tracey's manager. A few phone calls later, I had found myself at a coffee shop on Long Island, plotting my debut with the woman I'd run from months ago.

"So, you're gonna go out for twenty minutes. That should give you the chance to read a couple people. And I think you'll find that, the more you work your ability, the quieter it'll be when you're not using it. Think of yourself as a bucket—"

I interrupted with a laugh. "I'm sorry, that's just ridiculous."

Tracey rolled her eyes good-naturedly. "Hear me out! You're a bucket, Spirit is the tap, and your ability is the water. The tap is always running, always spilling water into the bucket, and if you don't drink, it'll overflow. The more you use your ability, the more satisfied Spirit is, and the easier it is to stay in control."

It made sense, that in order to relieve the pressure inside of me, I had to let some out every now and then.

Now, I took a deep breath, as I waited for my turn on stage. I found I was terrified and riddled with nerves. What if, for the first time since I was a child, the spirits decided not to communicate? What if they had stage fright? But there wasn't time to tuck my tail between my legs and back out. Tracey's manager called to me that it was time, and I walked on unsteady feet to the stage.

The theater was small with a capacity of only seven hundred, but standing on the stage beneath the bright spotlight, it might as well have been a stadium full of thousands. I couldn't see beyond the first few rows of faces, but the static volume was deafening. I came to stand before the microphone and the figures of the dead came into focus. They pleaded with their eyes, staring intently at me from the audience. They were too loud, too distracting, and I couldn't find a slice of free attention to introduce myself. Grabbing the mic in a firm grip, I pulled it from its stand, and walked to the edge of the stage, to face a woman and the ghost of her sister.

"It wasn't your fault you weren't there," I said, crouching at the edge of the stage. "She's relieved you didn't see her at the end. She was so sick; she didn't want you to remember her that way."

The woman opened her mouth and lifted a trembling hand to her lips. "O-Oh, God ... Is she, is she h-here?"

I nodded. "She's beside you, in the aisle. She wanted to tell you your parents are fine. She's with them all the time. And the baby, the one named after her ... she's honored."

"Oh, thank God. I thought she'd think it's weird."

"She loves it. She watches her often. When you hear that song, the Elton John one that makes you always think of her, she wants you to know that that's her, saying hi."

The woman's eyes spilled over as she nodded. "I-I thought so, but I wasn't sure."

I could've read her for hours, but there wasn't time. The tug of a young boy, dragging me toward his father, was too great. I cut myself from the woman and her grateful sister and let the static lure me instead of shutting it out. Smiling as I knelt before the withered man, I faced the little boy, who was no more than five years old. He was too young, too sweet, and he reminded me of Jamie.

"He was so glad to finally let go," I said gently. "He always knew he wouldn't be in this world for long and he was just so enthralled with the time he had. But he needs you to live. Give your wife another baby."

The man laid a hand over his shadowed eyes and released a quiet sob. "I can't replace him," he whispered, and the man beside him laid a hand over his shoulder.

"He knows that, but he doesn't see it that way," I replied gently, feeling the delicate fragility of his glass heart. "You have so much love to give, and you need to release it. Your life was meant to be spent on loving what you've been given, not on mourning what was taken away. Because he's not gone. He's right there. He always is."

The grieving father wouldn't face me. He wouldn't show me his eyes, full of pain and sorrow, but I could feel the reluctant lifting of his soul. And I could see the smile on his little boy, knowing I'd gotten through to his daddy, and that they were going to be fine. I let myself revel in that for just a moment, before moving on to the next.

I realized, in that brief, stolen moment, that this is what I've always been meant to do. Helping people by giving loved ones the gift of closure. There was so much satisfaction in finally listening and letting it happen without resistance, and I wished it hadn't taken so much time and pain to see it. But maybe that's how it had to happen, I considered. Maybe, in order to truly fall in love with our callings, we first have to explore and resist. Maybe we need to feel the pain of denial, to know how good it feels to give in and let it flow.

And, I realized, this was the greatest high of all.

***

"How do you feel?" Tracey asked in the car after the show.

I considered the question with a smile, staring out the window at the streams of passing streetlights and power lines. "I feel good," I said. "Like, really good."

She grinned from behind the wheel of her Mercedes. "I told you."

After just fifteen minutes of willingly receiving messages and passing them on, I was exhausted and ready to crash, but there was also a buzzing beneath my skin that couldn't compete with anything I'd ever felt before. Then, I was elated by the realization that the static had never been so quiet, or so calm, and I knew I'd need to do it again.

One time and I was already addicted.

"You hungry?" Tracey glanced at me from her side of the car.

I really needed sleep but my stomach growled in protest. "I'm starving."

"Same."

We drove aimlessly, looking out the windows at the passing restaurants, waiting for something to jump out and grab our attention. But burgers weren't appealing at the moment and I'd just had Chinese the night before. It wasn't until we drove by a dimly lit Italian restaurant called Vincenzo's that Tracey's face lit up with interest.

"I could really go for some pizza," she said, and although it reminded me too much of the man I used to know, the man I was still legally bound to, I agreed. It'd been so long since I last ate pizza, and after an exhausting night, I craved the comfort of hot dough and melted cheese.

Tracey pulled into the parking lot and we went inside, both of us weary with smiling faces and sagging shoulders. My legs felt heavy and weak, like I'd just run a marathon, but I felt so good and satisfied, that I couldn't complain. It was late and there weren't many stragglers left in the restaurant, but Tracey still found us a far table in a secluded corner.

"Less distractions," she said with a wink, leaving her bag on the bench seat. "What do you feel like eating?"

"Oh, um … I don't know. I'll find a menu—"

"I'll get it. You gotta be so worn out, especially when you're not used to it. Sit. I'll be right back."

She left me at the booth, browsing through my phone and enjoying the whisper of music playing through the sound system. I sank further into the cushy seat, too aware of how tired I really was, and as hungry as I might have been, I still couldn't wait to collapse onto my bed.

Lord Huron's "Louisa" began to play, barely detectable to unfamiliar ears, but I'd know that song anywhere. My vision clouded in the memory of dancing with Vinnie on a dark street in New York City, the night when he had first kissed me, and I'd first kissed him. I thought about all of the promises time had broken since then, and I spent the minutes of the song wondering where we went wrong. We had been so good together, hadn't we? He, the broken bad boy, and I, the innocent girl destined to put him back together. But tropes are meant for predictable movies and cheesy romance novels. They didn't fit into the real world, with real people and real problems. And no matter how deep I delved into it, I couldn't pinpoint any one pivotal moment that had ruined everything, and I wondered if maybe it had simply always been.

"How depressing," I muttered to nobody, before looking up to see where Tracey had gone.

She was at the counter, looking over a flimsy takeout menu and talking to a guy behind the counter. He was cute. Blond. Tall. It didn't take long for guilt to sneak its way in. I shouldn't have been checking out another guy, not when I was still married. But an annoying little voice in my head told me it was fine. It had been months since I talked to Vinnie and months since he'd sent Moe with that letter. I never sought him out, because I understood his need to fix things, by himself, for himself. Hell, I was doing the same thing. But how much time can go by before you realize you're not married anymore? How long can you remain faithful to someone, before you just have to let go and give up?

"You're seriously gonna sit there and check him out?"

I jumped, startled by the voice, and I turned to face the melancholic smile of the man I used to know.

"Hey, sweetheart," Vinnie said, wearing an apron and resting his chin against the broom handle in his grasp.

I gasped at him, unable to speak, as Tracey came back to the table. She was taken aback by my new visitor, and her eyes volleyed between us.

"You know each other?" she asked me, sliding into the booth.

"Um …" My lips pressed together firmly, as his eyes dared me to tell her the truth. "Tracey, this is Vinnie, my … my husband."

Tracey's eyes dropped to my hand, as if she hadn't thought to check if I was wearing a ring. When she found it there, where it had always been, she all but gasped. "I didn't know you were married," she said, then turned to Vinnie, extending a hand. "Hi! It's nice to meet you. I had no idea you worked here," she added, looking at him, then back at me for help.

"Neither did I," I said, not caring how that sounded to my friend, as I now angrily glared at my husband.

We were five minutes from my parents' house, and I had to wonder, how long had he been here? How long had he been working in my vicinity without so much as a knock on the door, or hell, a phone call, or text? Had he been watching me? Following my every move? God, I had so many questions, there were so many answers I wanted to demand of him, but all I could do was stare, mouth agape and eyes watering. Because above all the questions, demands, and anger, there was the bittersweet truth that, had he successfully taken his own life, this moment never would have been.

"What are you ladies havin'?" he asked, propping the broom against the booth, and pulling a notepad from his pocket.

"What are you—"

"Andy," he cut me off gently. "You'll get your answers, I promise. But you both look starving, so let me feed you first."

I couldn't argue that, so I did. I let him bring out a basket of garlic knots and a bowl of salad. Then, after we'd polished those off, he produced two heaping bowls of spaghetti and meatballs that I couldn't imagine ever having the stomach capacity to finish. Everything was satisfying and excellent, and when we were done and nearly bursting at the seams, Vinnie asked if we wanted dessert.

"Oh, God," I groaned, holding my hands over my stomach. "I think I'll die if I have anything else."

"Nah, you won't," he laughed, then turned toward the blond guy behind the counter. "Hey, Kev. Tell Marco to bring out the caramel gelato."

"You got it, boss," Kev replied, and disappeared behind the swinging kitchen doors.

Turning back to Vinnie, I raised a brow and asked, "Boss?"

His thumbnail tucked between his teeth and Tracey took that as her cue. “I need to get going,” she said abruptly, standing from the booth and grabbing her bag. “Thank you so much for dinner, Vinnie. What do I owe you?”

He shook his head and cut the air with a gesture of his hand. He was his father's son. “Don't worry ‘bout it. It's on me.”

She smiled and bowed her head graciously. “Thank you. And Vinnie?”

“Yeah?”

She lifted her head to look into his eyes and said, “This is why you weren't taken, to be with her. Treat her right this time, okay? Treat *both* of you right.”

He took a deep breath, as he studied her. Question creased the lines on his forehead as he looked from her to me, but then, he nodded. “I will.”

“Good.” Tracey turned to look at me and waved with a flourish of her fingers. “I'll call you soon. Maybe we should take this show on the road.”

With one last smile, she hurried out, leaving me alone with my once sad and angry, but always devastatingly beautiful husband. Marco brought out a pint of gelato and a few spoons and handed them over to Vinnie, who laid it all on the table.

Then, he sat down where Tracey had been and grabbed a spoon. I stared at him incredulously as he dug in, not knowing what was now supposed to happen, or what I should say, and came up with nothing.

Vinnie nudged the other spoon toward me and with a mouthful of gelato, said, “Come on, sweetheart. Eat. And while you're at it, ask me whatever you want. I won't lie to you, but you gotta do somethin' for me, too.”

“What's that?” I asked skeptically, taking the spoon.

“You gotta be honest with me.”

And for the first time in our months together, I agreed. To both him and myself.

CHAPTER FORTY-TWO

VINNIE

"What the hell are you doing here?"

That was her first question. Not how I'd been or what I'd been up to in the months since I'd last seen her. She wanted to know what the hell had brought me here, to this restaurant, in this moment. She probably thought it was all a set up, and I had to admit, it would've been a good one. But honestly, I'd been just as surprised to see her walk through the door. The moment had been nothing short of serendipitous and I knew that. But she didn't.

"I work here," I answered simply, digging my spoon into the tub of gelato.

"He called you boss."

"Right," I said with a nod. "Because I'm his boss."

"Since when?"

"Since I hired him two weeks ago."

Andy rolled her eyes and threw her head back with the motion. "You know what I mean," she groaned, before righting herself and staring straight into my eyes.

I couldn't help but smile at the way she slowly pulled her bottom lip between her teeth, a direct contrast to the steel in her eyes. A constant contradiction of bashful and fierce. She was back, the woman I'd fallen in love with, and I settled into the comfort of knowing I hadn't completely ruined her.

"Okay," I said with resignation, dropping the spoon and rubbing my sticky fingers on my jeans. "I'll tell you what happened, but you gotta help me finish this 'cause I'm not putting it back in the freezer."

Pinching her lips, she relented and dug in.

"So," I began, running a hand through my hair, "you got my letter. And I'm assuming you read it, right?" She nodded, and I continued, "Cool. So, you know I was really messed up. After rehab and a shitload of therapy in Boston, I came back home. First, I lived with Zach for a little while, knowing I'd need to get back to the city eventually. But the thing was, I didn't *want* to go back to the city. The more I thought about it, the more I realized I didn't have anything left there. Pops was gone, Zach was living his life upstate, and as often as Jenna was in there, her life wasn't there. And, I dunno if you've noticed, but I really hate being alone. Like, Z? He can spend hours by himself and he's all good, but I don't work like that. My brain is too loud.

"Anyway, I decided it was time to go. So, we let the lease run out on the apartment and packed everything up. Jenna invited me to come live out here in her basement for a while, and I went for it. I had these plans to commute back and forth, but I talked to Goose one night, and he gave me this whole spiel about letting go and living my life for me. I don't think I've ever done that before. The most selfish thing I've ever done was marry you, and despite everything that happened, I still think it's the best thing I've ever done. I realized I wanted to live the rest of my life like that, just doin' the shit that made me happy. So, I took my share of Pops's life insurance and bought this place."

Andy's jaw dropped. "But what about Famiglia Bella?" She sounded absolutely horrified, and I couldn't help but laugh.

"We still own it," I assured her. "But we put it under Moe's care and hired a few other guys to keep things going."

"Wow," she uttered breathlessly, shaking her head. "I just can't believe it."

Shrugging, I folded my arms on the table. "I decided I wanted to honor my father without living in his shadow. So, this is what I'm doin', and that's my story." I gently nudged her ankle with my foot. "Your turn."

Andy shrugged as the spoon slid into her mouth. I couldn't help but stare as she licked it clean with slow, purposeful nonchalance, completely unaware of what she was doing to me.

"There really isn't—"

"Oh, no, you don't," I interjected, shaking my head. "You don't get to drop a bomb like, 'I see dead people' on me without elaborating. So, spill it."

She shifted in her seat and I knew she was uncomfortable. But in order for this to work, we needed to come clean, literally and figuratively.

"Andy, come on. Just tell me."

"I ... I'm scared you won't believe me. That's all I've been afraid of this whole time."

"Well, I can't believe anything if you don't convince me. And if you don't tell me, how the hell are you gonna convince me?"

That seemed to do the trick. Her chest puffed with a deep inhale and as she exhaled, she nodded with determination and resolve.

"I don't know how or when it really happened, but I really noticed when my parents moved into their house when I was about six years old. There was this little girl who lived in my room, who couldn't speak verbally, but she talked in images. Like, little pictures that would pop into my mind, sort of like she was giving me her memories. She told me her name was Jamie, and that there had been an accident at the house. When I said something to my parents, they assumed I had just seen something about the house somewhere and that I had turned Jamie into my imaginary friend." She spoke rapidly, like she didn't want to be speaking at all, and I tried my best to keep up and retain it all.

"I believed that for a while, until it started happening outside of the house. I'd go to the grocery store with my mom and see the ghost of the cashier's husband. And at first, they were just there and I thought maybe they were imaginary friends, too."

I furrowed my brow and asked, "How do they look different? Are they like, translucent?"

That encouraged a little laugh as she shook her head. "They have a sort of a, uh, luminescence about them."

The corner of my mouth lifted in a gentle smile. "They sound pretty."

She nodded, finally giving me a smile of her own. "They actually are, but I mean, I'm kinda used to it now. But anyway, it eventually got to a point where I couldn't concentrate on anything because of the constant images and messages. I was failing my classes, my parents took me to a bunch of doctors, and I was diagnosed with ADHD."

"Why couldn't you just tell the truth?" I asked, cocking my head.

Andy sighed, flabbergasted. "Because the first time I did, they told me I had an imaginary friend. The second time I said anything, they told me I was too old for that stuff and to take responsibility for my own actions."

"So, you just kept it to yourself," I concluded quietly, beginning to understand. "Because nobody believed you from the beginning."

She didn't have to nod for me to understand that was the truth, and just like that, my love for her doubled in size. It occurred to me then that love isn't just the simple act of being with someone, it's also carrying the weight of their truth and making it your own. Just to lighten the load and make their life that much easier.

"I could never be in any kind of meaningful relationship," she explained, slowly twirling her spoon in the melted ice cream. "I tried a couple times in college, but I was always so distracted. There was this one guy," her lips turned up in the faintest hint of a smile, "named Logan, and—"

"You tryna make me jealous, sweetheart?" I teased, smirking.

"Hey!" She reached across the table and playfully swatted my arm. "*You* wanted the truth, so I'm giving it to you." A twinkle in her eye told me there was still something there, something to hold onto and build from, and I relished the relief in that.

"Please," I gestured with a hand, "go on."

Inhaling and turning her gaze to the ceiling, she exhaled like breathing was a chore. "Logan was my second boyfriend and I really liked him a lot. Like, he was the kind of guy I couldn't wait to introduce to my family. He was sweet and so smart, and—"

"So, the opposite of me," I snorted.

With an enthusiastic bob of her head, she laughed. "Yes! Yes, exactly. And I really tried to make it work with him. We would go out and I would just keep my eyes on the ground, just so I could avoid looking at the freakin' ghosts, and that worked for a little while. But the thing about ghosts is, I'm the only one that can see them. *I* knew I was ignoring them, but to Logan, it looked like I was ignoring *him*. So," she shrugged, folding her arms on the table, "he broke up with me. It was after that I decided I couldn't have a relationship, not with this shit going on, and I spent all my time at the hospital, helping old people and the ghosts that followed them. And in the meantime, I was on the hunt for someone who could help me turn this crap off."

Pieces clicked into place as I nodded. "So, when you first met me, outside of that show ..."

"I was there to see if she was the real deal, yeah."

Laughing loudly, I tipped my head back. "So, when you said she was a fraud, you really fuckin' knew she was."

"Yes."

"Holy shit," I chuckled, shaking my head. "And that Tracey chick? She's the real deal?"

Andy nodded affirmatively.

"So, she's helping you turn off your, um, power?"

Shaking her head, she explained, "There is no turning it off. That night we saw her and I told you I'd bumped into an old friend, I was really going out with her."

A sudden strike of suspicion narrowed my eyes. "Why wouldn't you just tell me you were going out with her?"

Shame crumpled her features as she said, "I just thought it would raise more unnecessary questions, and if she had the secret to turning it off, then there'd be no point in explaining anything. But, when she told me there wasn't a way to stop them, I figured it was inevitable that you and I would fall apart. Then, your dad died and I started seeing him, and you had the drugs ..."

I only hear you when it's quiet. Quiet is good.

"And that turned it off," I finished for her.

Quietly she nodded, and quietly I accepted that I might have played a hand in her destruction but I wasn't the cause. There was peace in that knowledge, and I exhaled like I'd been drowning in the blame all this time and unable to breathe.

It was an amazing thing, though, when I really thought about it. How all the horrible things in our lives seemed to be so perfectly choreographed, and maybe even designed to bring us here, to this revelation, and to bring us back together.

"When you sent me home, I talked to my dad and told him everything. He said that he would get me whatever help I needed, as long as I didn't speak to you during my recovery. He thought that we would just encourage each other to relapse or something."

I nodded slowly, feeling a new appreciation for her father. "Smart man."

"I don't know how he's going to react to me talking to you now," she admitted uneasily. "But I have missed you so much. Not the drugs or being high. Just you."

"I've missed you, too."

She shifted in her seat like she wanted to ask me something but didn't know how to say it, and I waited for her to find the words she needed.

"So, you've been at Jenna's house?"

I nodded, and another heavy pause wedged itself into the conversation, as she studied her hands and the wedding ring she still wore. I wanted to ask what was on her mind but felt I didn't have the right. The ball was in her court now, and I was resigned to letting her decide the fate of our relationship, despite how much I hoped this would end with us together.

"Then, I have to ask you something," she finally said, never allowing her eyes to reach mine.

"Anything."

"If you've been here this whole time, why haven't you reached out to me?"

"Sweetheart," I muttered, wiping a hand over my mouth. "I don't—"

"No," she cut me off, lifting her gaze to mine, to reveal the pain and rejection she held inside. "If I'm going to consider making this work with you, I need to know what kept you away. I mean, I got it, you needed to learn to be alone, but you've been *here*. How could you just ignore the fact that I've been living five minutes away? How could you hope for me to wait for you, and then never reach out once you were here?"

Scratching the back of my neck, I pulled in a deep breath, then said, "I haven't ignored it, but—"

"*But*, you have, because if it really bothered you, if you really wanted me back, you would've—"

"I *couldn't*," I interjected sharply, before raking a hand through my hair and shaking my head. "Andy, I treated you like shit. I fuckin' *hit you*. How the hell was I going to show up at your parents' house and beg you to take me back, when I don't believe I deserve your forgiveness in the first place? You just said you don't know how your dad's gonna react to you talkin' to me now. What if I just showed up at his door?"

Her blue eyes softened, as she asked, "Well, would you hit me now?"

"What?" I replied, exasperated. "God, no! Andy, the reason I—"

"I *know* why you did it. You thought I was talking like a crazy, strung-out junkie, and in *your* crazy, strung-out junkie mind, that's what you felt you needed to do to snap me out of it." She reached across the table, and to my surprise, took my hand in hers. "Vinnie, we both did things we never should've done, and in the right frame of mind, we never would've done them in the first place. But that's the thing; we *weren't* in the right frame of mind. We were *sick*."

"Yeah, well," I grumbled, with my eyes fixed on her hand in mine, "that's no excuse for bein' an asshole."

"No, maybe not," she agreed. "But you're not an asshole, I know that. And, believe it or not, my parents know it, too, even if they are skeptical of our relationship. So, if you had come to my door, I'm telling you right now, they wouldn't have turned you away. I wouldn't have let them."

The corner of my mouth lifted in a lop-sided smile. "Oh, no?"

Andy laughed, shaking her head. "Baby, the only reason I was staying away from you is because you *asked* me to, *not* because I *wanted* to."

Grief and guilt are heavy feelings to carry all the time, and my shoulders had been permanently slouched with the weight, or so I thought. But at that moment, when I knew our relationship and marriage hadn't been left to die with our addiction, relief helped to lighten the load, and I sat up a little straighter.

She smiled and squeezed my hand. “So, Jenna’s basement … what's it like?”

“Hey, Kev!” I called, and my cashier and dishwasher popped his head out from the kitchen. “Clean this up, will ya? I'm gonna get outta here.”

“You want us to lock up?”

“Yeah, man,” I nodded, standing up and leading Andy to the door. “I'll be back in the morning, but just so you know, I might be late.”

CHAPTER FORTY-THREE

ANDREA

Jenna lived on a quiet street a few towns over from where I grew up. Her house was a modest ranch, with a cozy front porch and stained glass door to welcome your entry. The yard was beautiful and clearly professionally landscaped, showcasing a series of white rose bushes and lavender that lined the flagstone walkway. It looked like a picture and something a family had never lived in, except for the toys on the lawn giving it away.

"It's so beautiful here," I complimented, as Vinnie pulled up to the curb.

"Yeah, well," he shrugged, "I mean, it's not as nice as your parents' place, but ..."

It dawned on me that maybe he had done all of this—rehab, therapy, moving, and buying a new business—to simply impress my family, and I gawked at him with a blend of hurt and pity blanketing my heart.

"Don't do anything for them," I said firmly, and he shook his head, incredulous.

“Sweetheart, don't take this the wrong way, but I don't give a fuck about your family,” he pressed. “I'm doin' this for me, and for Pops, but most of all, for you. 'Cause you deserve better, so I'm gonna give you better.”

A memory came to mind, something I thought I'd forgotten, from when I’d gone home after Vinnie made me leave. My father had told me that all we can hope for is to love someone enough to make a difference, and I realized then, that I had.

He was alive because of me.

He was doing better, because of me.

And I couldn't ask or hope for anything else.

“You ready?” he asked, killing the engine.

With a rapid blink, I batted the tears away and nodded. We left the car and I headed toward the walkway when Vinnie stopped me.

“This way, sweetheart,” he said, directing me to a smaller path off the paved driveway.

He led me through the white, vinyl fence and around the back of the house. There was a white door, illuminated by a single light, and Vinnie unlocked it with a key. He opened it to reveal another door and a dark staircase.

“Where does that go?” I asked out of curiosity, pointing at the plain, inconspicuous door.

Flipping a light on and brightening the stairwell, he casually replied, “Oh, that goes to the laundry room I share with Jenna and Nicky,” then, he headed down the stairs and I followed.

At the bottom of the stairs, was a small room with two doors. Vinnie nudged his chin toward one and told me that was where the hot water heater and oil tank was. Then, with his hand on the other, he said, “And *this,* is where I live.”

I'm not sure what I had expected from Vinnie's apartment, when he told me he was living in his sister's basement. I knew he'd have a bedroom, maybe a bathroom of his own, but anything more than that hadn't crossed my mind. So, stepping over hardwood floors into the living room was a surprise, and as Vinnie dropped his keys on a small end table beside the door, I took in the tasteful leather couch and armchairs. Then, the new coffee table and large flat screen TV. There were a few pictures on the wall behind the couch—one of his father, one of the whole family, and one of us from our wedding day. My heart swelled, looking at the room. This wasn't a bachelor pad. It was a home, well-decorated and warm, and I loved it.

“I'm just gonna get outta these clothes,” he said, gesturing at the sauce stains on his light-washed jeans. “You can give yourself the tour, if you want.”

Wordlessly, I nodded, and with a cordial smile, he turned and exited the room through an open doorway. I kept a close distance as I followed, watching as he opened a door at the end of the long hallway. Assuming that was his bedroom, my attention was drawn to the three other doorways. One, a wide entryway, led to a small but lovely eat-in kitchen with what appeared to be another door to the outside. The other two doors concealed a bathroom and what appeared to be a storage room. The tour was quick, as the apartment was fairly modest in size, but it was clean and perfect for a single guy—or newlyweds.

Not knowing if I should barge into the bedroom, unsure of where our relationship stood, I waited for him in the living room. I sat down on the couch and looked down at the coffee table, remembering what we had used his old coffee table for. I wondered what had happened to it and if he missed it.

I closed my eyes and shook my head. That was another life and there was no going back. I didn't want to ever go back, and I said a silent prayer, hoping that I never did, with or without him.

Taking a deep breath, I inhaled control and exhaled calm, and when I opened my eyes, I found that I wasn't alone.

Vincent stood before me, regarding my presence with a knowing smile, and I regarded his with a bow of my head.

"Hi, Mr. Marino," I said. "I feel like I owe you an—"

"Are you," Vinnie cleared his throat as he entered the living room, wearing nothing but a pair of plaid pajama pants, "are you talking to my dad?"

For the first time, I didn't try to hide it from him as I nodded. "Yeah."

Vinnie turned in a circle, searching for where his father might be, and I laughed. "He's right next to the

TV," I said, and Vinnie stopped his spin cycle to stare at the blank space of wall where, for me, his dad stood.

"You can see him?"

"Yep."

Vinnie's skeptical eyes flicked toward me, and I knew I needed to do or say something to truly convince him of my ability. He needed proof—people usually do—and so, I grasped for the first image Vincent fed to me.

"You learned to dance from him," I said, while seeing the image of a young Vinnie awkwardly slow dancing with his father. "You were twelve. There was a dance at your middle school, and you asked a girl in your class to go with you. Your father told you there would be slow dances, and you panicked and almost called it off. But your dad taught you how to dance in your living room, to Billy Joel's 'She's Got a Way.'"

It was a private memory only they knew, and it was one that made me smile. But Vinnie didn't smile. His jaw clenched and his eyes filled instantly with tears and recognition.

That was when I knew he truly believed in me.

I watched his Adam's apple work with a forceful swallow. "So, um, what does he look like?"

"What do you mean?"

"Like," he squeezed the back of his neck, "does he ... does he look sick? Or, um, like a, I dunno, like a zombie or somethin'?"

Laughing and standing from the couch, I shook my head. "He just looks like your dad."

It felt so intimate, being there with my husband and the ghost of his father. Vincent respected the moment of his son's acceptance and held off on passing along his messages. He simply watched; a somber smile drawn across his face. Before, in the old apartment, I had been too desperate to escape the nature of my ability to realize how much I myself missed him, but I felt it now. I hadn't been given enough time. But is there ever really such a thing?

"I wish I could see him," Vinnie finally spoke, after moments of silence and his voice was gruff, as if he hadn't used it in weeks. "Is he saying anything?"

"The, um ..." I cleared my throat. "The dead don't talk. I can only hear static, like radio interference. It's weird, like, like we're in the same world but not on the same frequency."

He nodded slowly, sliding his hands into his pockets. "It's not weird. I mean, that kinda makes sense, 'cause that's really how it is, isn't it? Like, they're here, but also in another dimension."

I couldn't help but smile at his attempt to understand. "Yeah. Exactly."

Taking a deep breath, Vinnie looked over his shoulder at me and said, "Okay, so how does this work? He's here to give me a message, right?"

"Usually," I said. "But sometimes, they're looking for something from you."

Nodding, he looked back to the place where his father stood. "If I talk, he can hear me, right?"

As Vincent nodded, I replied, "Yes."

Vinnie bowed his head and stared at his shuffling bare feet as he said, “Okay. Um, so … Pops … I dunno if you were around when I was in Boston—”

“He was,” I quietly interjected, as an image came through of Vinnie, sitting on a couch, across from a professional-looking woman in glasses.

“Cool, okay,” he continued, nodding toward the floor. “So, then, you know I had to write those letters. Dr. Travetti told me it was important, so I could let go of the shit I was holding onto. And I did write a few of ‘em, to Zach, Jenna, and Andy. I was gonna write one to you, too, but I didn’t know if there’d be a point, you know? ‘Cause if I couldn’t give it to you and say the shit I needed to say, why waste time on it?

“But,” he continued, looking up and facing the wall, “I still have some shit I need to say to you, and if you can hear me, then I’m gonna say it. Ready, old man?”

Vincent nodded, which I reiterated quietly, realizing I was there only as a mediator for father and son. Their conversation felt personal, and I felt like I shouldn’t have been there at all. But I had my purpose, and I knew they needed me, so, I stayed.

“So, I’m never gonna understand why you decided not to tell us about your heart. I’m never gonna get that. But I can accept it was your decision to make and I gotta believe you did it to protect us, for whatever fuckin’ reason. And it’s because of that, that I forgive you.” He took a deep breath and pinched the bridge of his nose, as he went on, “And I don’t blame you, okay? I mean, yes, choices I made were affected by the shit in my life, but that's the thing, Pops—they were choices *I* made. You once asked me why I decided to get into drugs, and I didn't really answer. Not truthfully, anyway. Andy asked me, too, and I told her it was to escape the shit in my life. And the truth is, yeah, it was for an escape, but it wasn't 'cause of the shit in my life. I mean, my life, all things considered, was pretty good. But it was the shit in my head I needed to get away from, and that, you had no control over. I don't blame you for that, and I don't blame myself for it, either. But I own it. I wasn't ready to do that before, but I own the fuck out of it now. I'm sorry you had to put up with all of my bullshit while I got there. I'm sorry I put you through hell. I'm sorry I wasn't more grateful for everything you did and all of the sacrifices you made for us. I mean, man, I bitched and moaned about giving up my life to take care of you, but shit …" His voice rose an octave as he shook his head and my heart creaked and splintered under the weight of it. "I'm such an asshole for not realizing everything you gave up, to take care of me."

He held a hand over his eyes and finally broke against his palm. As he wept, Vincent spoke in a montage of pictures. All showing me Vinnie's accomplishments. Him leaving rehab the first and second time. Working at his pizzeria and buying Vincenzo's. Selling their place in Brooklyn. Moving out of the apartment they shared in the city and moving into this one on his own. Marrying me. The things he was there for, in person and in spirit. Things that lifted my heart with light and triumph. And after that mental scrapbook, there was only one thing to say.

"He's proud of you," I interpreted, reaching out and placing my hand on Vinnie's shoulder. "For everything you've accomplished. And you've accomplished a lot."

Vinnie laughed, swiping the back of his hand beneath his nose. "Death turned the old man into a sappy motherfucker, huh?"

Nodding, Vincent stepped forward and laid a hand over Vinnie's arm. Vinnie shuddered at the touch, and I asked, "Do you feel that?" He nodded erratically.

Vincent pressed his hand to his son's chest and passed along a message. "He says, 'I love you, Junior,'" I croaked, the words nearly dying in my throat, but I still managed to choke them out in a quiet burst of emotion.

Vinnie exhaled, as a fresh tear trickled down his cheek and onto the floor at his feet, and said, "Yeah, old man. I love you, too. And you don't gotta worry about me anymore. All right? I'm gonna be okay."

The twinkle in Vincent's eyes told me he believed every word, and with a slight nod of his head, he turned from his youngest son to look at me.

The emotions bubbled up from my heart and into my throat, remembering the promise I had made to him. Knowing that I'd allowed his son to spiral, and for us both to slip into the darkness without any attempt to find the light until it was too late. So, what right did I have to stand here now, presenting the gift of comfort and reconnection? I was a failure, and I didn't deserve his forgiveness, when all I was supposed to do in the first place, was make sure that his son was okay.

But Vincent reached out with a gentle hand, brushing his weightless thumb against my cheek. He shook his head and reminded me of that image and premonition, of Vinnie, lifeless on the floor. He reminded me of the phone call I had made, of how I'd saved him in the nick of time. Of how I'd loved him enough to take what I'd been given and save his life. He shook his head, controlling my tears with the silent command, and I closed my eyes and nodded.

I'd like to think, that after we had parted ways outside of Regina Miller's show, I would have still run into Vinnie again. I liked to think our relationship would have still found another way to happen. But that's not how it went. We had found ourselves together again because this man, his father, had neglected to tell his children that he was dying. And I knew Vinnie and I had a long road ahead of us, and that the hardships we'd faced would take time to fully overcome. But while I stood in this clean, fresh apartment, I knew that we'd be fine. Because, for me, our love was the sweetness in the bitter reality of life and death, and I knew that if we could get through all we'd endured so far, we could survive anything.

"I don't feel him anymore," Vinnie said, fighting back the distress and hurt of losing his father a second time. "Is he gone?"

I opened my eyes to see my husband, blinking back unshed tears and staring in the direction of where his father had been just seconds before, but now, there was nothing but the TV and the wall it hung upon.

Swallowing against a mournful sob, I slipped my hand into his. “Let's go to bed, baby,” I said, tugging him toward the hallway.

He hesitated for a moment, continuing to stare stubbornly, as if he believed that staring long enough would give him one final glimpse of his dad. But I knew better, and I think somewhere beneath the hurt, he knew it, too. I tugged again, and this time, he slowly followed.

As we headed down the hall, to begin the new, honest chapter of our lives together, I swore I heard someone exhale, somewhere not here, and then ...

Silence.

EPILOGUE

VINNIE

"Are you excited?"

With an incredulous look, I rolled my head against the pillow to face my wife. "Are you kiddin'? Of course, I'm excited."

"Well, I mean, I wasn't sure," she replied. "Especially when you consider how it went the last time you were at a party with my family."

I snickered, leaned it to kiss her lips, and said, "That was then, sweetheart. Things are different now. And besides," I climbed out of bed to pull on a pair of sweatpants, "this time, we're hostin', and if I wanna bang my wife in the middle of my fuckin' kitchen, I'm gonna do it."

She groaned and pulled the blanket over her head. "Oh, God, please don't."

"Come on," I went on, grabbing my sweatshirt, "imagine the looks on your sisters' faces. They'd fuckin' love it."

Andy uncovered her eyes and leveled me with a hardened glare. "One day, you're gonna love them."

"Yeah," I snorted. "Maybe after I'm dead and need you to give 'em the message."

She wasn't amused. "Well, you can at least pretend."

"How 'bout this? I'll start pretendin' when they—"

"Daddy!"

The little voice came from the next room, and I couldn't help the groan as it passed through my lips. I looked to Andy, hoping she'd take one for the team, but she only shrugged and offered an apologetic grimace.

"He wants you, baby."

"He always wants me."

"You should be happy you're his favorite," she said, with a gentle laugh.

"I know, I know," I muttered. "But I can't help that I got other shit to do before this shindig."

"You go see what he wants, and I'll start getting the food ready."

Agreeing with a nod, I headed through the door and hung a sharp right into my son's room. He was sitting up in his bed, with a book in hand, as usual. The kid was incredibly smart and loved to read and learn. He was, for all intents and purposes, my polar opposite, and he was the best thing that could've happened in my life.

"Hey, buddy, what's up?"

"What time is the barbecue?"

"Uh, five o'clock," I answered, lowering my eyebrows with curiosity. "Everybody's gonna come by probably closer to four. Why?"

"'Cause I wanna pick a book for Natalie and Katherine to read to me, and I need time."

I narrowed my eyes and poked the inside of my cheek with my tongue, searching for the right words, before saying, "Uh, bud, Nat and Kat can't read yet. They're just learnin' now."

"I know," Vincent groaned, throwing his head back dramatically. "But they gotta practice."

Snorting, I nodded. "Well, I can't argue with you there. You got plenty of time, okay? But you better pick a good one."

My brilliant three-year-old little boy climbed out of bed with a surge of determination and headed straight for his shelves, stuffed with an array of books. And in his Spider-man pajamas, with his blond hair sticking up in every direction, he proceeded to pull each one out and throw it on the floor, as he searched for the perfect book to lend his four-year-old cousins.

I left his room with a chuckle and a disbelieving shake of my head. It still left me in a state of awe, to think that my son had taught himself to read at the age of two. He flew through everything Dr. Seuss and Eric Carle had to offer by the time he was three, and now, he was confidently consuming his collections of *Curious George* and the *Berenstain Bears*. Even Andy, who was far more intelligent than I was, couldn't believe how smart this kid was. It was a gift, and it wasn't the only one he possessed.

"Is he okay?" my wife asked, as I entered the kitchen.

"Yeah, he's all good. Just pickin' out a book for Zach's kids."

"Oh, good," she replied, breathing out a heavy sigh of relief. "I thought he might've seen your dad again."

I shook my head. "Nah. At least, if he did, he didn't say anything to me about it."

Just after his second birthday, when we were still living in Jenna's basement, Vincent began to have conversations with Nonno. And it wasn't until Andy had seen my father herself, that we learned that our son had inherited her ability to see the dead. But unlike Andy's parents, we never discouraged him, or took him to doctors to try and rid him of his gift. Because, also unlike her parents, we already knew what it was, and we knew there was nothing he could do about it. So, we taught him to embrace it, and that there was absolutely nothing wrong with him for being able to do what he could do.

Besides, who knows? He might one day decide to get into the family business.

"How's Tracey doin'? She comin' by tonight?"

Andy shook her head on her way to the fridge. "She's good, but she can't make it. Her producer has gotten crazy demanding."

"Hey, she's the one who decided to get her own TV show," I pointed out.

"No, I know," Andy replied, pulling out packs of ground sirloin. "I think she's just tired."

"She should settle down. Get married or somethin'. Have a kid. Buy a house."

"Oh, you mean, live our life?"

I shrugged innocently, crossing my arms. "I mean, it's not the worst thing we've ever done, right?"

Then, her eyes filled with the pain of memories that hadn't faded enough, as she replied, “Right.”

***

Time doesn't heal all wounds. I would always mourn my father. I would always miss him with an impossible ache, eating away at my gut. But time had healed my relationship with Andy's family, for the most part, and for that, I would always be grateful.

“You gotta flip those burgers, Vin,” my father-in-law commented, standing over my shoulder at the grill.

“I will.”

“They're gonna burn if you don't flip them soon.”

I turned to him, lowering my brows. “I said, I—”

“Daddy,” Andy intercepted, shooting a stern glare my way, “Vinnie has barbecued a thousand burgers. I'm sure he's fine.”

“Oh, I know,” he said, clapping a hand against my shoulder. “But he doesn't mind when I give him a few pointers, right, Vin?”

“Well,” I wobbled my head from side to side, “I mean, I guess it depends on what kinda pointers we're talkin' about here.”

“Oh?”

“Absolutely,” I said, as I began to flip the burgers. “Like, on the golf course? You go ahead and give me all the tips you wanna give, 'cause God knows I still don't know shit about golf. But when it comes to me and my cookin'?” I snickered, shaking my head. “Man, you're better off keepin' your mouth shut, 'cause I ain't ever gonna listen."

Once upon a time, if I had talked to Andy's father like that, I could've safely expected to never see the light of day again. But now, he only squeezed my shoulder and laughed heartily, bumping his arm against mine.

"All right, all right," he relented. "I'll leave you to it. Just don't burn mine."

"Have I *ever*?"

"Nah," he said with a chuckle and another squeeze of my shoulder. "You wouldn't do that to me."

Meredith and Willa sauntered over, carrying cans of diet soda. Ever since Andy and I had gotten back together, the two of them had kept their alcohol consumption away from us, and to say we appreciated it would be an understatement. I saw it as an olive branch of sorts, and a sign of their acceptance. They respected us, as well as the burden of our lingering temptations, and that meant more to me than they'd ever know.

"Let me tell you something," Willa said, poking one long-nailed finger against my shoulder. "Your son has a very special way of making us feel like idiots."

"I've taught him well, then," I jabbed playfully, shooting her a wide grin.

"No, seriously," Mer chimed in, nodding. "I cannot believe how smart that kid is."

Andy wrapped an arm around my waist, then said, "Don't feel bad. Vinnie has to ask him how to spell words on a regular basis."

“Thanks for that, sweetheart,” I grumbled, shaking my head.

At that moment, my brother and his husband headed through the gate and into the backyard, with both of their girls in tow. Their shimmering, blonde hair bounced in pigtails, as they ran toward me, with arms outstretched, and I handed my wife the spatula to drop to the ground.

Years ago, I had teased my sister for her role in donating her eggs and body, in order for them to have a family. Even though I had been mostly joking, there was a part of me then that couldn't understand how Jenna would ever be able to look at them as her nieces, and not her own children.

But now, I got it.

I could never see these girls as anything but the daughters of my brother and brother-in-law. They had Zach's eyes and sharp wit, as well as Greyson's hair and fiery temper. They were a perfect combination of the two, and I loved the hell out of them. And I loved that I could be here, free from the shackles that had once bound me to my addiction, to be the best uncle I could be for them.

“Uncle Vinnie, do you have presents for us?” Nat asked, flashing me her trademark doe eyes.

“Yeah!” Kat bobbed her head wildly, wrapping her arms around my neck. “Do you have presents?”

“Is it your birthday?” I asked.

“No,” they replied in unison.

“Is it Christmas?”

They giggled. “No!”

“Do I *look* like Santa Claus?”

“You're not even fat!” Kat laughed, shaking her head.

“Then, hell no, I don't have presents. Do I look like I'm made of money?”

“You're made of skin and bones and guts,” Nat informed me, so matter-of-factly.

“And *blood*,” Kat whispered, grimacing.

Taken aback, my eyes widened as I looked up to Zach and Greyson, as they came to stand by the grill with Andy and her sisters.

Greyson shot my brother with a look that could kill. “*Someone* let them watch *Child's Play*.”

“Excuse me, cupcake, but I didn't let them *do* anything,” Zach fired back, crossing his arms over his chest and hardening his glare at his husband.

“Oh, okay, I'm sorry. I just thought inviting them into the living room, while you were watching Chucky movies, was basically the same thing as saying, 'Here, girls, come on in and get scarred for life.' But I guess I was wrong.”

“I didn't think they would pay attention,” Zach replied through gritted teeth, forcing a smile as his daughters looked up at their bickering fathers.

“Oh, are you new to this fatherhood thing?” Greyson whispered. “Newsflash, babe: they're *always* paying attention.”

I stood up slowly, eyeing both men, and asked, “Yo, is there trouble in paradise here? Do I need to call my shrink and give you's a referral?”

Zach sighed and shook his head, as he wrapped an arm around Greyson's shoulders. "No, we're all good. It's just been a long ride, and Thing One and Thing Two over here wouldn't stop talking about killer dolls, and I kinda hate myself because of it. But we're fine."

"Good," I replied, clapping a hand against his upper arm. "Now, let's eat."

***

After everyone had gone home and Zach, Greyson, and the girls had gotten themselves comfortable in the guest room, I helped Vincent get ready for bed, while Andy took a shower. Once his teeth were brushed and his bedtime story was read, I tucked him in and got ready to finally say goodnight.

"Daddy," Vincent said, as I sat on the edge of his bed.

"Yeah, buddy?"

"Nonno says you did good."

I lowered my brows and took a quick glance around the room, then asked, "He said that, huh?"

"Yes," my son said with an affirmative nod. "He was here today. He saw you and Uncle Zach and Aunt Jenna, and he said you did good."

Over the years since Vincent had learned to talk, he had said things relating to my father often. I knew the old man was watching, and that he was proud, so this statement didn't come as a surprise. But with it brought a sting of emotion as my throat tightened and my eyes watered, and I wished I could see him myself. I wish he could say these things directly to me and not my son.

I wished it didn't hurt so much to miss him, even after all this time.

"Don't be sad," Vincent said, crawling out from under the covers to sit on my lap.

"It's okay, buddy," I assured him, as I wrapped my arms around his little body. "I just miss Nonno sometimes."

"He misses you, too."

I snorted beside myself. "Yeah, I bet he does. He misses what a pain in his butt I was."

"He says you still remind him of Jesse."

This statement was new coming from him, and I narrowed my eyes with curiosity. "What do you mean?"

"He says Jesse got away from the bad stuff. He says he finally got away, and so did you. That's why you did good. 'Cause you got better."

Vincent had never been made aware of the trouble I'd gotten into in the past, or the bad things his mother and I had done in the beginning of our relationship. I figured one day, he would know, but right now, he was too young and innocent to understand. Hearing him say this though, I worried that my father was showing him things, telling him the things I didn't want him to know, and I shot an angry look into the room.

"He did, huh?" I grumbled.

"Were you sick? Nonno says you were sick."

Relief washed over me and loosened my shoulders, as I sighed and said, "Yeah, buddy. I was really sick."

“But you're better now.”

I nodded and kissed his head. “All better.”

“'Cause of me and Mommy?”

I smiled, pressing my cheek to his hair. “Yeah, buddy. 'Cause of you and Mommy.”

Kissing his forehead again, I instructed him to get back in bed and get to sleep, and he complied without complaint. I tucked him in for a second time and told him I'd make pancakes in the morning, then headed for the door and turned off the light.

“Daddy?”

With a sigh, I looked through the darkened room and toward his bed, and asked, “Yeah, buddy?”

“Nonno is very happy now.”

Looking into the room and imagining I could see my father there, I replied, “Me, too.”

“Good night, Daddy.”

“'Night, Vincent.”

If you or someone you know is suffering from substance abuse, there are people out there who want to help.

Don't wait until rock bottom.

Don't wait until it's too late.

SAMHSA

(Substance Abuse and Mental Health Services Administration)

1-800-662-HELP (4357)

ACKNOWLEDGEMENTS

Thank you, Jude, for the naps you took, giving me the ability to write this book. I wasn't sure it was possible to write a book and have an infant at the same time, but we proved me wrong, didn't we?

Thank you, Danny, for being so supportive and encouraging, and for giving me the time to continue doing what I love most (apart from you and Jude, of course).

Thank you to my parents for everything. Just … everything. I will never, in my life, be able to repay you. I hope you're okay with that.

Thank you, Jess, for your speed and diligence in getting this book back to me ASAP. You're a good friend and the best editor a gal could ever ask for.

Thank you, Kate, for taking the time to read this wild ride of a story, and for your contagious enthusiasm. I'm *not* sorry I made you cry. Your tears are my joy.

Thank you, Dear Readers, for sticking with me through the years, and for giving me the freedom to write what I want. You are everything to me, and you are never taken for granted.

ABOUT THE AUTHOR

Kelsey Kingsley is a legally blind gal living in New York with her family and a black-and-white cat named Ethel. She really loves doughnuts, tea, and Edgar Allan Poe.

She believes there is a song for every situation.

She has a potty mouth and doesn't eat cheese.

Other Books by Kelsey Kingsley

Holly Freakin' Hughes
Daisies & Devin
The Life We Wanted
Tell Me Goodnight
Forget the Stars
Warrior Blue
The Life We Have
Where We Went Wrong

The Kinney Brothers Series
One Night to Fall (Kinney Brothers #1)
To Fall for Winter (Kinney Brothers #2)
Last Chance to Fall (Kinney Brothers #3)
Hope to Fall (Kinney Brothers #4)

Printed in Great Britain
by Amazon

51341732R00273